HEATSTROKE HEARTBEAT

MATT WEBER

COBBLER & BARD PRESS

'Veraamaka Navo': Or, How to Dogfight an Eldritch Horror and Still Hit the Finish Line First

In a kinder world, this would have been a racing story.

There's such a fine racing story here. There is. Struggle, defeat, grit, blood, victory, all punctuated by the flame-driven wingbeats of vast death chickens caroming like rubber balls off the stone and steel of this undeserving city. The sort of racing story so pure it's hard to write about with any originality: "The spear-straight surge of Shearwater's Dawn Wyrm slaughtered Shanhoon Krait on the straightaway, surging straight up the middle of the lane with a kraitlike spearing that sheared away all doubt about the coming slaughter..."

... and I did run this jewel by my editor, hoping to buy some time to breathe and bind my wounds, but no. Now she finally sees where this was all going from the start. Now we are writing it my way. And so I wet a cloth and wipe away the thin crust of dried blood that has oozed from the seven stitches in my forehead and try to get my eyes to focus on the piles of documents, the scraps of paper scrawled with story beats, the dot-and-line net of connections spiderwebbing the sheet of map-sized paper from the top of the pile I stole from the cartographer I was fucking for a few weeks that one autumn. (It's all right; that one ended badly; he won't read this.)

None of it wants to resolve in my field of view. I should be sleeping. I should be healing.

But, reader, it is a rare treat you are in for. Breaking news is one thing; I've broken so much news my old paper bought me a golden hammer. (Gold-plated.) What breaks for you here, though, now, is—with all respect to the other reporters going without sleep this night, and I know they are legion—no mere news; this is a breaking *feature*, a bird whose rarity is without measure, a journalistic deed whose existence is only possible because the context for all this news is known to me in advance for what honestly amounts to no particular reason except: It felt like it might come to this. I did not predict this, but it did not surprise me: Every piece in its place and in its time, like a blacksmith's puzzle where the shining ring slides over a knot of thick black steel the eye insists it cannot pass.

Fine, then. Now we are writing it my way. Here is why.

***

It was the kind of summer night—last night, that's to say, as you read this, and the night that's dissolving into grey and pink as I write it—the kind of night where the scent of jasmine hangs like a curtain in the thick, still air... but you wouldn't have smelled it, because the breeze had been shattered by the wake of a Dawn Wyrm the size of a healthy rhinoceros streaking overhead, and the scent of that crashing wake was sulphur.

On that Dawn Wyrm was the widow Zaya Shearwater, green-goggled and orca-jacketed, her hair a luminous azure that almost blended into the Dawn's plumage. She was pressed belly-down to the Dawn like a baby sloth—but her daughter, Vanako, held her hands up to the wind in victory. Vanako's head was turned towards the coal-feathered head of the Melanic Shrike gaining on them; if her hands were gesturing in some exultation of obscenity, I didn't see it... but the Dawn's nose crossed a healthy half-length before the Shrike's, and a roar rose into the night along with its twin, a poleaxed grunt of chagrin, as Zaya and Vanako Shearwater clinched first place in the Basting Stitch.

I should, in this narrative, spend more time with Zaya and Vanako in their victory. They're owed it, they've earned it. But my head is throbbing with a pain that whiskey won't cure, or hasn't anyway, and the rush of the crowd toward the winners and the bustle around the winners' podium is nothing but noise in my memory, the crash of waves on the shore. I remember the characters I'd marked in my mind and in my notes, exemplars of competing tendencies in the crowd: A too-well-dressed Mrineen, whose cool features screamed disappointment; a pair of Mrineen men dressed almost like day-laborers and built like cops, whose screams of disappointment were much more literal; a gaggle of mixed bright-haired kids, mostly Kayalim, who threw popcorn and elated swear words and drew some calculating gazes from the men who were probably cops.

And I remember Kaana te-Tekko: A Kayalim woman built like a gourd, with a face that looked like some mean god had squashed it flat under a divine finger, smart in a buff waistcoat and brick-red cravat. I couldn't see much of her, what with the two poles of meat flanking her, in the same uniform. I ran lines in my head, turning over what might work best to get past a man like that. One of them had a beautiful tooled leather satchel over his shoulder, decorated with an orca and a sailfish.

The other wyrms sailed in, all in a pack, and then there were enough 'streamers to stand on the nine-stepped winners' ziggurat, and I dutifully wrote out all their names, which did not make it out of the square with me—that's to say, they shared the fate of the rest of my notes. But I remember they stepped up to take their places one by one, creating a sense of false suspense that might have made sense once upon a long-lost time.

I remember the second-place step was not filled.

Maybe it never is, when Shanhoon Krait is the runner-up. He's never burdened himself with a reputation for grace. But now, in the post-midnight-pre-dawn stasis of this borrowed editor's office where I write, that absence yawns.

Here's what I was told was going to happen. Zaya would receive a fat sack of cash. With great ceremony, she would toss it to Kaana; one of Kaana's meat poles would catch it and, presumably, stow it in the orca/sailfish satchel. This would be an event of Journalistic Interest and would certainly be covered by the half dozen other reporters I'd sighted in the crowd, who had certainly received the same tip I had, perhaps in the same language:

> *For your information: Tomorrow night at the finish line in Inundinir Square, the point leader in the current season of the Brimstone Slipstream will donate her winnings from the Basting Stitch in endorsement of Kaana te-Tekko, the Travelers' candidate for alderwight in Ochre Precinct.*

Well, Zaya got the cash. She made that expansive gesture of inclusion or acknowledgement that people seem to do when they're up in front of a crowd, because how many things can you do in front of a crowd that everyone will actually see? She made eye contact with Kaana or one of the meat poles, I couldn't really make it out.

And then there was a scream, like the same god who'd squashed Kaana te-Tekko's face had sunk its fingers into the night sky and ripped it in two with its bare hands. The blue and yellow of wyrm-fire lashed over Inundinir Square, and a keening crowd began to flow away from the podium as a flame-licked thing the height of a good-sized giraffe seized the third-place winner, who later edits will have informed me is named Vanioun Ora, and engulfed the upper half of his body with an orifice that no reasonable human could possibly describe as a mouth.

By the time his kicking legs dropped away and the thing pulled the top half of Ora's body inside its own with a peristaltic pulse, the only winner on the podium was Zaya Shearwater, and her Dawn Wyrm, Bandit's Breath, was on top of the creature, flame and talons forward. The thing turned, a whole battle array of fully articulated limbs bursting from its skin to grapple with the on-rushing wyrm...

... and that was when I lost my fight against the flow of the crowd and went down hard on the cobblestones.

I don't know how long it took me to fight my way back up. My face and chest took hit after hit from shoes with none too soft soles; they immediately felt swollen, constricted, half numb and half in agony. I didn't feel the cut on my forehead as anything other than a piece of that generalized pain. The cracks of my own bones under the shoes of the crowd were louder than any noise I'd heard that day; so was the rustle of clothing passing over me, the slap of shoe leather on stone; the screams of panic five or six feet above my head were as far away as the calls of wild geese in flight. The screams of wyrm and demon and the odd flashes of wyrm-flame were grace notes to the slow flattening of my body under the soles of what felt like about a million and a half elephants who'd crammed their feet into human-sized shoes.

I was the road out, I felt at some point. Through some occult transfiguration I had become the path to safety; every impact on my thigh or chest or head was a new person (or mis-shod elephant) transported from danger to salvation. Why struggle against such blessed service?

Well, I am a journalist; self-sacrifice is not native to our mindset. When I did succeed in fighting my way to my feet, I certainly wasn't in the same place as I'd been when I'd fallen; my pen and notes were gone, so was one of my shoes. The other reporters were still there, mostly. There were a number of others who, realizing that Bandit's Breath had the creature pinned, had stayed to watch; a few 'streamers had mounted up and taken to the air while I was down, but they seemed unable to bring their wyrms in close.

One of Inundinir Square's famous features is the Hotel Ochre. It's been out of business for nearly a century, too expensive to run at a profit when our fair city isn't the destination it once was… but there are not many children in Yemareir who haven't taken the trip to Ochre Precinct to see the altorilievo masterpiece carved into the six stories of its façade, with a rush of Dawn Wyrms climbing up the left side and a similar crowd of Dusk Stalker wyrms plunging toward the ground on its right. We all heard a keen, thin and small in comparison to the screams of wyrm and demon that had swept over the square but unmistakably, in contrast, human. We all snapped our heads around to the Hotel Ochre in time to see a plummeting form, head down as though it were one of the façade's dragons, streak through the air; we all heard the slap and crack of its impact, and we all snapped our head back to the battle that had cleared the square, which now was over, one of the sides having vanished. Bandit's Breath lay on its back alone, panting and bleeding.

There was one open window on the fifth story of the Hotel Ochre, by the Dusk Stalkers. For a moment, I saw a face there.

Silence, or some near cousin of it, hung over Inundinir Square for the space of three deep breaths. A knot of black-robed necromancers rushed in from Scrivener's Street, their eyes glowing with the power of their discipline, bodies encased in some eggshell-shaped field that ran with translucent color almost like a soap bubble. They assessed the scene and let their protections down. I saw a pair of police on Argent Swordwings circling in the sky overhead, looking for any dangers they might have missed.

As casually as I could, I walked to the wreck of a body in front of the Hotel Ochre. I looked at what there was of the face to memorize it.

By the winner's podium, Zaya and Vanako Shearwater were tending to Bandit's Breath, which had rolled over to rest on its belly, its head held up but low to look at its riders. Kemreen Gharial, Zaya's ex-cop partner, joined them. Kaana te-Tekko and her meat-pole guards were nowhere to be found—which, as they'd begun the evening in the front row, nearer the slaughter than anyone except for the winners, spoke well of the meat poles' ability to get her to safety quickly, unless they'd all been eaten while I'd been getting trampled. (A few minutes before this went to press, I was able to verify that they had not been eaten.)

I thought about going up to the Shearwaters for a quote, but why? The one I'd like to get, I knew I wouldn't. I left down an alley before the police could land and detain me for questioning. I had a story to write.

***

THAT WAS THE LAST scene I visited for this story. This, six weeks ago, was the first.

Laurel Street, in Lilac Precinct, hasn't changed much in six years: A bodega at each end, a haberdasher with a number of shiny dag-gers in the window, a specialty store selling Kayalim ingredients, shade trees down the north side, date trees down the south, several free-standing residences, and a few modest four-floor tenements, one behind a low outer wall. On this particular day, Laurel Street looks like it's stumbling home hung over from a party held by some friends of friends that it's definitively learned it can't keep up with, but through the paper cups, coconut half-shells, orphaned shoes, and that one fast-asleep gentleman courting a sunburn in front of the haberdasher, its basic respectability is plain to see.

The mural is new, though. It's on that low wall around that one tenement, and words do quite literally fail to do it justice; every step closer reveals a new level of detail, whether it's the tiny stories in the rings that comprise the blazing sun or the faces, painted in a barely-fainter hue, that provide the texture of the sky. But the basic composition is simple enough. There's a woman on a dragon. Above her is the sun; below her is the city. It's a flattened side view, but the dragon is the shape and colors of a Dawn Wyrm, and the woman has bright magenta hair matching the Dawn, flowing behind her like a wake. In the sky, balancing the composition, are two huge, intricately detailed words in the Kayalim alphabet, painted in the purple and orange of the wyrm, and a few smaller ones, a sentence or so.

On this particular morning, I'm on this street for a while, and the mural gives me something to do. I pick up a cup of orxata at the bodega at the north end of the street and stare at it for a while; on the rear of the wyrm, painted subtly, in a shade of blue just barely fainter than the sky, a skeleton rides, girt with the 'streamer's talismans of goggles, jacket, and saddle-knife.

I spend a while savoring the orxata as slowly as I can—can't comment on authenticity, but it's rich and perfectly sweetened, hard not to gulp all at once and go back for more—then visit the bodega at the southern end of the street for a wax-paper twist of pork rinds, spiked with some kind of brick-red dust of chili, tamarind, and sugar. I return to the mural and eat and look at the rings that comprise the sun, each broken into panels that make it into a little comic. I can recognize scenes from races I've heard about or, sometimes, seen: The conflagration of butterflies at the Mariposa Annulus, the dogfight in the Omari Shadowrun.

I'm through the pork rinds, licking spices from my fingers and squinting my way through the sun-comic, when the gate to the low wall opens and a Mrineen woman walks out. She's short and fit, with arms that look like she spends her days wrestling orang-utans snarling at me out of a sleeveless shirt. The kind of person who looks like she could take a hit from a ton of bricks and not flinch—which is lucky for her, because the sun hits her like two tons of bricks, and I can see her roll back on her heel.

When she's off her back foot, I attempt journalism. I've guessed her name, so I use it: "Excuse me, are you Kemreen Gharial? I was wondering if you've got a moment to chat about Zaya Shearwater and her place in what seems to be a growing protest movement among the city's Kayalim precincts."

In response to these very reasonable questions, she says "Ehhhhhhh," which in fairness is more or less what you'd expect Laurel Street to say right now if it could talk, and turns her back on me. She can't walk as fast as she'd obviously like to; I can see her swaying a little bit as she hustles away, not realizing that I'm not trying to follow her. I know when I'm beaten.

***

I SAY AGAIN: THIS was supposed to be a racing feature.

I won't say I'm *not* bitter about how I've made my name in this city, the Rainbow on the Bay, the Boil of the Emerald Dunes, the Maw of the West. You people ought to know better than to pay perfectly good money for Sports Journalism if you have the option to read anything else at all. But I throw the rubies of historical exposition and trenchant political analysis before you, and you grind them under your cloven hooves to get to the trough, where your pig-keeper has dumped a steaming compost of underground drag-on-racing for your snuffling delectation. Luckily, that pig-keeper is also me—and a well-fed swine shits cash, if only you can wash the stink of the wallow off it...

... but this article is for a moderately good publication, whose audience will endure only so much good-natured abuse from even a Celebrity Sportswriter, and their fact-checkers will doubtless cry foul at the idea of a cash-shitting pig, necessitating that I waste my irreplaceable hours under this waning sun imploring a clutch of art-bereft bean counters to appreciate imagery and metaphor. So, reader, without further clearing of the throat: Know that you have my contempt! And know, for the last time, that this is *not* a racing feature. Because the most important conversation I had on that morning on Laurel Street where the air was so humid you could cut it and serve it in cubes as the world's worst thirst-quencher, was not with any member of House Shearwater: It was with the mural on their low outer wall.

***

How many of you know what "veraamaka navo" means? For that matter, how many of you read Kayalsho at all?

Before I wrote this thing, whatever it is, I could not have counted myself in either number. I now read Kayalsho in the sense that I can transliterate it, which is better than you. But if I can learn "veraamaka navo," then so can you; and what it means is "our wyrm-rider."

It's not a natural word. Kayalsho has words for lizards, winged snakes, wingless snakes, and dinosaurs, but "veraam" is just "wyrm" in Kayalim-compatible phonology, a loan word. And

Kayazē doesn't have a tradition of racing on animals, or even recreational riding; "-ka" is just someone who does a thing. It's a thin film of what readers like me register as foreignness on a concept that is purely Yemari.

Which is, of course, an irony, because what Zaya Shearwater, her late wife, and her adopted daughter have made of this purely Yemari concept is something that the 'stream has never seen, and is still flailing frantically to reject, like ants on its skin. And the reason for this is explained, as simply as can be, by the other word in this phrase that has come to synonymy with Zaya Shearwater.

"Navo" is, of course, the word that means "ours."

Every generation has had its celebrity 'streamers, some more influential than others. In the 200s, Mrajaan Taipan galvanized the city against the disastrous war with Cineladris Conurbation over water rights to the Rifil Aquifer. In the 500s, Nekaroon Skink and Kanjoon Goanna led a doomed expedition of 'streamers to discover the fate of Yynraan Colony, still unknown. Some of our grandparents fondly remember Fsalaan Tuatara as a front-line fighter in the crusade against a century-long revanche to the gender binary. 'Streamers have made themselves into avatars for causes good, evil, consequential, and trivial... but all of those causes have been prosecuted in the context of an organization of government and society that places Mrineen on both sides of every issue, and at the levers of power that ultimately decide.

We know a few Kayalim folk heroes as well, of course. And we, you and I, are not threatened by them. We praise them for their work, and although the praise is ritual, we mean it. Why not? Their success, such as it's been, is priced into our existences. If Zaya Shearwater wants to do something wholesome and benign, who are we to fuck with that?

***

ABOUT SIX YEARS AGO—THAT'S to say, a little under a year after Kiriki Shearwater was reduced to greasy cremains by an animal so inimical to human existence there exists no oral or written record of anyone even thinking about eating it—a creature of the sort we conventionally term a "demon" killed a dozen passersby near a wet market on Ariendor Street in Eggshell Precinct.

The summoner was found, because a level of amateurism is practically priced into any horrorshow like this. Practitioners of any nontrivial proficiency are discovered, bound, and regulated by one of a handful of professional guilds in a tradition we carried from Mlinivoun precisely so we could have the nice things attendant on dangerous magic like demon-summoning without random civilian massacres. The conventional definition of "nontrivial proficiency" is "can summon a demon without immediately being devoured by it," the prepositional phrase being more difficult by a distance than the independent clause, and so this all works because the wannabes are self-exterminating. Most demons, especially venial ones, will go after their summoner immediately for the same reason that you'd go after a person holding your head under the water: They in a very real sense *cannot breathe here*, any more than we can survive in whatever hells they come from, and they can feel the mind of the summoner holding them in this world as keenly and precisely as you could feel the fingers of your drowner's hand tangled up in the wet hair of the back of your head—and could follow them up wrist and arm to shoulder, if you had the flexibility.

So the summoner was found, and incinerated summarily by a police wyrm. But a broader problem persisted, because when a *non-guild* goetist pulls out a demon long enough for it to kill *anyone other than himself*, there comes a question of how he got past the guilds. And it soon became clear that this crushingly mediocre amateur had so little in the way of talent or prior achievement that any guild effort to audit practitioners at his level would subsume somewhere between half and a third of the city. He'd done it with a grimoire, a completely undistinguished mind... and a third factor; but that wouldn't surface until later.

***

THE SUN IS DIRECTLY overheard as I discover that the city in the mural is built up of people. To the first glance, there are buildings, which is how it's recognizable as a city—but even the buildings are basically stacks of people, thin rectangular cells in which some stylized figure seems to have just gestated, somehow sized to fill it completely without seeming terribly distorted. Because the buildings are made up of people, it's actually slightly hard to detect that, in the streets of the mural-city, many of the "people" are actually animals. Monkeys, hawks, dogs, owls, lizards.

The people are looking up, eyes and mouths wide. The animals are cowering: Gazes downcast, faces somehow, with marvelous economy of line in this sea of crowded, tiny profiles, full of noticeably animal aversion.

Before the shadows have quite disappeared in observation of the noon hour, a decrepit Kayalim man shuffles out of the gate in the low wall. He has a long braid in three colors as smooth and bright as I've ever seen in a person's hair: Royal blue, orange, purple. He sees me scrutinizing the mural and comes over. "You know who that is?" he asks.

I of course have many things to say on this topic, but I know better than to interrupt the social mating-display of an old man trying to teach something to a Callow Youth. "I don't read Kayalsho," I say, with a helpless gesture at the words that maybe he sees through, maybe he doesn't.

"That's a young woman named Zaya Shearwater. She thinks she can fight death and win. And what nobody realizes yet is that she's right."

"How so?" I ask. "We're all mortal, last I checked."

"Galhoun Tuatara was supposed to have been undefeated until his final bout against Terisheen Anaconda at the Twilight Cliffs in your homeland."

"... I'm not sure I follow."

"He lost eventually, but he's remembered for his victories."

"If that makes him a champion, we're all champions. Or at least I don't know of anyone who doesn't live until they die."

The old man looks at me in annoyance. "I'm not going to get killed in a sword fight today because I'm not going to be in one. If you don't get the difference between that and winning the fight you're in, maybe you should close your mouth and spend some more time staring at that mural."

I hold up my hands and show my neck. "All right, Galhoun, I yield."

He puffs a self-satisfied breath through his nose. "Damn right."

We've been doing this too long; it's now or never. "I do actually know who you are, te-Zuuno-zē, and I know who that woman in the mural is. I was hoping you and I could talk about her in a comfortable place of your choosing."

I meet his eyes with as piercing a stare as I can muster so he knows exactly what I mean, and I see him know exactly what I mean, and in the spirit of deserved self-flagellation I will cop to it here: I mean, and Zinji te-Zuuno knows I mean, that I will take him somewhere to get high and foot the bill. This is a call I'll come to regret over the months I spent on this piece, not because I suffered as a result of it but because of a basic inhumanity it seems to have revealed as a part of me as inseparable from me as the pit of a peach—which is to say, separable, but you'd have to cut me in half to get it out. I can see Zinji mull over the offer, because he knows as well as I do that he's cash-strapped and a decently well-off person implicitly offering to buy you *what the fuck ever* isn't an opportunity that comes along every day.

At last he shakes his head. "I read the article you wrote just before Kiriki died. You missed a lot, but you said the right things about the right people. I'm not the right person. And I'm not going to say the right thing."

"What could possibly be not right about anything you'd say about your daughter?"

Zinji laughs. "The last person anyone in this world needs to hear from is an old man coked to the gills moaning about his regrets. Zaya in particular doesn't need to read that shit."

"All right. If you did say the right thing, what would it be?"

He takes the time to compose his words. "I know what it's like to be a widower, and I know what it's like to fear for the life of a child. People like you who hear about my daughter winning the Omari Shadowrun and think it's a sports story are wrong. People who hear about at my daughter and find it inside them to paint murals like that—" gratuitously, he points—"are right."

"I'd really like you to say more about that."

Zinji laughs an old smoker's laugh, shows me the back of his middle finger, and stumps off, the same direction as Kemreen Gharial.

I go back to my shady spot and settle in to think about Zinji's words. They are, let's face it, the most predictable of dad-words: My kid is great, their achievements mean something real.

But it does make me wonder. When I covered the rise of House Shearwater leading up to the last Grand Bisai, there was no short-age of all the things you'd expect: the Kayalim community came through with inspiration, with pride, with big and foredoomed words about how this was going to change the "stream forever. But the discourse died quietly with Kiriki Shearwater, and I never saw art about her in the streets. When Zinji said "people who" and "murals like that," was that a hypothetical plural of which this was the only instance, or were there more? And if there were: Why now and not then?

I turn back to the cityscape that reaches across the bottom of the mural like a fungus. This time I can't help but notice an irregularity in the way the figures are spaced. The people are close together, but there's a regular buffer of space between them, a consistent quarter-inch. They're stylized figures painted to fit in non-overlapping, square spaces, so the painting induces almost a grid... but a few figures break it, bridging that last quarter-inch to almost fuse with each other. Across the whole sprawling thing, the pattern is the same: Each pair is a human and an animal. A monkey, a hawk, a dog, an owl, a lizard, each yoked to a person. They're not reaching out as though to seize prey; they're not snarling or covered in blood. Just a little closer to one side or the other than they should be, subtly disturbing the harmony of the grid design.

When you look, you see them everywhere.

***

THE MINOR MASSACRE AT the Ariendor Street wet market wasn't the last.

A cut-rate goetist summoned a demon in Incarnadine Precinct, in front of a luthier's shop where the girl who'd spurned him was apprenticing. Witnesses observed that it didn't really occur to the thing to go into the door, and the girl and the luthier survived by hiding in a closet, but the demon chewed on pedestrians in the area until a few adepts of the Grey Heron Society showed up to unsummon it. The motive for the malevolent conjuration was established by the goetist after the fact; the Grey Herons managed to keep him alive, although they managed to mangle his mouth and jaw in an "accident" during some sort of abstractly described wizardly altercation.

There were more incidents like this, mostly acts of petty retribution with large blast radii, the occasional inexplicable or at least unexplicated lashing-out like the Ariendor Street massacre. There wasn't enough of it that anyone was really worried for themselves, but there was enough of it that people were worried about others.

And then the Salt Road Desperadoes and the Knucklebones each brought a demon to a street fight in Damask Precinct, and people really started paying attention.

The Knucklebones had always had an undeserved reputation for goety; the Desperadoes were responding to a threat they had no real ability to evaluate. Only the Desperadoes thought it through. The Knucklebones' goetist was also their leader, Kaalo te-Kaalo; he watched *both* demons tear through his gang with an expression we observers of the historical record can only guess at, although the head of the Desperadoes, Ziyako te-Natuuvo, described it on the stand as "like a freshly gelded billy-goat." She lives free, as far as anyone knows, across the continent in the Kerkakan colony of Ajmawar, having accepted exile rather than death in exchange for giving up the secret that kept the Salt Road Desperadoes safe, if not from the law, then at least from the demons: A simple alchemical preparation of the pollen from the brightwick and datura flowers, which grow together only at the foot of the Supplicant, well east—but not too far east—of Yemareir.

***

IF, AT THIS POINT, you're asking what in all creation the secretions of a flower's gonads could possibly have to do with demon summoning, you're asking questions that very little of the journalism around this five years ago even came close to addressing.

Of the articles I found from that period, many mention things like "a protective talisman" (*Transpiring*), "what amounts to a sort of camouflage for summoners" (*The White Heart Testament*), even "a protective substance synthesized from the pollen of a rare jungle flower" (*City Crypt*). This makes it seem like some sort of holy or otherwise blessed substance that puts up a demon-proof wall around you and does nothing else in particular. But if you understand that brightwick and datura pollen, if subjected to certain processes that aren't so hard for a mediocre amateur to replicate in a back-alley laboratory, combine into a substance called "yliaster," which throws off resonances that disrupt connections between minds, a lot of other things become clear.

If you get that, you get why it protects summoners from demons.

If you get that, you get why it protects the hunted from their kers.

If you get that, you get why it prevents Kayalim empaths from establishing mindlinks with animals.

If you get only the first thing, you understand why "camouflage for summoners" is illegal inside the borders of Yemareir, and has been for, oh, about five years, during which time there have been almost no mass murders conducted through demonic proxies by yliaster-abetted goetists. And you're probably happy about it.

Zaya Shearwater—mother of a hunted child and, at present, the most famous Kayalim empath in the city—is one of the few people in this city who gets all three. She does not share your happiness. And now, maybe, neither do you.

***

AFTER THE DAY WHEN I wait on Laurel Street like a junkie looking to score—or at least to beg his supplier for a taste—I chase quotes fitfully for weeks, hoping to gain some understanding of the Dogfight Under the Mountain, the weird event that occurred during the last Omari Shadowrun, resulting in the death of veteran 'streamer Arhoon Pogona and Zaya Shearwater's first victorious race since her wife died in the Grand Bisai almost six years ago.

I do succeed, a little; a number of 'streamers are willing to talk on background, and a scion named Shanhoon Krait, the favorite going into the Omari Shadowrun, cheerfully puts his name to a number of calumnies and insinuations about Ms. Shearwater and various other 'streamers. Much of what I hear, from him and others, is talk of "dampers." There are no more dampers, so Zaya was able to cheat to win; the dampers were a profound injustice holding Zaya back from victory, and it's great they're gone; people *said* Zaya won the Shadowrun because there were no more dampers but really it just took her a few weeks to get back in the game.

Those of you who've been following the 'stream since the last Bisai will, of course, know what a damper is. But my entire value proposition for this very middlebrow publication is that my name will bring in readers who *don't* follow the 'stream—who might, in fact, not even know "the 'stream" as the conventional abbreviation for illegal underground street dragon racing and the scene that has developed around it—and if I didn't know what a damper was when I started working on this story, I'll hazard a guess that most of you don't either. (Or at least that my editor doesn't, which is why he'll pay me for the words explaining it... assuming I make it through the throng of dead-eyed freaks at the door.)

What a damper does is very simple: It disrupts the kind of mind-to-mind connection that's required for an empath, or a pair of empaths, to control a dragon in a race. The requirement of a damper was imposed by the Standards Board about a year after Kiriki Shearwater and the Mule died in the last Grand Bisai. None of the 'streamers I succeed in talking to knows where the dampers come from or how much they cost, except for Shanhoon Krait, who gives me a smirk that says he knows but isn't telling.

Meanwhile, Zaya Shearwater and her daughter, Vanako, are winning races—*without* dampers, just to add to the confusion, because the Standards Board reversed its own decision just before the Omari Shadowrun and decided they unduly hurt Kayalim 'streamers, who are less likely to have spare cash to burn on things like exotic dragon species or special diets or what have you. (When I ask about Cerminir Shearwater's role in managing the Shearwater wyrms' diets, I get a lot of confused responses; not only has any recognition of Cerminir faded from the scene, but none of the 'streamers I talk to actually take a particularly active role in managing their wyrms' diets. This makes me wonder if the market for 'streamer supplies has transmogrified Cerminir's contribution from the skilled application of Ililuë dietetics on a tight budget into some expensive product that can only be purchased for cash.) This reversal by the Standards Board has boosted Kayalim interest in the 'stream, as exemplified by several Kayalim 'streamers I talk to, who've entered the scene since the Shadowrun and are pleased to credit Zaya for it.

This, on its face, is weird. Why should Zaya's reentry to the 'stream have anything to do with the Standards Board?

On average, the Mrineen 'streamers answer this question like this: "Everyone knows Zaya Shearwater is one of the greatest racers in Yemareir. They couldn't retain a restriction that kept her from winning. There was too much public pressure to remove it."

On average, the Kayalim 'streamers answer this question like this: "When it came out that Shanhoon Krait had introduced the dampers and his brother's company was making money from them, the Board couldn't keep them. It was too much self-dealing, people were filing complaints and threatening to go to the press."

What's interesting here is, the Mrineen 'streamers are aware of the controversy around the dampers. Some of them, off the record, claimed to have filed the very complaints that the Kayalim 'streamers had talked about. And when I asked both the Mrineen and the Kayalim 'streamers how the information about the dampers and House Taipan had come out, they both had the same answer: After the White Steeplechase, Zaya Shearwater announced it.

The Mrineen 'streamers take this to mean that the Board knuckled under to a favored racer. The Kayalim 'streamers think it means a *disfavored* racer finally made an appeal to justice that the Board couldn't ignore.

***

I'll confess, though: I'm only half interested in these quotes. I pick them up almost by accident hanging around bars and plazas and other places where I know the 'stream will be congregating for post-race festivities, the places where new ground crews are made, tips are swapped, lamentations drunk down, and winners celebrated.

But Zaya Shearwater doesn't come to drink at Shizaki's in Rust Precinct. She doesn't come to dance at the Widow & Sage in Heliotrope. She doesn't come to smoke up at the Grove at the Center of All Things in Lime. Everyone else is there, but not her.

There are a couple of gentlemen I notice for the first time at the Widow & Sage. They arrive before the 'streamers, like me, drinking together and not talking much. They don't look remarkable in any particular way; one's a Kayalim, one's a Mrineen. But their shoulders are broad with muscle, their arms etched with it, their jawlines sharp, their eyes restless. They're cops, is what I'm saying, and the reason I notice it is because they were at Shizaki's too. And something else happens that I also didn't notice at the time at Shizaki's: A scruffy-looking Kayalim individual comes in, orders a small glass of the cheapest arrack on the shelf, tosses it back, and leaves. And I know I won't see the winner of the Mariposa Annulus that night, any more than I saw the winner of the Red Switchback at Shizaki's.

When those same cops show up to pretend to be the most incongruous hookah-smokers at the Grove at the Center of All Things, I find Zaya's scruffy scout, and I follow them.

They take an only slightly circuitous path to a small knot of people hanging in the mouth of an alley off Jrashivain Square, passing a couple of bottles of sour beer and talking. It's not the people I expect. Zaya is there; so's Kemreen Gharial, conspicuously armed with a falx and a broad main-gauche. But there's also a small retinue of four young Kayalim, all bright-maned like Zaya, none I recognize. Vanako Shearwater isn't there; neither is anyone else from the house. But there is one person who used to live there: Yyrreen Turaco, who used to design Zaya's training courses. She's dressed exactly like the up-and-coming entrepreneur she is, a crow among the kingfishers; she jabs a finger at a Zaya, who looks amused but also annoyed, and says, to the obvious irritation of the entourage: "Scarlet. Coral. Cobalt. Ochre. Amethyst."

I'm a journalist, not a spy. Kemreen Gharial sees me and nudges Zaya. Kemreen doesn't remember me, I think, but Zaya does. She smiles sadly and shakes her head, then waves me off. I think about asking a question, but those four Kayalim kids turn their heads toward me and Kemreen settles her weight in a way that makes the street lamps glint off her very large weapons, and I go.

****

EARLY AFTERNOON ON LAUREL Street in early summer is the worst. It's not as hot as it'll be in three or four weeks, but the moisture of spring is still in the air, except that feels impossible because the air should be bone-dry because every drop of that spring moisture is clinging like a tick to my skin. Not just clinging: burrowing in through my pores, each drop carrying a little glowing kernel of sunlight at its core, steaming my skin from the inside. I buy another orxata but it's like pissing on a house fire. (In terms of the futility of trying to cool myself off with it, that is. It's delicious.)

(Stop right there.)

The rattle of the front door is a benison, because anything to take my mind off my inexorable death by boredom and/or par-boiling, and then the gates rattle open and, cazart! It's Minshoon Shearwater! And then, Tiamat! There's a tiny child with him! They have matching broad hats, which make me immediately and crushingly jealous, and Minshoon is carrying a couple of panniers to lash to whatever rattletrap bike he might manage to find and OF COURSE his cute little companion has her own little-person-sized basket that she'll no doubt fill with tiny groceries given to her for free by enchanted grannies at whatever wholesome market she's headed to, probably the one by the border with Rust Precinct where the art students busk for the kids. I am completely uninteresting to this little person, and rightly so, but Minshoon meets my eyes from under his ridiculous hat, smiles coolly, reaches out for her shoulder and pulls her close. "Good afternoon, Agama-*cha*. I wasn't expecting you, but I suppose that was a mistake."

I shake my head. "You've got a kid with you. You've obviously got somewhere to go. I won't press it."

"That's decent of you."

"Not so fast." A theme's come upon me. It may seem obvious to you, but I didn't have the luxury of hindsight in the moment, so feel free to keep your opinions to yourself. "One question, quick answer."

His eyes get very focused and his lips start quirking like there are some words they're trying to keep from getting out. "If it's all right for the audience, go ahead." He squeezes the little kid once to make sure I know what he means by *the audience*.

"That's up to you. What's the most interesting part of this mural that someone might not notice if they weren't paying attention?"

Minshoon looks at the mural. "The wyrm's feathers."

"Bandit!" says the little person.

"That's right," says Minshoon.

I kneel down, because I know you're supposed to get on the level with the kids, and the little person shrinks away from me to hide behind Minshoon's leg. It seems more awkward to acknowledge this than to ignore it, so I ignore it. "Can you show me what's so interesting about the feathers?"

She looks me very seriously in the eyes and shakes her head, the thick black braids that pop up from her skull wobbling with the motion.

I look up at Minshoon, who is very tall even when I'm not squatting, and realize that I'm going to reel and have to steady myself if I get up, which I do not want to do. "Worth a try. I'll have a look. Enjoy your grocery trip!"

Minshoon casts me a sort of baggy-eyed pity that he had neither the range nor the taste for the last time I interviewed him, back when he was more of an esoteric dragon-race gambler and less of a conveyance for children and vegetables. He makes himself blessedly scarce.

I stand, half-black out, lean on the wall for what feels like forever until my blood pressure equilibrates from the sudden opening up of the blood vessels in my legs, and look at the drawing of Bandit. It takes me a second to see what Minshoon is talking about; then it is obvious. The feathers are not feathers. They alternate: half with the trumpet pattern that even then I identified with the datura flower, half with the trefoil of broad, leaf-shaped petals that I've since learned to identify with brightwick.

I won't understand anything about this until later, but you get it, so I'll spare you.

***

SCARLET. CORAL. COBALT. OCHRE. Amethyst.

Reader, the hypotheses I entertained. Yyrreen Turaco runs a business specializing in renovating and reselling apartments, so I thought perhaps this was a discussion on relocating House Shearwater out of Lilac Precinct; but I trudged to Eggshell Precinct one day to look at demographics, and none of it seemed right. Prices were lower in Coral and Amethyst, but higher in Scarlet and Ochre; not unrelated, Coral, Amethyst, and Cobalt had more Kayalim residents than Lilac Precinct, but the others had fewer. Nearby schools weren't obviously better anywhere, and much worse in Cobalt and Amethyst, although Amethyst did contain part of the campus of the University of Yemareir... which was where Kirono Shearwater worked, although his department was housed in Heliotrope not

Amethyst, and in any case moving to Cobalt Precinct would make that commute unbearable except by wyrm...

... and blind alleys quickly commence to look the same, so let me end this misery, especially as the actual answer will be obvious to many of you at this point. As my friend who works in the government and insists on anonymity explained to me over a pair of piously weak drinks at a clean-lined bar in Ivory Precinct, "It's an election year, idiot."

This was not news to me, exactly, but it wasn't like I'd thought about it. "So what do these precincts have in common that made you think of the election?"

"They all have alderwights in the House of the Stars."

This was a well deserved cut at my obliviousness, but I've learned from experience that you can't let these operative types bully you. "What else do they all have? Buildings? Residents, maybe?"

"Yes," my friend replied. "Good. Let your anger fuel you. Let the bright flame of rage be your guiding star."

I waited. I was pretty sure that just staring at them with eyes full of hate would get me what I needed faster than saying more stuff they would just make fun of.

"They all, dipshit," said my loathsome friend whose craven anonymity is the only thing that shields them from the righteous fury of my incredibly loyal readers, who might not die for me but would surely, surely kill, "have open seats this year, and the races all look close."

***

MY MISBEGOTTEN FRIEND IS a stain on the human tapestry, but that's just the type of person who'll get you an interview with a politician, if maybe not on the record. We meet over shaved ice at a hole in the wall in one of the blue precincts. My interlocutor recommends the cloudberry lemon with grass jelly and condensed milk; I take it with nutmeg, raisins, and sweet onion, because I'm an independent thinker.

There's prefatory material, but the fundamental question here is pretty clear, and I get to it just before I've picked the last raisin off my dessert: "Why is yliaster illegal?"

They smile and eat a spoonful of grass jelly, buying seconds to polish an answer that's pretty evidently already prepared. "An epidemic of amateur goetists isn't something this city can afford."

"Are you sure the epidemic of kerostasia is cheaper?"

"You'll have to draw that line for me," they say, but their expression makes it clear they know where it goes.

"Yliaster is a ker repellent. It works by severing the mental connection between ker and hunted, the same way it protects goetists from demons—"

"The pollen has to be collected in places where two flowers bloom together," says my interlocutor. "Which only happens at the foot of the Supplicant."

"Has there been any effort to make it grow elsewhere?"

Their voice grows sharp. "You need to talk to a goetist."

This is annoying. "What if I have?"

"You haven't asked the right questions."

"Which are what?"

"How big a massacre could someone do," they say, speaking just slowly enough to ensure that every syllable lands, "if there were enough yliaster in circulation to treat every hunted person in this city?"

"How many people is that, exactly?"

I'm already speaking to a bowl of melted cloudberry-lemon sludge. The answer is about twenty thousand.

***

"ME, PERSONALLY?" SAYS JEVOON (not his real name), a goetist of the Star Reader Cabal. "A few hundred, anyway. Take it to the right place at the right time, do the right preparations, put down the right wards, I could summon something that they'd need a whole wing of police wyrms to take down."

"Tiamat," I say, because it seems like that's what he's looking for and because, well, Tiamat; this kid might weigh ninety pounds, he seems to be constantly shivering, and one of his eyes nimbly scans the room while the other stays fixed on me. The prospect of a person like this having the power to mass murder thousands of Yemari citizens is terrifying.

"Of course, I'm not ever doing that," he continues. "I'm not doing it, no one even a tenth as good as me is doing it. Not because I'm a good person. I mean—I don't *want* to do it. But if I did: The Star Reader Cabal possesses and tracks the components I need for the right wards, they track any major summoning in the city in real time, and they'd have me inside out and probably... what's the word? Disintegrated?" I can't speak for the policies of the Star Reader Cabal, but Jevoon at this point certainly had the middle-distance stare of someone looking up a regulation in his head. "And the demon banished or killed. Long before the wing of police wyrms had a chance to get within breath-weapon distance of me." He looks at me as if remembering he'd been answering a question instead of spontaneously monologuing to the air. "I mean, nobody who's using *yliaster* to ward themselves could pull a demon anything like that dangerous. They don't have the training. But then again, they also don't have to focus on maintaining the ward." His eyes get lost again. "Actually, with that kind of focus, you could do a lot with a little."

"If you don't mind me observing," I mention after mentally composing my last will and testament, "it's an interesting flex for the Star Reader Cabal to let you speak so candidly about this on the record."

"The Star Reader Cabal is an ancient society devoted to the pursuit of deep truth and the correct use of profound power, not a neighborhood debate club that can't get quorum if we spook the clerks at the precinct office," my informant declaims, without taking a breath at the comma. "Our 'public relations' are inscribed in eldritch glyphs on the night skies. Our only constituency is the Archdukes of the Novae, the Margraves of the Quasars, to whom the quailing of the human breast is nothing more than the fearful chirping of crickets."

(Before this piece went to press, I was contacted by a very kind individual who claimed to possess a moderately high rank in the Star Reader Cabal. They asked me to emphasize that, although nothing my informant said was strictly incorrect, the Cabal does retain—as mentioned perhaps too glancingly by my informant—strict procedural safeguards to preserve the life and well-being of the many magical non-initiates with whom they gladly and responsibly share the city of Yemareir. They would neither confirm nor deny whether the clerks at the precinct office had threatened to take their clubhouse away, although they did concede a general organizational understanding that crickets don't chirp out of fear. When I asked them to name two Margraves of the Quasars, they made some sounds that I spent the next three nights dreaming about.)

***

FIVE POLITICAL SKETCHES IN a hundred words or less:

Scarlet Precinct will soon see the back of the Brightest Scale Party's Kyrleen Crotalus, a beloved elder stateswoman who has somehow survived having an arm chewed off by her ker, a sun bear whose fur is streaked with prehensile cilia and which boasts a giant blue sac under its chin that it can inflate when it's angry. She has declined to endorse her heir apparent, former Scarlet sheriff Avshoon Monitor; he is opposed by the Thread & Mortar Front's Etrimain Slider, a former architect who claims no current profession.

Coral Precinct's Sharnikeen Anole, also of the Brightest Scale Party, is stepping aside to take a peerage in House Pogona. Common wisdom holds that we'll probably see her in the House of the Moon before too long. The serious contenders for the race are Kuriaan Goanna, a commodities trader and the owner of a number of apartment complexes in the precinct, for Brightest Scale; and Yyvvoun Leatherback, a handsome young widower and a member of the Society for Inquiry, an independent.

Despite the testimony of my appalling friend, Cobalt Precinct's Jenishoon Terrapin is running unopposed. Cobalt Precinct has the highest rate of kerostasia in the city at almost two per thousand; the precinct is represented on a temporary basis by Mrahain Tegu, replacing her sibling Mrishtaan Tegu, who died late last year from wounds inflicted by an ora ker. Terrapin attests no party, but Cobalt is a Thread & Mortar precinct and if the party didn't like him, he'd have an opponent.

Ochre Precinct is likewise represented by a temporary candidate, Anroon Slowworm having resigned in disgrace some months ago due to the appearance of impropriety in his accounts. Brightest Scale's Tjalivain Taipan will run to keep her seat in the party, but she seems to have her work cut out for her with Kaana te-Tekko, a construction foreman who's worked on a number of new housing initiatives in the south and west of the city. Te-Tekko runs for the Travelers, a labor party you don't hear much from these days; Thread & Mortar's Fsanreen Slider is spoken of politely but generally viewed as a non-factor in this race.

Yyrreen Turaco's last precinct is Amethyst, where Thread & Mortar's wildly unpopular Ranjoon Whiptail has declined to stand for reelection after a disastrous protest where students were killed for demonstrating in solidarity with contingent workers. The student population in Amethyst makes it difficult to take the pulse of the precinct's voters from its general mood; the proprietors of Amethyst do share the sensibilities of their young neighbors, but less than you might imagine. So it's hard to know whether the edge goes to Brightest Scale's Kanivoon Gharial, a professor of politics whose readings draw crowds of thousands, or the Travelers' Kelloun Rinkhal, an adjunct instructor of theoretical sorcery whose signature style seems to be a jolting mix of populist slogans and incomprehensible mumbled analysis.

If what you've gotten out of that is mostly a long list of Mrineen names that are hard to tell apart, I can't exactly blame you. But the details, as my horrible friend confirms, make it make sense. Etrimain Slider in Scarlet and Jenishoon Terrapin in Cobalt are replacing successful alderwights soon to be lost to the hunger of their kers. Coral's Yyvvoun Leatherback is a sympathetic survivor, an attractive young man who's lost his partner to a panther ker. And as for the Travelers...

***

"The idea that widespread use of yliaster for kerostasia would lead to a rash of demonic massacres has no support in... anything at all," the Travelers' Felindir Ola-Kalenwë intones in complete confidence, over shaved ice because I've developed kind of a thing for shaved ice. "No one thought to make it illegal for centuries, and nothing happened. There were a few copycat incidents a few years ago that died out on their own."

"After it was made illegal."

"It's illegal to take it into the city, but it's not illegal to travel out to the Supplicant, and you don't need more than a knucklebone's worth of yliaster to do the kind of damage you're talking about," Ola-Kalenwë replies. This arrow is clearly the first in their quiver. "You can credit the law for it if you want. I can't prove anything about what everyone who's not killing anyone is thinking. But the penalty for possession is prison time. Whereas basically everyone who's summoned a demon with the help of yliaster has gotten messily executed in the street. On the list of self-preservation strategies for shit goetists, yliaster is empirically no better than saying 'please don't kill me' to the demon."

"Has anyone ever tried that?" I ask.

Ola-Kalenwë gives me exactly the kind of look this sort of irresponsible journalism deserves. "On the other hand, on the list of self-preservation strategies for kerostatics, yliaster is the only item."

Ola-Kalenwë says *kerostatics* like a nerd rather than *hunted* like a normal person, which I infer is due to their pedantic and humorless nature. Then I realize this inference is unfair and strike it from my mind completely, never to be seen again—much less memorialized in print.

In the moment, though, I make a rude scoffing noise. "Surely it's not *the only*—"

"You're trying to wind me up."

"Can I quote you on that? Readers love it when normal people catch me out."

This *really annoys* them, because they know I'm trying to annoy them and they're doubly annoyed that it succeeded. "Fine. But you're wrong. It's the only item."

"Standard dispellings have bought patients years—"

"The median effect of a regular course of dispelling is measured in weeks, and it runs a nontrivial risk of immediately provoking an attack."

I did know this, but I don't admit it. "Interesting phrase."

"Look—"

"I've spoken to a number of exponents of the efficacy of zissurû for kerostasia—"

"You have *not*. No one who knows the first thing about zissurû would think you could use it to keep a ker out if it actually wanted to get in."

"I said exponents, not experts."

Ola-Kalenwë takes a furious bite of shaved ice instead of leaving the table. I congratulate myself for thinking of this. They are correct again, though.

"Look," I continue, "I really appreciate you putting up with this. I'm just trying to answer readers' objections in the article so we don't have to do it in the letters column."

"It's infuriating," they say, but the next bite of shaved ice is more subdued.

"Can you speak to why the Travelers have taken up the cause?"

"Because you can only get yliaster if you're rich," they say, "or maybe if you're fucking the right dealer."

"Who's the right dealer?"

Ola-Kalenwë snorts, which is more polite than that question deserves. I follow up with, "What do you have to say to the police who claim you're signing their death warrants?"

"First, let's recall that the person who signs your death warrant, for those lucky enough to get them, is the person who's *attesting* you're dead, not the person who's killed you." This is humorless, pedantic horseshit at its apex, and I feel ashamed I didn't think of it myself. "Someone in a profession that deals with coroners should know this.

"Second, you're laboring under a false consciousness hand-crafted to prop up the existing cultural hegemony of ancestrally wealthy Mrineen colonizers and you should feel bad." This is like liquid gold in my veins. Felindir Ola-Kalenwë, if you're reading this, please know that I appreciate the purity of your fabulously antisocial character, I'm terribly sorry that you have no friends, and I wouldn't blame you if you saw me drowning in quicksand and walked away. Also, I do feel bad.

"Third, and related: I've seen your take-home pay. The colonizers like you because you're useful, but not enough to save you when you find that fuzzy little sloth bear ker sleeping in your kitchen. *That's* a death warrant."

"Which you've just signed."

Ola-Kalenwë looks at me as though I've spoken out of a mouth that just suddenly popped into existence in my neck.

"Because you haven't killed me, but you're *attesting* I'm dead."

They scoop up a big spoonful of shaved ice, put their forefinger on the tip of the spoon, and flick it at me like a catapult. Fair enough.

***

MY EDITOR IS UNDER the impression that not every reader of the *Damask Free Press* is clued in to the politics of Yemareir. I'm under the impression that all eighteen of you are the kind of person who corrected their teachers in civics class, but my editor is also under the impression that there are a few folks out front who've figured out I'm here and I need to turn this in before they realize there's a back exit out the cellar. Herewith, then, a primer.

The House of the Stars is the chamber of elected representatives, one from each precinct of Yemareir. The House of the Moon is the chamber of the peerage. The peerage is an imitation of the system of landownership and peasant-fucking-over that governed the Empire of Mlinivoun a thousand years ago; since our contemporary economic system leans a lot more on skilled craft and trade and a lot less on extracting plants from dirt, a noble title is basically a thin scrim between you and the blinding realization that you didn't earn any of that money you inherited. The Stars originate laws, the Moon advises and occasionally vetoes. The House of the Sun is currently defunct, but we'll probably get it back one of these centuries, when the people feel like getting ordered around in church isn't quite *binding* enough and decide they want priests in the government again.

The Brightest Scale party has held a majority in the House of the Stars since anyone currently alive was born. It's hard to identify their ideology—not because they don't have one, but because the way things are is pretty much the way they want things to be. It's like trying to smell air. They like giving food and shelter, but not money, to poor people; they like having Kayalim and Ililuë in the peripheral precincts to do work, but like having mostly Mrineen living in the central precincts; they like having power concentrated in the Houses and the property owners (but I repeat myself). They like magic and technology and dragons. They like trade, but they don't like getting spanked by Ililuë guerrillas on colonial ventures outside Yemareir. You get the idea.

The Thread & Mortar Front has been shouting from the sidelines for a number of years, and if you listen to what they're saying, you can get a sense for Brightest Scale's values by contrast. The Thread & Mortar Front thinks poor people should get money as well as food and shelter. They want the vote expanded beyond just property owners, and favor a property tax to fund social programs for the destitute. They're neutral at best on magic, technology, and dragons, all of which are largely out of reach for the tailors and bricklayers they say they represent. They don't like trade. You might think these positions would buy them a ceiling higher than a third of the House of the Stars; we'll get there.

But first: The Travelers.

In the House of the Stars, the Travelers are represented by Jina ze-Saibaka of Lilac Precinct and Mirwennë Oriadar of Viridian, which is weird; they don't, historically, win elections. Their positions on basic income, social support, and the vote are exactly what you'd predict from a party made up principally of Kayalim and Ililuë, a lot of whom are on the dole or out of work. Which, of course, is why they don't win elections decided by owners.

Now: A reader just debarked from Kerkakan or Jaidar might wonder what the difference is between the Travelers, as I've just described them, and the Thread & Mortar Front. A couple of illustrative examples.

In the last legislative session, Adraan Loggerhead of Thread & Mortar advanced a proposal for tariffs on textiles. The eighteen idiots who buy this rag on the regular will need no further context, but for those of you who were here for the sportswriting: Cloth is a massive import from surrounding Ililuë communities, and unlike (say) farming it's something that a solo practitioner or household team can support themselves on with very little investment up front. It's also a major source of income for Ililuë residents of Yemareir, who can differentiate themselves from the commodity market by taking custom orders and availing themselves of dyes produced only in the city. The bill in question departed from existing trade law in defining textiles produced by non-citizen residents as "imports." Most of the majority balked at the idea of raising commodity prices for pretty much any reason at all, so the bill is in its death throes, but my terrible contacts in politics assure me Loggerhead has boosted their margin in Crimson Precinct by a minimum of five points.

So much for "thread."

Three sessions ago, Kanjoon Ora put a bill on the floor limiting the use of nonhuman animals in construction. I don't think anyone who knows enough to read those words needs any further explanation of that one. It got closer to passage, thanks to a split within Brightest Scale; broadly, the precincts where there are a lot of construction *projects* aren't the same as the ones where there are a lot of construction *workers*, and the latter liked this idea—the workers mostly don't vote, but the landlords who collect their rents do—but the former didn't. There'd have been more of a floor fight if the House of the Moon and the Reeve's office hadn't been extremely clear that the bill was dead on arrival. But Kanjoon Ora has sailed to reelection in Cadet Precinct ever since.

So much for "mortar."

This kind of almost-plausibly-deniable offensive against Kay-alim and Ililuë residents of Yemareir is a relatively new evolution of some more forthright attacks. It's been eight sessions since anyone in the Thread & Mortar Front proposed tying any kind of social support to "descendants of the founders of Yemareir." The bill there was to fund a basic income measure for descendants by making non-descendants ineligible for the dole.

That was when Thread & Mortar had 10 seats, not 19, and there were a few weeks when it looked like it had the votes in the Stars.

Technically, who knows. It never did go up for a vote. There were riots in green, pink, and brown precincts, which delayed it; but what really sank the thing was a letter from the courts. Lawmakers had assumed that any Mrineen citizen of Yemareir is a descendant of the founders... but the judges warned that eight hundred years was enough time for plenty of migrants from Old Mlinivoun to find their way here, and that genealogical proof would have to be submitted and reviewed to qualify for support under the proposed new law.

So that's why the Travelers and the Thread & Mortar Front don't work together.

Here's the thing, though, this year.

Brightest Scale doesn't like yliaster. Or, they like it—as a component of lucrative industrial processes that can rake in money for the Houses and companies with the means to mass-produce and distribute products based on it. Not as a substance unpredictable individual humans can craft and use as they please without surrendering a cut of the value. They also have safety concerns for which, as an individual recently used as a pavement substitute by several thousand people fleeing a demon, I have developed a heightened if perhaps not complete level of appreciation.

The Travelers' position is obviously the opposite, well stated by Felindir Ola-Kalenwë: A lot of individual humans need yliaster or they'll be gruesomely devoured by invulnerable predators from other worlds. Yliaster-abetted goetic attacks are a problem, but balanced against thousands of otherwise inevitable deaths a year, they're not that big a problem. (Recent pavement substitutes have difficulty considering this position on the merits, but we can grudgingly concede there are merits.)

Thread & Mortar are interestingly positioned here. Their default, populist orientation ought to align them with the Travelers on the yliaster question... but alienating the police is a tricky decision for the Thread & Mortar Front. Most police are Mrineen, and a healthy fraction of them are on the dole, which makes them natural constituents for Thread & Mortar. On the other hand, the job is considered a way *out* of the dole, and indeed, very few senior officers are on it. On the next hand, most officers aren't senior. Maybe there's a hidden current among the force in favor of legalizing, or at least liberalizing, yliaster; but they won't say it where it might get back to their bosses.

So much for elementary education. We herewith return to journalism.

***

IF THE PUBLIC RELATIONS of the Star Reader Cabal are inscribed in the night sky, the public relations of precinct police forces are inscribed on the flinty eyes of thick-armed women and men whose highest fondness is the *crack* of a door slammed in an inquiring face.

The exception is in Cobalt Precinct, where an anonymous officer arranges a walk along the beach at dusk at a later date. They're good-looking; I think seriously about bringing flowers but opt, inevitably, for a steel flask of elderflower arrack, on the theory that if my interlocutor prefers to be professional in this interview I can at least enjoy myself.

Tide's low and we're backlit by the setting sun. We walk along the firm, wet sand by the waterline; the surf is loud enough to swallow our words before they wander too far.

"First," my interlocutor says, "no one believes they're going to find a ker in their kitchen until it happens. That's human nature, it's too horrible to think about that stuff when you don't strictly have to. That said, people in my line of work are prone to thinking it can't happen to us because we're living right. They know that's not how it works, but in their hearts they believe that's how it works."

"Why," I ask, "does 'living right' give you immunity to invulnerable soul-eating beasts from adjacent dimensions but not from incompetent baby sorcerers with chips on their shoulders?"

"I'm not the spokesman for the weird beliefs of the entire profession. If people in general felt like their beliefs needed to make an ounce of sense, we'd live in a very different world."

That's worth a nip from the flask. "You're cynical."

"I'm talking to you. That makes me an idealist."

"OK." I hold out the flask; my interlocutor has asked me not to describe whether or not they took me up on the offer. "You said 'first.'"

"Second," says my handsome subject, "if your 'representative from the Travelers' thinks they have any idea what our 'ancestrally wealthy Mrineen colonizers' won't do for their falsely conscious props for the cultural hegemony—did I get that right?"

I nod and hold up the flask in encouragement.

"If they think they have any idea about all that, they haven't been around enough precinct offices. Look for kers. Look for tattoos. They're not that hard to find."

"Sorry," I say. "Expand on that for my readership."

"Cops," my interlocutor says, "get treated."

Maybe it's contempt for me that makes them speak so slowly and distinctly; maybe it's the arrack. But, of course, whether they've drunk the arrack, I cannot say.

***

SCARLET. A RALLY FOR Etrimain Slider gets broken up by police.

Coral. Yyvvoun Leatherback invites the hunted and their loved ones to speak about their experience. A few minutes in, someone in the crowd attacks a pair of passing cops with a sword. A heathy few dozen are arrested. Days later, I informally interview a number of police in Coral Precinct with the question, "What kind of sword?" and get a number of blank stares back.

Cobalt. Torazoon Skink, formerly a lieutenant in Ivory Precinct, announces a late candidacy for Brightest Scale. Property records show he's only just bought a seaside villa in the precinct. It is painfully predictable and yet somehow necessary to write that police pensions do not support this kind of purchase for any position below precinct chief or at least a mid-level citywide administrator... especially not for those with art collection habits; Skink likes hippo-tooth figurines from the Long Arm Period. Torazoon Skink is way too smart to give me a quote, wherefore I am unable to attribute him the statement, "For that house I owe no one but my past self, who built up to it through to long decades of hard work and diligent saving." But I've met the man and I can assure you it's the kind of thing he'd say.

Ochre. A rally for Kaana te-Tekko is canceled because there's a police wyrm squatting in middle of the square where it's scheduled. When a representative from the campaign asks the cop in charge to leave, the wyrm immolates the stage and podium.

Amethyst. After Scarlet and Coral, the campaign for Kelloun Rinkhal implores attendees not to come to their events with weapons, alcohol, or basically any hard thing that can be thrown. In the midst of a fiery speech, Rinkhal himself is pulled from the stage on the grounds that he is inciting violence. The police escorting him from the stage are immediately thronged by a knot of rallygoers including a gorilla ker, which apparently unnerves the arresting officers enough to let Rinkhal go on the condition that the rally is dissolved. He tries, but his audience isn't interested, and for the rest you really ought to read Karalain Boomslang's feature in these pages on the events of that night, whose callous headline of "Class Dismissed" so neatly belittles a masterfully written essay of genuine conscience, compassion, and truth-seeking that, if you didn't know better, you'd almost think our editors did it on purpose.

***

I MAKE MY WAY to Eggshell to have another drink with my horrible friend in another minimalist bar whose every angle is perfection. "Give me five other precincts with close races. Nasty ones."

They rattle them off without thinking: Alabaster, Incarnadine, Heliotrope, Madder, Celadon.

That last one rings a bell. "Who's running?"

"Some house-flipper who owns a business around the corner from here. Apparently she's co-domiciled in Celadon so she's eligible. Some weird name. Toucan? Turaco."

"Have any of the events gotten violent?"

My friend laughs. Horribly, obviously; for nothing my friend does is not horrible. "I think you've confused Yemareir for a city where the residents care about politics."

Spend too long with primary sources, you forget how most people get their information. A few 'zines and underground papers reported on the clashes at the rallies in Yyrreen Turaco's five precincts, but the rest of the city's papers were as clean as water from a mountain spring. Including, let me not stint to point out, this one. When I brought this up with my editor three weeks ago, she asked me "What do your primary sources tell you about who won the Course of Birds?" And she's going to leave that line in because otherwise I'll spike this story myself.

The domed city-states of the unclaimed deserts have different microclimates in different regions, and so people sleep in shifts. The Spiral City of Gadijir is said to wind continuously around a pillar a mile high, so it is effectively laid out in a line a dozen miles long, except for those brave souls willing to rappel or climb.

Yemareir is a big city, but we're not that big. When I asked a couple of Kayalim construction workers about the riots in Amethyst, they didn't answer, but the look they gave me as they got away as fast as possible said that they knew exactly what I meant. What's your fucking excuse?

***

(To be fair, my editor does deserve the credit for greenlighting "Class Dismissed"—the article itself, not the headline. Better late than never.)

***

At some point, in the gathering dusk on Laurel Street, I notice a Kayalim boy loitering with me: Good-looking, on the tall side, one of those hard-mouth-soulful-eyes kind of deals with hair that's long enough you could mess it up. He's biked here from a precinct that's poor and not close, as your sharp-eyed correspondent could easily tell from his sweat stains and the death-trap-looking bike itself, which skulks near him like a spider. He's across the street, but right across the street, which makes me think a bit that he might have preferred to be where I am if I weren't already there. And his eyes keep going up to that fourth floor height, even when he doesn't think I'm not looking (I'm obviously looking).

"Hey, kid," I say, acting every bit the obnoxious, bored grownup who's identified a source of amusement, "how about this mural, right?"

"Fuck the 'stream," he says.

"Huh," I reply. "Care to elaborate?"

He curls a lip with such fluidity, I imagine him practicing it thirty times in front of a mirror every night with a tiny little weight attached. "It's nothing better than gladiator fights. People die just to amuse people like you."

"Yeah, I heard about that Pogona guy."

I can't see that well in the dusk, but I can tell that, to this kid, Arhoon Pogona does not count. Then he seems to change his mind. "Exactly. There was no reason anyone should have been racing in there. That course in particular is a known deathtrap."

"You know more about it than I do," I say, which is almost certainly true. "Not a fan of the mural, then."

He obviously wants to say something, but he knows better than to say it to a Mrineen, even on home turf. So what the hell, I call him on it. "I can tell you've got something to say here."

"She's a good person."

"That bad, huh? What'd she do to you?"

That actually buys me a caught-out laugh. "Remember the first thing I said to you? Before we got to know each other."

I do. "She's just getting by. Trying to keep a roof over her head. Isn't she?"

"Sure."

A girl with hair whose color I can't quite place in the dusk comes out of the gate by the mural. The boy's back straightens, his shoulders pull back. "Tuuro, stop talking to the reporter," she says to him.

He looks at me. I give him a shrug and an embarrassed grin. His face turns into lava.

The girl is sizing me up. She's maybe a little younger than the boy, and I guess they're going to go suck face in some alley by a square where there's a show, and since she knows who I am I think I know who she is. "Ms. Shearwater," I say, "if you've got a moment, I'd love to hear your thoughts on a number of topics including, but not limited to, the death of Arhoon Pogona, your mother's growing fame, and the future of your own career in the 'stream."

"She's definitely not telling you any of that," her boyfriend says, and I thank him silently, because her glance up at him tells me she has to say something just to prove him wrong.

She's not the type to compose her words. "My career in the 'stream is to support my family and buy treatments that my brother needs to live. If there's anything else you want to know, check us out in the Course of Birds next week."

I beg for a follow-up because I have a job to do, but I know an exit line when I hear one.

***

MY HANDSOME INFORMANT HAS agreed to a meeting in a green precinct that shall remain anonymous. We sit down over something that's rumored to be deep-southern Ililuë food; I can't comment on the authenticity, but there's a lot of bread, sauce, and beer, so why do I care? I ask them the obvious question, and their reply is this:

"The police departments of Yemareir don't demand our members vote a certain way, but institutionally we do think it's important to support the governing party in elections."

"Why?"

"Those are the people we work with."

"You also work with elected members of opposition parties," I point out. "Are you saying you support all incumbents?"

"I said what I said."

"So no love for the Thread & Mortar Front."

"Are they the governing party?" they ask.

"What if I said yes?"

They look at me as though I'd asked the same question in a very different context. I'm a doctor of journalism, so I don't blush.

"So no love for the Thread & Mortar Front."

"We save love for when we're off duty," my handsome informant declares without a trace of innuendo.

"You're really going to support Torazoon Skink just skating in from Ivory Precinct to take Cobalt?"

My handsome informant shifts their weight and puts their hands in front of them, fingers interlaced, the universal posture of an individual about to utter a pronouncement, as I have learned from innumerable bad third dates. "Torazoon Skink supports continued controls over substances that, we believe, threaten the lives and safety of members of our force as well as the citizenry at large."

"Very nice. Next time you pay someone for canned statements, please consider me. My rates are reasonable and I am a delight to work with."

"If I had any idea who commissions these things, I'd put your name in."

"Are there similar statements with the names of other candidates filled in?"

"Yes."

"Avshoon Monitor, Kuriaan Goanna, Tjalivain Taipan, Kanivoon Gharial?"

"Among others."

That's interesting. "How many?"

"I don't know. I just know I've heard other names than those, and more than one."

"So this is, like, a real fight. Not just a couple of precincts."

"You would know people who know the answer to that. I just arrest cats and rescue pickpockets from trees."

The conversation continues. Of course it continues. Do I ask them, at some point—perhaps even many points—why they have chosen to break ranks with their colleagues and snitch to the journalist? Of course I do. Will I divulge the answer? I will not. Could you guess it? Yes, reader, I think you could.

***

IN THE EVENING, WHEN the trees of Laurel Street glow with fairy lights and the proprietor of the bodega drags his grill outside to sell a walking dinner to people with somewhere to be, the heart of my story shows itself.

Perhaps it's the smoke from the grill that brings them out? Perhaps it's the dark, easy on hungover eyes, or the cool; it is, after all, that part of the evening of a hot day where the balance shifts, where the blessed shelter of indoors becomes a prison, too confined to dissipate the lingering day-heat or the itch to move that you were too hot to notice building up while the sun was out. Perhaps it's the orxata, although the bodega sold out of it around sunset; believe me, I checked. Whatever the reason, my bright-haired subject finally emerges.

She does not look older, but she is older. I'd say you see it in her eyes but horseshit; eyes are stones, I for one have never met any object less forthcoming than an eye. No, where you see it is in where she looks. Zaya Shearwater at nineteen had a target, a point in space different from the one she occupied, organizing all her movements around getting there whether she was thinking about it or not. Zaya Shearwater at twenty-five has a wider field of view, not scattered but consciously dispersed, scanning the environment outside the gate to the house she calls House Shearwater, in the way that every parent scans every city street to make sure it is safe for someone small and not very thoughtful to move through it.

Jaliki Shearwater is not all that small, and the head whose crown sits just at the point of Zaya's shoulder bears a face that is thoughtful indeed. Or maybe that's just how it comes off because the hound ker pops out with him, and one of the strongest, dumbest reflexes of the hominid brain, right alongside the delusion that getting drunk in public is ever a good idea, is to assume a death sentence has to confer a wisdom of some kind, a sight into corners of the soul denied to those of us whose end is not yet written in language we can understand. Whatever he's gravely contemplating in this moment, behind those soulful eyes, it has to be more consequential than "chicken or pork?", or what does all this suffering even mean?

"The last time I saw you, you were a baby," I'm about to say, but I can't choke it out. Why, honestly, I have no idea. I've interviewed the stricken and the grieving with as hard a heart as is required, because inside that hard heart lives the knowledge that truth is the kindness that pays for all. The presence of suffering children is a cord around my tongue, but one that I can cut through. If I had to give an accounting for this silence, I suppose I'd put it down to simple surprise. Because I did meet this child when he was a baby, and there was no shadow of the headsman then, not that there ever is.

Zaya and Jaliki do not see me, but the hound ker does, and there's no way I can not feel transfixed by that gaze.

They walk over to the bodega guy and get some grilled meat and some potato cakes that he's added to the grill while I wasn't paying attention, and my outrage flares when he does somehow find them a couple of cups of orxata, I mean folk hero and all but *what the hell*, her money's no better than mine, and they walk back and now Zaya sees me because of course she does and, I realize, it's evening, Minshoon and his little nugget would have been gone for uncounted hours by now, and if I didn't see him come back then he's obviously returned through the back door or something and informed her of who's lurking in wait.

She edges closer to Jaliki, bumping him gently with her hip, and looks behind me at the mural and raises her eyebrows in a way that clearly communicates *You saw that, right?*, and then nods her head, once, and then they pass back through the gate. Jaliki, whose neck was not strong enough to support his head the last time I laid eyes on him, has not noticed me at all.

Good for him. He has more important things to think about. I leave the street.

***

THE NARRATIVE HERE, FOR closure, demands I tell you where the tipoff to the event in Inundinir Square came from. Because that's where I have to end: back at the beginning, the terror and carnage from out of nowhere now tidily recontextualized as an escalation in a battle you never knew was being fought, to which my coda will add a further, final piece of information that casts the whole thing in yet a different light.

And it will! Carpenters get paid to join legs to tables, I get paid to do this. The frustrating thing about it all is that, if I did tell you, it would feel right, narratively. It's a person you know, now, a person who makes sense. But the other thing I get paid to do is protect my informants. And this one, through word or action, indicated it was confidential.

So, to close the loop, because it's an hour before dawn and my editor is roaring obscenities outside my door and any minute now I'm pretty sure the printer is going to send a goon of some kind with a hacksaw to break in and pull whatever draft I've got from my trembling hands, after which I'm sure that bastard will bill me for the repair... consider these:

At a bar in Ivory Precinct, my thrice-cursed political operative friend slides their empty wine glass over for a refill. Caught under it, a slip of cream paper, neatly folded.

In the cold morning light after Ililuë food in an anonymous green precinct, I wake up on one side of my bed, alone in tangled sheets. The cream paper is on my bedside table, folded into the shape of a rose.

I swan into my editor's office, collapse in a chair, and moan consumptively about the impossibility of this story I'm now several weeks late with on Zaya Shearwater's return to the 'stream. She looks at me over unfeeling spectacles and hands me an envelope, says she found it slipped under the door this morning. My name is on it.

Felindir Ola-Kalenwë hands me a card with information about the next campaign rallies for Kaana te-Tekko and Kelloun Rinkhal. It's not until days later that I check the back and see the tip. Thankfully, or not, it's in time.

Yyrreen Turaco finds me at the finish line of the latest Arc-en-Ciel, where I am still going even though I know Zaya won't be there. She gives me a raised eyebrow and silently drops the note into my glass of beer. I'm too busy scrambling to read it before the ink dissolves to catch her and ask about it; by the time I save it, she's long gone.

Zaya Shearwater, walking her son into the house with dinner in hand, meets my eye once more as she and Jaliki pass the mural, through the gate. She makes sure I notice the twitch in her hand, flicking the crumpled paper to land almost at my feet.

None of these actually happened—especially that last one; how would Zaya even know about the Basting Stitch that far in advance? Pick the one you like. Imagine another one. The truth isn't these, but it's like these. I'm not holding out on anything great. I just can't say exactly how it happened.

***

A SLICE OF A scene from Inundinir Square, because it's been a minute since you read it:

There was one open window on the fifth story of the Hotel Ochre, by the Dusk Stalkers. For a moment, I saw a face there.

Silence, or some near cousin of it, hung over Inundinir Square for the space of three deep breaths. A knot of black-robed necromancers rushed in from Scrivener's Street, their eyes glowing with the power of their discipline, bodies encased in some eggshell-shaped field that ran with translucent color almost like a soap bubble. In another three breaths, as they assessed the scene and let their protections down, I saw a pair of police on Argent Swordwings circling in the sky overhead, looking for any dangers they might have missed.

As casually as I could, I walked to the still wreck of a body by the Hotel Ochre. I looked at what there was of the face to memorize it.

The face of the body on the ground was one I knew. My informant, no longer handsome.

The face in the window was not theirs, but it was also one I know. I saw it at Shizaki's, at the Widow & Sage, at the Grove at the Center of All Things. I saw it one minute ago, from the window of the dark office I've crept into because it has a view of the front door.

***

I CAN'T WRITE MUCH longer. I need to be ready to move; and this manuscript needs to be ready for its steward, the sure and subtle hand who will guide it somewhere safer than this office has become.

And the question in your mind, reader, is surely the same as the one in mine: Will it be too much, for this officer to be involved in two acts of unsanctioned goetic massacre in one night? Or will the law gamble on the magical societies of Yemareir turning their eyes away—knowing, as one must imagine they do, that no further bloodshed will come once their target is acquired?

Let's make a deal: If I've given myself too much credit or the law too little, if I'm able to walk out of here and find these words again before they go to print, you'll never read this sentence. If it's not revised out, on the other hand—well, best not to think about it.

At least for me. You think about it all you like.

Pencils down. Godspeed.

***

SHENIREEN AGAMA HAS COVERED economics and culture for the *Damask Free Press*, lectured in the humanities at several of Yemareir's universities, and been a senior sports correspondent for

This Seasonal City. She is the author of two books of non-fiction, *The Linear Orchards* and *The Tusk-Mad*, and a memoir, *Surmises*. As this essay goes to press, her whereabouts are unknown.

PART I

CHAPTER 1

SIX WEEKS BEFORE BELL THE CAT

NO MATTER HOW FAST she pedaled, the slipstream of the bike didn't dry the blood on Zaya's dress. Maybe the sweat had kept it wet; the night was seasonably hot, the wind—when there was wind—blowing in from the east, bringing the wet of the cloud forest and the heat of the veldt to mingle in the streets. Embers of pain burned in her thighs, heralds of stiff stilt-walking tomorrow; she didn't realize until she dismounted, practically hurling the piece-of-shit bike across the street, that her forearms ached from squeezing the handlebars like a stewing hen's neck.

Stepping toward the compound made the world slow down. Neither wheels nor wings were here to make her fly now. The fug of the night was edged with harissa, mutton fat, and some syrup-sweet alcohol; the aroma sent a blade of thirst through Zaya's throat, and the taste-memory of shaved ice with lemon-cloudberry syrup followed like a lance to the chest. A thickly built shape stepped from the shadows by the gate, a scimitar jutting proudly from a sword belt. Zaya's mind *reached* for other minds and found them: A pangolin rooting through trash for ants, a dozing fennec, a brace of idly watching shearwaters—and a human, holding unnaturally still. Zaya seized the shearwaters and the fennec and fixed her eyes on the human, whom she still could barely see, and walked directly toward them until she could.

"Slow down, ma'am," said the other human, the one with the scimitar.

"Yeah, no," said Zaya, keeping her eyes fixed on the hidden person. She brought the fennec over with the scent-image of barbecue and had it look in the same direction she was looking. "Stop hiding, it's not working."

The hidden person didn't move. "Are you supposed to be here?" said Scimitar. "Because no one told me anyone was supposed to be here."

Zaya had the shearwaters land on her shoulders. They, she, and the fennec all stared into the shadows where the hidden person lurked.

They sighed through their nose and stepped out into the streetlamp-light. The lurker turned out to be a short, slight Mrineen woman, with a faintly glowing knotwork face tattoo of the kind you occasionally saw on some Mrineen who wanted to show how strongly they identified with their forebears who knapped flint and interfered with herd animals in the hills and hinterlands of Mrineendom a million years ago. Lurking in shadows while sporting a glowing face tattoo is the kind of thing you need magic to do, so there was that. Face Tattoo cast a quick glance up to her partner. "No appointment," she said, "but she's expected."

"Since when?"

"There's birds on her shoulders."

"I had leeches on my balls once," said Scimitar, "but it didn't get me in the boss' house at midnight."

"They're not there to scrape out her earwax, dipshit," said Face Tattoo. "She's telling us who she is."

Zaya felt a mind probing at hers. She lashed out with lightning and harsh static, and Face Tattoo flinched and hissed as if she'd been burned. The hiss faded to a grin, though. "All right, Shearwater-cha. The birds can clean out your ears for now, but they don't come inside. I'm getting a friend to verify you're who you seem to be saying you are, and then you and my employer can have the conversation."

"What conversation?" said Scimitar.

"If you don't know, I don't believe I'm authorized to enlighten you."

"She's got blood on her dress," said Scimitar. "Are you sure we ought to let her in?"

Zaya felt a familiar consciousness skitter into her mental field of view. She looked to the gate; a mandrill was staring at her. It looked at the lurker, who didn't look back, then left.

"She's the article," Face Tattoo said to Scimitar. She looked Zaya up and down, eyes lingering on the blood. "My colleague's right, though. You're in a touch of disarray. What happened?"

She didn't wait for an answer as she dug around pockets for a key and began opening the gate. Zaya felt Face Tattoo's mind just outside her own, though, watching. "Someone close to me is very badly hurt," Zaya said.

"Interesting," said Face Tattoo. "What do you expect himself to do about it?"

"If I give you the right answer, will you let me in?"

"Just making conversation," Face Tattoo said, palm out in conciliation. "I let in who the monkey says I let in. Even weeping women with blood all over themselves."

"I'm not weeping."

Face Tattoo chuffed a quick chuckle. Zaya swept past her, sending the fennec and the shearwaters on their way, and through the gate. It began to creak closed, but she felt the lurker follow.

The courtyard was small but well designed: A little pond with a fountain, a pair of benches, a banana tree. It was only a few steps to the front door of the house. Face Tattoo stepped in front of her to unlock the door, and they both stepped into a cramped, close waiting room. "You get the white glove treatment," Face Tattoo said. "Precious few guests who can pull me away from the door and back here into the *vestibule*." She pronounced the word with a deliberate twist. "Most people get the monkey. You know why, though, right? It's not because you're special. It's because you're dangerous."

Zaya looked down at her hands, still aching from squeezing the handlebars. What were they any good for? They couldn't keep their grip on what mattered most.

"You're really in no state, are you?" Face Tattoo said. Her voice was brash and jeering when she said it, but her mind was close enough in that Zaya could feel a thread of real concern. It wasn't all for Zaya; Face Tattoo wasn't sure how this would leave her with her boss, bringing in a woman who was obviously distraught, who perhaps couldn't execute, or follow through on, whatever transaction she was here for. "My name's Tanishain."

"Zaya." Zaya made herself look at Tanishain, tried to erase some of the ruin from her face. From close up she could see a dusting of fine stubble on her jawline. "Sorry about outside. It's been a rough night."

"Forgive me, Zaya, if I say I've seen women come in from rougher."

"Sure. I suppose I'm just unusually fragile."

"I doubt that. And, look, the mystery and the intensity got you in the door, didn't it? Showed us you're serious. But unless that blood's the blood of the last person beneath this sun who ever loved you... I mean, look, boss man's going to want to get down to brass tacks. Intensity's good for brass tacks. Mystery, though—"

"Tanishain," Zaya said, with a voice as clear as she could make it, "you're not going to regret bringing me in the door. I don't know whether Tjaroon and I are going to part ways with a deal or not. That was never going to be up to you. But you're not going to present your boss with a blithering sack of snot and regrets who can't hold up her end of a dessert tab." Cold pierced her again: Lemon and cloudberry syrup over shaved ice. "And you were right. I do have people waiting on me at home, and I plan on coming back to them." The words felt hollow, but she said them lightly, naturally, with no special emphasis. "You've got nothing to worry about." She glanced at the pale form at the top of the stairs. "Though I guess I should have just been talking to the monkey." Tanishain's face twitched a bit; that had stung. "Relay. Right? I used to do that once in a while. Much more useful for you, though; that's smart. Anything else I need to send along?"

Tanishain laughed softly. "Good spot. He wants to know what you're here for."

Zaya didn't try to keep the catch out of her throat. "My son. He said he could help out with my son."

"That's right."

"How long?"

"Five years."

"Not enough."

Tanishain looked off to the side a moment. "It'll have to be enough. And it'll be enough, he says. Things are changing."

Zaya closed her eyes against the sting of tears, then made herself speak before she could think too hard about it. "Fine. And what do I have to do?"

The mandrill stood and deftly opened the door at the top of the stairs. Tanishain jerked her head up toward it. "That one doesn't go through me, love."

Zaya stood and walked over to the stairs. Her legs, still so much slower than wings or wheels, made the journey an infinity. She thought the mandrill had disappeared into the room, but when she looked up, she saw a pair of flashing eyes and the ghost of a snout, watching to see what she would do.

She closed her eyes briefly, bit her lip, and placed one foot on the lowest stair.

CHAPTER 2

NINE WEEKS BEFORE BELL THE CAT

WHEN THE DOOR OPENED, Jaliki was already standing on the sofa, shouting: "Mom, there's this new place, Cerminir took me, you have to try it, Mom, it's called Snowcaps and they have this lemon cloudberry—"

It wasn't Zaya whose hand was on the knob, though, it was Shozo: Bald, boulder-shaped, and copiously scarred, with feather tattoos on his scalp in parrot-green. "Hey, Jaliki," he said. "All good here?"

"Yeah, is Mom back? Because—"

Shozo cleared the door and beckoned behind him, and a crew of seven shuffled in: Zaya, Vanako, Yyrreen, Taavi, Kemreen, slim Amiko with black hair down her back, and Chashu, whose real name Zaya still didn't know, with the grey hair dyed lavender and the potbelly and the knives on his belt big enough to gut a bull rhino. Zaya walked over to the couch and picked Jaliki up off it without a word, pulling him close; he was young enough to hug back with arms and legs both, no questions asked. She breathed him in: Skin and hair and sweat, his tight curls soft on her face, his shoulder blades sharp under her hands. She ignored the nose snuffling around her calves, the whining from the floor. It was only Jaliki's presence that stopped her boot from lashing out. The last yliaster tattoo paid for by Ziyuki had faded over the weeks since

Zaya won the Omari Shadowrun; the ker had no aversion to Jaliki any more, was as comfortable near him as it had ever been.

She set her son down and turned to Minshoon, who'd just gotten up from the armchair. "Sorry for the entrance. The race—" She turned to Jaliki, thinking they should talk somewhere where he couldn't hear. But his eyes were elsewhere: on Shozo and Chashu, who were standing casually by the door as though by the door was where one generally stood when one was a guest in a home, and Amiko and Kemreen, who were pacing back and forth between the windows. He was past being babied about all this. He should know. "Someone summoned a demon to hit the awards ceremony. None of us got hurt, Kaana's OK. Vanioun Ora is dead, but he might be the only one. Bandit's a little banged up—I don't think they were counting on it to defend us, I don't know if they'd have summoned something stronger if they'd known—"

Minshoon pulled her into a quick embrace, then put his hand on her shoulder and pressed down. "You should sit. Have a drink. What are you drinking?"

"Whiskey's good, not much. Thank you."

"Anyone else?"

A chorus from the room; Minshoon bustled over to the kitchen. "No sugar cane juice after dark, Jali."

"Awwww."

"Hey, when we get old, we need you to still have some teeth in that skull. Otherwise how will you chew our food for us?"

Black bile surged up from Zaya's heart; she bit it back. Minshoon knew to look at her, knew to look abashed. One of the rules of being around Zaya: You didn't joke about Jaliki's future. The ker was curled up at Jaliki's feet, right next to her. She kicked it a little. It didn't budge.

Yyrreen sat next to her. "Hey, Jali," she said, rubbing his head. "Zaya, we have to think about what this means for tomorrow. The rally in Cerise Precinct—"

"Call it off."

"What?"

"It's not worth risking people's lives if this is going to happen again. Call it off."

"We can't call it off."

"All right. Then what do we need to talk about?"

"Someone tried to kill you," said Yyrreen. "They'll expect you to have something to say about it."

"Who?"

Yyrreen looked at her as if she'd asked who the Reeve of Yemareir was. "People?" she said. "Who cast votes?"

A sharp rap came on the door. Shozo and Chashu glanced up toward it, and the ker looked up from its spot on the floor, tail thumping.

"It's fine," Zaya said. "Let them in."

Chashu looked unhappily at her. Shozo shrugged, loosened the chain from around his waist, and opened the door. Kaana te-Tekko strode in, lean and dry and sharply dressed, accompanied by a tuxedo-clad pillar of muscle as thickly built as Shozo and half again as tall. The bodyguard and Shozo shared the sort of nod men share who've been in the same line of work and seen some things. Kaana's composure was less complete. "This is an act of fucking war."

"Kaana," said Yyrreen, "what are you doing?"

"Declaring war!" said Kaana, storming over to the couch, kicking the ker out of the way—it disappeared with a brief whine a heartbeat before impact—and kissing Jaliki on the cheek before he could begin evasive maneuvers. "Hello, Jali my love."

"Kaana," Yyrreen said across Zaya, "stop."

"I wasn't the first one summoning demons to kill my political opposition," said Kaana, "but you can take it to the bank I won't be the last—"

"Kaana," said Zaya. "Stop declaring war in my living room."

"Fine. We'll do it in Cerise Precinct."

"Zaya doesn't work for you," Yyrreen said. "We need to figure out the message."

"If the message isn't 'cops, step off,' we're losing Cerise Precinct," Kaana said.

"We were never going to win Cerise Precinct," said Yyrreen. "The only voters there are slumlords. How many owners are going to be at that rally? But if we start declaring war on the government, we're definitely losing Scarlet and Coral, maybe Cobalt—"

Another knock on the door. Shozo, Chashu, and Kaana's guard all looked to Zaya. "Fine!" she said.

This time it was a crowd, which made Kaana's guard visibly tense, the muscles of his back pulling his jacket tight across his shoulders—but Shozo nodded and beckoned them in: Kiri, Vinaali, Zayeni, Zayeni's latest boyfriend, Jozai te-Naako, Seneppo Tchagra, and a few neighbors Zaya had seen around the block but couldn't place. They divided themselves between Zaya and Vanako, clucking and stroking and setting food on the coffee table. There wasn't room on the chairs and couches, and Zaya found herself standing to let Vinaali sit, and they exchanged words to the effect of

VINAALI: Oh, dear, please don't get up, you were almost killed!
ZAYA: No, please, I'm perfectly fine.

which, Zaya realized as she hooked around the couch to stand on the outside of the conversation that had coalesced around her, could not possibly have been less true.

The bustle of introductions, renewals of acquaintances, sharing of food, and bickering over precinct politics continued for some span of time—five minutes, ten, thirty—but when the question came, it was as predictable as sunrise, and like sunrise did each day, caught Zaya unprepared:

"So," Kiri said, "we're sure it was the police who did it?"

It didn't stop the flow of conversation in the house, but the house grew quieter. Every pair of eyes didn't turn to Kemreen, but the ones that didn't were making an effort not to.

"I'm sure," Kaana said into the near-silence.

"It *might* have been *some* police," Kemreen said, and Zaya's heart sank.

"We're not going to make that call tonight," Zaya said.

"Are they going to do the same thing here?" Zayeni asked.

Vinaali *tsked* and set a hand on her shoulder. "No need to worry about that, child," she said. "Jina ze-Saibaka's safe in her seat. This isn't where they'd be trying to swing opinions."

"Sure it is," Kaana said. "The hit on the Basting Stitch victory ceremonies was a message to every dissatisfied Kayalim in the city to back off and keep out of politics. It's also a message to every landowner in the city that yliaster is too dangerous to make legal. If that's the message—where do you think they're going to hit next? What would be a great way to show the owners what they're facing while not actually hurting any of their friends?" She gestured around the room. "Hit the Kayalim who've made good. Put Jina on the back foot, make her prove her precinct is safe instead of fighting for the poor in the House of the Stars. Not that she's ever had much of a belly for that, she'll be glad of the excuse."

"You're declaring war again," said Zaya. "On my couch."

"I didn't send a demon to eat everyone in Inundinir Square," said Kaana. "We need a plan to stop this when it happens at a rally. Because it will."

"That," said Yyrreen, "I actually agree with."

"I don't," said Kemreen.

"Read the room, colonizer," Kaana snapped.

Zaya walked over to Kemreen. Her steps felt unsteady; weaving through the room felt like walking down a long block where the only shade tree was on the corner, each step seeming to bring her no closer. She was never going to get to Kemreen in time to stop the fight from getting worse.

"My people were here before yours," Kemreen said, and the room erupted in groans and hisses.

"Oh, now we're talking 'your people' and 'our people,'" Kaana said. "If the people in this room aren't 'your people,' you're welcome to go find the ones who are."

There was a voice Zaya had used, more often than she liked, with the children when they were being deliberately intolerable: It was the one that didn't sound like a shout or even particularly like a raised voice, but it burst out from a ringing contralto root that made the words fill the room, coming at the child in question from all four walls, the ceiling, and the floor at the same time. "Kaana," she said in that voice, and now the room really did fall silent. "No more."

"We're all tense," Kemreen said into the pause that followed. "A lot of us came close to death tonight. Let's not forget that we're all working toward the same cause—"

"Fuck me," said Zaya, and seized Kemreen's bicep, pulling her toward the kitchen where the liquor was.

Kemreen went along; Zaya let her go and poured a mug of arrack, then took a sip. "Hey," Kemreen said. "Pour one for your girlfriend who just got her ass reamed like a grapefruit by that dried-up nutjob?"

Zaya closed her eyes and shook her head.

"What?"

"You didn't need the last word," said Zaya.

"What... what did I even say? We're all working toward the same cause? Sorry, am I wrong?"

"You're not convincing anyone that you're right."

"Zaya, what the hell?" Kemreen reached for her hand; Zaya made herself not move it away. "Whatever I did wrong, just tell me. Please?"

"I told you. In here, you don't have the last word. When you argue with Kaana te-Tekko about how we're all working together, you're not making anybody think twice about what Kaana is saying. You're actually distracting them from doing that, by making them wonder why you're in a room full of people working for change the cops don't like, talking like a cop, over the opinions of a leader they know and respect."

"What, again, the hell," said Kemreen. "You can fight with her, but I can't?"

"No—" Zaya reconsidered, took a sip, reconsidered. "Yes."

"Because I was a cop."

"You say that like it's not true."

"I left the force for you."

"I'm glad you did," Zaya said. "So are they."

"It doesn't seem that way."

"Glad isn't the same as trust."

"Do you trust me?" Kemreen said.

"It's not about whether I trust you."

Kemreen reached for the whiskey. "You could answer the question, though."

"I trust you with my life."

"Is that all?"

Zaya looked her over: Tall, broad, bare-armed, jawline sharp enough to cut glass, skin as clear as a noontime sky in summer. Thick hands with palms callused rough from knife-grip knurling—hands that had rocked Enwë to sleep, that had settled on Jaliki's shoulders to lend quiet support, that had made Zaya gasp and beg and shudder—held glass and bottle as though they were made of tissue paper.

"You can't show up like a cop in here," Zaya said. "That's all."

Kemreen nodded and took her whiskey back to the window.

***

"THANKS FOR THAT," KAANA said when Zaya rejoined her group. "I don't need you to help me scrap with cops, but thanks."

"Kemreen's put her body on the line for my family," said Zaya, "and I've never given her a flinder in return. You, I tossed a sack of cash. What are you going to do with it?"

"I don't question how you race. Don't question how I run."

"I win my races."

"Zaya," said Yyrreen.

"OK, Yyrreen," said Zaya, "you tell me. Is howling about some wild cop conspiracy going to help beat Tjalivain Taipan, or isn't it?"

"It's not *wild*," said Kaana—

—but Zaya cut her off. "You're trying to get elected. Do you have proof that will convince the owners in Ochre Precinct that the police sent a demon to kill us all, or not?"

"It happened five minutes ago, of course I don't have proof."

"You're too used to losing," Zaya said.

Zaya didn't know Kaana te-Tekko all that well, but she felt the satisfaction of knuckles hitting nose head-on, and the guilt of it. Kaana flinched as though she'd been bitten, and her eyes flashed. "Fuck you," she said. "Of all the people who should—"

"You found a way to survive anyway," Zaya said. "You found people, you found a cause. We have that in common. What we don't have in common is that when I was young, I had to learn the difference between everything and nothing. That difference is a feather's breadth between your wyrm's nose and the next one's. In your world, you lose and come back to fight again. Not in mine."

"Horseshit. You've lost before."

"I can only lose so many times before I'm done." Zaya's eyes flickered over to Jaliki, who was eating some kind of sweet bun and chattering to Vanako, pulling Kaana's with them. "My son can only lose so many times."

"How am I supposed to respond to that?" Kaana groused; but her heart wasn't in it.

"I don't need you to respond," Zaya said. "I need you to win. If you accuse the Ochre Precinct police of goety and mass murder without any evidence, you will lose."

"You don't win people over by being timid."

"You're not trying to win *people*. You're trying to win owners in Ochre Precinct."

"They should be worried about the cops on their streets summoning demons in front of their houses."

"If you prove that happened, they will be."

A blurry feeling that had been buzzing behind Zaya's eyes snapped into focus: With every word she said, she felt farther away from her body. Her words sounded flat and foreign, as though the bones of her skull had thickened to damp the sound of her mouth as it traveled to her ears. *Owners in Ochre Precinct.* Kaana te-Tekko knew as well as she did that the owners in Ochre Precinct weren't worried about what happened on the streets. Most of the owners in Ochre Precinct were professional landlords, renting on the open market if they could compete and to the city for the dole rate if they couldn't. There'd been a surge in Kayalim home buyers from Rust and Taupe Precincts moving west as a few large municipal construction projects paid out—that was why Yyrreen had identified Ochre as competitive in the first place. But *those* owners were voting for Kaana anyway. The tenement landlords, on the other hand, just wanted to make sure their properties weren't broken into and damaged. But demons weren't much for breaking and entering; and a renter dead in the street, Zaya thought, was just another deposit the landlords wouldn't have to return.

The conversation had moved on. Yyrreen and Kaana were talking strategy. If war was still in Kaana's plans, at least she wasn't talking about it.

Zaya took a look around the common room. This was how it was now, more nights than not: full of food, drink, and people, humming with the energy of discontent put to work. It was different tonight, of course, she began to think; but it wasn't. Tonight she'd seen a gate between worlds torn open, the incursion of a demon, the tearing and searing of flesh and feathers and whatever starry stuff demons were made of—and she, Zaya, who had been close enough to feel the demon's emanations raise the hair on her arms, who had been in the mind of the dragon who killed it, was talking about how the episode would be received by owners in Ochre Precinct.

She thought about tugging on Yyrreen's sleeve, but that was the wrong move. She got up and found Kemreen—still by the window, still nursing the whiskey, her own discontent somehow carving out a shield of empty space in the packed apartment. Zaya put a hand below her shoulder blade, not quite an embrace. "Hey."

"Hey."

"Where did Vanioun Ora live?"

Kemreen turned around. "Why are you asking me?"

"You're a fan of the 'stream? To me he was just the competition, I never learned anything about him that wasn't going to help me beat him." Zaya shrugged, using the motion to get a little closer. "And you were a cop, and cops know that kind of stuff sometimes.

Which maybe is a helpful thing about you that I could appreciate more often."

"When I'm in a better mood, I'll ask you to list more things about me you could appreciate more often." Kemreen took a sip. "He lived in Crimson Precinct, on the border with Ivory. He dated a guy on the force there for a bit, but he got married to like a chemist in the department of wastewater management or something like that. You're going to send flowers?"

***

WHAT IT WAS THAT made its way to Crimson Precinct, Zaya wasn't sure. It was ragged enough to be a mob, but its aim wasn't to do what mobs do. But it was too ragged from a long night of blood and fear to be a procession; the haggard eyes of its members were too full of grit to leave any room for solemnity. Whatever it was, it was big enough that the drinkers of Chartreuse Precinct's worst bars left it alone without so much as a catcall, and the neighborhood watch of Vermilion Precinct sent a deliberately conspicuous tail after it but didn't interfere. After Amiko pointed out the tail, Zaya kept her eyes on the sky, but the brushstrokes of dawn hadn't crept above the tops of the buildings yet. If a police wyrm had passed over, she might not have seen it.

Who was it who made their way to Crimson Precinct? Zaya and Vanako at the front, because they were the ones who had raced alongside Vanioun Ora; their tribute mattered most. Cerminir, Minshoon, Kirono, Yyrreen, and Kemreen in the second rank, because family recognized family. Shozo, Amiko, and Chashu, because you never knew when you'd need chains, blades, or bees, and Chashu's voice could carry for a block and still sound like he was shouting in your ear. Kaana te-Tekko and her meat pole, because the magnanimous acknowledgment of death was something voters expected from their elected officials, and it wasn't often you got the inside track on that. Kiri and Vinaali, because they were those kind of people; Zayeni and her boyfriend, who really weren't, but who knew how to read a room; a dozen others. Taavi and Gilthiniel were home with the younger children, Bandit was sleeping off its injuries at Saavero's. Zaya couldn't stop herself from missing Bandit, and she wasn't sure if it was because it belonged—it had raced alongside Ora, too; it should be there to speak for his life—or because she wanted backup if a police wyrm did fly down to block their path. Backup wasn't exactly what you wanted in a fight against a dragon; you'd rather have a quick getaway. But it beat getting chased down and carbonized.

She felt a hand on her shoulder, and put her own hand on it. But when she turned, expecting Kemreen, she saw Yyvvoun Leatherback instead, and snatched her hand away. "Sorry," they both said at the same time; and, at the same time, laughed the laugh of wanting to be anywhere but here, any time but now. Which felt like it should have joined them in some kind of solidarity against awkwardness; but it didn't.

Yyvvoun was short-haired, sad-eyed, only a head taller than Zaya; his skin was tan, his hair and eyes were light, and the grooves on his face hadn't yet erased his youth. (He was older than her, but a lot of young Mrineen were.) "I just wanted you to know—" he began.

"I can see you're here," said Zaya, putting just enough lightness into her voice that she hoped it didn't ring false. "We've established that."

"It's more embarrassing than that," Yyvvoun said. "I don't know the words."

Zaya managed to keep the deep sigh inside her head. "You're not supposed to know the words."

"Oh."

He sounded disappointed, or maybe hurt; Zaya was too tired to read people. "I didn't mean you're not allowed to know. I mean I wouldn't expect you to know. But no one can tell you don't know the words. You're going to look a lot dumber not knowing the motions."

Yyvvoun ran a hand over his scalp. "Are there a lot of motions?"

"Have you ever seen a haka?"

"I might have seen one in a play one time."

"Next time someone asks you that question, just say no."

"Unless they ask in the next couple minutes, the answer will be yes." Now it was Yyvvoun's turn to push some lightness into his voice. If his attempt was any better than hers had been, she might as well not have bothered.

"I have to be in front," said Zaya. "Get behind Kaana's meat pole, he's tall enough to mostly hide you."

"Who's Kaana's meat pole?"

"The meat pole in the tuxedo."

"Why do you call him a meat pole?"

"What else would you call a pole made of meat?"

Yyvvoun didn't have a response to that.

"OK," Zaya said. "When I call out *Siblings, I heard the wind over the breakers scream with mourning!*, you—"

"When you call out what?"

Zaya looked up at him. "You don't speak Kayalsho."

"They didn't teach it in my school."

"It's fine. I've never heard anyone speak Kayalsho worse than a Mrineen who's gotten top marks in it. Look, the movements mostly happen at the end of sentences, and we always hammer the ends of sentences. Almost always." She thought for a moment. "Look, this isn't going to work. You should just watch."

Yyvvoun's handsome features set into an obstinate look. If she wasn't scared and exhausted, it might have been cute. "I'll look like an idiot if I just stand on the side."

"You'll look like someone who knows his limits."

"I'm not going to ruin your haka."

"You couldn't ruin my haka with a hundred-piece brass band and a plague of frogs," said Zaya. "I'm not trying to gatekeep you out of somewhere you belong, I'm saying you don't know how to do it and I can't teach you before we hit Seventeen Talon Square. You can do whatever you want with that, but a pretty normal choice would be to butt out."

He cast an eye back to Kemreen, who returned it several degrees cooler. "Is she going to do it?"

"She knows the movements."

"So they're not that hard to teach."

"In an afternoon. We don't have an afternoon."

He looked over the mob, or procession, or whatever it was. "They really all know it?"

"They're not up here asking me how to do the second haka you learn in school when you're barely old enough to say the words right, so forgive me if my educated guess is yeah, they fucking do."

Something dawned on Yyvvoun's face, accentuated by the gentle light of a gathering sunrise. "I'm being a shit."

"Knowing is half the battle," Zaya said.

"If I shut up and take your advice, is that the other half?"

"Forty percent."

"What's the rest?"

"Unspecified acts of atonement."

Watching his face was like watching a succession of flowers grow, bloom, and die in instants, if instead of flowers you were looking at questionably witty ripostes. "All right, acknowledged. Can I ask you one thing?" He didn't wait for her reply, which wasn't wonderful. "Can you translate the words for me? So I know what I'm listening to?"

After the conversation she'd just had, Zaya did not want to do this. But, she reminded herself, he was here. He'd come out at the dark before dawn to join them, even if it would have been better if he hadn't. She recited, mumbling a little:

Siblings, I heard the wind over the breakers scream with mourning!
I saw the spray of the falls write words of anguish on the cliffs!
Siblings, what absence wounds the world?

"I say all that," Zaya explained. "And then the group says:"

Vanioun Ora is dead!
Vanioun Ora is dead!

"And then I say:"

Vanioun Ora is dead!

"Usually you let the silence linger for a while here," she said. "Then we go into a little call and response:"

Do your hearts not split, siblings?
—They tremble and tear in twain!
Are your eyes not bottomless salt springs?
—Great bitter rivers leap forth from our eyes—

"Hold up," said Yyvvoun.

"Questions at the end," said Zaya. Then she looked up and saw the Crimson Precinct police.

There were four of them, not quite blocking the stretch of... whatever street they were on, standing or leaning in menacingly casual postures. Zaya turned around. There wasn't anyone behind her group. That was good; leaving an escape route meant they hadn't decided to murder you. Usually.

"Look," one of them called—the different precincts designated rank in different ways and Zaya didn't know Crimson's, but in her head he was the Lieutenant. "I'll skip the hail-fellow-well-met shit. You're a large group of armed individuals out late at night. We don't know where you're headed, but we know we don't like what happens when you get there. Therefore, to improve everyone's evening, go home."

"We're allowed to be here," said Zaya.

"I'm telling you you are not," said the Lieutenant.

"We're here to mourn a death," said Zaya. "The man who was killed after the race tonight."

"You don't look like family."

"I beat him in the race. If I'd been a couple lengths slower, I'd have been eaten instead of him."

"Which is why you have the one guy with the chain whip and the other guy with the meat cleavers. What's that, tribute? Are they gold-plated?"

Zaya wasn't going to tell him they were for protecting her from cops, and she wasn't going to tell him that Shozo and Chashu were about as likely to drop their weapons right now as sprout spinnerets from their asses and build a web that said *We come in peace.* That left open what she was going to say. "Comfort objects," she said. "They snuggle up to them when they can't sleep."

That drew laughs from both sides, but not from the Lieutenant. "That's good," he said. His tone suggested it was something else. "They can leave them here when you go."

A couple of small things happened in a very short period of time, and Zaya wasn't sure which was first: Yyvvoun said "hey now," and warm breath lapped gently on her face, and steel clanked from one side and sang from the other, and a hand lay lightly on her bicep, and she couldn't see in front of her until she realized she could, it was just that all she was seeing was the Lieutenant, who was less than an arm's length away, whose fingers encircled her upper arm like delicate bangles, light and unbendable.

"I think I may have conveyed the wrong impression," said the Lieutenant. "We're not negotiating. I'm giving orders, and you're taking them."

"That's fine," Chashu said. "You let go of Shearwater-cha and everyone leaves."

This was infuriating, but it was also literally Chashu's job description—he, Shozo, and Amiko could make these calls in a crisis. They'd discussed it.

"I let go when you drop the weapons," said the Lieutenant.

"All respect, that's not happening," said Chashu. "You made the move, not us. Right now it seems like you're trying to start something. We're not interested in being unarmed when something starts."

Silence stretched over the air, and Zaya's thoughts began to catch up. The Lieutenant was, of course, trying to start something. This was how things started, and he knew it. He'd seen things start, maybe he'd started a few himself; either way, the starting of things was known to him. She'd seen that the police hadn't tried to block their retreat and been satisfied that they weren't in danger; but, of course, if your victims could run, then they'd do it, instead of defending their lives from a corner and finding a forgotten power nestled deep in the haze of their fear. At one to six, even Yemari cops might not like their own odds. And maybe there was a dragon in the sky to mop up the runners. Was that paranoid?

When was the last time police had used a dragon to mass-murder fleeing Kayalim? But the lieutenant wasn't talking. He was—was he?—uncertain; he'd expected them—had he expected them?—to make a move or crumble, not to hold the line—

"Officer," said Yyvvoun. "My name's Yyvvoun Leatherback. I'm a candidate for the House of the Stars in Coral Precinct next door."

The Lieutenant's grip didn't slacken, but he gave Yyvvoun his attention.

"The gentleman died in Ochre Precinct—you'll see the Travelers' candidate for Ochre in the group here as well, with her own escort. M. Shearwater and M. te-Tekko were both in Inundinir Square when the attack occurred, and they're understandably concerned about safety."

You're an idiot, Zaya said to Yyvvoun in her head. *They don't care. They've never believed anyone like us should be armed for any reason, and they're not going to start now.*

"But they also wish to stand with the family of the dead," Yyvvoun continued, "who was a respected opponent, according to Kayalim tradition. Can you see how it is? The armed gentlemen don't wish you any harm, they're only looking out for the safety of their employers."

You just read him the dictionary definition of a bodyguard. As far as he's concerned, any Kayalim with a weapon is a crime waiting to happen. He's about to stop your meat flapping with four knuckles to the teeth.

He didn't, though. And, of course, Zaya knew why: Yyvvoun was a *candidate.* It didn't mean much; but it meant the word would go out if he saw something happen that shouldn't have. Or if he didn't go home tonight.

The Lieutenant looked from Zaya to Kaana and back to Zaya, then let go of Zaya's arm. "Don't know why you didn't say something," he said. "Of course, if you're concerned for your safety, it's understandable why you'd have a bodyguard." He turned to his men and waved them off with a jerk of his head, and they parted to allow the group through. "Go ahead and be with the family. Who'd you say it was again?"

No one spoke; Zaya realized they were expecting an answer from her. "Vanioun Ora," she said. "The 'streamer who died in Inundinir Square."

"Of course."

The officers who now flanked them stared, annoyed, urging them on.

***

THEY COULDN'T VERY WELL *not* do it, after that.

Maybe the dawn redeemed the performance—or painted over it, at least. Zaya couldn't really see the faces of the Ora family as they gathered on the balcony to watch the haka in Seventeen Talon Square; so maybe she only imagined the puzzlement on their face at two dozen Kayalim dully relating the mourning scream of the wind over the breakers as though it were some senile neighbor's gossip, some news of mild and evanescent interest. When it was over, a couple of them raised their parted hands as if to clap, then dropped them, unsure as to the protocol.

Maybe it wasn't the Crimson Precinct police's fault. Maybe the whole thing had been doomed anyway. Or maybe it had been fine? Vanioun Ora's family was sleepless and reeling; they weren't in a position to care about nuances of delivery. The whole thing had probably been grey noise. Like wind over breakers actually sounded.

The mourners passed the Lieutenant and his men again on the way back. They hadn't moved. He opened his mouth, his face smeared with a pleasant smile; but he looked at Zaya's face and rethought speaking.

CHAPTER 3
STILL NINE WEEKS BEFORE BELL THE CAT

THE NIGHT HAD BROUGHT death, terror, and a sleepless dawntide march to Vermilion Precinct to chant uncomprehended words into the ears of the bereaved; but in the morning there was school for the children, and teaching for Kirono, and Cerminir had to take Enwë up to Celadon Precinct to see a few émigrés from Cildinior Amalgam, and Zaya had to get to Cerulean Precinct for a meeting with the Thread & Mortar Front.

Yyrreen had stayed over, at least, and paid for mate and breakfast beforehand and the wyrm to take them there. Zaya closed her eyes as soon as she hit the cushions of the massive Ranger Wyrm's surprisingly comfortable howdah; and if she wasn't actually asleep when Yyrreen said "I appreciate you doing this," she was close enough to fake it.

The Cerulean Precinct meeting place was an alehouse that reminded Zaya of the Blind Beggar, a sprawling establishment whose configuration of bar, booth, rooms, and corridors made for innumerable nooks and eddies where assignations could be had. It was easy enough to find the meeting room; Chashu stood opposite one of Kaana te-Tekko's meat poles by the door. They looked like they'd gotten exactly as much sleep as they, in fact, had gotten.

The Reef Room was wrapped in some kind of lumpy substance painted to approximate coral, with sculptures of anemones, bright fish, and eels scattered on the walls for variety; all of which would have had a much cheerier effect in a room with any natural light. As it was, the guttering candles threw twitching shadows under the clownfish and blue tangs, making it seem like they were shuddering with fear.

Zaya and Yyrreen were the last to arrive. The others were as far from one another as the round table would permit. On the right, Kaana sat with an Ililuë who looked vaguely familiar. On the left were Tenijoon Anole, a middle-aged Mrineen man whom Zaya knew, and a younger Mrineen whom she didn't. Anole was built and dressed like a dock worker, powerful shoulders under a thin red-and-yellow shirt, the kind of thing you'd wear if you wanted people to notice when you fell into the sea. The other one was built and dressed like a bureaucrat, although they were taller than Anole by a head or so.

Kaana wasted no time with introductions: "You all know me. My partner on the Travelers side is Felindir Ola-Kalenwë; they're one of our community liaisons in the Greens. The Thread & Mortar Front have Tenijoon Anole, who's the deputy elections director or some other fluffed-up shit their party's made up to sound important, and Ajishain Loggerhead, sub-lickspittle to the third vizier for policy atrocities—please, Ajishain, correct me if I'm wrong." Loggerhead declined with a shake of her head. "The puffy-eyed latecomers are Yyrreen Turaco, candidate for the Stars in Celadon Precinct, and Zaya Shearwater, queen of the Brimstone Slipstream. Zaya's the one with the purple dye job that's going grey. We were all up late mourning Vanioun Ora, but I still got here on time."

"You slept here," said Anole.

"That's called forethought. I think we're here to discuss Zaya's 'stream agenda and the distribution of winnings therefrom. Which is an unwelcome departure from the deal we struck when we forged this coalition, when you seemed very comfortable with the idea that the risk and reward of those races would all go to the Travelers."

"That was before you started cutting into our lead in key precincts," said Anole. "This one, for example. We can win it if it's us against the Scale. But when our people see the queen of the 'stream—" he nodded to Zaya—"tossing actual sacks of cash to the candidate from the Travelers, some of them wonder if they wouldn't be better off with you. Enantior can't take those three extra points to victory, but Sefhalaan can sure take them to defeat."

"Enantior Neduin's the Travelers candidate in Cerulean," Yyrreen whispered to Zaya. "Sefhalaan Skink is Thread & Mortar's."

"Why doesn't Enantior just drop out?" Zaya whispered back.

"Because the Travelers run everywhere," whispered Yyrreen. "It's their thing."

Kaana seemed to have just finished explaining this to Anole. "Look," she continued, "we can't be seen working with you. You know that. Our people will see it as a betrayal. I still haven't convinced myself it isn't one."

"It sounds to me," said Anole, "like you're saying you've got enough money for your operations in Cobalt and Amethyst. But I just wanted to make sure."

Yyrreen shook her head. "If we lose Cobalt and Amethyst to squabbling, we're handing Brightest Scale another majority. But if I want to keep those precincts, I'd rather lose your support than have Zaya publicly support your party."

"The chances of Zaya tossing a bag of cash to the 'descendants of the founders' people are slightly thinner than the padding on the crotch of her racing pants," said Zaya. "Which she's been told are an attack on public decency."

"I like it when Zaya talks," said Anole. "I like watching her people try to haul the conversation back where it's supposed to be.

It reminds me of this one steersman I saw try not to crash a ship into Pier 9." His eyes squeezed into a sour smile. "He dislocated his shoulder so bad they had to amputate. Didn't save the pier."

"Zaya's been pretty cooperative so far," said Yyrreen, "but I actually can't control her. So when she tells you what she's not going to do, she's not going to do it. But there's got to be something we can do to help Sefhalaan and some of your other candidates who need it." She tapped the table a couple of times and looked at Zaya. "Maybe organize something around the specific issue, instead of blanket support of the party."

"Neduin also supports the specific issue," said Loggerhead.

Anole looked at Yyrreen, then at Kaana. Yyrreen looked at Kaana. Kaana blew a breath out through her nose.

"Fine," Kaana said. "If Sefhalaan needs Enantior to step back, he'll step back."

"The specific issue is a problem," said Felindir Ola-Kalenwë.

Kaana rolled her eyes. "Look, I get it, but if I can get over working with—"

"I said the issue, Kaana. Legalization. Is a problem."

This got Kaana's full attention. "What?"

Felindir let the silence hang for a moment. "Lots of our people in the Greens have people back home at Cildinior Amalgam or Ettre Conurbation. They already don't like the harvesting operation out at the Supplicant. What if everyone who's sick decides to go out there themselves? That area's been taboo for centuries because the Ililuë communities know what comes of too many people using the árimori: too many people summoning demons without consequences. If you get your coalition, and you pass your law, what are you going to do with all that power?"

Anole looked at Felindir in disgust. "If we can't agree on the one thing we agree on, why are we here?"

"I'm not here to tell you why you're here," Felindir said. "I'm telling you what people in my precincts think. That's research you haven't paid for. But I guess that would only help you if you had the balls to run candidates in the Greens."

"If people in the Greens had the balls to vote for candidates who'd actually advance their interests, we'd run there."

"Arimori," said Zaya. "What's that, day-night? That's the word for yliaster?"

"Árimori," Felindir repeated, correcting her pronunciation. The *á* was an intermediate sound, somewhere between *yarn* and *black*.

"There are a lot of hunted people in the Greens, are there not?" said Zaya.

"There are shamans in the community who are trusted to break taboo and treat the hunted," said Felindir. They shot a glare at Anole and Loggerhead. "Speaking of research you haven't paid for."

"Do those shamans get harassed by cops?" Zaya asked.

"Do you mean more than anyone else in the Greens?"

"You know I do." Zaya said it lightly. It was an annoying thing to have to say, but Felindir came by their own frustration honestly.

"You know they do."

"That's a way in," Zaya said. "For you, too, if you want it," she said, moving her eyes to Anole.

He flicked his gaze over at her, surprised to be addressed; but she didn't have to spell it out. "Police who need yliaster but can't afford it arresting priests filling that same need in their communities. Double slap in the face. Yeah, maybe we can work with that. No cop likes working the Greens to begin with."

Zaya clenched a fist and waited to see if Felindir would slash back at Anole. They didn't. "The community already sees the need for shamans not to get arrested," said Felindir. "They need to trust the government to protect the taboo area and not use demons against the Ililuë communities. But the candidates can go a distance on that. If they unite behind a message of responsible harvesting and use…"

"Like having police issue permits?"

Felindir shot Anole an icy look. "Don't make jokes."

"Then what's the message?" Anole asked.

"Regulate and limit harvesting so it doesn't harm the area. Commit to no goety in wars of aggression."

"Wars of aggression," said Loggerhead. It wasn't quite a snicker.

"If you policy folks have trouble with nuance," Felindir said, "I'm sure we'd accept no goety at all."

"Famous last words when we get invaded," said Loggerhead.

Zaya drew breath to speak, but Yyrreen laid a hand on her forearm. "We're talking a lot about situations that haven't happened in centuries," Yyrreen said. "As Yemareir's grown, we're more dependent on the Ililuë communities than we've ever been. And they've gotten more from us as well." She looked at Felindir. "I don't mean this to say they shouldn't ask for assurances—and get them. But the message has to be, we're trying to help people *now*. We're going to get police off the shamans' backs *now*." She turned to Anole. "We're going to get help for the longshoremen of Cerulean Precinct *and* the construction workers in Ochre Precinct *now*. That's why *this* election matters."

Felindir and Loggerhead both looked as though they'd been served a mug of spoiled milk, but Tenijoon Anole looked at Yyrreen with a new appreciation. "That's right," he said. "They only vote today if they think they'll get something out of it tomorrow. I think we can sell them on how to get something out of it tomorrow." He didn't quite manage to look at Felindir, but he did include them in his *we* with a tilt of his head. He did look at Zaya. "And we'll send an invitation to the Queen of the 'Stream to come to Cerulean and… what do we think? Hand out cash to the families of the hunted?"

Zaya shook her head. "If you're really serious about this, I have a better idea."

***

"WHAT DID YOU THINK?" Yyrreen asked Zaya over chicken with chocolate after. The cart that had sold them the food had a few tables under a tent nearby; but in the rising heat of midmorning, they were the only customers.

"I think if you have to babysit every time the Travelers and Thread & Mortar get in a room together, we don't have a chance."

"They're almost never in a room together," Yyrreen said cheerily.

"That's not a recipe for good cooperation."

"I always hated recipes anyway."

"Interestingly, you're a shit cook."

"But I'm good at this." Yyrreen pointed a morsel of dripping chicken at Zaya; dark sauce fell on the wooden table. "They can be made to see the benefits of working together—for the short term, to get this done. You saw it yourself. You got them there. And your idea was genius."

"It's common sense," said Zaya. "Which means there are probably a hundred stupid reasons people will refuse to do it, ten good reasons they aren't doing it already, and at least one fatal flaw that makes it a dumb idea to begin with."

"It's real work. People can sweat a morning away, and see the future they want coming into being. You don't understand how potent that is."

"For a lot of people, it's how they live, and they hate it."

"Not people who own property in Yemareir."

Zaya rubbed a forkful of rice in the bitter chocolate sauce, then ate it. "I don't think Tenijoon Anole's as smart as he thinks he is," she said. "I think he's figured out how to be important in an organization that doesn't win. That's a different game than the one he's playing."

"You said that about Kaana."

"I don't think Kaana's as smart as she thinks she is either."

"You can't dismiss everyone we're working with because they don't already control the government," said Yyrreen. "That would have been like dismissing you and Kiriki before you'd ever won a race."

"People did dismiss us. You remember the odds Minshoon was getting, right?"

"Sure. And the people who dismissed you were on *the wrong side of them*. Which made you a shit-ton of money." Yyrreen reached across the table to take Zaya's hand. "I know you could be doing other things with that money. Things that would be certain to help Jaliki, for a little bit. But then nothing changes. This is every meal we skipped to set aside the money for an entry fee, except the stakes are a million times bigger. Instead of gambling a meal, you're gambling Jaliki's life. But instead of life-changing cash for one family, the upside is literal life for tens of thousands of people."

Zaya squeezed Yyrreen's hand. "When we were racing, I had to trust you," she said. "Now I'm putting Jaliki's life in Tenijoon Anole's hands."

"Remember what you trusted me to do."

It took Zaya a moment; it had all been so long ago. Yyrreen had been their surveyor: the person who understood the shape of the course, and its relationship to their dragon's strengths and weaknesses, better than anyone else. As far as Zaya knew, it was a role their family had originated, and Yyrreen was the first and last person to do it for anyone.

Was an eye for dragon races the same as an eye for political ones? Yyrreen wanted her to believe it was. But what it took to win them wasn't the same. "What if I got into one of these races?" Zaya asked. "I don't want to shove some other candidate aside, I'm just curious. Do I have a shot?"

"People know who you are," Yyrreen said. "That's always better than being unknown. A lot of owners don't like the 'stream because they worry about frequent races driving rents down, but that could be balanced by the number who just like it for what it is. Personality-wise, your liabilities are that you're too intense, too unpredictable, and too honest. But that all changes in a world where non-owners have the vote."

Zaya took a sip of lukewarm water from her none too spotless glass. "Oh yeah?"

"Sure. They've been cut out of this whole thing, this whole time. They're going to vote for you because they know you and like you; that's the only thing they know how to think about. You'd swallow any precinct in the Pinks or Browns whole, maybe in the Greens as well. And there's others you'd obviously have a shot in—Lilac, Incarnadine." Yyrreen's eyes got wide and her mouth made a tiny "o" shape that she'd have dragged without mercy if she saw it on anyone else. "Maybe you could even pull Umber back in—"

"All right," Zaya said. "You don't need to do the whole analysis. I was just curious."

"Next election," Yyrreen said. "Six months in advance. Talk to me. By then, we might just have delivered that non-owner vote."

Zaya smiled, mostly to stop the conversation. Yyrreen took the hint and started eating in earnest.

When they'd talked about voting for the first time, Yyrreen and Minshoon and Kirono and Cerminir and Kiriki, they hadn't talked about how they knew or liked the candidates. They'd talked about the privilege of choosing who would fight for them, and whom they'd fight. Minshoon and Yyrreen especially had religiously attended the speeches delivered by Lilac Precinct candidates, had asked their friends to tell them all they could. There'd been arguments; Kiriki, Kirono, and Minshoon had favored a protest vote for the Travelers' Jina ze-Saibaka, and the other three had preferred Thread & Mortar's Zenisheen Terrapin, who'd seemed to be more viable by virtue of attracting more votes from Mrineen owners. Terrapin had campaigned hard on expanding the vote, but also on cutting the dole; ze-Saibaka had struck back by proposing to increase precinct support for schools and apprenticeships; Brightest Scale's Anjoon Monitor had stayed above the fray, promising more of the same in only slightly more elevated phrases. The fault lines were what they always were: Did the candidate mean what they said; and Isn't it better to ask for a little and get it, than ask for everything and get nothing? When the votes had been counted, Monitor had won easily with a plurality—but Jina ze-Saibaka had edged out Zenisheen Terrapin for second.

Kiriki had been so tired, by then—she would live one more night after that, before a Cinereal Vore Wyrm would burn her to cremains under a bright blue sky in Ashen Precinct—but she had hauled herself into the post-mortem around the House Shearwater kitchen table to say one thing. The other five had been so surprised by her joining that they'd fallen silent at her presence.

"This proves that we can ask for what we want," she'd said. "People know what's good for them. When we take away from what we want—what we need—by asking for what we think we can get? That's when we get nothing."

And Zaya had said into the still-hanging hush, "Knowing how to come in second has nothing to do with knowing how to come in first."

It was one of her shittiest memories, coming as close to Kiriki's death as it did. But, the Dancer keep her soul, Zaya still believed it.

Back in the hot tent, over a too-hot hit of spice from a stray shard of unground chili, Zaya said one more thing. "When we talked about getting the vote, back before the Bisai. It wasn't about who we knew, or who we liked."

"We've all learned a lot since then," Yyrreen said.

***

WHEN ZAYA GOT HOME that afternoon, Kirono was passed out on the couch. Eäril was sitting with him, stroking his hair like she might a baby's. The house smelled of spice and oil—there was a big bowl of sausage and potatoes on the kitchen table, half full, and some sliced oranges—but no one else was in the kitchen or the common room. "He was having nightmares," Eäril said solemnly to Zaya. "When I pat his head, it help him sleep."

Zaya sat beside Eäril and kissed the crown of her head. She barely had to bend her neck to do it; Eäril was getting tall. "Who's home?"

"Jaliki and Mom Cerminir and Enwë. Jaliki's reading, Enwë's eating." Enwë didn't really need to nurse any more, but she sometimes did it for comfort before she slept. "I was reading too, but then Papa Kirono had a nightmare, so I helped."

They were speaking quietly, but not quietly enough; Kirono's eyes fluttered, then opened. "Sorry," Zaya said.

"It's OK," Kirono said.

"Don't you teach today?"

"Not the first time this has happened. I always leave them with an assignment in case I don't show."

"You spent too much time with the knife again?"

Kirono nodded.

"Don't touch it for a couple of days," Zaya said. "Please? I never would have asked you to look if—"

"Zaya," said Kirono. "It's fine. I loved her too."

"But you'll leave the knife alone for a bit."

"Yeah."

"Who?" said Eäril.

"Who what?" asked Kirono, raising a hand to scratch her head.

"Who did you love?"

"Kiriki-kana," said Zaya. "My wife."

"Why Papa Kirono loved *your* wife?" Eäril's eyes narrowed. She knew grownups weren't any better behaved than children, but you had to look harder to catch them at it.

"We were friends," said Kirono. "Mom Cerminir and Papa Min-shoon and Yyrreen-kana and I, we all lived with Kiriki-kana and we all loved her. Not the same way Mom Zaya did. But she was just as important to us, in a different way."

"What happened to her?"

Eäril had heard the story, more than once, and for a moment a slug of molten anger rose in Zaya's throat. It was a gruesome, horrible loss, not a fairy tale for bedtime. But Eäril was little, still. She might really not remember; she might want to practice remembering. "I was racing through Ashen Precinct with her and my old dragon," Zaya said. "We were attacked by another dragon. I got away, but they didn't."

"Why?"

"No reason. Just luck."

"Why does Papa Kirono love the knife if he loves her?"

It took Zaya a moment to sort through that tangle of thoughts; Eäril wasn't old enough to ask *what does the knife have to do with Kiriki.* "It's a little complicated. The knife is a lot like one that used to belong to Kiriki-kana. We know who gave her the one we used to have, but we want to know where he got it."

"Who gave it to her?"

"My old friend Arhoon Pogona."

"Did he died on a dragon race too?"

"Yes. Not long ago."

Eäril looked away. The corners of her mouth turned down, and her face looked fragile, like the surface tension on a pond where something large was swimming too deep to be seen.

"Hey," Zaya said, putting a hand behind Eäril's head and planting a kiss firmly on her scalp. "I'm here."

Eäril didn't speak, but she also didn't cry. She hooked a hand around Zaya's neck, pushing Zaya's head against her own. Kirono found her hand and squeezed. Zaya stayed there as long as her back could take it.

When she separated from Eäril, Kirono caught her eye. "I think I have a lead," he said, as softly as he could.

Chapter 4
Seventeen weeks before Bell the Cat

After Zaya had recovered from the Omari Shadowrun—before the litter from the party on Laurel Street was fully cleared—two things had happened: Zaya had started throwing herself into any race she thought she could win, and Yyrreen had started showing Zaya off to owners.

***

The Ogres' Amphitheater was a stone-clad hole in the ground more or less cattycorner to Umber Precinct. As Shenireen Agama's travel guide to Yemareir put it, "if you've ever wondered what it would be like to be the runt of a litter of voles, or possibly an underfed skink, and go watch something in one of the more conventional amphitheaters of Yemareir, you should visit the Ogre's." Ancient scorch marks on the stone led archaeologists to infer that the thing had been used for rituals involving dragons in the pre-Yemareir season-city, although "sending dozens of them orbiting at top speed for twenty-three laps where the audience was supposed to sit" probably hadn't been one of them.

Where it got interesting was when you switched from counterclockwise laps to clockwise at sixteen and a half. This variation had been codified actual centuries ago when courses were fewer and more often repeated, and some Tuatara had complained that their very expensive Argent Swordwing was suffering asymmetrical shoulder strain from winning it too many times in a row. Legend in the 'stream was that the mid-course switchback was intended as the Standards Board's fuck-off to said Tuatara, but the Swordwing in question nimbly dodged all the oncoming racers to notch a two-lap victory, and the spectators had been thrilled. (The rest of it was legend in the 'stream as well; surely there were primary sources weighing in on some of it, but Zaya and Vanako hadn't read them.)

Zaya and Vanako had been far enough ahead at sixteen and a half that they had a clear course for almost a quarter lap; but even from behind, Vanako could see the midnight-black wyrm on a collision course with them. *Mom—*

"He won't do it," said Zaya.

Even if he doesn't crash into us, Monsoon's spikes—

"Don't worry about it."

An image formed in Zaya's mind, too scared to be as detailed in its gruesomeness as it should have been—a spike-clad black tail slamming into her face and chest.

"Nah," said Zaya.

Monsoon drew closer. Its chest swelled as if preparing a burst of flame.

MOM—

"Pick up Bandit's mind and do not deviate. I've got this."

And they were in range, and Zaya was out of Bandit's mind and into Monsoon's, and the muscles of its tail stayed strong and straight as it passed over them—even over the series of squeezes from its rider that signaled a tail-lash.

It didn't take much. The wyrm wouldn't do it, but it didn't really want to do it.

Krait's heart wasn't in the race after that. They were less than a lap ahead of him, so they didn't have to cross paths with him on another lap, and he never got close. Vanako complained about walking in circles for a week, although she never settled on which clockwise or counterclockwise.

***

Fourteen weeks before Bell the Cat.

The gala for Yyvvoun Leatherback was under the stars the hot night after the Ogres' Amphitheater, in Coral Precinct's Goanna Succulent Garden. Zaya was in a light linen shift and skirt, unadorned to set off her hair; she had thrown herself on the mercy of Papa Zinji, whose sense for hue, shade, and the properties of dye were the best she knew. From a base shade of rich violet at the roots, he'd coordinated a symphony of plum, violet-blue, and magenta that played off each other beautifully in a braid and, worn down as she did that night, fairly blazed. In honor of the venue, the cocktails were all cactus-based, although Vanako was disappointed to hear that no peyote was on offer. She and Tuuro had said a few hellos, eaten and drunk an amazing amount, and crept off to a quiet corner somewhere. Zaya was hearing from a Coral Precinct landlord waxing philosophical about kerostasia. He had the broad shoulders of a man who'd once been an athlete, the skinny legs and comfortable belly of someone who'd left that part of his life behind some time ago, and a glass of chili mezcal he'd freshened at least once during the conversation, which meant he was about keeping pace with her.

"Death's a part of life," he said. "This is nature taking its course. Kers need to eat too."

"So do crocodiles," said Zaya. "But when they attack people, we kill them. Defending our people is also nature taking its course."

"We'd do that to kers too, if we could."

"We can."

"With the same kind of goety we use to summon demons." He shook his head sadly, although Zaya wasn't sure if it was a performance for her benefit or just a lamentation of his now empty mezcal glass. "I feel for you, Shearwater-cha, but it doesn't sit right with me."

A hand landed on the landlord's shoulder. "Come on, Malihoun," said a handsome young Mrineen man—tall, sharp-featured, a tattoo at the corner of his left eye that looked like a tear, until Zaya looked more closely and realized it was a feather. "You were at Dzaroon's funeral. You wept with me, or looked like you did. If you really feel for Shearwater-cha, try to feel a little harder."

Malihoun the landlord's eyes narrowed a fraction. "Are you sure you want my vote, Yyvvoun?" He sounded more resigned than threatening, as if this were a conversation he'd had before.

"Of course," said Yyvvoun. "But you can't brush this one off with platitudes. You don't like goety, and I don't blame you; but I watched a buzzard ker bury its beak in my husband's guts up to its eyes and eat his insides while he lived. That's the future Shearwater-cha is seeing for her child, and if you're going to condemn them to it you owe her a little more than pearl-clutching about whether using yliaster 'sits right with you.'"

Something shifted in Malihoun's face; when he looked at her again, it was with eyes that seemed to see more than they had before. "Of course," he said.

"Anyway," Yyvvoun said, "Kuriaan's your competitor, and I've heard things about their business practices. You don't really want them passing laws, do you? They'll own every brick in Coral."

"You're one to talk about self-interest," Malihoun grumbled.

"My self-interest means that organizations like the Society and Taipan Invotechnic can start working on things that will benefit everyone. Like ways to process yliaster so it can't be used in goetic applications. Kuriaan Goanna's self-interest means good businessmen get driven out of my precinct. Don't take my word for it, though—you know both of us. You'll make the right decision. Just remember who's got the Queen of the 'Stream on his side."

Yyvvoun clapped Malihoun on the shoulder. Malihoun seemed to take that as an invitation to disengage, and homed in on the waitron with the tray of chili mezcal glasses. Yyvvoun, at a loss, looked at Zaya and shrugged. "Pleased to meet you? Yyvvoun Leatherback."

"The candidate," Zaya said, then took a sip of mezcal and sloshed it around so she wouldn't have to say more. Unfortunately, the candidate didn't fill the silence. Zaya swallowed. "You've got a good yliaster speech," she said. "You're a sorcerer?"

Yyvvoun held his hand palm down and swiveled it: *Sort of.* "Pretty weak on the practical side. Also on the theoretical side. When I'm working, I'm working in industry. But I like the Society. They have an Old Mlin cream tea with a nice spread, and occasionally you really learn something from the talks. Like that thing about anti-goetic yliaster."

"Have you worked for Taipan Invotechnic?"

Yyvvoun smiled, a little tightly. "No. I don't think they hire Leatherbacks into jobs I'd want to do. Which isn't the reason you'd like me not to work for them, I think."

"If you want me to shit-talk Shanhoon Krait," Zaya said, "just ask."

"I might at that." A waitron glided by; Yyvvoun Leatherback seized two glasses and sniffed one. "Lime, I think?" He offered it, and Zaya took it; they raised the glasses and drank. She wouldn't have noticed the lime flavor if he hadn't pointed it out. "I know how to handle Malihoun," Yyvvoun said, "but he speaks for a lot of the people I need. You've put some of us in a tough position, Shearwater-cha. I hope yliaster is the winning issue you think it is, because I'm having a lot of conversations like that one, and they don't all go that well."

"Don't they?"

Yyvvoun chuckled. "Most of them do, actually. But not everyone's lucky enough to run against a slumlord like Kuriaan Goanna."

An arm slid around Zaya's waist, hard and solid; the scent of grass tinted the air. Kemreen, in a plunging silver sheath that put a lump in Zaya's throat every time she saw it. "The donor meets the candidate," she said. "What do we think, donor?"

"We're not yet regretting sending him a fat sack of cash," said Zaya.

"Stolen directly from the money bin of Shanhoon Krait, by the way, in a masterful victory at the Ogres' Amp... Amfit— " Kemreen made a face and shook her head. "Am-phi-the-a-ter. Just think about who he'd be donating it to right now."

"I think about that a lot," said Yyvvoun. "I was there; I saw you dodge Monsoon's tail. That's incredible bravery to win money you weren't going to see a sherd of."

Kemreen's arm tightened around Zaya's waist. "Incredible," she said.

"In the moment, it's just a calculated risk," said Zaya. "You don't really have time to think it through until after."

Kemreen looked at Zaya; her smile was like a dawn sun, soft and bright and unstoppable. "Yeah you do."

Heat bloomed through Zaya's chest. Her own hand, resting on Kemreen's hipbone, drifted lower. "Maybe you do," she allowed.

Yyvvoun's smile was real, but visibly confused. "I don't think I've had the...?"

"Kemreen Gharial," said Kemreen, "formerly of the Azure Precinct Police. I'm the donor's gentleman friend."

"Formerly?" Zaya asked.

"Yeah. I was planning to tell you at a sort of random and inappropriate time, so now seemed good."

Zaya looked over at Yyvvoun, who was continuing to look polite, interested, and confused, then back to Kemreen. "We talked a little about this, but—"

"—but you live with a million people, so everything you do has to be three committee meetings and a floor vote. As a gentleman friend, though, I'm a free agent. So I can do big, romantic things like resigning in the morning and dropping it on you in front of some candidate, just to show my faith in you and what you're trying to do."

Kemreen let that announcement rest, and for a moment, nothing filled the silence. "It's an impressive show of faith," Yyvvoun said. He sounded like he meant it. "It's not every cause that can turn someone away from a steady livelihood. I can't make any promises about winning, or about how my votes will go if I do, but you can take it to the bank that I'll remember this."

An arm slipped around Zaya from the other side, and a head rested on her shoulder. She realized she recognized it by the smell of the hair: Vanako, a little unsteady from a glass or two of mezcal more than she could handle. "Hiiiiii, M. Leatherback," she said. "You should do what my mom says. Because she handed you a bunch of money, but mostly because she's always right. And because my boyfriend brought you a drink."

Tuuro stepped forward and bent silently at the waist. He'd somehow expropriated a tray of durian mezcal from one of the waitrons, and it had at least ten glasses on it. Four pairs of eyes landed on the candidate.

"Don't wait for me," Yyvvoun said.

But they did, until he took one.

Then there was a glass in everyone's hand, and then it was down everyone's throat, and no one spoke, not because they didn't know what to say, but because it was clear that what to say was nothing. The heat of the mezcal mingled with the heat of Kemreen's body against Zaya's; her skin had grown sticky under her shift from Kemreen's closeness, and her forehead was growing damp as well, but that was only a sign of skin and sweat to come, and she squeezed Kemreen hungrily, feeling her own bicep tense and press on her *gentleman friend*'s, who replied by claiming a palmful of Zaya's ass for herself. Zaya turned toward Vanako and took a deep draught of her hair. This was where she should be: Caught between lover and daughter, decorated by her father, winning over the men who could make the world more like it was meant to be. It was everything that should happen. It was everything.

***

TWELVE WEEKS BEFORE BELL the Cat.

The Vravali Market had nucleated, centuries ago, around a loose throng of rough-hewn standing stones about two stories tall, bridging what are now Amber and Amethyst Precincts. Their lowest few feet were graffitied with glyphs unknown, slogans and aphorisms in old Ililuë, and profanities and propositions from any number of contemporary languages. Touching them brought visions of unknown people speaking unfamiliar tongues, often performing acts with an air of sorcerous ritual and enchantment; and it was these visions, early in the history of Yemareir, that prompted frauds and hucksters to set up tables among the stones, offering treasures that promised to decode their secrets. The treasures soon acquired the reputation they deserved, but the tourists and seekers still came, and eventually were joined by the theoretical sorcerers of Yemareir's first learned societies, who didn't care for snake oil but did very much enjoy a good meal in the middle of the day.

Visitors began coming for the food as much as the stones, and over years and decades the area began to fill with stalls and carts.

It was the fishmongers, not the scholars, who discovered that the thaumaturgic potential of the stones could be harnessed like a battery.

Or maybe it was the shaved-ice carts? Or the butchers, or the performers. By the time anyone respectable inquired into how the fish and meat stayed so fresh, the ice so cold, or the singers so smooth and clear-voiced over the roar of the crowd, the power of the Vravali Market standing stones was an open secret among the vendors. You couldn't do a lot with it, but you could do a little for a long time; the potential was self-regenerating and, at known bandwidth limits, limitless, like a vast underground sea pushing up through a forest of finger-thick wells.

A later application, innovated by the long-dead 'streamer Haniveen Skink, was levitation.

You couldn't levitate a person above the standing stones, not using their power alone. But a charm weighing a few ounces could stay up for hours. Enchant a charm to glow a certain color, and to release a cloud of colored sparks when hit with fire, and you had the Vravali Market Skyte: A zigzagging course above the market, where each spark-belching charm you missed notched you one lower in the rankings, and each one you hit got you cheers and catcalls from the crowds below.

Zaya didn't know if Shanhoon Krait and Monsoon had missed any; but they were hot on Bandit's heels, and Bandit had just missed the red spark-charm.

It's fine, Vanako fed forward. *He has to have missed one by now.*

"Smooth out Bandit's energy and stop talking about it."

I can't smooth out its energy if you're pushing it to sprinting speed. Bandit was a long-hauler; its body had adapted for sprints and maneuvers over the last months, but its strength would always be maintaining a fast pace for a long run, and too many surges left it exhausted.

"I'm not sprinting. Just do your job."

I can't do my job if its lungs are exploding!

"That's the course. Turns and burns. Find a way."

It's a bad course for Bandit—

An explosion of light and smoke blinded and deafened both of them.

Zaya checked frantically for Vanako; she was there, she hadn't fallen. A dark shape surged past them in the night sky. "Fuck me with a spike-weasel, they're shooting fireworks—"

Spike-weasel?

Zaya shot Vanako a finely detailed image and enjoyed the deeply stupid and pointless satisfaction of feeling her daughter's gorge rise. "Now keep your eyes on our tail while I figure out how to get back in front of this idiot."

As if Krait had heard them, Monsoon's spike-girt tail swayed tauntingly in the slipstream.

Had Krait heard them? He hated and scorned psionics in the 'stream, or at least that's what he always said to the Standards Board. That, Zaya decided, would probably not make a stitch of difference as to whether he'd use them to his advantage.

Head out of ass, Mom.

"Don't even—oh, shit!" A shower of sea-blue sparks exploded ahead of them—not crowd-shot fireworks this time, but the next spark-charm. Zaya made her mind slow down, drew a careful bead, and launched a burn.

Another shower of blue sparks; relief loosened the muscles of Zaya's stomach.

Then Bandit lurched. They lost altitude; Monsoon seemed to shoot ahead. Zaya heard the scream of fireworks and squeezed her eyes shut. "Come on, Bandit, pull back up. Vani!"

It's exhausted! This is too many burns!

"It is exactly the number of required burns!"

That's why we never should have raced this course!

"We're almost at the finish. Bandit can do this." Zaya tamped down Bandit's air-hunger, tamped down its pain, pushed its wings.

Mom. You're going to hurt it. This is too much.

"Bandit trusts me. Time for you to trust me."

They were gaining on Monsoon again. The last charm was double the size of any of the others, and double the brightness: A white moon among the roofs of the city.

Carnaug is on our ass—

"It doesn't matter."

It did matter; the huge wyrm could wrestle them out of the sky if it chose—and, if it did, Bandit might be too exhausted to stop their fall. Zaya began gathering breath for a burn.

What the fuck, Mom, this is too soon. You're not close enough—

"Just stop saying things to me."

Vanako threw back Zaya's image of a spike-weasel, this time decorated with the kind of bloody scraps you'd see on a butcher's counter at the end of the day. Zaya pulled in all the breath she could into the burn-lung. Bandit's vision began to narrow, blackness scratching at its edges.

YOU ARE GOING TO KILL MY DRAGON—

Zaya watched Monsoon gather breath for its own burn. She'd seen more Eyrie Shrikes breathe fire than she could count; she knew exactly what it would look like the second before it released the flame.

Didn't she?

"Burn!" she screamed, letting the word tear her throat ragged. Only the slipstream would hear it. But she imagined pushing the power of her scream into the stream of flame that licked from

Bandit's mouth, stretching it longer than it had any right to be, holding more heat than it had any right to hold.

It hit the charm before Monsoon's burn could begin. The Melanic Shrike veered instinctively away from the heat; its burn sprayed wildly off-target, scorching the standing stone instead.

Bandit lurched again, and then they were in free-fall.

Zaya and Vanako kicked in as one, tensing and flexing alien muscles in perfect concert. On its own, their best effort couldn't have done much more than soften their fall; but Bandit's consciousness came back, and they were flying again.

Carnaug roared over them like a feathered avalanche, and the downdraft nearly ripped Zaya from her saddle; but Bandit's calm abided, its wings hauled air, and then they were over the line, past a charm unkindled by a second burn.

Bandit would have to rest for a week just to recover from the landing, much less the race. Zaya knew that before they landed. Whether it was worth it would depend on Monsoon and Carnaug.

***

ELEVEN AND A HALF weeks before Bell the Cat.

"I should have known Yaulë would be hopeless at the Skyte," said Zaya. "Carnaug missed four targets, it was barely in the race. So technically Monsoon was in second, we were in fourth, and Carnaug was in sixth; and since Lerikaan and Arrow missed blue, that moved them down to fifth. So nobody did better than second or fourth—because even a perfect finish in fifth place or lower would tie them with Arrow at best—which meant second was first and fourth was second, which is why I'm handing Professor Rinkhal the runner-up prize. Does that make sense?"

"I just find it all so absolutely fascinating," said the landlord.

Zaya thought she'd explained the rules of the Skyte reasonably well, but it was possible she hadn't been trying that hard. "To bring it back to what we're here for, though: I don't think anybody should have to run all those numbers just to buy their child's life."

This took her interlocutor a moment or two to compute. Zaya was trying to figure out how much of the landlord's airy stupidity was an act. Some of it had to be; but her on-paper qualifications supported the act impeccably. Her husband had built a small shipping empire that funded a comfortable life for their family, and she'd taken an interest in student housing as her own children had aged into university and reported the difficult choice faced by their less blessed classmates from more remote precincts: Spend money and time on a daily commute by wyrm, or less time but more money on a flat near the university. She'd already joked insecurely about the unprofitability of her ventures into dormitory housing; it turned out that students would choose the daily commute because it was all they could afford, and even a slightly more expensive option wouldn't register. She'd chosen red ink in the books over empty rooms, and while Zaya could, abstractly, understand that this was a good thing for her tenants, it was just a gilded frame around the portrait of a woman rich enough that she didn't have to worry about the money she was dumping in a blast furnace.

Then again, the dining hall at whose long table they were eating was run by this woman. So maybe Zaya could at least run on appreciation of a free meal.

"We all must buy life, though, mustn't we?" said the landlord. "And the cost isn't so unreasonable, all things considered, is it? I mean, what's too expensive in exchange for the privilege of living? Life's priceless!"

A *clack* sound distracted Zaya for a moment; someone had dropped a fork, maybe. "We, ah, don't all, really," she said. "The dole's actually a godsend to quite a lot of our neighbors. I lived on it myself for a while."

"It's true," said the landlord, running a finger around the rim of her arrack glass. "Unfair competition, though, my husband points out. A small business like mine can't compete with housing run on the scale of the city government, can it?"

"A small business like mine could hardly compete with you if you were driving up the prices on black-market yliaster," said Zaya. "And, look, I'd do the same if I were you. I'd do anything to save my child. But rich people outbidding poor people for the *priceless privilege* of living isn't justice."

"You are a small business, aren't you?" said the landlord. "I never thought of it that way. Oh, but surely these criminals don't have auctions? They just set a price and you pay it or you don't, I would have thought."

"They charge what the market will bear." Another *clack* on the window; Zaya thought she caught a flash of motion outside.

"Well, I don't think the well-to-do become hunted on purpose, any more than anybody else. And you can't blame people for making money. Especially not in a world where you need to buy life, as you say."

"I'm supporting Prof. Rinkhal because I don't want the world to be like that," said Zaya.

The landlord laughed. "It's true he's a sorcerer, but I think changing the nature of the world might be beyond him."

"May I ask, then, respectfully, why you're here?"

"Oh, I enjoy meeting candidates. It's so important to understand who might be representing you in the halls of politics! Speaking of," and, without obviously looking behind her, she reached out to clutch the sleeve of Kelloun Rinkhal himself, who was headed somewhere in a hurry. "Have you met your most ardent supporter, Professor? M. Zaya Shearwater, the so-called fastest woman in Yemareir?"

"Pleasure," he said. "Please excuse me, Shearwater-cha, M. Boomslang, I'm afraid I'm, ah, asked for out of doors."

M. Boomslang's knuckled whitened just a touch as she tightened her grip on his sleeve. "What brings you out there in such a hurry?"

He looked down in annoyed perplexity at her hand on his sleeve. "Later, if we could."

"Now, Kelloun."

The words came out so fast that Zaya wasn't sure if she'd heard either their sounds or their tone correctly; they were still pleasant, still spoken in that half-singing lilt, but it might have been a different woman who spoke. Something seemed to click into place behind the professor's eyes. "All right, Zariveen, if you like." He looked at Zaya. "Students are protesting this little gathering of ours."

The *clacks* out of nowhere: Rocks on charm-hardened glass. They were throwing things at the windows.

"Come on, then, M. Shearwater," said Rinkhal. "Ask me why."

Zaya couldn't help glancing at Zariveen Boomslang, whose face was cool and calm. "Why?"

"The University of Yemareir auxiliary doesn't think the Travelers should take money from slumlords," said Rinkhal.

"That's a hurtful term," said Zariveen, not visibly hurt. "Why do they say that?"

"I'm sure I don't know."

"Kelloun."

Instead of a *clack*, the next noise was a *crack*; heads turned, and Rinkhal grimaced. "The same reasons anyone else gets called a slumlord. A squatter would take better care of those buildings than you do."

"I've been losing money on them for years," said Zariveen Boomslang. "I'm supporting my tenants out of my own pocketbook."

"That's the tale, yes. Will you make me tell her what I know?"

"You've got a crowd to calm, Kelloun."

Kelloun Rinkhal pulled back his freed arm as though he'd seared his palm on a hot panhandle. "You've heard enough anyway," he said as he scurried off. "Ask anyone if you want the details."

Zariveen Boomslang watched him go. "You've heard him speak?" she asked Zaya. "He's a firebrand. He has a ragged eloquence. He'll calm them down. Or at least distract them. He can make a fleabite sound like a noble sacrifice. You know the saying?"

"About lying down with dogs?" said Zaya. "That's how you think of yourself?"

"That's how he thinks of me. But he knows who wears the collar."

"You seem to think this has something to do with me."

"I think it's *lovely* that you want to help his campaign."

"But?"

"M. Shearwater, I'm not sure what you mean." The quickness had gone out of her voice, and the steel with it; if it hadn't been for the last minute, Zaya would have taken her at her word.

***

ELEVEN WEEKS BEFORE BELL the Cat.

Cotton Pass, in the foothills north of the city, was a long, deep gorge lined with abandoned pueblos, so named because of the woolly clouds that filled it no matter the dryness of the day or the brightness of the sun. The Cotton Pass Blindway was simply a race from the west end to the east.

About the race, the less said the better. Vanako held tight to her control over Bandit's vitals, her attention focused there rather than on extracting what signals she could from the sights and sounds doled out in stingy portions by the clouded pass. Neither wheedling nor telling-off would shake her from her ticklike concentration on the wyrm's biology, which left Zaya the only one looking out for things like the rope bridges of the gorge's old inhabitants, or the walls of the gorge themselves. That alone might have bought them second place; but trying to work with Vanako in this state was like running a sprint with a foot you'd been sitting on. When Kshalain Honu on Javelin tried to smash them into the wall, Zaya just dropped back and let them pass; when Yaulë on Carnaug shot over them and tore through a bridge that would have clotheslined Bandit, Zaya didn't try to overtake them. With Shanhoon Krait sailing to first place on Monsoon's echolocation, they came in fourth. Vanako stormed off silently as soon as they landed.

"What in the Limper's bum leg happened to you two?" Yyrreen whispered to Zaya as they watched Krait and Honu receive their prizes.

"We're having a fight." Zaya shrugged. "Vani just realized she hates losing more than she likes being right. It's fine."

"How are you going to explain that to Jenishoon Terrapin?"

"Which one is he again?"

"Cobalt Precinct. Independent."

"Great. Please inform Jenishoon Terrapin that I race lizards through the air for money. If he wants guaranteed income, he can sell pancakes."

"He's going to say you came through for the Travelers and not for independents."

"Yvvvoun Leatherback seemed happy with his sack of cash," said Zaya.

"That's not all he's happy with," Yyrreen muttered.

"What?"

"Don't play innocent. You saw how possessive Kemreen got. You were doing it on purpose."

"I was directed to play nice with the candidates."

"Whatever," said Yyrreen. "Summon up half that niceness for M. Terrapin, if you can spare it."

"I can do way less than half, if that helps."

Yyrreen bent her head and covered her face with her hands.

"Hey," Zaya said. "What makes Zariveen Boomslang a slumlord? It's been bugging me for days."

"Who said—" Yyrreen shook her head. "I should know better than to do the song and dance with you. Look, it's not a complicated grift, if you're rich. Your husband's money gets you the down payment on your buildings. Your contracts include the right to bill tenants occasionally for certain types of improvements. A fair few of them have the means to just pay, and they do. For the ones who don't, the contract specifies that you can silently convert non-payment into high-interest debt. You could hire some shin-crackers to collect, but that's expensive; instead, you sell the debt at ten percent of its value to a shin-cracking agency that thinks they can collect twenty. That sounds like a bad haircut, but remember, this is debt you made up out of thin air in the first place; it's pure profit."

"She never improves the buildings at all?" said Zaya.

"I don't live in her balance sheet. I assume she does what she has to do."

"And Kelloun Rinkhal takes that money? How does he survive in class?"

"Plate mail?"

Black flame licked up Zaya's throat; she dug her fingertips into Yyrreen's upper arm. "I'm serious."

Yyrreen locked Zaya's eyes for a split second, and the blade of her hand wiped Zaya's fingers away. Her hand was hard, the move as assured as a cat snatching a bird from the air; Zaya was reminded that Yyrreen had grown up in dole-flats and neighborhoods as bad as hers, and had done worse than she had to survive them. "If he got more from people like you," she said, turning her eyes back toward the Shanhoon Krait and Kshalain Honu, "he could take less from people like her."

"I am doing *literally everything—*"

"I know you are," said Yyrreen.

It seemed like she was about to say more; and when she didn't, Zaya thought of things to say. But they had all been said, or else were the sort of thing that seemed like they shouldn't have to be said, and Zaya kept her silence.

***

Ten weeks before Bell the Cat.

For the gala for Jenishoon Terrapin, they'd set up a plank pavilion that straddled the high tide line, so you could feel as if you were out to sea if you kept your eyes west. The salt air and the shush of the breakers brought a calm to Zaya she hadn't felt in... well, the last time she'd visited the shore. She and Kemreen sat quietly in two chairs, facing the horizon with fingers loosely tangled and small dirty plates balanced on a knee each. Without a donation, there wasn't much call to mingle, and that was fine.

Kemreen examined Zaya's scalp. "Your dye's fading."

"I'll have Zinji touch it up."

"Could do new colors. A sunrise. Match Bandit's plumage."

"If I go new, I'll go simple. I wanted to impress all these grandees and marquesses, but I don't think they care."

"Pink?"

"Purple. For yliaster."

Zaya felt the sigh through Kemreen's fingers more than she heard it from her breath. Then Kemreen's hand came free of hers. "Can I get you a drink?"

Zaya looked up at Kemreen. The moonlight cut her into soft planes and facets; she was like a gem. "One of whatever you're having."

That brought a small smile forth, at least. "Famous last words."

Zaya took her hand back. "You look beautiful. In the moonlight." She waved her other hand up and down, trying to indicate the wholeness of her—why did people do that? "Like, someone who knew how to use words would say some really good ones. To you, right now. Because you're beautiful."

"Save some of that poetry for later," said Kemreen. "It's wasted on these grandees and marquesses." Her grin made it clear exactly what "later" meant, and where, and how much clothing would be present (minimal, and exclusively as furniture decoration).

The moon piled in snowdrifts on the water; spray shot through the gaps in the planks. She'd had the conversation with Vanako, and it hadn't gone *well*, but the Cotton Pass Blindway had made the impression Zaya had thought it would. Vanako had grudgingly conceded that pushing Bandit at the Skyte had done no long-term harm, and that her own hoarding of Bandit's energies during the Blindway hadn't helped. She'd declined the invitation to this thing to spend the evening with Tuuro near his flat in Damask Precinct, which Zaya probably shouldn't have said yes to, but what was done was done. Kemreen had been moody since the gala for Kelloun Rinkhal, and she wouldn't say why, but it wasn't hard to find out. A question to the Lilac Precinct police's newest young patrolman confirmed it: Kemreen's old beat-mates were freezing her out. They'd decided she'd joined the enemy, and they were treating her like it. That hadn't led to any fights, but Zaya sometimes wished it would. It would be better—maybe?—than the sour silences that felt like abscesses, breeding grounds for fights that would erupt too violent and venomous to control. Zaya could, of course, wield the lance, and she wasn't sure why she hadn't, except that the immediate pain of doing it felt more dire than the long-term cost. That kind of calculation was always wrong, she knew, but that had yet to move her.

But neither Vanako nor Kemreen was the worry most weighing on Zaya's mind.

"Bold of you to come here empty-handed," said Yyvvoun Leatherback, taking Kemreen's seat.

"Bold of you to assume I wouldn't stab a candidate with a canapé toothpick for bitching."

Yyvvoun chuckled. "If you're going to do that, do it to me. M. Terrapin won't be nearly as philosophical about it."

"He's running unopposed. Why does he need my help anyway?"

"Conditionally unopposed. Having strong financial support helps maintain the conditions."

"Is that why you're here?"

"We independents have to support one another."

"That sounds like code for something," said Zaya.

"It is, which is why I'm not going to explain it. Ciphers and utensils aside, Zaya, how are you?"

She laced her fingers behind her head and looked at the moon. "Losing races, bleeding money. Just like old times, honestly."

"As someone who's perfected the art of deflection, let me acknowledge a fellow master. What I'm asking is, how is Jaliki doing, and how are you feeling about it?"

Zaya didn't literally feel the sea air sting her skin as though her clothes had suddenly evaporated, but that's the image she'd have used in a poem about that moment, if she were someone who knew how to use words.

"I think it'd be best if you answered," said Yyvvoun. "That sounded like a threat. Sorry. What I mean is, I think it would help you if you put it into words. Even if you don't say everything. It would help if you said anything."

"He's my son," Zaya said. "He's a little boy."

"And that makes you feel…"

"Poisoned."

That wasn't the word she'd been expecting to say. It wasn't a word she'd ever thought.

"That's a good word for it," Yyvvoun said. "I mean, not to critique the diction of the terrified and grieving. But it has a specificity. When Dzaroon was dying, I would think of what I felt as feeling sick, or full of dread, or crushed. But 'poisoned' hits something real that's lacking in those other words. In this candidate's opinion."

"The last treatment's worn off." Zaya spoke quietly; she wasn't even sure if he could hear her above the rush of the sea. "The ker won't leave his side now. It's like it missed him. I'm sure it missed him." Her mind bloomed with the usual, impossible thoughts: strangling it, gutting it with a kitchen knife, seizing it by the tail and bashing its head against the wall until it stopped moving. "Everything I do for him takes me away from him, and I don't know if any of it is giving him any more time."

Yyvvoun put a hand on her shoulder. Zaya pressed the back of it with her palm. She wanted to touch her face to see if it was as wet as it felt; but then she'd know, and that might be worse.

"I don't know how to phrase this delicately," he said. "Why are you helping us, when you could be helping him?"

I'm so tired of explaining this to Mrineen. She was trying to figure out how to say it without saying it, but Kemreen's voice came from above and behind: "I'd have brought an extra chair, but I've got a drink in each hand." There were worlds in which her playful tone showed no signs of strain or irritation; this wasn't one of them.

Yyvvoun was out of her seat in a flash. "M. Gharial," he said. "I should have known this was yours."

"Where goes the queen, there goes her consort, right?" Kemreen sat down and handed the drink to Zaya. "So what's going on with the candidate from Coral Precinct? It'd be kind of rude to hand you cash at someone else's party, you know. That's if we had any."

"We were just sharing experiences of having a loved one who's hunted," said Yyvvoun. "I've found it can help."

Kemreen turned to look at Zaya. "I love Jaliki too. You know that, right?"

The spear of the Slayer give me strength. "I know," said Zaya.

"I left the—"

"Babe," said Zaya, finally giving in and wiping at an eye with a fingertip. "Whatever you're trying to say, please just say it."

"I'll leave you to it," said Yyvvoun. "M. Gharial, I'm sorry I took your seat."

"My name's not on it," said Kemreen, standing. "You're right, though, this isn't the kind of conversation we should have around a candidate. You two go back to bonding over death and grief, that's much more festive."

Breakers washed over the silence. Kemreen stared into the glass she was holding, then turned and, with a graceful snap of her arm, tossed it into the sea. It went farther than it had any right to go; Zaya didn't hear the splash.

"Listen to me," Kemreen said. "I'm sorry. Really. Neither of you deserved all that."

She left, and Zaya said *Babe, no,* but she knew it wouldn't stop Kemreen leaving. She could absolutely have gotten up and taken her hand and stopped her, or else followed her; but she didn't. Instead she looked back at the moon again.

"Entrances and exits, she's great at," Zaya said. "What's between them maybe needs work?"

"One of the things this does," said Yyvvoun, sitting back down, "is cut you off. People don't understand, and it's exhausting. So you withdraw, because you're already exhausted enough."

"The Yearner, yes," said Zaya. She decided she wasn't too good to drink the drink Kemreen had bought; it was some kind of gin cocktail, dry and herby. She made herself sip instead of gulp. "I don't want to push her away, but... 'I love Jaliki too'? He's my *son*. I raised him from a little baby. And not alone, but... the only one of us who knew how to be a mom was gone. And she was my wife, so he was mine. Oh, sure, the rest of them know what they're doing now, but when Kiriki was in the ground and someone had to feed the baby, it was *me*."

Yyvvoun looked out at the horizon. If you went far enough in that direction, Zaya thought, you'd hit Kayazē. "Sometimes you also start inventing reasons that other people's grief doesn't count."

"Of course it counts—"

"How could it?" said Yyvvoun. "Dzaroon didn't even like his parents; he hadn't lived with them for years. They didn't really know the man who died. They weren't there when it happened. How could their grief be the same as mine?" He turned to look at her. "And how strong, how special, was I, to hold a grief that great?"

Zaya closed her eyes and looked at the ragged afterimage of the moon.

"I'm not grieving," she said. "My son is alive."

He might not be, though. The ker didn't avoid him any more. Unless he got treated, it was only a matter of time. Maybe that wasn't what Yyvvoun was thinking into the silence; but she felt like she could hear it anyway.

"I promised Kaana the winnings from the Basting Stitch," said Zaya. "Then I have an Arc-en-Ciel. I'll find something for him after that. And then you need to get yourself elected and pass a law so my family doesn't starve."

"They'll say you're only out for yourself."

"Fuck them." She drank. "Who are they?"

Yyvvoun shrugged. "No idea. I actually can't imagine anyone saying that. I just wanted to hear you say 'fuck them,' so the ocean and the stars could hear you and you couldn't take it back."

"The ocean's not the boss of me," said Zaya.

Yyvvoun chuckled. "No, I don't believe it is," he said.

Her hand was hanging at her side, the empty cocktail glass held loosely in it; she felt the backs of his knuckles brush the backs of hers. She shot a glance back to the party. Kemreen's shimmering silver dress was nowhere to be seen. She let the glass drop and hooked a pinky around his.

He looked at her; she looked at him.

"Come on," she said, and stood.

CHAPTER 5

EIGHT WEEKS BEFORE BELL THE CAT

THE ROOF DECK OF the building that housed House Shearwater wasn't completely clear; there were a couple of neighbors Zaya didn't know, drinking and smoking and passing a guitar back and forth. Shozo had given them a stern once-over as they'd come up the stairs, she was sure, and would have kept them off the deck if he'd been told to. But he didn't strictly have the right to do that, even if he was a big guy with a chain-whip. Amiko sat off in a corner, reading a book, but Zaya knew her bees were keeping their compound eyes on the air around them, and any hint of a wyrm getting too close would draw her swarm before she had time to close the pages.

The table where she and Kemreen were sitting was on the opposite corner from the guitar-playing neighbors, and far enough from Amiko that they had some privacy if they spoke softly. They'd laid out a tablecloth and taken some of the nice place settings, although Zaya had still not figured out how to get the water spots off the glassware. The meal was cobbled together from leftovers and market staples—cold roast pork and mashed epazote, extra egg bread rolls that had been better that morning, julienned potatoes in chili oil. Kemreen had brought some syrupy pudding thing studded with figs and apricots, and a bottle of absinthe without a label. When there was food on both plates and drink in both glasses, Zaya couldn't help but blow a sigh into the silence.

"Nice to see you too," said Kemreen, smiling around a mouthful of pork.

"I feel like I don't know what to do with myself," Zaya said. "I feel like I should go downstairs and find whatever's wrong."

"Why does something have to be wrong?"

"There are ten people who live in my house and a bunch of needy politicians who won't leave me alone unless they've gotten the last drop of marrow from my bones," Zaya said. "There's at least one person who wants me to be doing something specific for them, right now."

Somewhere in there, the joy had drained from Kemreen's face.

"What's up?" Zaya asked.

"Needy politicians," said Kemreen.

"I mean. No disagreement. But I feel like you've got something specific in mind."

Kemreen took a bite from a roll and chased it with a sip of absinthe. "At that beach party for that Cobalt Precinct fogey, I told you I love Jaliki and I care about him. You didn't seem like you wanted to hear it—and I actually get that," she said over the words Zaya was about to say, even though she didn't know what they were yet. "It wasn't great in context. But it is true. And I don't get what you're doing. The Cobalt guy doesn't give a shit about Jaliki. None of them do."

Zaya took a bigger sip of absinthe than was maybe wise, and washed it down with water. "Have I ever told you how I met Kiri and Vinaali?"

Kemreen looked apologetic. "Remind me who Kiri and Vinaali are again?"

"Some bodyguard you are."

"OK, OK. They're... not the neighbor girl and her boyfriend, that's Zayeni. The couple who bring all the food?"

Zaya nodded and looked over to the other side of the roof deck. There they were, sitting in a couple of low chairs with broad arms, talking. Kemreen followed her gaze and saw them too. "Huh."

"When we were on the dole in Madder Precinct, they lived across the street in Incarnadine. You know I talk a lot about how we'd go to the beach to pull a wyrm and then go knock over a liquor store. It's horrible, it's funny, it's the thing people who don't know me know about me."

"It's not funny, it's child abuse."

"Sure. But, like, there aren't enough liquor stores in Yemareir to keep a family fed. Even if we sold everything we stole at market rates, which is impossible—the wyrm wants its cut, you fence the rest or sell it at a discount—you can cover maybe one day in two, one day in three? More if one of your dads is doing time on a crew, since he's eating for free, but that didn't happen often. And at the time, mind, they're both spending a lot on recreational substances, you wouldn't hire them to dig ditches without a week of drying out beforehand.

"So Kiri and Vinaali lived on the quickest route to Scarlet Precinct from our project. Up Caskmaker Street, through some alleys over to Sarain Tuatara Street, and a right on the Boulevard of Wings would take you straight to the Moonturn Moultwyrm broodspire. They were brooding at the time, so Scarlet was empty. I couldn't sit in an algebra lecture for ten minutes without climbing the walls, but I could sit on a bench in the Square of Forgotten Dances and watch for baby Moultwyrms—do you know they're black and white until they're almost a year old? They brood in winter, and they stay black and white until that next winter moult, where the black feathers come in blue..." A little Moultwyrm hopped up on the table, as starkly black-and-white as Zaya had described. It circled like a cat, then curled up to rest its chin on its tail and slept.

Kemreen stared at it for a moment, then looked at Zaya. "Is it Moultwyrm brooding season now?"

"I don't think so. They can't fly, anyway, I don't see how one would get up here."

"Then how's it here?"

"Don't overthink it," said Zaya. "Anyway, it was peaceful, just being on my own in Scarlet with the Moultwyrms. Whenever I was around a human, they wanted me to be doing something I wasn't. On my own…" She smiled, remembering. "I faced down what must have been an eighth-cohort wyrm, two stories high, blocking the street. I don't even know how long we looked at each other. I remember it turned away first, and I realized it had somewhere to be and I didn't. I don't know if I've ever felt that good since. The only wyrm that ever attacked me was a pup, barely bigger than this guy."

The Moultwyrm on the table reared up and spat flame at Zaya.

Kemreen shrieked and swatted at it, tagging it in the eye; it squeaked and flew off. Zaya's forearm was protecting her face. The skin of it wasn't charred, thankfully, but it was an angry red, and a few strands of her hair were smoking where the flame had licked over. She grabbed Kemreen's hand with hers and said, "Sssshhhh. Neighbors."

"We have to get you help—"

"No, we're good. Where'd you get the absinthe?"

"I don't think you should use—"

"Oasis & Mirage?"

That made Kemreen go very still, like a lizard that's just seen a raptor overhead. She looked at the absinthe.

"Oasis & Mirage on Kemreen Loggerhead Street," Zaya said. "Halaizen puts worldvine in a lot of his homebrew. It's his thing. I figured it out when we saw Kiri and Vinaali. I should have told you."

Kemreen twirled an enormous claymore, its gem-studded grip wrapped in beautifully tooled blue leather, then leaned it on the table. "My little friend here agrees you should have told me."

"Always knives with you."

"Always."

Zaya couldn't help but stare at Kemreen's arm, each muscle clearly visible. (Of course they were; she wasn't actually resting her hand on the grip of her hallucinated sword, she was holding it up by herself, to the neighbors' confusion or amusement depending on how much they'd deduced.) She thought of kissing her way from the tips of the fingers to the heel of the hand, over the soft skin of the wrist where the heartbeat pulsed, out over the point of the elbow and up the plane of the triceps... and stopped herself, before she found a hallucination of herself—or her actual self—doing it. Instead she turned her forearm over to show Kemreen where the wyrm-flame had hit. Their shared hallucination of the burn had faded, replaced by the scar she'd had there since. "I hit the pup in the eye after it flamed me, just like you did, and it ran away. I almost felt sorry for it. Didn't realize how badly I was hurt until I started getting dizzy on Sarain Tuatara Street. Kiri and Vinaali saw me and took me in, found Papa Zinji, gave me food and water. I don't think they'd ever seen a hurt kid eat like that, I was starving. And after that, whenever I went to watch the Moultwyrms in the morning, I'd find food on their front steps.

"When the Moultwyrm brooding season was over, they could have just let it pass. I wasn't coming by any more, they didn't know where I lived, no one could possibly have blamed them if they stopped helping. But they didn't. They found us—I'll never forget the day because it was one of the normal ones, where Papa Kaalo was pretty sober and Papa Zinji was happy about it, and I was happy about them being happy, and the three of us were playing cards over snacks with the window open..."

Zaya kept narrating, she supposed, but the words seemed to fall away as they both watched the story play out: Zaya, young and painfully thin, and Zinji and Kaalo, drawn and haggard but bright with the happiness of men who know to suck the moment's marrow from any crack they can find, trash-talking and bickering over rules and tossing scraps to a knot of monkeys gathered outside the window. A knock came at the door and they all froze for a moment. Kaalo rose to answer, and of course it was Kiri and Vinaali, two middle-aged Kayalim with cropped black hair, with a basket and a towel-covered pan, the smells of oil and bread and spices thickening the air. Words flowed back and forth; Kaalo looked to Zaya, Zaya nodded, and dinner began. When it ended, there was at least as much food left as had been eaten, and Kiri and Vinaali left all of it, including the pan. The scene flowed, dreamlike, into their next visit: A pot of jeweled rice and a tray of chicken legs, the not-yet-clean pan reclaimed with no comment on its state. Next it was a meat pie big enough for a fourth-cohort Ranger Wyrm. Leftovers piled up, then disappeared; pots, pans, and trays came in filled and left (this time) clean; two fathers and a daughter filled out, the daughter growing visibly taller as if her body had seen an opportunity to slip the chains of a lifetime's scant eating and bolt as fast as it could.

The paint and windows and view of the flat changed, and the pans stopped coming. Kiri and Vinaali, too, faded away. But now Zaya and her fathers were bringing food in themselves—food they burned and overboiled and mis-seasoned, food they ate with resignation and disgust as often as pleasure, but food at least, a steady stream of it.

A change of place again: the familiar dark hardwood walls and soft light of the House Shearwater common room. Minshoon and Kirono entered, each holding the hand of one of what appeared to be two young mixed girls, their faces stony and solemn. The two adults and two children walked over to the sofa, whose back was facing Zaya and Kemreen, and only then did a head and shoulders pop up from it: a tear-ravaged Zaya, holding a tiny bundle that could only be Jaliki. The transformation on Zaya's face was quick and clear: Her expression grew, if not happy, then at least alive; she leaned down and showed the baby to the children, who were not one molecule more at ease.

"Taavi and Gilthiniel?" Kemreen asked.

"We took them in after Kaalo and Kiriki died," Zaya said. "I told Minshoon no, I couldn't do it. And he told me they needed us. And I told him no. And he did the right thing."

Kemreen was quiet, but not silent; the air around her hummed and spat with sparks.

"Say it," said Zaya. "You can't hide from the gods of world-vine."

"You're the only one who'll fight for Jaliki. He needs you."

"I know. I'm going to."

"Not like electoral politics. Like getting him treatment."

"I know."

The sparks around Kemreen turned from spitting yellow to flowing blue; she leaned forward, her shoulders and elbows loosened. "I'm so glad. What changed your mind?"

"I talked to Yyvvoun."

The sparks disappeared abruptly, without a trace. Zaya wondered what the air around her looked like. "Needy politicians," Kemreen said.

"He's been there."

"I've been telling you this." Her voice echoed, but the echo said something different: *Why didn't you listen to me?*

"It means something different when you've been there."

There was light coming from Kemreen, but it was black now, muting colors where it shone, obscuring everything behind her.

"Whatever," she said. "I should just count my blessings you're not supporting legalization any more."

"What?"

Kemreen examined Zaya. "Right. Of course you are. Even if you don't need to."

"It's the right thing. I can use my image, my reputation—"

"I understood you supporting it when it was your kid on the line."

"It is my kid on the line! Maybe not this month, but what if I die? What if I can't race? I'm doing what I can, but that might not be—"

"What I don't get," said Kemreen, "is we were *there*. Vanioun Ora died in front of you. Bandit still has the scars. You still wake up yelling in the middle of the night. What is it going to take to convince you this fucking stuff can't be every—"

She finished the word, probably, but the roofdeck was Inundinir Square now at the height of blood and fear, Ora's trunkless legs still kicking and spurting on the cobblestones, Bandit's bright feathers wrapped in the night-sky blackness of the demon's fluid body, its cobalt-and-cadmium flames painting the stampeding crowd with shadows. As they watched, Kemreen sprinted in the wrong direction, fleeing spectators falling in her wake as if to a thresher, her body landing in front of Zaya's with a knife in either hand. Zaya, for her part, stood slack-jawed, but the moment sprang back into being in her mind: Managing Bandit's pain and fatigue, blunting its animal urge to flee, giving it information from her vantage point that it couldn't perceive from the melee. She hadn't known what the endpoint was, whether Bandit could kill the creature. She still didn't; some unsung sorcerer in the audience had banished the thing mid-combat.

Then the scene swung around to a body falling from high up in the Hotel Ochre. The *crack* and *slap* of his body hitting stone reverberated in their shared hearing.

"I was there," Zaya said softly.

They hadn't really talked about Shenireen Agama's feature, the one rushed to print the day after Inundinir Square. Zaya had read it, and had told Kemreen she read it, and the darkness in Kemreen's eyes had been the end of the conversation.

"If that was police at all," said Kemreen, "it was a couple of bad ones acting on their own. Nobody would put that many people's lives at risk just to make a political point."

"You're covering for your people," said Zaya, "in a way you'd never cover for mine."

"Someone always brings it back to 'your people' and 'my people,' but it's never me."

"No. You just told me your people don't abuse yliaster, even though they do; and my people do, which is why they have to die instead of live."

Kemreen's eyes flashed; she leaned forward... then checked herself. "You know what?" she said. "Maybe you're right. Maybe cops can't be trusted with yliaster either. What about it? How does a demon biting Vanioun Ora in half show me that it's safe for every idiot in this city to be able to summon one?"

"It isn't. It never has been. It's about justice."

"Still not seeing the justice in Vanioun Ora being dead."

"The cost of not doing anything about kerostasia is tens of thousands of lives every year. The cost of no regulations on yliaster for centuries has been like a double handful. *Your people* count the double handful as tragedies, because they're at risk, but the tens of thousands as just the cost of doing business."

"Cops aren't any less likely to be hunted than anybody else."

"'Cops get treated.' That's what Shenireen Agama says." Zaya held Kemreen's gaze for a moment, then two. "Is she right?"

"I don't know. I never saw a ker at the precinct."

The answer was quick enough to be the truth, but not so quick it sounded like a lie. But the air around Kemreen shimmered like the air over a hot cast-iron pan, although the sensation emanating from it was a draft of cold. Zaya caught the ghost of a shudder in Kemreen's shoulders as well. She wasn't lying about what she'd seen, or hadn't seen, in Azure Precinct, but she couldn't deny Agama's accusation. She hadn't seen it happen, but she knew enough to know it might, and more than might.

But she wouldn't say it.

Zaya reached out a hand. "I'm sorry." She *wasn't*. Not about saying the truth. But—"This isn't how I want it to be with you. I don't care more about being right than being with you."

"You do." The words were gentle. Kemreen put her hand out and interlaced her fingers with Zaya's, absently tracing the soft skin between knuckles with her forefinger. "You should. I don't want to stand between you and what you care about."

"That's—" Zaya did not dare say *breakup talk*. "Don't say stuff like that. I care about you."

"I know." Again, the gentleness, saying more than Kemreen could or would in words: *I know you care about me, and how much, and what I matter more than, and what less.*

They stayed a while, connected by their interwoven fingers, each tiny motion and change in tension a caress. Each moment that passed seemed to solidify what that silence meant; but Zaya could not think of how to break it, and more moments passed.

They drank more of the absinthe from Oasis & Mirage and watched seas and cities etch themselves on the darkening sky. They said things like "after the election" and "I'll still come by" and "I love you." They laughed bitterly about how it was that this moment of all moments, when something was ending, could be filled with such calm and peace and purity; and the clouds formed up into dancers, performing a funeral haka for their love as the worldvine in Halaizen's absinthe turned the thunder into drums; and there was a piece of Zaya that was walled off from all of it, screaming and weeping behind thick glass, and although at first Zaya thought that confined soul *was* Zaya, that her pain and her alienation were what was true about Zaya Shearwater, there was no denying that the heart that leapt at the cloud-haka was also hers: that, fuck it, when the love between a dragonrider and a war-rior snapped like an overburdened bridge, it was *right* and *correct* for the skies themselves to pay respects, to drench the city in a lamentation of noise and tears. When the lightning struck so close that they went flash-blind and the thunder nearly capsized the table, they ran inside laughing down the stairs leaving puddles be-hind them like a pair of wet dogs and then, quietly (they thought), stumbled to Zaya's room and made love, and if everything was a little numb and clumsy from the drugs, the worldvine didn't let them know it, wrapping them in noise and color until they had to stop because their heads hurt from the brightness of it all. At some point, pulling Zaya's shirt over her head, Kemreen had whispered "I won't stay the night"; and, although Zaya fell asleep with her there, in the morning she was gone.

So was the headache: It didn't take all that much of Halaizen's absinthe to make for a hell of a trip. So, Zaya thought, was the rain; but the streets outside were dry, and so was the soil in the window-box. There'd been no storm. The part of her walled off in glass gave a knowing shrug; but the part of her that had reveled in the wildness withered a little.

"You're the part that believes in things that are too good to be true," she said to that part of herself, and it withered a little more.

***

ZAYA WOULD RATHER HAVE stayed in her room and let the dullness of her heart leach from her veins into her muscles until her entire body was lifeless stone. But after a few minutes of that, she realized she couldn't stop thinking about the food and dishes they'd left out on the roof, and she put off petrification until they'd at least been reclaimed. When she woke, Jaliki was reading on the couch under a blanket, the ker curled up next to him. Zaya swatted at it, and it winked out of existence to appear back on the floor.

It was only when Kirono came in the front door, while Zaya was still cleaning up soiled glasses and dishes from the night before, that she realized she hadn't seen him at all the prior day. She heard a growl from the couch and turned her head in time to see the ker disappear. She looked back at Kirono; he waved a knife.

It was the saddle-knife that Jenirain Gila had found in Arhoon Pogona's belongings, that she had come to House Shearwater at spring's end to deliver, thinking it had belonged to Kiriki—because it was nearly identical to the one Pogona had given Kiriki a few weeks before she died. "Please tell me you weren't working with that all night," she said.

"No, I spent all night catching up on the work I get paid for," he said.

"It feels like there's a 'because' coming."

"Because I spent the day confirming that no smith in this city who works regularly with psychoreceptive materials made the thing."

Zaya made her way to an armchair so she could properly collapse into it. "Well," she said, collapsing, "fuck that."

"Language, Mom," said Jaliki, not looking up from his book. Zaya reached over and rubbed his head; she felt him lean into her palm.

Kirono walked to the kitchen and took two mate gourds out from a cabinet. "I was thinking about this. We should have expected it, honestly. These people I've been talking to, the ones I know from the university, they know how to work these substances. Not yliaster in particular, but weird inlays with nonstandard crap mixed in the metal. They all say this is an amateur mistake."

"What's an amateur mistake?"

He seemed to be concentrating extra hard on grinding the leaves. "I probably shouldn't touch it for a while."

"*Kirono.*"

"They mostly don't live or work near the university or here. I just wanted to get it all done."

"You already didn't sleep last night."

He brought two gourds, each filled with steaming mate and paired with a straw, and put one on the table by Zaya. "Go look at it."

She got up, walked over to the door, drew out the knife, and looked. The similarity to Kiriki's cut her as surely as if she'd squeezed it by the blade. But she could see what Kirono meant. The inlay was curling out in spots from the knotwork pattern, pulling away from the groove in others. She resisted the urge to pick at it. "Could that be related to the design?"

It had taken her a minute to notice, after Jenirain Gila had given her the knife, that although the shape and balance of the blade were the spitting image of Kiriki's, the inlaid design wasn't. They were about the same size and shape, but Kiriki's had had a winged serpent inlaid—obviously drawn by a Mrineen, for which they'd given Arhoon Pogona endless and well-earned shit—instead of the complex knot on this one.

"That was another thing I learned on today's expedition. It's not just any knotwork pattern. You've seen ones like it."

"Have I, Professor Shearwater?"

"Don't kid yourself. You have a lot of studying to do before you can pass the entrance exam for my classes."

"Kirono. Where. Have I seen it."

"Definitely after you won the Omari Shadowrun."

"I don't remember a solitary thing about that day other than being chased by an eldritch horror over a lake under a mountain. So unless the horror was wearing a cummerbund with this knot-work and I just forgot in the heat of the moment…"

"Ziyuki," said Kirono.

"Ugh."

"Ziyuki-kana?" said Jaliki, looking up with interest, and Zaya regretted her reaction.

"This is why I wasn't saying it straight out," Kirono said under his breath.

Zaya thought back to the night after the Shadowrun, when she and Ziyuki had talked after the victory haka, out in the street. There had been a subtle pattern to her tunic, glossy black on matte; Zaya remembered curves and crossings that echoed the ones inlaid into the knife in her hand. "All right," she said. "So this is what, a House mark? Do they have, like, a registry or something?"

Kirono smiled tightly and raised his gourd. "There is a registry."

"Is this in it?"

"There aren't many copies of it. There's a Ministry of Marks that has the registry, but to get a look you have to come with a commission from a scion for a specific mark. They don't let folks just thumb through for research, they don't want plebes to knock them off."

"What's 'plebes'?" said Jaliki.

"Normal people," Zaya said. She put the knife back in its sheath, then got back in her chair and sipped her mate. Jaliki took his book and blanket and climbed into her lap. She rubbed his head again, then kissed his scalp. "Kirono, you work at a university. You can't tell me there's not someone there who knows—"

Kirono looked down into his mate. "It took me all day with that thing on my hip to get this far," he said quietly.

Zaya let the silence hang to show she'd heard him. "I'm sorry."

"It's—" He didn't finish the sentence; it wasn't true. "I understand," he said instead.

"Do you think there is someone who knows?" she asked.

"Maybe not in the department," he said. "But I probably know a historian who knows a historian, or something."

"If you could find out which House, or tell me what I can do to find out," she said, "I'd be grateful. Which I am already, for you getting this far."

Kirono looked at Jaliki for a moment, then back at Zaya. "You're OK with this getting out? I know I already talked to a bunch of blacksmiths, but academics are practically professional gossips."

"I'm not doing anything wrong."

"Sure. But what are you going to do once you get your answer?"

"I'm going to find out how that knife got to Arhoon to give it to Kiriki."

"I know. But what then?"

She looked down at Jaliki's face, still seemingly absorbed in his book. "If it's who I think it is, it's grounds for a lifetime ban. Even Kanivoon Taipan can't sit back and let his little..." She caught herself and took a breath. "Let *some 'streamer* just get away with sabotage."

"And is that something you want to let everyone know you're doing? Taipan Invotechnic is all over the university right now. They stole a student right out of my Theory of Material class—before they even passed. Not the best student, by the way." Kirono sipped his mate with a little shrug. "But they were a Boomslang. What are they going to learn from some crusty old professor that they won't learn better from a bunch of money-drenched boys out to flip a quick slab?"

Jaliki looked up at Kirono. "It's wrong to judge people on their heritage," he said. "They deserve the credit and blame from their own actions."

"That's right," said Kirono. "But I wasn't judging my student because they're a Boomslang. I think they were picked because they come from a high-ranked family in a rich House, not because of how well they were doing in my class. And I know they weren't doing too well, since I grade the exams."

"You didn't teach them all their classes, though," said Jaliki. "Did you?"

"You're right that there's a lot I don't know about why they were picked," said Kirono. "Maybe I should be less judgmental about things where I don't know the whole story." *No way*, he mouthed silently to Zaya.

"If I don't want to ask the professors," said Zaya, "then who?"

"You could go straight to the source," said Kirono, "but you'd have the same problem. They only know the marks for the Houses they work for. A lot of them have shops close by one another, but if you go knocking on doors up and down that street, it's probably going to get around. But you could get lucky?" He took a sip of mate, opened his mouth to speak, then closed it again.

"Say it."

"You won't like it."

"Name the last thing I've liked."

"I'm hurt that you don't like my mate."

"Ziyuki-kana," said Jaliki.

Zaya wasn't sure what she wanted to say to that; Kirono took another long sip and looked at her over the steam from his drink. Jaliki twisted around, digging a knobby knee into her thigh, to look at Kirono. "Was I right? You want Mom to talk to Ziyuki-kana."

"You're right, that's what I want."

Jaliki looked up at Zaya, questioning.

"Your uncle's entitled to his opinion."

"She's your sister," Jaliki said. "She'll help."

"No she won't," said Vanako, wandering out from the hall of bedrooms into the common room. "Everyone knows that the only good sister is me. What are we talking a—oof!" A one-kid stampede of blanket-draped Jaliki cut her off, one good jump getting his arms around her neck and his legs around her sides, his book abandoned. He hadn't exactly made an effort to be a comfortable presence in Zaya's lap, but the loss of his weight and warmth left her pining. Vanako responded by taking Jaliki to the ground, pretending to pin him with her weight so he could wrestle her off and get on top, then bounce on her stomach; she made an obliging couple of sucker-punched noises before getting a corner of his blanket and wrapping it around his face. He shouted "No fair!" while she wrapped the rest around his arms, then squirmed somehow so she was still on the bottom but had him in a bear hug from behind. Tickling followed. "Please don't suffocate your brother," Zaya called.

"It's him or me," Vanako said with mock ferocity; but the blanket fell away from Jaliki's face, and then he was out of the bear-hug and punching Vanako a little harder than he ought to be, just to show he could. She let him batter at her forearms for a minute before saying "Ow ow ow, OK, I give in."

"I took away your coal magic. You can't use it to hurt or threaten anyone else ever again."

Vanako looked up at him, confused.

"Now you say, 'I am the Volcano Emperor!'"

"I am the... Volcano Emperor?"

"Volcano Emperor? More like a lava of... I mean, more like a whole lava nothing!"

"That's not Wing's line," said Vanako.

"Only because the other actors get mad if Wing gets all the good lines," said Jaliki. He got up and stood on Vanako's stomach, pulling a sucker-punch noise out of her that sounded very real to Zaya. "Balance! Has been! Restored!"

"Hey Volcano Emperor," said Zaya.

Vanako pushed out her stomach suddenly; Jaliki stumbled off and caught himself. "Hey!" he shouted, but she was on her feet before he could get back on top. "What?" Vanako asked.

"Can you draw something for me?"

"Not before breakfast."

"That's fine."

Kirono stirred in his seat. "She shouldn't spend that much time near the knife."

"That, professor, is where you come in."

CHAPTER 6

SEVEN WEEKS BEFORE BELL THE CAT

"I'M A DRAGON-RACER," VANAKO said to Zaya out of the side of her mouth, hopefully out of earshot of the crowd.

"Shut up. He's speechifying."

He was; in front of Zaya and Vanako, Tenijoon Anole was telling the crowd packed into the vacant lot on Whelk Street in Cerulean Precinct about the virtues and accomplishments of Sefhalaan Skink, their next (in Anole's considered opinion) alderwight in the House of the Stars.

"Before I was a dragon-racer," Vanako continued, "I picked through trash in the back alleys behind restaurants for extra food. That sucked, but I don't hide it. I wasn't a farm girl, I wasn't some kind of hunter-gatherer. I don't belong anywhere near a garden."

The sun was directly in Zaya's eyes; she was trying not to squint, not to sweat, and not to pound her daughter into the ground like a fencepost. "I'm sure the Sculptor will give you strength to dig a row or two if you ask nicely."

"The Limper could grant me a stroke if that's easier. I'm not picky."

"Stop being a baby."

"And now," said Anole, "the candidate!"

"More like can't-didate," said Vanako. "Or, uh, can't-didn't-eat?"

"He's not even skinny."

"At least I'm trying."

"This is the opposite of trying. Shut up, I'm listening."

"You can't be serious."

"Also that kid in front is starting to stare at us."

There was a Mrineen child around Jaliki's age toward the front. They'd been staring at Zaya and Vanako for a while; but Vanako didn't have to know that. What she did have to do was stir the pot. She wasn't quite brave enough to go all out making faces, but waggling her eyebrows and surreptitiously sticking out her tongue at the kid would keep her busy for a few minutes.

Zaya hadn't gone to an event for a Thread & Mortar candidate before. She was expecting the crowd to be overwhelmingly Mrineen, which it was; she'd been expecting that to be uncomfortable, which it was, but not as bad as she'd thought. The longshoremen, boatwrights, and fishers were easy to spot; their work darkened the skin and thickened the arms and chest. The landlords weren't so easy, but Zaya had to believe they were there, if only to see how their tenants were responding. There were several kers in sight, a bushpig and some kind of eagle and a jackal.

And there were precinct police, of course, nearly a dozen of them in a thin ribbon at the back.

Sefhalaan Skink wasn't a bad speaker, and even better, they kept it short—a few good digs at their Brightest Scale opponent, who owned a shipping concern and probably employed a number of the crowd; some over-lyrical stuff tying the tilling of the soil to the fishing of the sea. Then it was Zaya's turn.

"Some of you folks might know who I am," she said. "For the rest, I'm Zaya Shearwater, and I fly dragons. Sometimes I win races. On really bad days, they write articles about me." There was a ripple of recognizing noises: chuckles, hmms, whispers. "I'm guessing you've put together that I don't actually know your candidate very well. No disrespect, of course, but if you know me, you know where

I live and spend my time, and it's not here. I'd love to spend more time on the water, but I get the feeling a lot of you are ready to tell me it's not all fun and games out there." That got a laugh and a couple of whoops; good enough. "But even though we don't get together for drinks at the Dulse & Laver... look, I see some kers out there. It's no secret that my son's hunted. There's a treatment that'll keep his ker away, and I know it works, because I've seen it work. It could be cheap, if we let it; but it's not, and you folks who live off the sea know broke follows rich just like storm follows calm. If I could afford to treat Jaliki now, I'd sleep better, and I'd be less worried about making sure Sefhalaan Skink made it to the Stars. But I can't, and I lie awake at night, and I'm out here for Sefhalaan because I'm worried for my son. I'd love it if the next time I came to Cerulean Precinct, that bushpig ker and that eagle ker and that jackal ker I see out there had fucked right off and given up. That's why I'm here. Let's hear from our master gardener and get our hands dirty." That got applause a little more vigorous than it had to be, and Zaya ceded the lectern to Fsalain Crotalus, the gardener.

The goal was to set up the whole garden in a day; some of this might have been better done in spring, but waiting wasn't going to help anyone get elected. The basic setup was a high trellis for the brightwick, with ample space for sun to shine through on the datura. The garden would be rimmed with transplanted four-o'clocks, so the moths could feed while the datura grew, and a hive would be constructed in the back corner away from the street. False flowers with pollen-traps for the moths would be planted throughout. So anyone who wanted to help could dig, build, or plant, and the capstone of it all would be Eshiveen Goanna, a boatwright who kept bees on the side, donating a queen to the hive. (Less discussed, and to be implemented later: The fence and gates to keep honey, hive, and datura safe from passersby with loose scruples, to say nothing of the watching and watering schedules.) The brightwick would be the slowest piece of it, as the long creepers connecting blooms to soil couldn't reliably be transplanted; they had to grow *in situ*, inch by inch. But those inches would mark progress in the weeks ahead, the upward march of green showing to any passerby who cared how close the Cerulean Precinct yliaster garden was to fulfilling its potential.

There seemed to be plenty of thick-armed men interested in putting the trellis and the hive together, and the four-o'clocks had been commandeered by a gaggle of children since they were easy to plant, so Zaya figured she'd help dig furrows for the datura. Tuuro had arrived, or maybe he'd been there all along, so Vanako wasn't working. This was technically fine, since there were neither enough shovels or enough soil for everyone to dig, but it was annoying. Zaya stole glances at Vanako and Tuuro while she dug. She'd never liked how Vanako seemed to become softer around Tuuro—more prone to laugh, more open—while Tuuro seemed to recede further into the kind of low-affect bravado favored by insecure boys. It looked to Zaya like Vanako was giving up more than she was getting. But Zaya supposed she'd been the Tuuro to Kiriki's Vanako, back when there was a Kiriki, and maybe that had been all right. She'd never know whether it would have been, in the end. Or if the end hadn't been what it had ended up being.

She wiped sweat from her brow with her forearm, then got up and filled a half-gourd from a dipper in the shade by the hive, returning a few pleasantries of recognition from strangers. When she turned back toward the garden, two Cerulean Precinct cops were talking to Tuuro.

He was almost their height, which you didn't see often in a Kay-alim kid, and he was starting to get some thickness to his shoulders and some hair on his face. She was at his side faster than she could have been if she'd been walking as casually as she'd meant to be. "... is going to last?" the officer was saying.

"I don't know," Tuuro mumbled, his eye on the officer's cheekbone: Not daring to look him in the eye, not wanting to embarrass himself by looking away.

"Sure you do," said the other officer. "All that thornapple. What do you figure, ten rows with twenty plants each? I mean, you do the math. What's the going rate on all that?"

"He wouldn't know," said Zaya.

"Shearwater-cha," said the first cop, nodding. "Looking forward to the arc-en-ciel."

"Me too. What are we talking about?"

"Just worried for the future of this project," said the second cop. "There are some addicts in this town who'd smash the whole thing up just for the datura. Hate to see you break your back for nothing."

"I don't think my daughter or her friend have a single thought on that topic," said Zaya. "You're in for a boring conversation."

"A man speaks for himself," said the second cop. "Unless he's a chickenshit."

He looked at Tuuro. Tuuro shrugged and looked over at the garden.

"Come on," said the first cop, tapping the second cop's bicep. "We'll talk to him again when his balls drop."

Zaya braced herself to block Tuuro with an arm; but it was Vanako who stepped forward, livid. "I watched cops run like rats from a starving dog while my mom stood her ground against a demon in Inundinir Square. Without the law and your dumb juiced muscles to hide behind, you're as chickenshit as anyone else. If you weren't, you wouldn't come here with your dicks out trying to scare people out of putting *plants* in the *dirt*."

The second cop's face grew ugly; the first's eyes moved from Vanako to Tuuro. Zaya wasn't in his mind, but the calculation was clear enough: If he couldn't get a rise out of Tuuro directly, maybe he could he do it by threatening Vanako. Then his eyes moved to the wider area, and Zaya's followed: There were a lot of eyes on them. A lot of thick-armed longshoremen, and a lot of mouths that could talk. "Show some respect," the first cop said. His hand moved to his partner's bicep again, but now it gripped instead of tapping. "If anyone keeps those addicts out of your garden, it's going to be us."

"Thanks in advance for your service, then," said Zaya.

That seemed to be enough to let all parties off without further repartee. The police went back to the ragged line of their colleagues, talking amongst themselves and watching from the edge of the lot.

"Good job," Zaya said to Tuuro. To Vanako she said, "You should know better."

Vanako opened her mouth, but Tuuro said, "Your mom's right."

Vanako looked from him to Zaya and back, then quirked her mouth once. "Sucking up to my mom isn't going to get you in my pants."

"Please," said Tuuro. "You wish you could have my baby."

Zaya's eyes widened, but Vanako was ready: "If some *evil sorcerer* cursed me with your *ugly baby*, I'd *drop-kick...*" Vanako kept going, but Zaya didn't catch the rest of it, because she'd caught Tuuro's glance over at her and realized that he wanted her to do exactly what she wanted to do, which was get the hell out of this conversation.

There were still rows to dig; Zaya went over to her shovel and got back to work. It wasn't long before a familiar shape bent down beside her, sinking a spade diffidently into the dirt as if he'd never done a day's honest work in his life. "Young love," said Yyvvoun Leatherback. "An inspiration for us all."

I'm begging you not to get inspired was the phrase that materialized, every dot and serif in place, before Zaya's eyes. Instead, she turned toward Yyvvoun and breathed a quick draught of a sweat whose taste she remembered; and that little bittersweet rush was enough to kick a smile to her cheeks. He was dressed for the heat, in a sleeveless shirt that let her see muscles move under a thickening film of sweat as he dug. He wasn't as strong as Kemreen, or even Thelendil; and that had been a strange thrill, to be with a physical equal, the kind of body she hadn't been close to since Kiriki. "I can't handle emotions that pure any more," she said. "Gives me the galloping shits."

"The protective layer of irony and world-weariness is key," said Yyvvoun. "Doubly so for folk heroes, I imagine. You don't want to get high on your own supply. I mean, I would, but a real hero wouldn't."

Zaya chuckled. They dug in silence for a moment.

"What I really meant to say there," said Yyvvoun, "is, you're amazing, and if I'd done half of what you've done I'd be insufferable about it."

"We just did a whole bit about pure emotions and digestion," said Zaya.

"I know. It was a pretty good bit. I just don't want it to get stale, you know?"

"Think of it as giving it some time to breathe. Exploring its potential."

"I have this feeling what you're saying is 'not getting ahead of myself,'" said Yyvvoun.

Zaya twisted her trowel to get through some stubborn root. "Not getting ahead of the situation."

"*That* sounds like 'it's not you, it's me.'"

"Who do you think hung the curtain?"

Yyvvoun stabbed the ground a couple of times, cutting through a root or maybe getting the tip of his spade under a stone. "What?"

"The curtain you keep trying to peel back. The one between you and all the stuff I'm not saying. Who hung it? And why is it there?"

That held him over for a few more spadefuls of dirt. "For someone who could send a killer lizard to eat me any time she felt like it," he said, "you're being very patient."

"Apology accepted."

"Dzaroon and I fell in love when we weren't much older than your daughter and her gentleman friend," said Yyvvoun. "Everything I felt seemed so impossibly big, and saying anything about it felt like…" He weighed the words, then went for it. "Like summoning a demon, if I'm honest. Bringing something into the world that would change the direction of gravity. Something that I couldn't control, that could pull the moon to earth and fling the sun out into space. And then I finally said it, and I *did* summon something, and it *was* massive and powerful… but I could control it. Or at least enough that it didn't scramble the stars and tear the ground up beneath my feet. So I really believe in getting straight to it. That sounds so smug—I'm not trying to—"

"I know," said Zaya. "That was me and Kiriki too. It was like letting someone throw a spear at your heart and having it bounce off your chest like a rubber ball."

"That is exactly what it was like."

"It didn't bounce off, though," said Zaya. "It left a spearhead in your chest. You didn't notice, and it became part of your heart. Which was fine, until it got torn out. And now there's a messy hole there, and you don't let people throw things right at your fucking heart any more. You put up a curtain."

Yyvvoun tossed a spadeful of dirt to the side. "Some of us are gluttons for punishment."

"You'll wise up."

"You can't fool me. Talk all you want about a curtain around your heart, but you're here digging a garden you know those cops are going to stomp to pieces before dawn."

Zaya looked over at the police. They seemed perfectly happy to be where they were; no one was throwing baleful glares around or giving sinister speeches to the gardeners. Then again, they'd tried that already. Maybe they were just biding their time. "All the more reason to get one started in Coral Precinct," Zaya said.

Yyvvoun chuckled. "Hell no."

Gentle, insistent memories of that beach in Cobalt Precinct had been bringing her attention to the friction of her clothes against her body. Yyvvoun's words were almost exactly a bucket of cold water all over her, except cold water would at least have brought relief from the heat of the day. "Whatever you say, candidate."

"Don't?"

She hadn't meant to look at him, but the plea in his tone drew her eyes. "You want my spear?" she said. "I love my son more than I'll ever love you, and this is what he needs. You're asking for the votes of all the Zaya Shearwaters in Coral Precinct. They know what their children need."

"Their children need the House of the Stars, or *this* never lasts long enough to grow anything for anyone."

"The House of the Stars isn't going to stand watch at this garden at midnight."

"Right," said Yyvvoun. "They pass laws. Then the nice folks with the swords and crossbows over there enforce them."

Zaya sunk her spade into the ground and twisted it, putting as much force into her forearm and shoulder as she possibly could. Eventually a chunk of dirt broke off. "It is *already against the law* to vandalize someone else's garden. It is already against the law to push people out of hotel windows. It is already against the law to summon demons and set them loose on crowds."

She stood up and threw down the spade. In her mind, it spun twice and hit point-first; reality wasn't so obliging, and it bounced and hit her foot. The police were absolutely all looking at her. Of course they were, she realized; it wasn't just their strength and speed that were enhanced, their senses were as well. "I'm headed home to get some rest, candidate," she said, turning to Yyvvoun as if it were him she was really talking to. "It's going to be a long night." She turned to face the rest of the gardeners, and the wholeness of the moment struck her: The knot of men bickering over some quiddity of beehive construction, the children and their parents planting the false flowers that would serve as pollen-traps for moths, the small teams holding the trellis-posts up in their holes and obsessively checking that the angles were square. Even Yyvvoun Leatherback, candidate, idiot, and fuckboy, tolerating the dirt on his hands and the sweat in his crevices to do a good thing here that he was afraid to do where he lived. "I'll be back at sunset with a dragon. We made this thing; we'll protect it." She found the first and second cops who'd talked to Tuuro and looked them right in the eye, one by one. "Maybe I'll see a few of you."

***

THE NEWS OF ZAYA'S midnight vigil in Cerulean Precinct wasn't well received at House Shearwater. Chashu liked neither the idea of her going alone nor the idea of going with her; Kirono was teaching and Cerminir was out, which meant Taavi, Gilthiniel, and Vanako would have to pitch in with the younger children. Jaliki, for his part, was hurt beyond measure that she'd forgotten tonight was the night she'd promised to take him to the Sweet Soldier, just the two of them. "Vani can take you," Zaya said, but the look he gave her said more than any words a kid his age could muster. So she followed up with "I'll take you there soon" and a kiss on his cheek, then left it alone.

Bandit, for its part, was pleased to see her sooner than it had been told it would, but its enthusiasm dulled on the scene. The cobblestones were hard, the air colder than it liked, and the boredom total. Eventually it slept—but not deeply: Its head snapped up and its eyes open, and Zaya realized it had noticed the shadow approaching from her shoreward side before she had. It let out a lick of cobalt-and-cerulean flame, not because she'd asked it to, but because it knew that was what she'd want; which she did.

"Stand down," called a voice that didn't belong here.

Zaya quickly combed the area, found a mind, and jolted it with a quick burst of static. The shadow winced. Bandit's head rose higher at the scrabble and thump of a bundle of fur and limbs falling from a roof, although it rolled in the air and landed on its paws just in time.

"You could have broken my monkey," called the shadow, resolving under a streetlamp into a muscular, short-for-a-Mrineen man with carefully mussed brown hair.

"I let him catch himself," said Zaya. She scanned the area again, but there weren't any other minds that she could find. Did Tjaroon's gang have more empaths? Not many, but it would only take one. Then the bottom of her belly went cold: He might not have empaths, but he had plenty of yliaster. He could block his men's minds completely—or summon something much more lethal than a man. Behind a veil too strong for Tjaroon to pierce, she cursed herself for an idiot. To the police, the yliaster garden might be a danger, but to Tjaroon and gangs like his, it was their dinner on the line. "What brings you here? Checking out the competition?"

Tjaroon laughed. He had a nice laugh; Zaya had hated that since she met him. "Is that what you're worried about? This isn't competition."

"Are you out of the business?"

"The business is good, for now." He stopped at a cordial distance: Close enough to see and hear her clearly, but well out of reach. "But I've never operated in Cerulean Precinct. Anyone who does isn't selling yliaster. They could worry about your datura, I guess, but you've made it very clear you're not selling that. You're getting good at getting messages out."

It occurred to Zaya that she had a decent shot at turning the man who'd taken all her family's money and nearly broken them apart into a screaming pillar of greasy cinders. It would have been a satisfying thing to point out. Instead she said, "Why are you here?"

"I bring the gift no one can take away." He waited a couple of seconds. "This is where you make a witty reply."

"I don't banter with people I hate. What gift?"

"The gift of knowledge." He paused for effect. "The smith who made your wife's saddle-knife is called Fanoun Makar. He works out of the Street of Bonded Smiths in Alabaster Precinct. Go ahead, ask me why I'm telling you this."

"I'm more interested in what makes you think I care."

"You mean why I'm spying on your people."

"I thought we might have to work up to that, but all right."

"We're not. But we keep lines of conversation open with the smiths in the city who work with exotic materials. Sometimes we can help, you know? We like to help."

"Gross," said Zaya. "But fine. Kirono talked out of school, you got wind of it. I'm not going to ask you how you figured out it was this Makar character because you'd just give me the world's shit-eatingest grin and tell me you have ways. So now you're helping me. Why?"

Tjaroon looked to the stars for a moment, considering. "We've had a checkered history, you and I."

"The idea that you're *balancing the scales* with this is—"

"Nah," he interrupted. "Balancing scales isn't how you make a profit. But—stipulating our checkered history—if I were approaching you with a joint venture, I'd have to provide a token of good faith. Wouldn't I?"

"There's no joint venture."

"The upside for you is yliaster for Jaliki," said Tjaroon. "Five years. Guaranteed. He won't need more than that."

"There's no such thing as a guarantee from you."

"Get a good-faith estimate of the monthly rate and I'll put twelve times that in escrow with a third party of your choosing. A year's supply. You can withdraw the cash whenever you want, or you can release it back to me when you're satisfied. Make whatever provisions you want for transfer of the debt so I don't have an interest in killing you to get it back." He shrugged and gave her a very serious look with his surprisingly soft hazel eyes. "Of course, if you withdraw it for anything other than breaking the deal, I will kill you."

Zaya took a moment to take this all in. "Sounds like I could set this up so you'd never get it back."

"You haven't asked what your side of the deal is."

"I'm trying to figure out what I could do for you that's worth what you're talking about laying out."

"Our lines of business are diversified," said Tjaroon. "One of them is bookmaking. The volume of gambling on the 'stream has risen over forty percent since you came back. Did you know that?" He chuckled. "You'd be doing us a favor if you went through partners faster, you know. Idiots love to bet on how a new pair of cheeks in the rear saddle changes the game."

"No sale. Parting suckers from their money is your business. Mine's winning."

"About that," Tjaroon said.

And there it was.

She took three long steps to close the gap between them, collapsing the mandrill's legs out from under it when it tried to lunge for her, then sliding in a quick spinal block that would be easy to maintain. "Do not talk to me about that," she hissed in a low and level voice. She didn't dare say *throwing a race* out loud. "Even bullshitting about that could catch me a lifetime ban."

He put his hands up in conciliation. "There's nobody here."

"Not that I can see. But I seriously doubt you came out here alone."

The breadth of his grin told her she was right. "Sleep on it, talk it over with your people. My residence is the House of Vines in Chartreuse Precinct. I work late."

She stepped back. "Thanks. It's good to know where the bad neighborhoods are. Get out of here. Unless you're going to help me watch for vandals."

"Give my monkey its arms and legs back, please."

Zaya dissolved the spinal block, but kept her mind inside the mandrill's in case it chose vengeance. She felt Tjaroon noodle at the edges of her presence in the ape's mind, then withdraw. He didn't even try to eject her. "Boss doesn't give one lonesome shit about you," she said, echoing the sentiment inside the mandrill's mind. She didn't have to say it out loud, but she wanted Tjaroon to hear. "I'm inside your brain and he's not doing a thing."

"Boss picks his battles," Tjaroon said, audibly annoyed.

"Boss loves a distinction without a difference."

"You did this, you know."

"You exploit kids and the pain of the dying," said Zaya. "I don't care what you think I did."

"If you hadn't gone whining to the Standards Board about the Krait dampers," said Tjaroon, "the government wouldn't be all over black market yliaster and your sister could still support your son's care. You wouldn't have a problem for me to solve. You know it's true."

It was exactly what Ziyuki had said over cups of gin and mint, after Zaya had won the Shadowrun. And it was true.

"You know it's bullshit from end to end," said Zaya. But the night felt very large, and her voice felt very small inside it.

"Whatever you say, Zaya Shearwater," said Tjaroon. "I'm sure your hate for me will heal your heart after that dog ker's torn your son to pieces."

He turned on his heel and posted up a middle finger over his shoulder, then walked the way he had come, the mandrill trotting at his heel. They faded into the dark.

CHAPTER 7
SEVEN WEEKS BEFORE BELL THE CAT

VERMILION PRECINCT IS DIVIDED from Scarlet by the Road of Calm Seas, an artery in the original season-city extended early in the period of Mrineen overbuilding to reach out to Sapphire Precinct, where Yymroun Tuatara's ships first fetched up a century before any Mrineen had so much as heard of dragon-racing. It was represented in the House of the Stars by Tishaan Anole of the Brightest Scale Party, an actuary and a lay minister elected time and again by a constituency of boutique-owners and restaurateurs who took advantage of the lower property values that came with a border on Damask Precinct but always concerned about the influence of that southern neighbor on their clientele—

Mom, Vanako's mind-voice said, *looking to overtake on our left, keep your head in—*

"My head is firmly rooted in my sense of place," said Zaya.

Great, because the team on this Ranger Wyrm is about to root our asses firmly in last *place—*

The Ranger and its crew tried a feint-surge that would have totally worked on an above-average solo 'streamer with no rear visibility and no mental control over their wyrm; but there was no delay at all between Vanako noticing the lunge and Bandit moving to intercept it. Zaya panicked for a moment—it was a Kayalim team, if Bandit had overcorrected they would be preparing for a counter-feint—and then they *did* counter-feint, and Bandit moved to block them again as if it had seen them coming. They broke out onto the expanse of the Road of Calm Seas ahead, and when the Ranger team took advantage of the wide space to hook around them, Bandit surged straight ahead, freed from the need to concern itself with fine adjustments, and Zaya could hear the other team's profane cries as they crossed the border into Vermilion.

The owners here just want police who'll keep the undesirables from Rust and Damask out, Yyrreen had said. *Tishaan Anole promises that, they deliver, and they get elected. We can't break that cycle.*

Vermilion Precinct was proud of its color; the bricks of the storefronts on Inkmixers' Row were glazed in brilliant red. The street was narrow enough that Bandit could easily dominate it—not that it mattered much, the Ranger behind them seemed to be flagging. Zaya saw a child pointing and gaping from below, and waved. They made the right onto Fig Tree Street and sailed toward the broodspire; a gate of red banners framed the opening from Fig Tree Street onto the square, and a gate of orange banners framed the opening onto Kshaleen Ora Street on the far side. There were small crowds by the gates, cheering and waving.

Not this election, anyway, Yyrreen had amended, seeing the dark look on Zaya's face.

Mom, Vanako said in Zaya's mind. *Time to slow down.*

"Slow down?" Zaya said. "Are you high?" A wyrm had rounded the corner of Inkmixers' Row and Fig Tree Street—it wasn't the Ranger, Zaya couldn't quite make out the variant from Vanako's mental image—but it was gaining fast.

Remember why we're here.

"Fucking hell."

She felt Vanako's mind recede as she fussed with a shoulder bag. They swept through the red gate and bore right, around the edge of the square, where the race-watchers gathered; whoops and cries of excitement began as Vanako scattered the contents of the bag, a rain of soft red loops. Armbands in the color of Vermilion Precinct, decorated with the compass rose of the Travelers.

A black wyrm streaked across the square, missing the broodspire by inches as it made for the orange gate. A mix of cheers and boos arose; it was hard to say which dominated.

Don't even think about it, Vanako admonished her. *We've got a job to do.*

They showered the entire perimeter of the square, returning to the red gate before shooting across to the orange. There was no trace of the black wyrm by the time they gained the orange gate; but Zaya had seen its tail, girt with eight gleaming spikes.

Why is he *in this race?* Vanako asked.

"It doesn't matter," said Zaya. "But you know the answer."

Because we're here?

Even Bandit's mind hummed with agreement.

***

"Tuuro says there's an arc-en-ciel coming up," Vanako had said weeks ago to Zaya, Kaana, Yyrreen, and Yyvvoun Leatherback over beers at House Shearwater, with children familiar and strange playing shrieky, unapproved games of hide-and-seek in the back rooms. To Kaana and Yyvvoun, she elaborated: "It's like a rainbow. You go red, orange, yellow, green, blue, purple. The course changes every time, so you can't use them to qualify for anything and no one likes betting on them. So they run them at low fees and low prizes, and the competition is…" She put out her hand palm down and wiggled it: *Not so much.* "Tuuro and Zetaala ran them for a year before they entered a r—a major race."

"I'm not seeing the appeal of a low prize," said Kaana dryly.

"It's not about the money," said Yyrreen, "it's about show-ing you care about every part of the city." She looked to Vanako. "Right?"

"Yeah," Vanako said. "And it would be easy to win, so you could do something cool."

"Winning's not cool enough for you?" said Zaya.

"Winning only matters to people who already care about the 'stream," Vanako said. "Or who already care about you. I mean something that would be cool to any random idiot who's just pass-ing by. Something an idiot would talk about to their friends."

"'Something an idiot would talk about to their friends' is ab-solutely what our campaign should aspire to," said Yyvvoun.

Vanako looked away, not at anything in particular.

"He's not making fun of you," said Zaya. "He meant that." Her tone was free of comment, mostly.

"And he's not wrong," said Yyrreen.

"Yyrreen-kana sometimes finds *levels* of generosity—" Zaya be-gan, but Kaana cut her off. "In your estimation, young lady, what kind of thing would get the dumb-dumbs talking?"

"Fireworks?" Vanako ventured.

"Dumb-dumbs," Yyvvoun said, testing out the mouthfeel.

"I don't think unexpected explosions will do much to get our message across," said Kaana.

"It's a dragon race," said Yyrreen. "Zaya and Vani can't pause for speeches."

"Pretty sure explosives and combustibles are banned by Stan-dards," said Zaya.

"Like you've never done anything banned by Standards," Vanako snorted.

"Kiriki and I never ran an arc-en-ciel," said Zaya. "The 'stream-ers in those races mostly stay there, and the ones that move to real races don't do well. Tuuro and Zetaala are the exception. Practicing against poor competition just lets you kid yourself into thinking you can have bad habits and still win."

"I solemnly swear I won't let beating the snot out of a few bad 'streamers go to my head," Vanako said.

"I know you won't," said Zaya. "I'm worried at the political operators here thinking they can take chatter to the ballot box."

Yyrreen sighed and set down her beer. "What you insist in not getting about politics is that more than one thing can happen at a time. You think about competition as a series of decisions where you either do everything right and win, or you do one thing wrong and lose, because that's what you do on the wing. But we can do more than one thing at a time. When we take one risk, we're not gambling everything on it." She leaned back in her chair, the ghost of a grin playing on her face. "Also, can you even imagine what it'll do to your odds if you lose an arc-en-ciel?"

"They'll ban me for throwing a race," said Zaya. But, she thought, they wouldn't. Not when there was no money on it, not when she was clearly using it to send a message and not to manipulate the betting markets. But the odds might respond anyway... "But it doesn't matter. We're not gambling on races."

"Speak for yourself," said Yyrreen.

***

AMBER PRECINCT IS TUCKED in the city's southwest corner, home to the Amber Gate, where traders who don't plan to stay enter to sell, and the Souk of All Worlds: Not the city's largest outdoor market, but the most legendary. It's also the only precinct walled off from the rest. Ostensibly this is to limit the ability of Ililuë merchants to sneak into the rest of the city. Anyone who believes that, joke's on them; nine out of ten Ililuë wouldn't sleep in Yemareir if you paid them. Really, the walls—amber-adorned, of course—are to keep certain people out of the souk: People who aren't seen much in the continent; who might put off a less cosmopolitan Ililuë pharmacist or an eremitic Ranyar scrimshander or a mid-level executive of a Kerkakani silver mining concern; people who are poor or desperate or otherwise unlikely to buy; people who are, in short, Kayalim. Telivoon Honu, the precinct's alderwight, set aside taxes for the maintenance of the wall each year: He conscientiously released a report to his constituents, detailing repairs major and minor, the cost of greasing the hinges of the massive gate, of replacing removed glass shards on the wall's top edge. "The owners here are massively rich," Yyrreen had told Zaya. "Generationally, ancestrally. Maybe genetically. Telivoon Honu is immovable."

Mom. Stop.

"I can't help it," Zaya said.

Help it.

"Tell me you don't love it," Zaya said, "when we blaze over the Souk and all the rich little antiquers pissing their lives away under those yellow tents run screaming for the gates."

They crested the wall and dipped to stay below roof level; the buildings here were no taller than three stories, another quiddity of the residents. Some gate-guard barked orders, but the slipstream ground them into nonsense before they hit Zaya's ears.

OK, said Vanako. *I'm loving it a little.*

The orange gate opened out onto the Souk of All Worlds, where the running and screaming had already commenced; Shanhoon Krait and Monsoon had gotten there first—and they were still there, halfway through a loop around the square, the exact path that Zaya had planned to take. It was the wrong path; the yellow gate was a hairpin turn to the right, but Shanhoon had turned Monsoon left to take the long way around. She saw tents knocked over, smashed fruit and scattered gemstones on the cobbles. She could have sworn she saw Shanhoon catch her eye across the square a moment before a massive burn poured forth from Monsoon's mouth, bringing a freshet of screams and setting small fires on the tops of a dozen tents. Monsoon had been flying none too slowly already, but the burn gave it a burst of speed; it cornered so hard at the yellow gate that, for a moment, it seemed to fly backward.

He's poisoning the well for us, said Vanako.

"I knew we should have gotten ahead of him," said Zaya.

How?

"Craft, guile, and good looks are all that come to mind. Let me know if you have any other ideas."

She *reached* out to Bandit and had it fill its lungs—but all that came out was sweet air, blowing at the fires atop the tents. Between its breath and its wingbeats, the fires winked out, leaving holes rimmed with papery ash where they had been.

Yyrreen had decided on the gifts for Amber Precinct. "There's always an area for children," she had said, "around the broodspire. There's toys, usually a musician. People here won't appreciate the Travelers, but they'll appreciate something for their children." After the fires were out, they cut across the square, straight for that open area near the broodspire. It was empty now except for the band, who seemed to feel their tent was as much safety as they could manage, crouching over their tambourines and woodwinds. "Here we go," Zaya said to Vanako.

This time the gifts were bright orange marigolds, embroidered in thick felt. Inside wrapped in wax paper, were pieces of honeycomb. Zaya caught the eye of one of the band members, a young woman in bright billowing silks. "Something for the children!" she shouted as loudly as she could. Then they were past the opening, and through the yellow gate.

I guess that was good looks? Vanako said.

"Close enough," said Zaya.

We doing craft or guile next?

"Craft is what gets you on the next 'streamer's tail," said Zaya. "Guile is what gets you past them."

She waited for an empty street before she *reached* out to Bandit and said "Burn," and the smell of brimstone washed over them.

***

Six precincts, six prizes. Kaana te-Tekko coordinated their assembly: She knew the tailors and beekeepers, the miners and tinsmiths, the inkmakers and tanners and glaziers.

"What do you think we'll actually accomplish with this?" Zaya said to Yyrreen one night, as they filled five dozen tiny green felt pouches embroidered in the shape of purslane leaves. "You told me yourself, five of these six precincts aren't competitive. You think throwing a dinky little gift at someone is going to change their mind? Or anybody else's? Ziyuki could get on a wyrm and drop money on the same precincts. They'd like her better for that than they'll like me for this."

"Of course it's not going to swing Amber Precinct," said Yyrreen. "The idea is just to create the contrast. Veraamaka navo gives, Brightest Scale doesn't."

"I think you mean the Travelers give."

"Is there a difference at this point?"

"Yes." Zaya let it hang until Yyrreen looked up from her work to meet her eyes. "Veraamaka navo is me, who is a person. The Travelers are a political party."

"But you want the same things."

"No. The Travelers want to take over the government. I want to jeopardize public safety by riding a killer lizard through the streets for money. And I don't want my son to die."

"And the Travelers want you to have that freedom and that opportunity."

"No they don't."

"Why would you say that?" Yyrreen asked.

"Because what they're actually asking me to do is drop this stuff on crowds of people."

"While racing the killer lizard. See, you're one for two on your goals already. Objectively, that's incredible effectiveness."

"Just because it's one of two goals doesn't make it fifty percent."

Yyrreen sighed. "Every candidate standing for Travelers *or* Thread & Mortar has pledged to sign a bill legalizing yliaster for personal use in Yemareir."

"Because that's their path to becoming a kingmaker in the government. Watch what they do once Brightest Scale starts courting them to get things passed."

"That will force Brightest Scale to give a shit about something that matters to people for once."

"Do you really believe that?"

Yyrreen threw a purse on the floor and glared at Zaya. "Fuck it. You want me to convince you why you should do this? I can't. It was your idea. I don't know where else you saw it going. You change lives with laws, laws with lawmakers, lawmakers with votes, and votes with money—which includes stupid little tokens like this. It's a bad game. But if you do this, there will be some little kid who spends a morning standing bored on Date Street in Jade Precinct, hating her life and wondering why her dumb parent brought her here to piss away these precious, crumbling moments under the stars—and then there'll be a dragon soaring toward her, all magenta crest and orange wing feathers, piloted by a woman with bright purple hair and green goggles, and as this little girl gapes in open-mouthed astonishment, a gift from that woman will land in her hands. And she will put this stupid little charm on her wrist and hold this stupid little felt leaf like it's her own baby, and when she goes to bed in her terrible dole-flat with her shitty parents fighting in the next room and addicts gutting each other for flinders in the courtyard, she'll put this thing up against her cheek and remind herself that veraamaka navo is here, and she cared enough to give her something. And that will matter, not because the gift is important or useful or worth enough to buy her a meal if she sells it on the street, but because somebody who is strong and brave enough to ride a dragon gave it to her when she didn't have to."

"How little were you," Zaya said, "when you'd seen too much to fall for an act like that?"

Yyrreen laughed: a small bitter thing, but not without warmth. "Littler than I like to think," she said. "But not as little as all that."

Zaya sighed and stuffed a leaf. "I know. But that girl's going to wake up one day and realize veraamaka navo isn't coming to save her."

Yyrreen's eyes met Zaya's. They had always been her best feature, a crystalline cobalt blue warm as a clear summer sky. It was those eyes that had allowed her to pass in the business world of Yemareir's White Heart, that quietly led the landowners and builders she worked with to ignore her short stature and blunt features and dismiss her skin's base shade as the light tan of someone a little too fond of the outdoors. They had struck Zaya as well, nine years ago, at the after-party for the Ourobouros, when Yyrreen had buttonholed Zaya and Kiriki and begged for a place to stay because she'd just had to kill her boyfriend. Zaya had assumed it was a joke, at first, to cover something worse and more shameful. By the time she'd learned enough about Yyrreen to believe it could be true, she'd resolved to let it lie. They had been easy around each other's bodies, once, Zaya remembered, with a cold electric pang at the base of her throat; walking arm in arm, leaning on one another, more than once drawing complaints of mock jealousy from Kiriki to hide a slender but real jealousy. It had never gone anywhere, and the shock of Yyrreen's leaving the house hours after Kiriki's and Kaalo's deaths had so completely severed it that Zaya had never questioned where it had gone. It sat badly in her skin, now,

"But you are," Yyrreen said, her cobalt eyes wide and steady.

***

CADMIUM PRECINCT WAS NEIGHBOR to Amber, run by a career civil servant named Felireen Slider, popular in the precinct due to the arrangement she'd brokered with the Amber Precinct police: A card certifying residence in Cadmium that gets you through the gate to Amber, no questions asked. The broodspire is surrounded by a grove of massive yellow rose arbors, with head-sized blossoms and finger-length thorns; shrikes hang carrion from them, shrews and songbirds and young monkeys. Bandit cut Monsoon off, darting neatly through the grove and bursting out in a cloud of yellow petals, drawing a shriek and slash of claws from the black wyrm and a stream of curses from Shanhoon. The claws met only feathers, and the curses were shredded into monkey-shouts by the slipstream. When they circled the broodspire to drop felt purses in the shapes of dandelions, stuffed with tin-nibbed yellow quills, Shanhoon followed them and overtook them, tacking toward the center of the square while Bandit sailed expansively around the edge. Monsoon entered the green gate some lengths ahead, but not many.

Jade Precinct is across the city from Cadmium, on the north edge. Shanhoon and Zaya both took the route direct, Yymroun

Tuatara Street, the major north-south artery that divides Argent from Alabaster Precinct. Jade Precinct was empty, of humans at least, the residents evacuated to co-domiciles in Rust and Azure and Damask; the new cohort of Banshee Lianas had hatched a week or so ago, and the air was full of bright sinuous wyrms the size of garter snakes hunting, bickering, or taking the air. It was too dangerous to linger close to the broodspire, but a small crowd of spectators was gathered by the green-bannered gate to the Square of Unflinching Reflection. Zaya pushed Bandit to overtake just as they approached burn range of the crowd; she could see Monsoon drawing breath in for the burn as they approached—but Shanhoon clocked Bandit's move before the fire streamed forth, and then they were wrangling for the lane, crashing neck-and-neck through the gate as Vanako frantically showered felted purslane-leaf pouches stuffed with green jadeite charm bracelets on the watchers. Zaya feinted east, drawing Shanhoon and Monsoon after them, then looped Bandit elegantly under the black wyrm to streak off west, toward the blue gate. When they passed through it, they had two lengths on Monsoon and gaining.

Ultramarine Precinct is on the north shore of the bay, just south of Cold Point. Too far from the city center to attract much density of population, its owners are proprietors of small piers; parts and repair businesses that support the precinct's fleet of individual fishing concerns; and residents attracted to an area where they can buy a little house without a landlord strolling in to try to buy them out. They vote for Artimarain Goanna of Thread & Mortar out of impatience for patrician airs and, for some of them, be-cause they'd sooner the city feed and care for their Kayalim and Ililuë day-workers than do it themselves. There is nothing special about Ultramarine Precinct—no uncanny feature of the environ-ment, no particular landmark left by nature or the builders of the season-city—but the broodspire is the only one in Yemareir that looks out directly on the bay, and the Dawn Wyrms who hatch there sometimes return, even outside the breeding cycle, to renew acquaintances. There were two as Zaya, Vanako, and Bandit passed through the blue gate to the square, sunning their bellies at the base of the broodspire. They didn't so much as stir when Bandit came through, and the surge of jealousy from Zaya was so strong that Vanako laughed out loud. For the crowd it was felted blue poppies, with coils of thick blue thread inside, strong enough for sails. When they passed through the purple gate to Amethyst and the finish line, Shanhoon was nowhere in sight.

***

"THE ONE THING," ZAYA had said to Vanako, flying Bandit to Silver Precinct to start the race, "the solitary thing redeeming about this race, is that Shanhoon Krait won't be in it. We'll probably lose, but at least we'll lose to a 'streamer I don't hate."

***

THE LAST LEG OF an arc-en-ciel is always the longest, from the blue precincts on the shore that form Yemareir's west edge to the purple in the northeast. Long stretches down straight roads like Green Sand Street and Dawn Boulevard were a strength of Bandit's, trained for full days of straight-line flying over weeks and months; but Zaya coasted, letting Monsoon creep up length by length as they approached Amethyst Precinct. *What are you doing?* Vanako asked, the third time she moved to pour some reserves of energy into the wyrm's wings.

"Setting up some excitement at the finish line."

Excitement is bad.

"We're here to put on a show."

We should leave that to the professionals.

"I have bad news for you about who the professionals are."

They were in Amethyst Precinct now, Monsoon trailing by three or four lengths. The finish line would be on the main lawn of the University of Yemareir, surrounded by residential buildings, the main library, and the chapel; the last minute or so of the race would be through narrow alleys and tight corners where a straggler wouldn't have much opportunity to gain ground, especially against a team who could direct their wyrm at the speed of thought.

They streaked past outlying dormitories, their wake upsetting books and coffee cups and turning stacked papers into clouds around shocked students working on their balconies. Students pressed against the narrow, arched glass windows of a of a lecture hall, or pointed from the thoroughfares. And then there was the construction site—stripped to the beams, a skeleton with no roof, walls, or floor—

"Shit!" said Zaya.

The heat of Monsoon's burn bloomed behind her; in the corner of her eye she saw a black shape weave through the frame of whatever new building was rising beside them. Bandit's own burn swelled. It knew what to do.

"Hold off," said Zaya. Just for a second; just so Shanhoon wouldn't have time to pull any more surprises out.

Monsoon was flitting through the framed building's high-ceilinged lower floor. It would try to sneak out below her. She'd cut it off when it emerged, force it to brake, then burn. She dropped altitude to draw even with it.

Vanako's mind shouted—but Monsoon's jaws were inches from Zaya's face, the wyrm screaming in frustration as Bandit fouled its maneuver, and Zaya released Bandit's burn to take them to the finish.

Monsoon's scream was joined by a chorus.

The surprise in Bandit's mind brought Zaya's back to the lawn of the University, where the lane that should have been cleared for the 'streamers was full, instead, of people—full, but rapidly emptying, as hundreds of terrified students tried to clear the path below the wyrms. A few, the brave or the fallen, stayed in their places, rolling on the grass to put out fires on their hair or clothing, or helping others in the same frantic endeavor. Bandit's wings beat, and several of them fell, staggered by the blast of air.

Vanako reached out to brake, to rise, but Zaya shut her down. "Ten more seconds."

People are hurt!

Zaya could feel Monsoon's hot breath on Bandit's tail. Had Krait done his own burn, or had shock and horror slowed Bandit enough to let him gain? For eight more seconds, it was the wrong question. She reached to switch Bandit's tail into Monsoon's too-close eyes—

—but now it was Vanako blocking her. An image flashed through Zaya's mind, bloody and insistent: Monsoon stumbling from the blow, unable to recover lost altitude before a wingtip hit the ground and permanently fouled the rhythm that kept it in flight. Monsoon plowing a furrow into the lawn, knocking students left and right, leaving crushed bodies in its wake.

"Fine," said Zaya. Vanako was right; the risk should have occurred to her. She'd punish herself for missing it later. Maybe.

Five more seconds.

She braced for the next stupid thing, the next desperation maneuver: Fangs splitting the flesh of Bandit's tail, a lash of sorcerous flame or lightning slamming the middle of her back. A demon interposing itself between Bandit and the finish line.

None of it came. Monsoon didn't even surge up or around to overtake. Bandit's muzzle crossed the finish by a clean length; no contest.

No cheers either. Zaya didn't wait to unbuckle herself from the saddle; her knife was already out, the straps cut before Bandit touched the ground. She ran as fast as her legs would take her, toward the people she had hurt and left—for ten seconds, only ten seconds, ten yawning, irreversible seconds—to burn.

CHAPTER 8

SEVEN WEEKS BEFORE BELL THE CAT

ZAYA DIDN'T SHAVE HER head the night after the arc-en-ciel. She thought about it, got as far as setting a basin of hot water before the mirror in her room; but when she went to Minshoon to borrow a straight razor, he gave her a stern look and asked her "who'd you kill?" and she had to say "no one," because "I fucked up the election and yliaster's going to be illegal for a thousand years and Jaliki's going to die" was obviously going to sound dumber and more dramatic out loud than it did in her head, where it was ringing and damning and self-evidently true.

"You made a mistake," said Minshoon, "but you weren't the only one. They knew dragons were coming through. You didn't know they'd be there. And no one's dead. Don't torture yourself over this."

Since he had said not to torture herself, she didn't try to explain what she was actually thinking. She should have been thinking what she thought he was thinking: About the kids she could have killed. But she hadn't learned how many people had been hurt by Bandit's ill-timed burn, or any of their names. "What if I only shaved half my head?" she said. "Compromise?"

"I'm not your dad," he said. "But not with my razor."

***

IN THE CHAOS OF the spooked crowd, there hadn't been much Zaya could do. Near the finish line there was a roil of scared kids, but it was hard to tell whether anyone was hurt; there was screaming, but how much was from pain and how much from fear was impossible to tell—and should she be looking for where the screaming *wasn't*, for those whose chest might be too hurt to scream, who might have gotten a lungful of flame? Her mind leapt briefly back to another fear-filled crowd, not long ago at all, running from a dragon and a demon and the raggedly bisected lower half of Vanioun Ora, and for a moment her feet rooted to the grass. But this wasn't that, and what was needed wasn't a bulwark to Bandit's mind as it fought a possibly unkillable enemy, it was getting these fucking kids out of the way so no one else got hit by some dragon sprinting to the finish line.

She raised her voice to say exactly that, but no one heard her. So she started pushing.

That got people's attention long enough for them to listen to what she was saying. Then an Eyrie Shrike with a pair of Kayalim women shot over the crowd, the wing-blast knocking more people to their feet, and Zaya's shouts of "move aside!" began to echo and multiply even over the redoubled screams. The crowd in the wyrm-lane began to thin out, and she could start to see the people who'd been hit by the flame or toppled by wings on the other end of the lawn.

She wasn't sure how long she spent bustling people out of the path of the race—the boom and blast of wing-beats began to run together—but soon the lane was clear, and she found herself with a shoulder under the armpit of a weeping Kayalim girl who was using her other arm to shield the other side of her face. When the wind of the next wyrm blew over them, she screamed and hiccuped. "The air hurts my face," she said. "Why does the air hurt my face?" The tone of her voice said she knew.

"Where's the infirmary?" Zaya said.

"Behind Galliwasp Refectory," the hurt girl said, pointing toward a high-ceilinged building with a long nave full of stained-glass panels. It took a moment for Zaya to realize what it was: She'd eaten there weeks earlier with Zariveen Boomslang and Kelloun Rinkhal, during the protest against the Boomslang slumlords. There were a few other students and pairs of students limping in that direction. Zaya began helping the hurt girl move. "What are you all here for?" she asked, because distraction was good for pain.

"Rhetoric and poetics."

She'd misunderstood the question; whatever. "That's good," said Zaya.

"My parents think I'm studying physics."

"They'll come around," said Zaya. "We need more Kayalim in politics."

"No shit, right? How long are we going to settle for weird Mrineen sellouts like Kelloun Rinkhal?"

"As long as most of us can't vote, probably." They were close to the refectory; the crowd had begun to thin. "Is that why you're all here?"

The girl didn't turn her head toward Zaya, but the eye on Zaya's side rolled round. "You weren't here for the protest?"

Zaya took a look at the hurt girl and realized, or remembered, that she wasn't much older than these students she was thinking of as kids. She could blend in—physically, anyway. But since she'd just blown her own cover, there was no point drawing out the coming revelation. "I just won the race. It was my dragon's fire that hit you. I'm so fucking sorry."

The hurt girl stopped in her tracks. Zaya felt the pressure of the girl's arm ease off her shoulders. "Fuck you so much." Then her weight came back down. "Don't think this gets you out of helping me."

"I'd never."

"Don't talk."

They had to veer to the left to get around the near side of Galliwasp Refectory. Zaya idly wondered where the protestors had gotten the pebbles they'd thrown against the windows. The hurt girl locked her face in a snarl and breathed through clenched teeth, tears streaming freely from the eye on Zaya's side.

They were the first to make it to the steps of the clinic, but there were others close behind, some visibly burned and some nursing ribs or ankles damaged by the crowd. The hurt girl seized the railing by the door and thrust Zaya's shoulder away, then knocked, putting her whole shoulder into it. "A dragon breathed fire on the protest and there's a shit-ton of hurt students out here," she said, her rough voice ripping easily through air still humming with far-away crowd-roar. "My face is half off, I need help now!"

"We didn't *breathe fire on you*—" Zaya began, but the door opened, a white-faced medic pulled the hurt girl in, and Zaya felt the footsteps behind her. She stepped aside to let them through.

***

ZAYA VERY NEARLY ANSWERED the door when Sgt. Loggerhead of the Lilac Precinct Police knocked on it; but Minshoon elbowed her smoothly out of the way before she could. It was a swift and polite conversation. Sgt. Loggerhead could have pressed the issue of whether Zaya was really out on her morning constitutional, or waited until she "returned," but he seemed relieved to hand over a piece of paper and be done with it.

"It's a summons from the Amethyst Precinct Police," said Minshoon. "Loggerhead says he delivered it as a professional courtesy."

"They could have just let Amethyst come knock themselves," said Zaya.

"Yeah."

"Nice of them not to. Probably cost them something."

"Probably means they're worried about what happens if Amethyst Police come to the house," said Minshoon.

"Worried about what Amethyst Police will do, or what I'll do?"

"I think it's more of a worry about the general volatility of the situation."

Zaya's eyes flickered over the living room and kitchen; no one was there, for now. "Yeah. But they'll get here eventually."

"Not for a while," said Minshoon. "They have to exhaust reasonable channels before they go to the city. Maybe it ends up not being worth their time, or getting stuck in some bureaucratic bear trap. A lot of things can happen when you have time."

"I'm going to say something I need you to not blow off."

"OK."

"You didn't see the face of that girl I burned."

Minshoon's spine stiffened; so did his face. "We'll give her all we can."

"No we won't," Zaya said. "We're saving 'all we can' for Jaliki."

"Yeah."

"So—"

"I know." Minshoon drifted over to the living room, collapsed in an armchair. The easy, personable expression on his face had evaporated; he suddenly looked as if he hadn't slept. "We should do something for her. But we can't. You should face justice, probably? I don't even know. But I don't want you to. And it doesn't really matter whether you should or shouldn't, because there isn't any."

"I'll figure something out."

"Don't." His voice was ragged. He caught Zaya's eye and held it. "Just—there's already too much. You need to race for Jaliki, you're spending nights at the Cerulean garden, we need you here. Don't do more."

The smell of the girl's burned face; the whisper of her breath through clenched teeth. "Yeah," Zaya said.

***

THE RESPECTABLE PARENTS AT the Lilac Precinct schools had never, as a group, been warm to Zaya. Everything set her apart, from her hair to her name to the gaggle of co-parents who were not her romantic partners, and that was all before she'd returned to earning money through races that were, technically, crimes. But there were a few good ones, mostly neighbors whose children played with Eäril or Jaliki in the square when school wasn't in session. So when Halaino te-Kaizo guided his daughter Varu to the other side of the street when Zaya crossed paths with them to pick Eäril up, Zaya noticed. And when Aara ze-Itama pretended she didn't know them at the wet market, Zaya noticed. And when Eäril started coming home after school droopy and mute, she noticed.

She knew the other parents noticed, too, and she let them ask. Eäril might not be old enough to try to save Zaya's feelings by hiding what was happening; but, then again, she might—and if she didn't, she might attack Zaya for it. If she was angry at Zaya, it would probably be best for her to let it out. Kids were allowed to be unfair, it was parents' job to take it and turn it into something better. But Zaya wasn't sure she could take a child's pain and anger right now. She did not know what she would turn it into. She did know she felt like a solid block of some rare earth or radioactive mineral, something that would belch sparks and fumes at what ought to be no provocation at all—a spray of water, a scratch from a shard of some common metal. She didn't want to poison her children.

CHAPTER 9

SIX WEEKS BEFORE BELL THE CAT

JERIOUN CROTALUS: SOME OF your fellow students have been organizing in protest of the Brimstone Slipstream, saying it's become a tool of the rich to silence protest. They talk a lot about you in that context. Do you share their view?

ASHAVA TE-KAIZO: First of all, I unconditionally support my fellow students' efforts, and indeed all efforts, to raise consciousness about class in Yemareir. Any disagreements between us are matters of tactics, where disagreement is generative and also impossible to avoid. Our shared strategic goal of illumination and liberation will never be sundered.

JC: You know that saying, that everything that comes before the word "but" is just window dressing?

ATK: Fuck you.

JC: Yes, correct.

ATK: ...you're right, though, I don't share their view. I'm not sure if what happened was an accident, but I think it's a mistake—a *tactical* mistake—to focus on the 'stream, at least as a tool of class violence. A 'streamer helped me to the infirmary when dozens of students in earshot of me were quaking in place like hunted rabbits—

JC: Zaya Shearwater, if I'm not mistaken?

ATK: Sure. I didn't know who she was until that day and I wouldn't have learned if I hadn't been burned by her dragon. The point is, she was horrified by what she'd done. She wasn't there to hurt students. If someone orchestrates a horrible accident at another protest, it's not going to be the 'stream again, it'll be something we weren't expecting.

(*Note from JC: Sources within the Brimstone Slipstream Standards Board indicate that they're considering new procedures for warning 'streamers about unanticipated downstream conditions. I didn't ask te-Kaizo whether she'd been in contact with Standards, but that would seem to corroborate her speculation.*)

What I think is important about Zaya Shearwater isn't that she burned half the skin off my face, it's that she contributes campaign funding to Kelloun Rinkhal and Yyvvoun Leatherback and other candidates beholden to financial vultures like Zariveen Boomslang. I don't blame her for it, she's got a hunted son—

JC: For someone who doesn't know anything about Zaya Shearwater, you know a lot about Zaya Shearwater.

ATK: People keep telling me things! She sounds like an exceptional woman. And I feel for her family. I had an aunt who was hunted by a tiger ker, and I saw how it just destroyed my father. The idea that Rinkhal and Leatherback and so on could provide a legislative magic wand to just... save her boy? My father would have thrown them all his money if they'd been around to take it.

I believe in the Travelers' cause. I support their candidates, at least the ones who aren't in bed with slumlords. But this city is built to not care who I support, because I don't own my home. And thanks to Zariveen Boomslang, I probably never will, because I'll be servicing debt to her for the rest of my life.

***

"You can stop reading," said Zaya.

She and Yyvvoun Leatherback were on the roofdeck, sitting in low-slung, broad-armed chairs side by side, a bottle of grapefruit arrack between them. The sky was rose and orange to the west, full black to the east, the clouds in their finest.

"Did you like how I did the voices?" asked Yyvvoun.

"I liked how you did Crotalus. Who's he anyway?"

"Seems to be covering Shenireen Agama's sports beat at the Damask Free Press."

"Is he any good?"

Yyvvoun shrugged. "If you liked what she did? Not really."

"Did you?"

"Didn't you?"

Zaya shrugged. "I never really forgave her that the portrait of Kiriki she gave to the world was her at her worst. Ground down to a sliver of herself."

"Shit." For lack of further words, Yyvvoun reached for the bottle of arrack and took a sip.

"It's not her fault. She wrote what she saw. That's her job. But I don't have to forgive her for doing her job." Zaya reached for the arrack and took her own sip. "Why'd you read me that?"

"Because Yyrreen and Kaana seem like the type of people who'd ambush you with it, and I wanted you to be prepared."

Zaya looked at Yyvvoun with narrowed eyes. "You know something."

"I actually don't. But they can be kind of like those students Ashava was pretending she wasn't disagreeing with. They think that something's important because it's new and people will be talking about it. So like, do we have to put out a response to this one kid's ideas about politics, do we need to tell her to get Zaya Shearwater's name out of her mouth, do we need to double down on our support for Kelloun Rinkhal? And, you know, no to all. But Yyrreen and Kaana are high-strung people who really want to win and don't know how, so they assume everything is a catastrophe and everything needs to be managed. And they think of you as their big celebrity weapon, plus you're named directly by this girl, and so they'll figure you need to be the one to manage it."

The words hung for a while in the cooling evening air. "That was a lot of ideas," Zaya said at last.

"I thought them up all by myself."

"I didn't say they were good ideas."

"That's OK. I know compliments don't come naturally to you."

That stung, but of course she'd be playing right into it if she snapped back. And then there was the question of whether it was true; and if it was, should it be? "I didn't *say* they were good ideas," said Zaya, "but I was thinking it."

Yyvvoun chuckled. "You don't have to—"

"I don't want to be someone who doesn't appreciate people."

Yyvvoun reached for the arrack, laid a fingertip on the neck of the bottle, then let his hand fall away. "I'm trying to figure out how much to read into this."

"Nothing. Look, your message got through. And… I'm cautiously considering the idea that I've started being terrible to you as a habit. Rather than being terrible to you for good reasons, which are legion." She sighed a little. "But it's complicated, because you're also a dumb politician with bad ideas that can't be allowed to live to adulthood or they'll go sticking their ovipositors in everything."

"Phallic, yet feminine," said Yyvvoun. "I like it."

"But at least I can say shit about your bad ideas and their girldicks," said Zaya. "Even if I do it more than I should. I can say what I think is wrong and not have you acting like I said you, personally, should die."

Yyvvoun's chest rose and fell. "Thank you," he said.

"I won't lie, it took some effort."

"But also," Yvvvoun continued, "if I may… I'd rather not be around for any shit-talking of your ex. Not least because she could snap my spine just by blinking in my direction. But mostly…" He made an irresolute gesture.

"You don't like getting near messy drama. I get it."

Yvvvoun gave her a polite, uncomprehending frown. "I'm a politician. Messy drama is like… krill, or something, we survive by sucking it in and concentrating it into a nutrient-rich slurry." Dissatisfaction crept across his face. "I feel like I need to learn more about whales now. Some key whale-related question is going to come up in Coral Precinct and I'll fail my constituents due to a deficient education."

"I have children who can help with whale facts."

"But no, it's not about the mess. It's about the feeling that I'm here—with you—because of how I compare to her, and not just for… myself."

She looked at him, and the differences between Kemreen's lean, muscular body and his softer one couldn't help but come to mind. Kemreen was aggressive, creative, skilled; Yvvvoun was still working through the differences between fucking a man and fucking a woman. But none of that was what he wanted, or deserved, to hear. She got out of her chair and straddled him in his, putting a knee between his legs so she could grind on him properly, then spread a hand across the roughness of his jawline and kissed him deeply. He smiled under her mouth; his hands crept under her shirt to touch the skin of her back. She felt herself melt into him a little. She could do this long enough to figure out what she needed to say.

"Come over tonight?" he asked when she pulled away to take a breath.

"Can't." Zaya tried to cram as much regret into the syllable as she physically could. "I have to stand watch at the Cerulean garden." She could see him try to hide the disappointment. "Tomorrow?"

He took a breath to answer—but she was on her feet so fast, it felt like she was moving before the scream split the air.

Yyvvoun's eyes widened. "What was that?"

"Jaliki," she said, not turning, not waiting, through the door to the back stairs before his name had left her mouth.

***

ZAYA FELL DOWN THE stairs from the roofdeck at least once, but she was on her feet and sprinting again before Yyvvoun could catch up and help her.

Taavi and Gilthiniel had Eäril and Enwë in the common room. Enwë was crying into Taavi's chest, and Eäril was petting her and saying "It's OK, baby. He'll be OK." Taavi looked sick; Gilthiniel was crying and trying not to look like he was crying. "Vani wouldn't leave," he said, and Zaya said "Thank you, breath of mine," without looking at him or stopping, because if she did either one she might not be able to go to her other son, whose screams still tore the sky to shreds, making ice-shards out of the thick summer air.

Kirono was in the kitchen, wrapping a towel around his forearm. "What happened?"

"It didn't like the saddle-knife when I got close to it. Bit the fuck out of my arm." His face looked grey. "I left it on the floor by the ker. It doesn't seem like it's doing much."

Jaliki's room smelled like sweat and metal; arrack roiled in Zaya's gut. He was on the floor, the thinness of his body painful beneath the lean bulk of the ker, which rooted at the flesh of his right thigh like a pig at a promising tuber. Vanako knelt next to him, her hands around his, forehead to forehead with him; his face and hers alike were slick with sweat, twisted with pain, and tracked with tears. Cerminir was on Jaliki's other side; as Zaya entered, she said "Here, baby, swallow this if you can" and pushed something into his mouth with her thumb, then held his other hand. He closed his mouth around it, and the ker found something tough and yanked, and Jaliki screamed into a closed mouth, then sobbed into a closed mouth, then swallowed.

"Where's Minshoon?" asked Zaya.

"Out hailing the hospitalers," said Cerminir. "Jaliki, Mama Zaya's here. Do you want her?" Jaliki sobbed again and did not answer.

"It's all right, breath of mine," Zaya said. She was only half-listening—to Jaliki's tear-drenched screams, to Vanako's quiet sobs, to the ker's wet snuffling. The saddle-knife had grown to fill her field of view. She had kicked the ker a few times, although it hadn't much cared; it had felt like fur and flesh under her foot. She could feel, smell, and taste the warm release of blood springing from its flank, the thrill of serrated steel catching on bone, the sweet song of its pain as she imagined twisting the knife. It wouldn't make up for the year and more it had harried her son, but it would be a down payment.

"Don't do it," Vanako said, her voice torn burlap, rough and ragged.

Zaya's eyes flickered up to meet Vanako's. She found herself bent halfway over, hand outstretched for the knife. Vanako and Cerminir both had their eyes on her; Jaliki's were still screwed shut with pain.

"You can't hurt it," said Vanako. "It seems like you can, but you can't. It already hurt Kirono. We need you."

"The knife could drive it away."

"Kirono tried that."

Zaya did not say anything about Kirono's strength or his resolve or his tenacity that she would regret later.

"Vani's right," said Cerminir. "We need you healthy."

The ker's shoulders lowered. Zaya could see its long face relax as it raised its head. It looked around the room with its wet, red muzzle split into a doggy grin, as if it was happy to see so many friends all in the same place. There was a gobbet of something stuck to its tongue. Zaya picked the knife up and threw it at the ker. It whined and disappeared.

"Mama," Jaliki gasped, and Vanako stepped back, and Zaya wrapped her son's thin chest in her arms. They wept together into each other's shoulders as they had done before. She felt Cerminir push in to pack something into Jaliki's leg and place Zaya's hand to hold it down. When Cerminir tried to withdraw her hand, Zaya seized her forearm and squeezed, as hard as she could, for just a moment. Her eyes were still buried, soaked and stinging, in Jaliki's neck; she did not see Cerminir crouch down to hug her from behind, arms easily wrapping around both Zaya and Jaliki. She felt Cerminir's chest jerk with one quaking sob against her back; then Cerminir was up and moving.

Time passed; Jaliki's air-ripping sobs receded, replaced by gentler ones, sobs of pain but not of fear.

"I just want it to stop," he said, his voice tear-soaked and shaking.

"Me too."

"Why does it do this to me?" he said into her shoulder, the motion of his jaw rubbing tear-slick skin against hers; she could see as clear as ink on paper the squalling infant rooting in her shoulder for someone else's breast; in his voice was the same wail of incomprehension, the same unhidden hurt. "I'm nice to it, I don't kick and yell at it like you do. Why does it want to hurt me? Why doesn't it hurt you?"

It wasn't the first time these questions had dug her heart out in scoops, leaving a wet red hole under the shards of ribs. But in all the nights she had lain under sheets that seemed to scratch her skin no matter where they lay, the moaning of the wind through that crater keeping her awake, she had never found an answer.

Cerminir separated them gently and gave Jaliki a tea that smelled like grass. Zaya found her arms ached. Cerminir looked Jaliki in the eye; something about that gaze slowed the heaving in his chest, quieted his sobs to soft whimpers, and the hole that had been Zaya's heart filled briefly with black poison jealousy. It drained as quickly as it had come, but left a film that stung the ripped rag-ends of her arteries and charred the splinters of her split ribs.

"The hospitalers are on their way," Cerminir said. "Mama's going to have to leave the room when they come—not enough space in here, and it's better not to move you. But she can stay here until they come, and she'll be right outside when they're here. All right?"

Jaliki nodded, and Zaya realized why Cerminir had asked him instead of her: Because she would have fought to stay with him, even if it made the hospitalers' jobs harder. Cerminir pried her bloody fingers up from the balled cloth she was packing into his wound, replacing them with her own hand. "Go wash up, Zaya," she said.

"Don't dismiss me."

"I didn't mean it like that."

"I know."

"If you know, then why—" Cerminir shook her head. "OK. Go wash up. Then you can stay until the hospitalers are here."

Zaya kissed Jaliki's forehead one more time and said a tangled ball of words about love and pride and bravery, and then she practically knocked over a broad-shouldered Ililuë man in hospitalers' powder-blue. Two colleagues rushed in after, questions began, and she was left in the living room, staring at her family staring back at her from around the coffee table.

There was coffee. Vinaali had brought it, steaming in a tall ceramic pitcher, too hot for the night, and Zaya hated the smell. Forgetting about the state of her hands, she took a cup anyway. As she watched, Shozo entered, without knocking but with whiskey.

Zaya went to the basins in the kitchen, ladled up the clean water and poured it over her hands into the dirty, which was already red. The next steps on a night like this were laid out from too many before it: Sit with the family, pour too much whiskey into too little coffee, talk, cry. Have a slurred conversation with Cerminir about wound care that she'd have to revisit in the morning, because the whiskey would dissolve it in her brain. Sleep in Jaliki's bed whenever he got home, wrapped around him as tightly as he'd allow. Which would be as tightly as she wanted, since he would be too weak to protest. Wake in the morning to the ker licking Jaliki's face, its muzzle still brown from the attack, not yet clean.

"I need to get some air," she said. No one seemed to hear her, but that was fine.

When she left the gate of the tenement, she saw a bike about six paces from the hospitalers' bell. Good omen or not, she was on it in a moment.

Fast as she pedaled, the slipstream of the bike didn't dry the blood on Zaya's dress. Maybe the sweat was keeping it wet; the night was seasonably hot, the wind—when there was wind—blowing in from the east, bringing the wet of the cloud forest and the heat of the veldt to mingle in the streets—

PART II

CHAPTER 10
ON THE DAY OF BELL THE CAT

THE SHADE OF THE mahogany trees cooled the afternoon air to perfection. The wyrm under Zaya coasted, its feathers smooth as steel against her legs. The police officer before her sat as still as stone, their eyes wide open in the face of what they had thought, until a moment ago, was death.

"Congratulations," Zaya said. "I surrender."

***

NOTHING THAT HAPPENED NEXT was what should have happened.

Cops liked a perp walk when they could get it, or at least all the ones in the Pinks and Browns did, but the Ivory Precinct Police quietly surrounded her, put two dampers over her head—two!—tied her hands behind her back, and got her on a wyrm. Once she was secure in the saddle, a cloth sack went over her head. As sacks went, it was kind of nice: clean white linen with a loose enough weave that she could feel, at least at times, like she wasn't suffocating, and a drawstring that they drew just enough so she couldn't shake it off her head.

Shit, she thought. *This is where they kill me.*

Once the thought came, Zaya just wanted to wait for it to happen—her arms hurt, and her heart, and she hadn't slept, and she could smell the blood of the Sepia Precinct cop on the ground—but she tore thoughts of Vanako and Jaliki from the hole at the bottom of her mind that they were waiting to fall through, and she fought.

It was embarrassing. Against the physical restraints, she never had a chance. As for the dampers, she noted with distant interest that the two fields were subadditive; and in a different world that might have bought her something, but in this one she couldn't think of a single thing she could do with a tiny whisper in a strange wyrm's mind, which was currently the limit of what she might, just barely, push through. So she exhausted herself, which wasn't hard, and then waited for the bite of iron in her neck or, worse, her gut.

But it didn't come, and someone finally mounted up on the saddle in front of her, and the Swordwing took flight.

Her effort to keep track of where the wyrm was going died a death inside a minute. The shavings of perception she could scrape from its mind gave her no information on its speed, position, or trajectory. Weren't criminal masterminds supposed to be able to do this stuff? More to the point, weren't dragonriders? Thelendil would know where he was going.

These were the kind of thoughts she could have dwelt on for hours, but instead she jolted awake when the wyrm landed.

What came next was more similar to what should have happened: Getting dragged around the inside of an administrative building, getting chained to chairs and tables for hours, getting questioned. But there were a few differences. It wasn't a busy building, for one, and there weren't any cops in it, other than that one Ivory Precinct cop who brought her in, who was responsible for most of the dragging and tying—but not the questioning. For another, no one would tell her where she was. For a third—

—well, maybe more than a third. When Zaya left the building, they put two dampers and a sack on her, for a total of two dampers and one sack. Which meant the others had been removed at some point. That felt right—she had a general impression of having been able to see things—but what had she seen? Plenty of not-people—but had she seen any people? She felt like she had. What had they said? They'd asked her questions. What had she said? She'd answered, except when she hadn't. Why had they taken the dampers off? For all she knew, they could have told her; but she didn't know. What had the colors of the walls been?

Zaya was on wyrmback now, her legs spread wider than they had been, over softer plumage than the Swordwing's steel-hard feathers. By the size and the smell of its breath drifting back, it was probably an older Ranger Wyrm. She was exhausted, still, so heartsick that the sick had spread to her stomach—but there was nothing vague about anything now. The light was cloudy through the linen over her eyes, its weave was blurry in the specific way that a fine pattern ought to be blurry that close up. The sun beat her skin and the wyrm's ribs expanded and contracted with its breath, and the sack caught against the stubble of her scalp.

"You shaved my head," she said to anyone who might have been listening.

"That was you," said a voice with a Mrineen accent, probably a man. "Or, you asked to. We had someone else do it."

"Why did I ask for that?"

"You kept asking after the officer that fell. We finally got word that he died."

"Why don't I remember?"

Zaya felt the minor postural adjustments of a wyrm getting climbed on by a person. When the voice came again, it came from a few feet in front of her. "I don't know what they do here," it said. "And I don't ask."

"Where are we going?"

"There's a bag on your head for a reason."

"At least tell me whether we're going to go dump my body somewhere."

"I mean, yeah," said the voice.

Zaya's gut clenched, hard and cold. She began worming her mind through the doubled damper field, knowing the wyrm could take off any minute, knowing that she might not be able to make it do anything even if she penetrated.

"But we're not going to kill you."

She'd have bitten his throat out if she had it in range. Maybe. She was marrow-tired, tired enough that she could have fallen asleep mid-lunge, dreaming of blood on her tongue before she hit the ground. And there was a sack on her head.

Zaya didn't say anything else—to someone like this, there was no point—and the voice didn't volunteer anything further. The wyrm gathered its strength and leaped to catch the air. *Fly!* she said to herself, in the voice of an announcer at a race, a voice she wondered if she'd hear again.

CHAPTER 11
FIVE WEEKS BEFORE BELL THE CAT

WHEN ZAYA GOT HOME from the House of Vines, thighs aching from biking, somewhere around the midpoint between midnight and dawn, the guests had mostly cleared; but the clutter of the common room made it seem more crowded, somehow, as though the artifacts of visitation held some trace of whoever had drunk from the smudged glass, eaten with the crusted fork, wiped their lips with the oddly placed napkin. But it was just Minshoon, Vinaali, Vanako, and—new to the scene, his arm around Vanako—Tuuro te-Kaneva, his cropped hair now a shade of azure that didn't, in Zaya's opinion, suit his skin tone. Minshoon got up and, without a word, embraced her. He smelled newly washed; in a corner somewhere, wadded up, there would be a pile of bloodstained clothes waiting to be burned. "You're all clean," she said. "I'm sorry I'm sweaty."

Minshoon disengaged, put his hands gently on her biceps. "Where'd you go?" The gentleness of the question was a thin veil draped over its urgency. Minshoon was good at draining tension from an interaction—good, especially, at not having pointless fights with kids—but he knew that she knew that no one ever just disappeared in the wake of a kerostatic attack. That wasn't what you did, when a child was bleeding, maybe dying.

Except, of course, it had been what she did. To keep everyone breathing and eating, she had left, over and over again; while Jaliki grew up, while he grew closer to being hunted by the creature who would eventually be his death.

She looked over at Vanako and Tuuro. She hadn't wanted to have this conversation with them here. Then again, she couldn't hide it forever. "Vinaali, Tuuro, I'm sorry," she said. "I need some time alone with my family."

Vinaali got up to go; Tuuro moved to follow, but Vanako's arm tensed around his shoulder. "I don't want him to go. He can hear whatever I can hear."

"It's OK," said Tuuro.

"It's not," said Vanako, her eyes lances.

"Good luck with everything," Vinaali said, receding eagerly toward the door.

Tuuro gently removed her arm from his shoulder. "I'll see you tomorrow."

"No," said Vanako. "I'll come with you."

Zaya sighed, at least half in exasperation, maybe half in relief. "All right," she said. "I can tell you tomorrow."

Vanako's stare grew twice as sharp and twice as cold. "You're not shutting me out of…"

Taking advantage of Vanako's uncertainty about what she was being shut out of, Tuuro got up and put some distance between him and her. "It's OK, Vani. Stay with your mom. You can find me when you need me."

"I need you now."

"Your brother could have died tonight. I know what it's like. You need to be with your family."

Vanako turned her face away from Tuuro like a baby from a forkful of broccoli. He shrugged—his blank face showed that he was more hurt than he cared to let on, and for the first time in a long time, Zaya felt for the boy—and made for the door.

She made herself speak as soon as it closed. "I went to the House of Vines in Chartreuse Precinct."

Minshoon's face quirked with curiosity; Vanako's gaze bored into her like an auger. "Mom," she said. "What the hell?"

"Tjaroon wanted to make a deal with me."

"I didn't know about this."

Zaya sighed. "No, you didn't. He made me the offer at the Cerulean Precinct garden. Offered to help Jaliki in exchange for services. I sent him packing."

"You didn't tell me he made you an offer," said Vanako, "and you didn't tell me when you went to talk to him. What did he want?"

Zaya had walked into the candlelit study to Tjaroon with his feet up on a desk, the mandrill curled up under it staring at her with baleful eyes. Tjaroon had been nursing a bottle of whiskey from a single glass. He hadn't offered her any. That was the kind of discussion it was going to be; that was the kind of discussion it had been. She'd seized the bottle and swigged directly from the neck before she left, because she wasn't above displays of childish defiance and, mostly, because she'd really needed the drink. "He wants us to throw a race."

Revulsion sprang up in their eyes; but in Minshoon's, it writhed alongside calculation. "And in exchange, he'll treat Jaliki?"

Zaya nodded.

They both turned to look at Vanako. She looked back at both of them, disbelieving. "You didn't seriously take it."

"What would you have done?" asked Zaya.

"Obviously not taken it!"

"And then what?" she said. "I went to Tjaroon fresh off shoving a towel into a hole in my son's leg to slow down the flow of arterial blood. My hand was where his muscle used to be. I could feel the edges of his skin on my knuckles—"

"Why," Vanako said, fury building visibly within her, "does everyone seem to want to forget that I *also* lost someone—"

"I can go back," Zaya said. "I can be at his door in twenty minutes and tell him the deal's off. Tell me to do it and I'll do it."

"*Zaya*," said Minshoon.

"Of course," Vanako said to Minshoon. "Don't give the kid any power over this decision. All you're asking her to do is ruin her integrity and her reputation. Why should she get a say?"

"You're the best older sister Jaliki could ever ask for," said Minshoon. "But you're not his parent. And his parents aren't going to give you that power because one of us—" he looked pointedly at Zaya—"feels the need to prove a point about how hard it is."

Zaya hadn't realized she'd been leaning forward, letting her neck and shoulders tense into rock as she spoke. She leaned back in the armchair, letting the cushion support her weight. The release of tension in her muscles was like a pile of blankets had dropped on her from a height; immediately her arms and legs felt heavy and perfectly placed, immovable. She closed her eyes. "It's too late for that," she said. "I already gave it."

"What?" said Vanako.

"Zaya," said Minshoon. She knew the voice well; it was the one she used when the children were about to do something that they should not do, and that she had no will to prevent or punish. *I will be very upset if you do that, Jaliki.* The voice of a threat with absolutely dick to back it up.

"If you want to blow the deal," Zaya said, her closed eyes still facing straight up at the ceiling, "just spread the word. Your mom's going to throw the race. If enough people believe you, you can get me banned from the 'stream entirely... but just the rumor'll be enough that no one will take bets against me. You can start right now. I can't stop you."

The silence rested easy on the room, cottony and perfect. It sat for a long time.

"I'm sorry, Vani," Minshoon said. "This isn't how we should have done this. She's exhausted, she has every right to be—I don't even know if she's awake—"

"She's awake," Vanako said, at the same time Zaya said "I'm awake."

"—I don't want to make excuses for an adult woman who is right here and apparently can speak for herself," Minshoon said through his teeth, "but even if I don't agree with the method, I think the call was right."

"We don't leave family behind," said Zaya, the words falling sleep-slurred from her lips. "I fought for you because of that. I lied to people I love for you. Because I thought you were worth saving."

"Don't hold that over me," Vanako said, her voice as dull and dense as a brick.

"I'm not. You don't owe me anything."

"You don't mean that."

"I do," said Zaya. "But you're on the other side of it now."

"Zaya," said Minshoon, "she is not and should not be responsible for this decision."

"Yes I should," said Vanako.

"No you shouldn't," said Zaya. "But you are."

She felt Minshoon take his breath in, heard him release it. "I feel like there's not much more to say."

Zaya reached out, blindly, caught his hand as he was standing. She made herself open her eyes and he was looking at her, tired and angry and sad and scared, and she squeezed his hand, and his face didn't change, but he squeezed hers back. "I did this all wrong," she said. "I'm sorry. You're a good father. So much better than me. I probably should have kept this all to myself. But I couldn't lie to the family again."

"Maybe not," Minshoon said. "But the rest of us will have to do a lot of lying until this is over."

He let her hand go, and she let him let it. When he left, Vanako was still there, leaning her head on a hand that covered her face.

"Go ahead," Zaya said. "No better time."

"We were working to change this for everyone," said Vanako, her eyes still hooded by her hand. "That was the whole idea. No one gets lifted up until everyone gets lifted up. We were working for our people, as a people. Not grabbing to get our own like—" She looked in the direction Minshoon had gone.

"Like a Mrineen family would," Zaya said. "I know."

"Then how—"

"Because Jaliki will die if I don't."

Her eyes were too heavy to leave open, so she closed them again. She had to think of something else to say; those couldn't be the last words to her daughter tonight. She might run away to Tuuro's and never come back; she might never speak to Zaya again. But that balming phrase, that magic, wouldn't come, and when Zaya opened her eyes next the light was streaming in.

***

AFTER BREAKFAST THAT DAY, Zaya, Minshoon, Cerminir, and Kirono took a walk to discuss what would happen next. Taavi and Gilthiniel watched Eäril and Enwë; Vanako sat with Jaliki, who still slept, the ker curled at the foot of his bed.

The walk they planned was long: To Chartreuse Precinct, to see the House of Vines. It only seemed fair to bring them into the route Zaya had traveled the night before. Too late, surely, and too little, but only fair.

The first stop on the route was the Blind Beggar, past the Dawn broodspire in Lilac Precinct and across that unmissable border between the respectable neatness of a northerly purple precinct and the weary shabbiness of a southerly green. It was there, picking their way over a handful of sleeping drunks by the stoop and handing cash to a panhandler sitting and shaking in the cool of the morning, that Zaya told them what had transpired at the House of Vines, why they were walking there, what they needed to do before they crossed the threshold of House Shearwater once again.

There was pain, and fear, and concern. Cerminir fretted over what might happen if the fraud was found out; she also, in her direct but oblique way, mourned what Vanako had raged against, the taking of this decision from the family's hands by Zaya. Kirono's misgivings were for the family's financial future and Zaya's own well-being. She would have to quit the 'stream, would she not? How would they support themselves on Kirono's salary alone? How would Zaya's mind adapt to a life off dragonback? Zaya had already burned bridges as a caravan escort and long-haul courier; without the 'stream, what would she do?

Zaya listened closely to her family, explained what she could, apologized where she felt she should, wept where she could not stop herself, and expressed no certainty she did not feel. As to the revelation of the fraud, the main concern was for before it happened; the Standards Board of the 'stream had no legal authority, its only power was ostracism. As to Zaya's choice of career, she spoke briefly and simply on the possibilities of working as a construction foreman, an industry where her reputation had not been ruined as it had in long-hauling. She did not speak on her near-certainty that no Mrineen builder would hire her, a woman visibly aligned with workers and against police; she did not mention the thoughts she had had of joining Tjaroon for the long term, an empath enforcer in his ranks who might, through craft and guile and superior understanding of the minds of animals, one day supplant him. She did not say that either option felt like a kind of death, or at least a fate that might have been open to some Zaya who might, even recently, have been, but not to the one who now walked up Jujube Street with her family and tried her best, which was not very good, to tell them the truth.

They were quiet when they reached the House of Vines. They did not get close enough to it to make the gate guards nervous. They did not stand and stare for long. If her family had asked why she had brought them there, why it was important for them to see the place where she had gone to bargain away the 'stream for her son's life, she could not have answered; but they did not ask, only spent the time looking, inscribing the gate and courtyard and vine-crawled walls on their memories.

***

THEY MADE SURE THEY were out of earshot of the House of Vines before they turned to discussing strategy. The plan was easy enough: Drive up Zaya's odds by winning a few long-shot races, then lose badly in one where the odds would favor her. The races would be determined by Tjaroon, based on his subordinates' analysis of the odds. Zaya would receive instructions on the races to attempt and the race to throw. (Minshoon bristled at this; Zaya told him that Tjaroon had insisted, which was a lie; Zaya had, in fact, insisted to Tjaroon that Minshoon stay well away from the problem of which race should destroy her career.) There was a target for the odds she needed to achieve, and a proration schedule for the yliaster treatments Jaliki would receive based on the extent to which she might fall short.

"This is generous," Tjaroon had explained. "The treatments you get sooner are the most valuable."

"How's that?" Zaya had asked. "The prices go up every week."

Tjaroon had given her a look of disdain, shadow-painted by the flickering candle, and informed her that a treatment for Jaliki sooner, while he was alive, was more valuable than waiting until later, when he might be dead. But that was not what he meant by "valuable," and his face showed he was afraid she knew it, so she did her best to show she didn't. The mandrill glared at her from under the desk, still full of hate for when she had turned it against its master months ago, and although she knew it had not understood what had (or might have) passed between her and Tjaroon, her thoughts felt exposed, seizing on any shift of air pressure in the room as though her brain itself had been laid bare. ("Your brain can't feel the breeze," Cerminir would have said, if Zaya had confessed the image.)

"So he thinks the price is going down," said Minshoon, after Zaya had related that piece of the encounter.

Zaya nodded.

"Sounds like he likes our chances in the election."

"Not just the election, I don't think," said Zaya. "But the election will force the issue if it goes our way."

"But we can't wait that long," said Minshoon.

"Absolutely not," said Cerminir.

"No way," said Kirono.

Zaya cast a grateful glance at her co-parents, who knew her well enough to know she didn't want to be the one to have to say it.

***

WITH THE IMPLEMENTATION SET, the guarantees articulated, there was one great question: Who should know?

Most cases were clear-cut. Zinji te-Zuuno should not know. Enwë and Eäril obviously should not know. Taavi and Gilthiniel, after some heated discussion, it was decided, should know. Shozo, Amiko, and Chashu should not know. Kaana te-Tekko and Yyvvoun Leatherback should not know. As they approached the border of Lilac Precinct, two and a half hours after they had left their children to take care of one another in the house that bore the name they had chosen, there remained three questions on which they had not yet agreed:

Should Yyrreen know?

***

WHEN THEY GOT HOME, there was a note in their letterbox.

Cerulean Precinct yliaster garden destroyed last night. Where were you? We need to talk. KtT.

"It's not your fault," Minshoon said, reading it over her shoulder.

"I can't do this," said Zaya.

"You don't have to. You've got one thing to focus on now."

"The 'one thing' is exactly why I have to keep helping Kaana and Yyrreen. I'm already fucking a bunch of people over. I can't just hang them out to dry."

Zaya didn't see Minshoon turn to Cerminir and Kirono for guidance, didn't see the look they shared; but she could imagine it, as clear and fine as the edges of clouds on a bright day. "All right," he said. "In a couple days. When Jaliki's stable. When you've gotten some sleep."

"You're not my dad," she said; but she reached back to find his hand and squeezed it.

CHAPTER 12

FOUR AND A HALF WEEKS BEFORE BELL THE CAT

ZAYA HAD COME KNOCKING at Yyvvoun's three consecutive nights before she got him. He had a floor of a neat, well-maintained tenement in Coral Precinct, with lush kitchen-garden plots in the back and herbs in window boxes on all four floors; when she pushed up against him and hauled his mouth down to hers, his hands smelled like rosemary. His fingers tasted like dirt, though; she made him wash his hands before she'd undress. Or let him undress her. Whatever it had been. She didn't remember. They switched off making each other come until their hands and mouths ached from the effort, and then they lay too exhausted to care about what they stuck to, or what was sticking. Zaya traced the fine arcing scar under his nipple. He said "Stop," more playful than annoyed, but he did push her hand away.

"Sorry," she said. "My dad has these too, but he'd never tell me what they were."

"If he wouldn't," said Yyvvoun, "I certainly won't."

"Ha ha."

The effort of talking seemed to have winded Yyvvoun again, or maybe he was just thinking about what to say; either way, he took two deep breaths, then sighed. "Your dad who's dead, or the one in Azure Precinct?"

"Papa Zinji. In Azure Precinct."

"Perfect. You can go molest him instead of me."

"I'm sorry! Really. I won't do it again."

"It's all right. I just…" Yyvvoun paused again, still catching his breath. "Enh. I'll tell you later. Just a touchy subject."

"Or a no-touchy subject?"

A pulse in Yyvvoun's ribs stood in for a laugh. "All the other touching is good. Kind of a surprise, but good."

"You're the only one who's surprised. All your neighbors saw me knocking for three days in a row. Did one of them write you a letter or something?"

"That's the kind of thing Tzalijain on 2 would absolutely do. But no."

It was Zaya's turn to pause, and then to notice the work it took for her own breath to catch up with her heartbeat. Had it quickened? Or had it the silence just allowed her to notice how fast it was? "Why is it such a surprise? That I'd come here?"

"It's just… so soon."

It took her a moment to realize what he was talking about. "I guess," she said. "Some people turn away from fucking when bad things are happening. I'm the opposite. I want to remind myself what the good things feel like."

"I guess I don't know which one I am," said Yyvvoun. "When Dzaroon was dying…"

"I can't even imagine. He must have been wrecked."

"No. I mean, yes. I don't know." Zaya let Yyvvoun work through it. "He was more like you. He wanted to use the time he had to feel the good things. I did the best I could, but eventually… I couldn't. The scars piled up, he ended up losing a leg before the end." He shuddered, as if shaking a mass of flies off his torso. "I'd better stop."

"We don't have to talk about it," said Zaya. "But I won't judge you."

"Have you met you? Of course you'll judge me. You've already judged me."

Zaya decided to allow it.

"And probably you should," Yyvvoun continued. "But it's not your judgment I'm worried about. I think... talking about this has reminded me that the court of Yyvvoun has delayed a lot of verdicts on the conduct of Yyvvoun in the matter of the death of Yyvvoun's husband. And I don't think the defendant is going to react well when the sentences come down." His chest moved up and down in a deep sigh. "But I can't afford to do that before the election. So the court of Yyvvoun isn't handing out sentences just yet."

"Jaliki's ker changed. After the attack."

Zaya had to say it quickly; inside six words, her voice had already roughened, nearly cracked.

Yyvvoun let the words sink in. "If you mean what I think you mean, I'm so sorry."

"It's what you think. It has these... Cerminir calls them cilia. Whippy little blue tentacles all over its body that point wherever it's looking. When it's asleep, they stand up and wave around. And it has two new legs, and an eye in the middle of its forehead."

The hospitalers had explained what the changes meant, but Zaya knew it from those long-ago support groups: The ker had metabolized enough of Jaliki's ba to initiate the end of this instar. Its adaptations to tolerate this world were falling away, allowing its physical form to drift into far-flung corners of the phenotype space as it prepared for metamorphosis. The hospitalers emphasized, using very simple and clear words, that this wasn't the whole of the metamorphosis; if the ker was a caterpillar, this was the part inside the cocoon where its body began to break down and regrow. Most of that process was occurring in dimensions other than the four that humanity existed in. When it was ready, it would attack again, and this time it would need the surge of energy that came from the severing of the ba from its physical host. From killing Jaliki. There might be a penultimate attack, if the ker hadn't taken enough to bring it to the brink of metamorphosis; but, more than likely, the next would be the last.

Which Yyvvoun knew, from experience.

She should tell him that they had a plan, that Jaliki would be safe for some time anyway. It was easy not to say, because it didn't feel true. Tjaroon hadn't done his end yet, for one thing; for another, they were truly at his mercy. There was no margin for error now. Anyway, how would she explain it without giving the game away?

His chest moved more slowly now; his eyes had drifted shut. Zaya could look in if she wanted, see whether he'd really fallen asleep so suspiciously fast. But hiding what she shouldn't seemed bad enough without seeking where she shouldn't; so she didn't. When their bodies had cooled, she dressed and crept away.

CHAPTER 13

FOUR WEEKS BEFORE BELL THE CAT

THE STREET OF BONDED Smiths in Alabaster Precinct woke up early: Thick-shouldered dogsbodies crisscrossed the street with loads of coal and water, and the air was thick with smoke and the sound of hammers on steel. Zaya had met up with Chashu and Amiko outside Yyvvoun's—"the rules don't change for booty calls" had been in the ground rules from the beginning—and taken a wyrm to avoid the questions that might hit a heavily armed Kayalim man like Chashu cycling into Alabaster near dawn. At the east end of the Street of Bonded Smiths was a smithy called the Scute & Talon, elaborately adorned with fine wrought iron art, on the south side, and one without any obvious signage on the north. As they approached the smithy on the north side, Zaya saw thick, neat letters carved into one of the posts holding up the awning: *Fanoun Makar, Metalworker.* They were inlaid with steel, dull and dark but unrusted.

A chain of bells rang, harmonizing, when she opened the door. The front of the shop was a small reception area, spare and tidy but for the dirty dishes on the round table, the walls hung with both rough blades and finished. The finished blades were adorned with different knotwork patterns on the flats. Zaya held up the draft saddle-knife and compared it, lighting at last on one patterned in copper and abalone. It seemed the most similar to Arhoon Pogona's old knife, but there were differences.

"Help you?"

The question came from a Mrineen man, maybe in his forties, broad-shouldered and bare-armed, with knotwork tattoos covering both arms up to the shoulders. He carried a plain broadsword that shone softly in the morning's half-light. He wasn't pointing it at Zaya, but he carried it as easily and confidently as a chef might carry a ladle.

"Yes, please. Fanoun Makar?"

"Zenthoon. What brings you here?"

Zaya flipped the knife around to hold it hilt-out, then presented it to Zenthoon Makar for inspection. "A dead friend of mine had this knife in his possession. I want to know who had it made."

Zenthoon didn't look at it. "There's two dozen other smithies on this road alone. Why us?"

"I was told it was probably you who made it. Or your... ?" She let her voice trail up in the way Mrineen did when they didn't want to presume a relationship.

"Brother. Who told you?"

"Someone familiar with House patterns? You won't know their name."

"Try me."

"You haven't even looked at the knife. You don't know if it's yours."

"What's your name again?"

"Zaya Shearwater."

Something shifted in the muscles of Zenthoon Makar's face. He looked around the room for a moment, then gently leaned the sword point-down against the back wall to face Zaya with empty hands. "Give it here."

Throat dry and stomach tight, Zaya approached and handed him the knife.

Zenthoon ran his thumb over the curled-out inlay and laughed softly. "I remember who commissioned this. Not one of our client Houses. I had to go across the street to find his House knot, and then *this* happened." He thumbed the fouled inlay to underscore the point. "When he came to pick it up I was getting ready for war—you know how it is with these scions, they'll find ways to skint you even for mistakes you didn't make, forget about gigantic fuckups like this. But this one, he was half terrified but mostly relieved. He didn't ask for anything back, just wanted to keep the castoff and put a different design in for the inlay."

"Not one of your client Houses," said Zaya. "Who was he?"

"Tall fellow, grey for his age. Carried a sword around. Goanna, I want to say?"

"Pogona?"

Zenthoon snapped his fingers and pointed at her. "That's the one. I knew it was a lizard name."

"Did your brother have any bad dreams when he was forging the knife?"

"My brother?" Zenthoon shook his head. "Pogona told us to be careful how long we spent with the inlay. Said that would happen—bad dreams. He looked like he'd had a few himself."

"Who was with him?"

"Say again?"

"Who came in with him? Who else was there?"

Zenthoon shook his head. "It was all Pogona. He always came alone."

"What did he say the knife was for? Or who?"

"Research and development." Zenthoon examined Zaya with a slightly cocked head. "I'm starting to think that wasn't the whole story?"

"You're sure Arhoon gave you the inlay? And it was him who told you to keep away from it or you'd have bad dreams?" Zenthoon dug in a pocket and extended a stained, crumpled rag. Zaya blinked and realized her eyes were stinging; her cheeks were wet. She waved the kerchief away. "Can I speak to your brother? I need to know…"

"My brother won't help you," Zenthoon said. "He didn't make that dagger. Couldn't, then or now. That inlay's a bitch to work with."

"Fuck my life," said Zaya, wiping the tears off her cheeks. "I should have known. Of course there's another fucking layer to the onion. All right, then, Zenthoon—where should I have been while I was wasting my time here? Who'd you subcontract to?"

Zenthoon shook his head. "No subcontractor. This is a family business. Fanoun Makar was our father. Died a year ago. Eaten by a dhole ker." He cast his eyes back down to the knife. "Is it true this stuff can save the hunted?"

"This stuff?"

"I asked around," said Zenthoon, but Zaya's mind was already moving. She'd seen the metallic purple of the inlay before: In the ink of Jaliki's tattoos, in the psionic dampers. It didn't block empathy, but it gave bad dreams? Kirono had talked, months ago, about the early uses of yliaster to push minds closer together rather than pull them apart. Uses that had been abandoned because the early practitioners had driven themselves and their subjects insane. That was what spooked the ker when it was near the saddle-knife, what made it aggressive rather than driving it away; that was what gave the dreams.

Of course it was yliaster. What wasn't?

"When you asked around," said Zaya. "Who'd you ask?"

"Kajishain Slider," said Zenthoon. "She does work for House Krait."

"Think she'd talk to me?"

"I don't think you'd get much use out of what she'd have to say. If you've got questions, I can take them to her."

Zaya leaned on the counter, putting all her weight on the heels of her hands. She rocked back and forth gently on the balls of her feet. "Zenthoon," she said, "I feel like we've gotten to know one another." She sucked on her teeth, delaying the question. "What do you think Arhoon Pogona was doing, making this knife? And giving it as a gift to someone?"

"I thought it could drive a ker away. I figured that was what it was for." He looked at Zaya as though she were a crystal sculpture he was about to throw a rock at. "But if it can't do that, then I guess he was trying to give someone some really bad dreams."

"It really seems that way, doesn't it?" She leaned forward, letting her arms support all her weight, then pushed herself back upright.

"These rich fucks," said Zenthoon. "They think they can do whatever they want, don't they?" He pointed at her with the hilt of the knife that he was still holding by the blade. "That's what I like about you. You're taking the fight to them. They want to hoard the cure for themselves. You want everyone to have it." He remembered what he was holding, and set it down on the counter. "Not just people who can spend House money on cursed knives to screw up people's dreams. Why would anyone do that?"

"Why would anyone make a knife like that?" Zaya said. It took the saying of it before she felt the hot, coppery plug of anger in her throat. "Why would anyone make anything for people like that? Why are you all so eager to fall in line for people who act like money or swords or magic makes them better than you?"

Zenthoon's face went blank and hard, and the right things to say wrote themselves in the air in front of him: *Forget I said it. I long-hauled for the trade companies. I drank gin House Pogona paid for. In a couple weeks, I'm going to fuck over every sorry idiot unlucky enough to bet on me so I can cure my kid of the same thing your father died of. I'm not better than you.*

But she stood here before a man who lived off a business that had made the knife that killed Kiriki, and he never asked why. So, fuck it, maybe she was.

***

Zaya threw open the door to the Makar smithy and boiled out onto the street. This would have been more satisfying if she hadn't forgotten Chashu and Amiko were standing guard. As it was, the door slammed into Amiko, who squealed and fell on her ass, sending bees out of the pouch at her waist in a protective swarm; Zaya yelped and recoiled from the bees, only to be calmly pushed back by Chashu, who interposed himself between her and the swarm until Amiko had the presence of mind to call the bees back into their home. Chashu came around to Amiko and offered a hand to help her up, which she ignored, and then pushed her hair back to examine the growing lump on her forehead, which she allowed, although she eyed him like Eäril looked at Minshoon when he told her to try just one bite of something new he'd cooked. Chashu turned to Zaya. "Do you think those people have something cold we could put on her?"

"I don't know."

"Are you gonna go ask? Or do I need to do it?"

Veraamaka navo, Zaya told herself. *You are a grown woman who risks her life for money every week. You hurt one of your people. You can go into the shop you just stormed out of and ask the guy you just insulted for something to help her.*

"You should probably do it," she said.

Chashu went in, spoke quietly with Zenthoon for a minute while Zaya apologized nonstop to Amiko, and came out empty-handed. "He said they're a smithy, they don't keep ice around. I think he could do better than that. But I guess getting down to brass tacks with some House wage slave in Alabaster Precinct might not be great for our health."

"Here," said Zaya, heading east. "Let's just find a fountain. It's hot, some of them will be charm-cooled."

When she took them south at the next cross street, she could feel Chashu stick a little on the turn. They should have been continuing east to catch Aloe Boulevard, which would take them northeast to Chartreuse Precinct, just west of Lilac. But he didn't ask about it until they found a little park with sculpted hills, an orchid garden, and a fountain that a few Mrineen kids were using as a wading pool. Zaya could feel the adults' eyes on them as they sat on the rim, as far from the children as they could, and ran water over Amiko's goose egg as though she'd been burned instead of smacked by a door.

"Where we headed?" Chashu asked.

"Incarnadine. Yyrreen's office."

"Isn't she coming to yours for lunch today?" Amiko asked. She was sitting on the ground, her head leaned back on the rim of the fountain to try to minimize the wetness on her clothes. It wasn't working that well.

"Sure. We'll walk her."

"Isn't Jenishoon Terrapin supposed to be coming by for drinks beforehand?"

Jenishoon Terrapin had been running unaffiliated and unopposed for the open seat in Cobalt Precinct. Then he'd publicly thrown in with the Travelers and a challenger had materialized, a Cobalt cop with an enthusiastic following among the shore precinct police. Now Terrapin was having second thoughts. "Jenishoon Terrapin can drink on my couch without my help. I don't know what he ever expected from me."

Chashu shrugged. "You're the boss."

"Technically, Yyrreen's the boss," Amiko said from her prone position on the fountain's rim. "And, technically, the only reason I'm following Zaya around and throwing bees at anyone who looks at her funny is because I am trying to help you get the Moon and Stars to vote to improve the lives of normal people. So maybe be nice to this Terrapin guy even if you don't feel like it."

"Sure," said Zaya. "But if I get attacked in Incarnadine Precinct and you're not there to throw bees, Yyrreen will still be mad."

Amiko lurched to her feet. "Talking of."

Zaya swung her head around; Chashu was already stepping in front of her. Two Alabaster Precinct police, both women, were stepping toward them.

***

THEY SLOWED A BIT when Chashu interposed himself; but not much.

"Shearwater-cha," said the smaller one. "I'm Lieutenant Narioun Angonoka; this is Officer Ora. On behalf of our colleagues in Amethyst Precinct, we'd like to invite you to the station for a conversation about the events at Yemareir University, during the protest a few days ago."

There it was: The thing that had never happened yet, that they'd been drilling for. That Shozo, Chashu, and Amiko followed her around for.

"No thanks," said Zaya.

Angonoka looked around. That was good, in a bad way; she was checking the environment for any opposition Zaya might be able to summon. There wasn't much. Chashu was big and fast and not afraid, but his chances against one cop from a standing start weren't good, and of course they could snap an unaugmented woman the size of Amiko like a twig.

A rising hum in the air indicated that Amiko wasn't waiting to get snapped. Zaya couldn't help but steal a glance back. A dense cloud of bees, just slightly too big for Officer Ora to wrap her arms around, hovered above Amiko's head.

"Oh, come on," said Ora.

Angonoka looked back at Ora with the same sizing-up gaze she'd used to take in the square. Then she turned back to Zaya. "Kids got burned and trampled because of you."

"Are you charging me with something?" Charges were legally bad but physically safer; they kicked off a paper trail and a set of procedures involving witnesses. They also meant Angonoka and Ora could legally put their hands on Zaya, which she didn't love, but which was safer in the parameters of an arrest than it was in a "conversation."

"I'm making an observation as a private citizen," said Angonoka. "Likewise, you've got to know that bee thing won't work again. It's creative, but countermeasures are pretty easy against those little guys." She met Amiko's eyes. "Look, I guess you'll probably find this insulting, but I have to say it: You and your bees could just walk away. Officer Ora may seem like a bit of a squish right now with those bees in her face, but she's curb-stomped men who make your boy look like a sugar glider. You're really the deciding factor here."

"I'm not insulted when a bird shits on me," said Amiko. "It's just how birds live."

"OK, that's extremely rude, but I guess I asked for it." Angonoka addressed herself to Zaya again. "So, Shearwater-cha, congratulations on the ill-advised loyalty of your people, but what's the long-term plan here? Charges aren't in play because our colleagues in Amethyst Precinct are still investigating what happened on the lawn at Yemareir University when you and your dragon swooped in, but that's a matter of time. Meanwhile, you've made a strong case for yourself as a threat to public safety and declined a surprising number of opportunities to present your own case, which—I mean, I know you know how it looks. All I'm saying is, at some point there's five of us in anti-bee suits, carefully selected for bravery in the face of exotic threats—" Here she threw a withering glance at Ora, who pretended not to notice—"and, you know, in light of what Officer Ora and I are facing here, today, the focus shifts very much toward the preservation of our own people's safety, and things overall look very different than they do right now."

"OK," said Zaya. "If we're not allowed to leave, you'd better tell us, because that's what we're doing." She made herself turn her back on Narioun Angonoka, even though every shred of her brain screamed not to take her eyes off the cops, and began walking.

Once they'd turned a corner, she looked behind her; Chashu and Amiko were with them, the bees lagging several paces behind. They took the first turn they could, and the first turn after that, and after that, although Zaya kept them walking away from where they'd met the officers, and toward the border with Eggshell Precinct.

"Your head OK, Amiko?" Zaya asked at last.

"Fine," Amiko said. "What are we doing about that?"

"You're the muscle," Zaya said. "What do you recommend?"

"Stop leaving Lilac Precinct."

"Next."

"Do what they want."

"If I go to the station for that 'conversation' in the morning, I'm not sleeping in my bed that night."

"Stop walking."

"That sounds a lot like 'stop leaving Lilac Precinct.'"

"No, I mean stop walking and look at me."

Zaya stopped walking and looked at her. She was shorter than Zaya, slight, wide-eyed, intense; there was a little grey in her short black hair. "The kind of people who have little personal armies that can scare off police are not like you. Your constituency is people who need help, and you pay in snacks. You do not have access to enough violence to out-violence the police."

"So what should I do?"

"I told you what you should do."

"I'm not doing that."

"Then we're counting the hours until Narioun Angonoka does exactly what Narioun Angonoka said she'd do," said Amiko, "and we surrender or die."

"Fine," said Zaya. "You don't have to die for me."

"The fuck I don't. I'm not here to play."

The road this argument could go down unfurled in Zaya's mind, clear as a shining stream through red rocks: Zaya could say "And you think I am?"; and Amiko could say "Well, are you?"; and Zaya could say something about Jaliki, and Amiko could say something about her sister who died eaten by a hyena ker, and maybe it would end with them coming to a peace and maybe it wouldn't. But that wasn't what Amiko needed from this, was it? It wasn't what anyone needed.

"I'm sorry, Amiko," said Zaya, looking directly into her eyes. "I don't know if I can do what you're asking. But I hear you when you say you're willing to die. I won't take that lightly. I promise."

Amiko nodded briskly, breaking her gaze. "Come on," she said. "Let's get out of here before Narioun Angonoka's pet squish comes back in a beekeeper suit."

***

"LET ME SAY IT back to you," said Yyrreen, angling her gaze down just a shade.

They were sitting at the round table in her back office, architectural drawings pushed aside to make way for their elbows. Zaya followed Yyrreen's eyes and realized they were on the knife, which she was aiming at Yyrreen like a pointed finger for emphasis. She set it down. "You're not allowed to make me sound like a crazy person."

"I don't think you're a crazy person," Yyrreen said, which was especially kind under the circumstances. "I just want to make sure I get it. You got this knife from Arhoon Pogona's possessions, Jenirain Gila recognized it as Kiriki's. Which it is, almost."

"Correct."

"You waved it at Jaliki's ker, and that scared it off. And then you gave it to Jaliki, to see if it would help, and it did, but after a couple days, he couldn't sleep because of the dreams. Which is exactly what happened to Kiriki a couple days after Arhoon gave her the knife."

"You remember."

Yyrreen couldn't quite keep the haunted look off her face. "I remember thinking, if this is what the nighttime screaming is like before the baby comes, what is it going to be like after?"

"It's not supposed to be like that, turns out."

"I know."

Yyrreen held Zaya's eyes with her own—they were dark green, Zaya noticed, not their natural cobalt blue. Yyrreen filled her chest as though she was about to say something she'd been preparing... but when she spoke, it was only to unspool more theory: "The bad dreams are the result of the yliaster inlay in Kiriki's knife, which was probably smelted down and eaten when she died. And since yliaster is involved, you're pretty sure House Taipan and House Krait are involved—"

"—because Kanivoon Taipan was a contender to win the Bisai and he wanted us out of the way. They tricked Arhoon into using it in the knife—"

"Everything up to that actually makes sense," Yyrreen cut in. "Not, like 'an event that would happen in a sane world' kind of sense, but 'a thing that a couple of butthurt rich boys would absolutely do to a girl who was in their way.' But Kanivoon Taipan didn't win the Bisai. Arhoon Pogona did."

"Arhoon couldn't have gotten yliaster on his own," said Zaya.

"He was a scion of House Pogona. They could have given it to him as a favor. They didn't have to know what he was going to use it for."

"You can't be trying to tell me Kanivoon Taipan didn't have a reason to fuck us over."

"I'm telling you the only person you've connected to the making of this knife is Arhoon Pogona."

Zaya caught herself about to white-knuckle the handle of the knife. She ground her fist into the surface of the table instead. "Arhoon died saving lives he didn't have to save. He was far enough ahead to get out of the Shadowrun—he probably would have won—"

"I'm not talking about whether Kanivoon Taipan and Shanhoon Krait are better people than Arhoon," said Yyrreen. "And maybe I shouldn't care if you want to use them as a scapegoat for Arhoon. But I think it matters whether you're going after Taipan and Krait because they're bastards and you hate them, or because you really have good evidence that they killed Kiriki."

"I saw Shanhoon Krait kill a man and a dragon with my own eyes. He sent cops to ambush me and Vani in Rust Precinct after the first time I beat him. He got the 'stream to outlaw psionics so they'd pay his company for dampers—"

"All things we're supposedly not talking about." There was no sign of yielding in Yyrreen's new green eyes.

"Fine," Zaya said. "What do you think we should do?"

"We?"

"She was your family too. Don't you care if she was murdered?"

"That's not fair," said Yyrreen.

"Fine. You care. So? What?"

"Normally I'd say, if there's new evidence that she might have been murdered, we should go to the police."

Zaya sighed and rocked back in her chair. "Fine. What's the next best thing?"

"Do the investigation for them."

"What if they don't buy it?"

"Then you can feel good about taking the law into your own hands, if that's what you decide to do."

Zaya leaned back in the chair, laced her fingers under her breasts, and nodded.

"And you can start," Yyrreen said, "after the election."

"Always with the jokes, you," said Zaya, because she was trying to repair this relationship and *you can curl up in a latrine and drown* didn't seem conducive.

"Zaya. Look. We've spent months trying to make this election about one simple thing: Legal yliaster is good, actually. That's the level on which public persuasion functions. You take one idea and you say it's good or bad. What I'm hearing from you is that ver-aamaka navo, our most charismatic mascot for 'yliaster is good,' is now trying to throw in a soupçon of 'yliaster is *also* bad,' because bad rich people use it to do bad things."

"Which is *true*—"

"You're about to tell me that people don't think like that, that they can tolerate nuance or whatever, and yes, sure, sometimes, when you talk to them *one at a time*. But you can't. You have to talk to them all at once. If we're taking them on an intellectual journey, it has to be as short as possible, with no weird bends in the road—and you are adding a *detour* to a *scenic overlook*—"

"I love talking about how we can't trust the people whose votes we're asking for," said Zaya, "but what I'm talking about is going after the people who murdered my wife."

Yyrreen pointed her index finger at Zaya. "One, you still don't know that anyone who killed Kiriki is still alive." She added her middle finger. "Two, you don't know if you can prove anybody did it, much less who." Her ring finger. "Three, you're never going to bring Kiriki back. But if you can get revenge out of your head for just a few more weeks and keep winning races, you might save Jaliki."

You don't believe I will. Zaya examined Yyrreen's face, because that felt like what you did when you had a thought like that, but really it just let her focus on what Yyrreen must be thinking. If she thought they needed to hide simple truths to win, she didn't really think they could win. She liked the fight, she liked the influence, she liked the feeling of progress.

And maybe it was progress. But progress wasn't enough. They would win, or they would lose; Jaliki would live, or he would die.

Zaya looked down at the table and nodded slowly, as if she were swallowing the bitter pill of Yyrreen's wisdom. Close enough.

Yyrreen reached across the table and put a hand over Zaya's. "We'll do it," she said. "We will. We'll figure out who gave her that thing, and why, and if the courts won't give us justice then we'll find it somewhere else. We will. But right now, we've gotta rescue Jenishoon Terrapin before Cerminir tries to get him to go drink for drink with her."

Zaya looked to the side and smiled, small and rueful, like you did when you were giving in. Yyrreen meant it, now. Zaya squeezed her hand, and met her eyes for just a moment, and those eyes were green.

Chapter 14

"Bees are charismatic," Cerminir said. She tossed back a shot of arrack. "Bright colors, poisoned weapons, top-down command structure, obsessed with building things and hoarding gold. Not," she said, raising her glass in an unasked-for concession, "literal gold. But a valuable golden substance. There's a psychographic *type*, Jenishoon, that really identifies with bees. And that type? Is a fascist."

Jenishoon Terrapin sat on the sofa, holding a not-much-sipped mug of light gold lager and nodding along with Cerminir, who was standing and pacing with a glass in hand. Taavi and Jaliki sat cattycorner to Terrapin, reading; a blanket covered Jaliki's injuries, and the ker was curled up at his feet. Minshoon was in the kitchen, toiling grimly over potatoes that had boiled too soon and a chicken that wasn't roasting fast enough. Kirono was with him, chopping like a man getting paid by the diced carrot. Yyrreen, who'd just stepped in with Zaya, took a breath and raised a finger to interrupt; but Cerminir was off and running:

"Pageantry, violence, monuments, *geometry*. What's a hexagon but the architectural version of that bundle of sticks they like? We do all this myth-making, Jenishoon, about how bees are useful because they're busy. They're organized, they're out there all day with their semaphore and their thirst for the blood of their enemies. What, by comparison, is a moth?"

She let the silence swell until it was clear she would not answer her own question. "A... pyromaniac?" Jenishoon Terrapin ventured.

"Maybe. Maybe." Cerminir poured herself some arrack, then stared meditatively into the shot glass, as though it held some cryptic summary of the future. "Who knows what a moth would do if those six legs could bear the weight of a burning brand? If those papery wings could stand the heat? Not I. The minds of insects are a closed book to me, Jenishoon. But we can agree, can't we, that in comparison to the clockwork-like operations of these fascists we call bees, a moth is no more than a drunken vagrant? Stumbling from bloom to bloom, instantly obsessed with far-off light no matter the danger to its person. Or moth... son. Incapable of self-defense or even outrunning anything—to say nothing of securing territory, holy shit, can you even imagine? Nothing but tufts and suboptimal wings hanging off a six-legged death wish."

"Thorax," said Jaliki. "The legs are on the thorax."

"But the flowers don't care," Cerminir said, as if she hadn't heard. "No, more than that. The flowers *insist*. Not all of them, oh no. Some flowers love to be stomped on by fascists, to get fucked by heavily armed infantrymen slaving away to enrich their authoritarian governments. No accounting for perversions. But then there are the ones that open up in moonlight." She held her fingertips together in front of her, then slowly allowed them to blossom, like a sped-up opening of a flower or a slowed-down explosion. "Whose colors only stand out in the dark. Who only put out for the vagrants in their funny outfits, the defenseless ones who chase the light at any cost." Her eyes were far away and brimming. "No matter what they do, Jenishoon, those bee fascists will never produce a grain of yliaster. Not on their own. You need the moths as well. The unification of disparate principles, the furious spite-fucking of fascism and anarchy—"

"Cerminir!" said Yyrreen, with a shrill edge of false cheer just sharp enough to cut into Cerminir's declamation.

Cerminir looked up, finally, to see Zaya and Yyrreen, flanked by Amiko and Chashu. "So, as I was saying," she said, her voice growing deep and resolute, "you should stick by these women and give them all…" She squinted slightly at Jenishoon, trying to bring him into focus. "Whatever it is you might have been thinking about not giving them. There's an election on, you know."

"I'm a candidate," said Jenishoon Terrapin.

Cerminir's eyes widened and a giggle leapt from her mouth, which she promptly covered. "Good luck with that!"

Yyrreen took a seat by Terrapin, sitting on the edge of the couch beside him so she could interpose herself just the slightest bit between the candidate and Cerminir. "I'm sorry we're late, Terrapin-cha. Hopefully our friend's lecture about pollinators was informative."

"I didn't like it," Amiko said quietly, putting a protective hand on the pouch by her side.

"I can't sell 'the furious spite-fucking of fascism and anarchy' in Cobalt Precinct," said Terrapin.

"I think Cerminir was attempting an evocative description of the alchemical principles underlying the properties of yliaster," said Yyrreen. "For your consideration as an alderwight casting votes on these matters, not really as a public relations strategy."

"I also can't sell accepting prize money from an illegal sport and promising to enable amateur demon summoners."

"If that's how you talk about it, you're definitely going to lose," Yyrreen said.

Terrapin flinched as if she'd sunk a fork in his thigh; Zaya tried not to chuckle. "This cop they have running against me, that's how he talks about it. I can't stop him."

"Have you tried asking nicely?" Chashu said under his breath. Zaya glanced at him and grinned; he met her eyes. "That's how you win your races, right?"

"—the frame," Yyrreen was saying when Zaya started paying attention again. "They're fear-mongering. They care more about the tiny possibility that a cop might lose their life than about the certainty that the hunted people in your district will. Almost everyone who might vote for you knows someone who'll benefit from this."

"I say that," Terrapin objected. "He's got all the parents convinced that someone's going to summon a demon in their living room if this passes. He has this one mother, she and her ugly little baby come up on the stage—and the baby's ker trots up after them. Every time, she break into tears and talks about how she'd rather lose the baby to the ker in a few years than a demon in the streets tomorrow. How am I supposed to compete with a circus act like that?"

"Terrapin-cha," Yyrreen said carefully, "you have to know that's not a real ker."

"The things I know would fill a thimble," said Terrapin. "I can't go call bullshit on this weeping mother, they'll roast me on a spit in the street."

"Shoot the monkey," Zaya said.

"VERaMAKa NAvoh," said Terrapin, getting the stresses all wrong. "It's a pleasure. What am I going to get out of shooting this poor defenseless baboon? The crowds already bring rotten durian to throw at it, it's the most hated creature in the Blues—"

Zaya grabbed Chashu's knife from its sheath and told herself she didn't enjoy it when Terrapin flinched. She took it over to Jaliki's ker, who was curled up on the floor not far from Terrapin's feet. It looked up at her with three wide, liquid eyes, and its cilia all oriented to her like a classroom of little blue snakes.

She brought the knife down with a swift overhand strike, aiming the heavy blade's point for the spot where its skull joined its spine.

What if it's this easy? she thought, in the moment between letting the blade fall and feeling the impact. She'd cut apart lamb legs at their joints—not with quite this passion, but the mechanics must be the same. Dig the point into a fissure, a quick twitch side to side to make sure she'd really found the joining of bones rather than just nicked one, then one strong thrust to part them. A lamb leg didn't have light in its eyes to watch as it faded, but that was fine. As an everyday experience, for an innocent animal, you wouldn't want that. But here, just once, she could look forward to it.

No such luck. The ker disappeared without so much as meeting her eyes, reappearing by Jenishoon Terrapin's feet curled up with its nose under its tail. She pulled the knife back up short of the floor.

"Mom," Jaliki sighed.

Zaya straightened up and flipped the knife in her hand, reaching over Jenishoon Terrapin to hand it back to Chashu pommel first. She looked down at Terrapin. "If we could just kill them," she said, "they'd all be dead already. Shoot the monkey, you'll prove it's a fraud." She didn't add *dumbshit*, which she thought was praiseworthy restraint.

"It's dangerous," Terrapin snapped. "That baboon is always near the baby. I'm not putting a baby at risk for some stunt."

"You're a grown adult," said Zaya. "I'm not going to stand here listing ways to kill a monkey." They queued up in her mind anyway: Shozo, wrapping his chain-whip around its neck from the front row; Amiko paralyzing it with her mind while Chashu got up on stage and filleted it like a fishmonger; Zaya herself sending a hungry Merlin Wyrm to flame it in the face and eat it while it kicked. "But the next time I'm flying in a tight pack of enormous fire-breathing animals trying to win money to give to politicians, I'll think really hard about what's worth risking for *some stunt*."

"Feel free to quit burning the faces off students before you talk to me about *risking* anything," said Terrapin.

Black anger burned up her throat into her mouth—and sorrow with it, a little, at the fact that she knew she wasn't going to hit him. He was seated, and old, and slow; she could make it count. But her self-control was just a little too good.

Not perfect, though.

"I see through your *bit*, Terrapin-cha." The word *bit* flashed and rang—she'd used that voice she used when the kids were in trouble, the one just low and loud enough to echo in a small room—and everyone's eyes turned toward her. "You can't outflank this fraud cop on the merits, you can't compete with his circus act, you can't shoot a monkey, you can't take money from Zaya Shearwater."

"Zaya," said Yyrreen.

"You want people to beg you for help so you can say no. And the only reason you occasionally say yes is if you never did, they'd stop begging. No wonder you're getting lapped by some last-minute candidate and the world's worst one-act play. Nut up and shoot the monkey, Jenishoon!"

The silence didn't linger long; Terrapin spat a laugh. "Truly, spoken like the hero of Lilac Precinct," he said, and stood. "Murder the monkey yourself if you like. And keep your money."

He stalked toward the door. Chashu and Amiko parted to let him leave—but not quite enough; somehow, he managed to bounce off Chashu's shoulder before he got to the door.

When he left, Yyrreen stood, smoothing down the white dress with embroidered serpents in brick red and cerulean—a more Kayalim outfit than she usually wore, Zaya thought, although she as pretty sure she was thinking it to keep the hive of bees (*fascists!*) in her stomach from flying up out her mouth and into her brain. She felt like a kid in trouble, just waiting for a teacher to tell her she'd never be an empath if she couldn't pass a simple test.

When Yyrreen finally looked at her, it was almost a relief.

"The thing is, Zaya," she said evenly, "if we let him get scared off, he'll take others with him. They don't think he's a cowardly old man who can't handle a little pressure. They're going to look at him as a basically normal person who's doing his best to win an election."

Chashu laughed. "But you repeat yourself."

"I don't have time to repeat myself," said Yyrreen. "If I can't keep Jenishoon Terrapin from going wobbly on this one, I'm going to have to have three dozen separate conversations with other candidates so the 'movement' doesn't die before it's born."

"I'm sorry—" Zaya began, but they all knew she didn't mean it.

"You can stop there," Yyrreen said, getting up. "You have to take the allies you get, Zaya. You can't send people out the door just because they missed a question on some test they didn't know they were taking. You're supposed to be a hero of the common folk, not everyone's shittiest teacher."

The door slammed again, and Yyrreen, too, was gone.

***

They all thought Yyrreen might come back, with or without Jenishoon Terrapin; but she didn't, and she didn't, and eventually Eäril started getting whiny with hunger, and by that point no one felt good enough about the candidate returning to make her wait. So they passed out plates of chicken in chili sauce, and yogurt with apple and cucumber, and fried potatoes, because Jaliki wasn't supposed to move unless he had to and if Jaliki got to eat in the armchair, then Eäril was going to want to eat on the couch. Which was bullshit, but fuck it. The couch had seen worse; so much worse.

Zaya pulled a chair over by Jaliki and pestered him to eat and asked how the wound was doing. He said "good" every time she asked him, with only the barest hint of impatience at the third time, and it was always true and always beside the point. Ker bites always healed cleanly. They were extradimensional creatures; their microbiomes didn't support parasites that could live on human bodies.

But they always healed slowly, because the bite took more than meat and blood: It took a piece of ba, of vital energy, that would never grow back. Or maybe it would? Flesh did, up to a point. But it grew back scarred. Jaliki drifted off between bites, while Eäril was just asking for seconds, and after she checked his pulse and breathing Zaya set her own plate quietly on the floor and leaned her head on the back of the armchair so her forehead touched the back of his head and her nose was buried in his hair. She wept quietly for a while, grateful for the easy chatter around her, grateful that Jaliki's exhaustion was too deep to be broken by the shaking of her chest.

***

Zaya started awake at the sound of her name—Minshoon and Taavi were chatting over the washbasin. The twilight had deepened to full dark while she'd slept. "What are you saying about me behind my back?" she asked.

"If you'd really wanted to know, you wouldn't have asked?" said Taavi, tossing a quick grin over her shoulder to salve any accidental sting. The performance of it stole Zaya's breath for a moment—the just-rightness of her hooded eyes, her quirked mouth, the angle of her head. She was almost as old as Zaya had been when they'd taken her in, and surer in herself than Zaya had ever been, or at least had ever thought to seem. Six years had passed for all of them, but somehow Taavi had grown from barely older than Jaliki to barely younger than Zaya. Zaya squeezed Jaliki with the arm draped over the chair-back, resting on his chest; he stirred and smacked his lips but did not wake.

You will grow to be a man, Zaya thought fiercely to the boy whose mouth still moved like a baby when he slept, and Minshoon said "We're talking odds."

"You need to beat them and win?" said Taavi. "For the biggest upside when... you know?"

Zaya wanted to say it for her—but Jaliki was there, and it wasn't necessarily certain he was asleep. Which is probably why Taavi hadn't said it outright. So Zaya didn't. Instead she said "Accurate."

"So we need to find races where you're cheap?" said Taavi.

"Undervalued," said Minshoon. "Where you're more likely to bring it home than the market thinks."

"She can say cheap," Zaya said. She got up, resting her hand once on Jaliki's head, and uncorked a glass growler to pour a mug of warm beer. "You used 'cheap' the same way when I was racing before. I knew what you meant."

"'Cheap' was a synonym for 'survival' back then," said Minshoon. He took a quick, stock-taking look at Taavi, and Zaya imagined she saw some of the same amazement she'd just felt: How whole and perfect a woman she'd not at all suddenly become. "And I think I never really noticed how it sounded when some snot-nosed kid said it." He bumped Taavi lightly with his hip; she flicked dishwater in his face. He squeezed her around the shoulder and planted a kiss in her hair.

Zaya breathed in the yeasty scent of the beer, then took a sip. "So what's your analysis? I've been racing all summer. What are the markets missing?"

Taavi looked to Minshoon, who twitched his head in a "go for it" motion. "You've leaned hard on endurance races?" Taavi said. "The Annulus, Mend the Streets, the arc-en-ciel? And that maps to a difference between Bandit and your old wyrm that everyone knows about, so if anything you're kind of expensive there? But races with strong environmental factors haven't been good for you? Stone Forest, the Course Fabricant, Cold Point—"

"The Annulus has an environmental factor I'm famous for exploiting," Zaya said. "And I would have run away with Cold Point if not for the cops."

"The markets don't classify the Annulus as a race with strong environmental factors?" said Taavi. "And anyway, you didn't flame any exploding butterflies last time and you still won? There's some recognition of your near success in Cold Point, but it's still one of two races you didn't even complete, and you were with a more experienced empath than Vani—"

"OK," said Zaya. "I should know better than to question the geeks. Environmental factors."

She saw Taavi smile to herself a little bit at that. "And agility courses? To a lesser extent? Also anything involving retrieval? Between Cold Point and the Angels' Tribute the markets don't like you for that at all?"

"They're running Eleven Goats pretty soon."

"Meh?" Taavi shrugged a little as she dried a dish.

"You just said retrieval, child."

"It's all high-up stuff? No agility, no environment? And it's all about your map?" Eleven Goats was a challenge where tiny goat figurines were placed on top of the eleven highest points in Yemareir, three with a moon on them and eight with a star. The 'streamer with the most goats won, as long as they had at least one with a moon—which were usually placed the farthest apart from the starting line and from each other. You could try to rack up points on the star goats, gambling that you'd be able to pick up one of the outer three later; or you could focus on blocking the 'streamers who started with the inner eight by trying to collect the outer three first, and so on. "Anyway, no one gets good odds on that, it's too random? Yaulë won Eleven Goats once?"

"Our top three," said Minshoon, "are the Cascade Climb, the Narondo, and Bell the Cat."

Taavi glared at him. "I was getting there?"

"Now you're there."

"Bell the Cat," said Zaya. She looked into her beer at the bubbles rising to the surface and bursting: Perfect spheres, formed from nowhere, traveling through a calm amber sea and then... what? Rejoining the air their substance was made from. "You weren't kidding about looking for long odds. What makes you think I'm cheap on that course?"

"The usual strategy on Bell the Cat is for the leaders to stay together in a pack until they buzz the Department?" said Taavi. "Or to let some eager sucker take the lead and draw the chase?"

"You think I should be the sucker."

"That was the analysis at first?" said Taavi. "But it's priced in? The assumption is the Department will get tipped off if you sign up, they'll have their best pilots on duty when the race happens, and being in front won't help you much—actually, they'll probably have an ambush somewhere down-track just to really make sure that play won't work?"

"So what do you think makes me cheap in this race?"

A light grew in Taavi's eyes, and she began to explain.

***

Zaya didn't wake up screaming the night that Jenishoon Terrapin stormed out, but she knew if she went back to sleep, she would. She'd held the saddle-knife too long that day; not long enough to remember the nightmare that had sent her shooting out of bed, filmed with cold salt sweat and moaning as though she'd been stabbed in the stomach, but long enough that real sleep wouldn't come. She scribbled a note, left it on the kitchen table, and went out.

Amiko's words haunted Zaya on the ride to Saavero's: *Stop leaving Lilac Precinct. We're counting the hours.* She added a half hour going through alleys and side streets rather than down the main thoroughfares to Rust Precinct. Bandit was pleased and surprised to see her—although it probed with concern at the fatigue in her mind—and she took it on a quick loop over the bay before they landed. She nearly lost herself in the feel of the wind over its feathers, the pleasant burn in its shoulders, the subtle smell of fish from the water. She realized at some point that it was the saddle-knife: The same effect that left her mind open to the stray thought-fragments that seeded her nightmares also opened the floodgates of her empathy with Bandit. It was almost worth the lost sleep. If Kirono hadn't told her that repeated exposure carried the risk of all-devouring insanity, she might do it on purpose.

It was the first Zaya had seen the Cerulean Precinct garden since she'd gotten the letter saying it had been destroyed. It looked only half-wrecked; a few of the trellises were back up, and about half the fence was visibly repaired. Her tired heart swelled at the noticing. She'd assumed Cerulean Precinct had given up on it. There was one person standing guard, and she prepared all the effusive phrases for that person, who didn't have to be here, who might be risking their life if another gang came to finish the job.

Zaya landed and dismounted, and the phrases fell away. The guard was Kemreen.

"Hey," Kemreen said. "Pardon my knife."

She had, in fact, just gracefully re-sheathed a large, wickedly pointed knife. "I didn't even notice," Zaya said, truthfully. She'd been too surprised by Kemreen's presence at the yliaster garden to notice what she was doing.

"Bandit did," said Kemreen. "It looked like it was thinking seriously about whether to flame me."

If I was really thinking about it, Bandit said, *I would have asked.*

"It says it wasn't as serious as it looked," said Zaya. "How are you?"

"Can't sleep."

"Same. What brings you out here?"

"Same reason I can't sleep," said Kemreen. "I was going to tell you in the morning, actually."

"That sounds bad."

"Some police in some of the more heavily Kayalim districts are planning something," Kemreen said. "Apparently you had some run-in with Lieutenant Angonoka in Alabaster?"

"How do you people all know each other?"

"She's a gunner. Pretty young for a lieutenant, people think she'll be tapped by the city in a year or two. It doesn't matter. They don't like that Amiko threatened her and Shalineen Ora with bees. Not many people knew you guys could do that."

"It's pretty rare," said Zaya. "Amiko's the only person I know who can."

"You should go to the guys in Lilac," said Kemreen. "Talk to them. They like you. They'll keep anything bad from happening in their jurisdiction."

"I do that, it's just a matter of time until I'm detained somewhere awaiting trial."

"Not necessarily."

"Ashava te-Kaizo named me to the *Damask Free Press*. It's out there in black and white."

Kemreen's smile quirked again.

"You know something," said Zaya.

"The one thing Ashava te-Kaizo has consented to tell Amethyst Precinct police," said Kemreen, "is that she lied about you helping her. She told them she's never met you, that she was helped by a fellow Kayalim student who looks a little similar to you, and that she decided to go with the rumor that was spreading about you being the one who hurt her because it was drawing attention to the cause. No other student has named any other 'streamer or wyrm that they saw, either in the air or on the ground. That's why the police want to have a 'conversation.' They don't have anything other than that you won the arc-en-ciel area at about the time that people were hurt. And if they bring you in on that, they have to bring in the other 'streamers who placed high in that race."

Zaya chuckled. "And they don't want to bring in Shanhoon Krait."

"They do not." Kemreen delivered the news with a smile, but it quickly faded. "So they're not going to get much out of that conversation unless you give it to them. Now they know you won't, which is why they're planning something else. To send a message. I don't have any specifics, I don't hear enough. But I would be very careful about doing anything..."

"... at all," Zaya said.

"No. Just..."

Zaya waited.

"... just, if you leave Lilac Precinct and it's widely known where you're going to be..."

"I should hide in my house and sneak everywhere I go."

"Maybe?" Kemreen allowed. "For a bit? The election's in a few weeks."

"If the election doesn't go their way, I think they look for revenge."

"Maybe."

"Kemreen," said Zaya, "I don't know. Half of me says fuck these people, I refuse to hide. Half of me is appalled that I'm still walking around free after I did that to a girl's face, even if it was an accident. All of me is disgusted that the only reason I'm free is that the cops are scared of House Krait."

"The girl you hurt is smart enough to understand that you're worth more to her cause in the sky than you are scooping chunks out of a silver mine somewhere," Kemreen said. "Especially if you feel like you owe her one."

"Two. I burned her face *and* she didn't rat me out. I owe her two."

"Twice as useful, then. But not on a work crew. Talk to the guys in Lilac. Please."

"I'll think about it."

"Your *thoughts* won't do shit against Narioun Angonoka."

Zaya's ability to raise a single eyebrow on command was spotty, at best; but she managed.

"You know what I mean," Kemreen said. "I'm not insulting your spooky mind powers."

"Thank you."

The silence that followed was easy. Kemreen was good at quiet. When you had a body that could do anything, whatever you were doing was what you wanted to be doing; so there was no such thing as an awkward silence. Or at least that was how it always seemed to Zaya. Her thoughts strayed back to that body: the ridges of her triceps, the softness of her inner thighs, the crispness of the hair under Zaya's fingertips—

"Zaya?"

She managed not to jerk her head in surprise. "What?"

"Whatcha thinking?"

"Nothing."

"OK."

Zaya drew in a deep draught of cool, jasmine-scented night air.

"Only, I was just having some thoughts about myself that I don't usually have."

Shit. "Sorry. Spent too much time with the knife today."

Kemreen nodded; and, more than the memory of her body, that brought a pang to Zaya's throat. Yyvvoun didn't know about the knife yet. She'd have to explain to him what it could do. In the first few days she'd had the knife, Kemreen had held her through more screaming horrors than she cared to count.

"Awww," said Kemreen.

"*Dammit*. I'm really sorry."

"And how is your new gentleman friend?"

"Busy running for office. It's hard to find time. Which is fine, really."

"Yeah?"

"No," Zaya sighed. "He was there the night of Jaliki's attack. I haven't heard much from him since. I think... I mean, he understands what it's like to have a hunted person in your family." Zaya hadn't put it together until just now. "That's part of what I like about being with him. But I think maybe he's realizing that if he's close to me, he might have to go through it again."

In the quiet dark, some of Kemreen's thoughts slipped through, abetted by exposure to the prototype knife: *He's not a strong person. He's not what she needs. I could help her better. I can't help her better. Who am I to help her? I don't have money for yliaster, I can't kill a ker. I could be there for her. But she doesn't want a cop. Her people don't want a cop. Her people want demons in the streets! She doesn't need that to help Jaliki. Why doesn't she understand that?*

"I'm sorry," Kemreen said. "He should be there for you. You deserve that."

"Thank you," said Zaya. "I won't forget that you were here tonight, either."

She sat to lean back against Bandit's flank, let its breath rock her body back and forth. It didn't take long for the fatigue to catch up with her; her own breath fell in step with the wyrm's, their ribs expanding and contracting at the same pace. She thought about getting up, but even the thought of another nightmare couldn't overwhelm the sweetness of rest.

When the sun warmed her skin, Kemreen was gone. The nightmare hadn't come.

CHAPTER 15

THREE WEEKS BEFORE BELL THE CAT

"I DON'T KNOW ABOUT Bell the Cat," said Tjaroon.

They were in Viridian Precinct, in an open storefront separated from the street only by a row of tall, densely-leaved bushes in separate pots. Jaliki was in the back, getting a protective tattoo from one of what Tjaroon had represented was a stable of artists; Zaya and Tjaroon were chatting by the hedges, both nursing mugs of water that didn't do much to cool them on a day that felt like being wrapped in hot, wet wool. Shozo oiled his chain-whip and cast the odd glance out at the street through the potted bushes. The mandrill was watching Jaliki. The ker, for once, was nowhere to be seen.

"The Narondo, the Cascade Climb, fine," Tjaroon continued. "Bell the Cat is incredibly risky. If you get caught..." His eyes darted around the storefront, and he shrugged. "Zaya, I have cultivated a lot of interest in this play."

"Risk is part of this," said Zaya. "Nothing you're asking me to do is guaranteed."

"The thing is," said Tjaroon, "my odds-makers agree with you on the other two. They're not just herding to the market, they'll buy you for some races, including the Narondo and the Climb. But Bell the Cat never even came up. And since the market doesn't like your chances, I guess I don't either."

There's a story, Zaya thought, *where you and I fall in love.* He wasn't bad-looking, for a man; he dressed inconspicuously well, he was fit, and if his grooming leaned too hard on interesting facial hair, well, that was the kind of flaw that would get fixed in a story where they fell in love. Kiriki had liked to read those stories; and Zaya, who'd had a few frankly pretty hot experiences with women she'd hated, didn't think much about them one way or the other. She still didn't, because one of the things she'd slowly learned, when she was a widowed mother still shy of her twentieth birthday, was that realism wasn't fiction's highest calling. But it still made her skin crawl to sit across from the man who'd roped Vanako into running contraband for him, who'd extorted money from her family on pain of ruining their lives, and find herself appreciating his intelligence.

"So I just wanted to start off this rebuttal," she said, "by saying I have a lot of respect for the sheer grit and ingenuity that goes into exploiting desperate, sick, and poor people on the scale you've achieved."

"That's kind of you to say," Tjaroon said, raising his mug of lukewarm water in salute. "I couldn't have done it without your family's help."

"Good burn," Zaya said, to disguise the fact that it was a good burn. "If your odds-makers had talked about Bell the Cat, they would have mentioned two strategies. One: Go for broke, accept that the cops will be on your tail, try to win anyway. Two: Let a sucker go for broke and take the lead when they've flamed out. For Bell the Cat, that's where the market starts, and the question is what happens given the pool of streamers."

"OK," Tjaroon said, with the *I'm-getting-bored* edginess of a born middle manager.

"And the market will have ruled out sucker-takes-the-lead, on the theory that the police will hold out for me anyway. So it has me in front, with everyone else happy to let me be the sucker, and most of the uncertainty is around how long it'll take some cop to force me to disqualify myself."

"And you're about to tell me why those odds are wrong, or I'm going to wonder why we're talking about this. I'm not bribing the cops to go easy on you, by the way."

"Ugh, no." Zaya actually felt stupid that she hadn't thought of this; but she never would have asked him for it, so it didn't matter much. "But here's what I can do."

***

SHE EXPLAINED IT. TJAROON asked good questions. She had good answers. It was a conversation, she realized, like the ones she'd had with Minshoon, Yyrreen, Cerminir, and Kirono in the old 'stream days, when they had no money to do anything, but enough time to figure out how to win without money. Of course, the time wasn't worth as much when Cerminir couldn't think through the caul of hunger, or Yyrreen had half an eye on the door in case an ex came bursting in with a knife, or Minshoon was nursing ribs bruised and cracked by creditors for a bad bet he didn't yet have the reserves to shore up. But that was what made the back-and-forth so precious: the chance to ignore all those workaday pains and fears, to work alongside friends—family— to build something that just might take them away from all of it.

House Shearwater hadn't done that, of course. But there was so much it had done; and it, too, had been a long-shot plan once.

Tjaroon was on his feet, eyes scanning through the potted bushes.

***

"WHAT?" ZAYA SAID.

A Mrineen woman with a familiar face tattoo slipped into the shop. "Boss, we gotta go."

"Shit, really?" Tjaroon asked.

"Yeah."

"All right." He nodded to Zaya. "Just stay here, OK? No one's after you."

"Who specifically isn't after me?" she asked.

Tjaroon and his bodyguard turned to go without answering. She thought about bitching them out, then had a better idea, and reached into the mandrill's mind to flood it with curiosity—heavily spiced with food scents—about the street.

"Damn you—" said Tjaroon, but she turned away his mind's attempt to dislodge her own as easily as blocking a little kid's punch, and the mandrill thrust its head between two of the tall potted shrubs to see.

It caught the burnt-rubber scent first; Zaya noticed it in her own nostrils once the mandrill's more sensitive nose picked it up. Then it saw something push around the corner, out of a back alley—a smooth black surface, shot through with threads and motes of every color—

—and, inevitably, she snapped back into her own mind like a baby tooth jerked free from the gum. She caught her own reeling mass with a stutter-step and barely didn't fall.

When she had her balance back, Tjaroon, the bodyguard, and the mandrill were all gone.

Zaya turned to the tattoo artist, a young Ililuë woman with dark walnut-brown skin and fine geometric designs in some ivory pigment all up and down her arms. "How close are you?"

"What?"

"To done."

"You're kidding."

"I'll accept answers in minutes or seconds."

Jaliki twisted to look at her. "Mom—"

"This is your life we're talking about," Zaya said. "Tjaroon might be meatloaf the next time I see him. We need to finish this tattoo."

There was a circle of white all the way around the artist's eyes now. "We could *all*—"

"Minutes or seconds, please."

"Five."

"Minutes?"

The tattoo artist nodded.

"Do it. We'll keep you safe." She met Shozo's eyes; he snapped a length of the chain-whip straight between his hands with a satisfying *clank*.

"Mom!" said Jaliki, looking panicked.

"It's OK," said Zaya. "We're not going to jump out there and get its attention. I'm not actually planning to die."

"It's after him," the artist said. "This is the last place he was."

Zaya gave her best dagger stare and, before she could let her better instincts stop her, reached into the artist's old, deep brain and kindled a pulse of blood-freezing fear that crackled through her entire mind, so complete that she could only freeze wide-eyed and feel her heart knock on her ribs. When it passed, the artist bent down to work without another word. Jaliki shot Zaya a look that said he knew exactly what had happened.

When Zaya turned toward the street, the bushes separating them from the street were withering before her eyes.

Leaves melted into black sludge, then shriveled into dry twisted husks, then fell, exposing branches whose bark was flaking off into ashy scales. Behind the branches it was like staring into a night sky, with stars and comet-tails in every color and more besides. She heard the *clank* of Shozo's chain-whip.

The demon wasn't as big as the one under the Omari range, or even the one from Inundinir Square. Its shape was more primate; it walked on all its limbs, however many there were, and used the longer forelimbs to manipulate the environment. But its neck was longer than any gorilla or baboon, with no particular swelling or expansion at the end, and only that neck's sudden orientation toward Zaya gave any suggestion that it might contain the faculties of sensation you'd expect in a head.

Zaya reached out for an animal, any animal, to do anything at all; if she couldn't persuade one into a surprise attack, then even a surprising noise would help. Everything had fled the scene, except Shozo and her son and the innocent kid she'd bullied into staying.

"Ready when you are, boss," said Shozo.

"Hit it on my mark," she said. "But not before. It's after Tjaroon."

"Sounds like something Tjaroon would say to get us to sit still and buy him time while he runs," said Shozo.

Something about the demon's posture had changed. The neck leaned forward a bit; it wasn't focused on Zaya and Shozo any more. If anything, it was looking...

"If Tjaroon's behind us, I'm gonna be mad," said Shozo, and Zaya realized what it was looking for. It might have been told to kill Tjaroon, but it didn't want to kill Tjaroon. It wanted to kill the human that was holding its head underwater, keeping it from returning home.

And that human wasn't a goetist protected by a proper summoning circle. That human was an amateur hiding behind the concealment of yliaster.

The exact stuff that the tattoo artist was putting into her son's skin.

"No," said Zaya, "it's not us, please, this isn't what you think," as if the demon wasn't an abductee from a literal other reality; as though, if it did understand her, it wouldn't notice that her pleas sounded guilty as hell; and when it lumbered forward with one starry black shoulder and then the other, as though to shove its way between her and Shozo, she screamed "Mark!"

She lashed out with a frantic flare of psionics, doing her best to time the strike with Shozo's chain-whip—that was what Vani had done under the mountain, not enough to kill that demon but enough to repel it. This one was smaller. Did that mean it was weaker?

The question and everything else left her mind as it contacted the demon's—a shifting cloud of planes and angles that fractured the visual world into whirling shards and filled her mouth and nose with a cloud of coppery dust so cold it burned. The sensory assault lasted a fraction of a second, if that—she wasn't sure whether it was the demon that expelled her, or her own mind's will to self-preserve that sent it running—but if she couldn't understand the structure of a demon-mind, she could throw a pulse of entropy to destabilize it, and on the way out, that was what she did.

She didn't know if it impacted at the same time as Shozo's chain-whip, didn't know if precise timing mattered. But the air filled with the sound of a million locusts inside a tin-walled shed, and the demon staggered back, rearing up on its hindlimbs to escape the pain.

Then its forelimbs, freed from bearing its weight, split into a thousand tentacles and flowed like an army of mambas toward Zaya and Shozo.

She tried to dodge and counterstrike; but a few agile tentacles still tagged her in the calf, fouling the dodge, which in turn fouled the counterstrike, and her mind was forced out from the demon's again. She felt more tentacles find her; she heard the clatter of chain-links on the floorboards. The cold numb stinging of demon-flesh began to overwhelm her.

Then it came away, and that was worse, because she knew it meant the demon had switched targets. It had stepped between her and Shozo. Jaliki and the artist sat, transfixed. Zaya screamed some syllable through an already-raw throat and threw both body and mind at the thing as hard as she could.

Her weakened mind could barely even disturb the whirling geometry of the demon's, and her body bounced off its flesh as though off a polished marble tomb.

She wasn't sure how long she was on the shop floor before she could lever herself up and look with vision that could resolve objects to more than a smear of color. When she did, she saw a figure standing between Jaliki and the demon.

It was the ker.

Its hackles were raised like a dog's, it was growling with head low and teeth bared like a dog; and like no dog that had ever lived, the long blue cilia scattered through its fur had come to life, glowing and rearing up to orient toward the demon.

For its own part, the demon stood like sculpture. Zaya wanted to scream at Jaliki to run—but would that ruin the standoff? Who knew whether a demon could overpower a ker, which one held higher authority in the peerage of otherworldly predators? Someone did, probably Cerminir. All Zaya knew was her son's life was now a subject of negotiation between two things she couldn't touch, of which one wanted to exterminate him now and the other wanted to eat him later.

She almost closed her eyes and lay back down. But Jaliki was watching, so she hauled herself up to her feet.

"Mom! Behind you!" Jaliki shouted, and she turned in time to be bowled over again by another mass of smooth, hard, stinging flesh, moving with all the alien smoothness of the demon—which, she supposed, barely saving her skull from a shattering impact with the shop floor, she would now have to think of as the *first* demon.

The new demon was dark gray instead of black, a thicket of ciliate tentacles sprouting from a central mass, its flesh shot through with nebulas of color rather than stars and comets. It clung to the first demon and the tips of its cilia plunged into starry black flesh like fingertips into wet sand. Locusts sang in a tin shed. The first demon bucked and reared, then fell, and the two of them rolled through the pots of rotted bushes and into the street.

There was a reversal of some kind; the nebula demon disengaged, then began rolling away like the world's worst tumbleweed, the stars-and-comets demon loping behind in pursuit.

***

Zaya watched them leave, then watched the corner they'd turned for a minute until it felt like they wouldn't come back. She sat with Shozo, who was testing out pushing his torso up to sitting. "How are you feeling?"

"Like every one of Amiko's bees stung me at the same time, but for some reason my body's decided not to die."

"You don't sound happy about that," Zaya said.

"Give me five more minutes on this nice floor and I might be OK with it."

"I can probably help with some psionics, if you'll let me in."

Shozo shook his head. "You don't want to be in there."

The tattoo artist made something between a scoff and a puking noise.

"A lot you have to say about it," Shozo said, elbowing up off the ground, then visibly regretting it.

Zaya touched his shoulder. "Leave it alone, OK?"

Shozo left it alone. A minute or so later, after he'd managed to sit up, a pair of people with shaved heads and long coats inscribed with glowing runes shot over the street like kestrels on the wing. The air wailed with a buzzing roar; the world's colors reversed for a swift moment, then switched back. A minute after that, the smell of lemon and cordite wafted over on the wind.

Zaya walked over to Jaliki. "I didn't put the bandage on yet because I knew you'd want to see the work," the artist said. Zaya looked at it: A grid of dots and lines, adjacent to the first one, about the same size. In a couple of months he'd have a band of them wrapping around the meat of his forearm. The only difference she could see between new and old was the fading of the ink; the new was a deep purple-black, the old had faded to a charcoal grey. "Did it change at all?"

The artist pointed to two spots on the grid. "We'll close more lines each time we treat him," she said. "When the grid's complete, we'll start to fill in squares. He'll be an old man by then, though. Assuming someone doesn't get him eaten first." She started bandaging the tattoo.

"I'm sorry."

"You're not, and I don't care."

"I should have let you run. I put all four of us in danger."

The artist was looking more intensely at the bandage than she needed to. "This is a performance for your kid and your thug now that you've gotten what you wanted," she said with a singsongy lightness, "and I don't want to be a part of it."

Zaya knew there was nothing she could say, in that moment, that wouldn't make it worse. But she said "it's not," because it wasn't.

"Great," said the artist. "Let that heal for a day, keep it out of the sun for a week. It won't work as well if it scars. Don't ever come near me again."

Jaliki looked at the artist, hurt. She turned away from both of them and started cleaning up her station. He looked at Zaya. "It's her choice, my breath," she said, and helped him down from the chair.

The three of them stepped through the toppled pots of rotted bushes and into a street that seemed to be waking from a dream. Residents peered fearfully out of window to assess the damage; shopkeepers inspected signs and storefronts. The demons had left few marks: A patch of iridescent fluid in the middle of the road, two broken windows, a palm tree with a dot in thee trunk that looked like a rubber sole someone had tossed in a fire. The cordite-and-lemon smell grew stronger as they walked.

Jaliki looked up at Zaya; he'd noticed the smell as well and drawn the obvious conclusion. "Can we see?"

No, she wanted to say. *This is everything I've ever worked to keep you from. No child should ever have to see a scene like this. You should be doing nothing but eating shaved ice and reading Wing Windtwister today, not piling whatever trauma's over there on top of what you went through five minutes ago—watching your mother bully a poor innocent girl into risking her life for you, then watching death on legs take down that same mother not six feet away, and getting saved by an animal that only wants you alive to eat you later—*

"Yeah," she said. "We can go."

"Yeah?" said Shozo, with a careful glance at Zaya. "I don't know, buddy—demon carcasses smell pretty bad. Or so I hear."

"I don't care!" said Jaliki, and if he didn't actually come out and say *I'm not a little kid*, Zaya could hear it all the same.

"He's going to be reliant on yliaster for the rest of his life," Zaya said. "He should know what it can do."

***

IT WASN'T HARD TO find where the demons and the sorcerer's guild—whichever one it was—had faced each other down. Viridian Precinct police in green armbands blocked the street from both ends; between the two blockades, demon parts lay scattered. There were many smears and a few deep pools of the same iridescent liquid they'd seen outside the tattoo parlor. Sorcerers with long coats and shaved heads poked at the cremains with slim metal wands; a police officer sat on the curb with his arm around a shaking Ililuë woman. Two human-sized shapes lay under splotched shrouds, and a charred circular ridge marred the cobblestones, less like a crater than a ripple in a pond, flash-frozen. Or maybe, Zaya thought, it was still moving, but very slowly; in a day or a week it might hit the foundations of the buildings on the left side of the street, and then what would happen?

"They sent our demon back," Jaliki said, "but not the other one."

Zaya saw it too: The slate-grey flesh strewn in the street all had the novae-and-nebulae pattern. "I think you're right."

"I think that means they found the sorcerer who sent it and killed them," Jaliki continued.

Ah yes, this was the conversation she hadn't wanted to have.

Zaya sighed; Shozo gave her a knowing look she probably deserved but didn't need. "I don't know if they killed them," Zaya said. "They have other ways—"

"I wish they'd killed the other one too," Jaliki said. "That other demon didn't want to be here either. It just wanted to get back home. I don't think either of them wanted to hurt anyone."

Zaya put an arm across his back and pulled him to her. "They did, though," she made herself say. "They hurt me and Shozo, and they did worse." *Don't make me point at the dead bodies*, her craven heart whined.

"And I guess they might have killed us," said Jaliki. "If the ker hadn't saved us."

She'd feel the sting of that later, Zaya knew; kids wielded plain truth like playing blind tag with knives, no idea who they might hurt. She was still sore and half-numb from the hits she'd taken failing to save her son, and that would hurt worse later too. But, for now, she fell back on the miracle of breathing.

"The funny thing about that is that it did it even though I was getting a tattoo that would stop it from biting me," Jaliki continued. He looked up at Zaya. "What happens if I die before it can transform? Because I was thinking, maybe it saved us because it would die if I died. But then I thought, maybe if I die, it's free. Maybe it can take what it needs from my ba, or maybe it can start over with someone else. And if that's true, then it's funny that it saved me, because it would have been better for it if I died. I hope," he continued, as though all this were a monologue of facts about sharks, "it can grow when I die, and it doesn't have to start over. Because one day I will die. But when I die, I don't want it to hunt some other kid. I just want it to grow to its next stage and not hurt anybody else. I think that's fair. It has to wait until I die on my own, but then it can use whatever it needs from me. I think that would be fair."

Zaya looked for the ker, but of course it wasn't there.

"I don't think it would be fair, personally," she said, her voice hoarse. "But it would be OK."

"Yeah. It would be OK."

"OK."

She squeezed his hand; he squeezed back. The grieving woman broke into a burst of fresh wailing; the sorcerers conferred gravely over a quivering gobbet. Zaya let Jaliki decide when it was time to go.

***

ZAYA HAD COLLAPSED AS soon as she'd gotten home from Viridian Precinct. She wasn't sure how long the constellation of pain and numbness in her muscles had kept her from sleeping; but she'd felt unable to move in any case, or at least desperately in need of rest, even if sleep itself wouldn't come. When the sun woke her, though, she was still stiff but only barely sore. Whatever poisons the demons exuded couldn't long survive contact with this reality; or that seemed as good an explanation as any.

She opened her eyes to the violet petals of the irises on her balcony, winking in the dawn. *Why don't I see these more often*, she wondered—not for long; the answer was at hand. The angle was wrong from her side of the bed. She only saw them if she slept on Kiriki's.

When Kemreen slept over, it was usually on Kiriki's side. Yyvvoun hadn't been here yet, but the one time Thelendil had been here, he'd been on Kiriki's side. When the children came to her with night terrors, they came to Kiriki's side; and so did the occasional guests she'd taken home, when a conversation in a bar or a street festival or the locker room of the depot had felt worth taking past the words, to skin and sweat and the closeness that made move-ment a language of its own. They must all have cast their eyes out that window, in the light of dawn or midmorning or noon, to see the flowers Kiriki had left for Zaya.

There was a desk in the room, although Zaya mostly used it for clothes she'd wear again and books she'd read any day now; there was paper, there was a wood-and-charcoal pencil and a heron's quill pen and a bottle of black ink, all in different places that she had to go digging for. The desk had a view of the irises. She watched them as she wrote, a hit of relief for her eyes between phrases.

It wasn't a long letter, but questions flowed in to stop the words from coming easily. What would Kemreen think about her quest to solve the mystery of the saddle-knife? Zaya hadn't mentioned it to her—she'd mentioned the strangeness of it, not long after Jenirain Gila had delivered the draft knife to her door, but she'd said no more and Kemreen hadn't asked. Could that be the answer? Kemreen didn't want to know. She'd had the opportunity to ask, and she hadn't.

That probably wasn't the answer.

She'd say she understood, if Zaya told her. But what else could you say? You're not allowed to tell someone they can't care about how their wife died. Not when the question's open, not when it could be murder. Even if that's how you really feel.

Then again, Kemreen never did go in for subtlety. Her forthrightness and self-assurance felt like an extension of her physical strength, all driven by the same engine of no-fucks-giving that was Kemreen at her core. Maybe she'd say it. "Zaya, I love you, but you need to live in the present, not the past. You need to leave the dead girl behind." Especially now that their own love had broken, she might say it.

Zaya didn't want to hear it.

All this daydreaming on what Kemreen might think, and she hadn't even thought about Yyvvoun. Maybe that was all she needed to know.

She signed the letter, folded it, sealed it, addressed it. It was a pretty morning, cool with the coming autumn; she'd take it to the post box on Vasha ze-Mekume Street and bring back some bread for breakfast.

When she got up, a shape caught her eye: A graceful arc of white among green iris-stems. She leaned across the desk to look more closely, then got out on the balcony so she could get her eyes right up to it.

It was an egg, about as long as her hand from wrist to the tip of her middle finger, lightly flecked with brown specks the size of ground black pepper.

She almost reached in to pluck it out. By the size of it, it must have been laid by a condor or a vulture; whenever the mother came back to brood, it would crumple the irises like drafts of a sonnet. And if the mother didn't come back, some egg-sucking monkey would, and the mess would be even worse.

But she let it be. The irises were a memory of Kiriki, one of her most precious. But this new life was worth something too. She could let it stay. And if the irises didn't survive, she could always plant again.

It felt like progress, thinking that way. She congratulated herself a little as she pulled on pants and shoes and padded carefully down the tenement stairs so as not to wake the neighbors: She could let go, if she chose.

Chapter 16

Two weeks before Bell the Cat

You who hear my voice may have heard the story of the Queen who Flooded the Garden, the storyteller said, wide-eyed, crouching down and passing a spread-fingered hand across the audience as if casting a spell, *but not the way I will tell it to you.*

"So corny?" said Taavi. "They always say this and it's never true?"

"How do you know it's not true?" said Jaliki.

Once upon a time, a girl lived with her mother and a pig that was always sick on a shitty little farm in a valley full of lush green plants whose names I know, but they'd sound like animal noises to you.

"OK," said Taavi, "they don't tell it like this in school?"

The girl hated her life sometimes, but only the parts she spent hungry or sore from digging or mashing potatoes or grinding corn, or when she got bitten by a snake and almost died, or when the pig threw up in the house. Which was a lot of the time, except for the snakebites, which only happened twice. But there was also a little river in the valley, with a low waterfall that poured into a deep pool so you could jump off the rocks, and sometimes the valley gave her pineapples and elderberries and bananas, which were best when she was alone because her mother wouldn't make her save some for later.

And sometimes they would go to the city for festivals and eat the feasts that the emperor gave, and they would stay in her mother's friend's house which was made of real stone that didn't leak when it rained, and had a bed, so that the pig wouldn't step on her at night. (They did bring the pig to the city.) And the girl's mother and her friend would drink mate in the morning, and the friend would ask why they didn't come back to live in the city, and the girl's mother would shake her head like it wasn't worth the effort to explain, and the girl would know better than to ask questions or offer to stay, because getting smacked so hard her teeth rattled wasn't going to get her any closer to an answer.

So that was the way the girl grew up, until it wasn't. Now, often, in these stories, you get the emperor's soldiers stomping through and demanding money from poor subsistence farmers like our heroines, but the fact is that the girl and her mother and the pig were so dirt poor that anything a soldier could take from them couldn't possibly pay the two days' salary for walking out there and back, and that's assuming nobody got bitten by a snake or thrown up on by the pig, which would cost extra. And for those of you out there thinking "there's one thing they could take," let me remind you there are children in the audience, and I've now forced their parents to explain what somebody could possibly mean by that. Shame on you.

"Wait," said Jaliki, "what does he mean?"

"When you're older," said Zaya.

One day, in the rainy season when the stream had grown to a river and the girl was digging rows in the earth to plant sweet manioc, she heard a chirpy voice that said "just tell the earth to move!"

"Must be my wishes talking in my head," the girl thought to herself, and she kept digging.

"Tell the earth to move!" the voice said again.

And the girl said, out loud this time, "The earth doesn't move just because I say so."

"It does for me," the voice said, and then: "Soil of the jungle, form rows for roots!" And before the girl's eyes, the earth furrowed into trenches. When she looked behind her, where the voice had come from, she saw the pink snout of a boto sink beneath the water of the river. Barely thinking

about it, she said "Mud of the river, give me that boto!" And damned if the riverbed didn't heave up and fling that dolphin up onto the river shore! But when the girl ran over to it, it wasn't a dolphin at all, but a young man perhaps a few years older than herself, strongly built and well padded, with a long nose and short arms and a head of curly hair that did nothing at all to hide the blowhole on the crown of his skull.

At this amazing transformation, a cry rang out—not from the girl, who was too shocked by all that had happened to do anything so ordinary as scream, but from her mother, who had emerged from the hut at the incredible noise the stream had made when it disgorged the boto-man. "His little boy," she said. "You must be his little boy."

And at this, our girl finally recovered enough to say, "What in the name of Heaven, Earth, the eight great rivers and the three cloud-piercing peaks is going on here?" And the young man lurched up out of the mud, and the girl's mother said, "It's time for me to talk about your father."

It was a long story, but I can tell it quickly. The girl's father was an irukaama; the same irukaama had fathered the young man. And the irukaama—

"What's an irukaama?" Jaliki whispered to Zaya.

"What's an irukaama?" yelled Cerminir.

"Oh," said the storyteller, placing a cupped hand to his ear, "someone in the audience not educated in the songs of our people? That's all right; you're here to learn, I'm here to teach—"

"*Mom*," Jaliki said, shocked. "That's *rude*."

"No it's not," said Cerminir.

"You interrupted!"

"Someone has to ask," said Zaya. "That's the tradition. These storytellers didn't use to have to explain these things, back when we lived in places where everyone knew the stories. Now they do—but it's better if someone who isn't Kayalim asks. Or a child."

While they whispered, the story had continued:

The irukaama are boto—that's river dolphins, honey, you don't have them here—who choose to leave the rivers of the place of our birth in human form, seeking love and meaning in the society of Kayalim men and women. Their home is a place without pain and without death, filled with magic that the irukaama sometimes bring out to the world to relieve the pain and death they find—or, if we're in a certain kind of story, to make it worse, whether they mean to or no. They love magic, they love music, they love the flaws and passions of their human cousins, and they love... well, since there are babies here, let's just leave it at they love babies, or at least they love the play that makes them. But they're creatures of the river, and when you spend your life in moving water you sometimes don't know what it means to stay.

Where was I?

"'It's time for me to talk about your father,'" called Jaliki.

Ah, yes. The irukaama—the young man from the river was also an irukaama—and the girl and the mother sat down in the shitty little cottage along with the pig, and the mother began to speak, and like I said before someone *made me explain—here he wagged a finger at Cerminir, who responded with a gaze of serene defiance—it's not a long story. The irukaama who'd fathered the girl had spoken of another child, fathered on a woman of his own kind, born and raised in the rivers. He'd spoken with love and longing of watching the child take his first breath, and his first suck, and lurch about in the water for the first time... but when the girl's mother had asked where the child was* now, *and the irukaama had shrugged, she had known that she would be raising her girl alone. And she had moved to the valley to do it, in a cottage far from the waterline so it would not be swept away by the floods, so her child could live by the water and perhaps catch a glimpse of her father one day.*

And then the irukaama spoke, and his part was just as simple. His father had spoken from time to time of the human woman whose company he had most enjoyed, who had lived in the great city a day's walk from a certain bend in a stream that flooded into a river when the rains were high.

And when all was said, the lover and the son abandoned by the same man embraced with sobs of joy, and the girl waited patiently while they did. And when they were done, she pointed at her brother and said the same thing so many of you have been patiently waiting to say: "So what about the magic?"

And the irukaama who was her brother gave her a grin full of little fish-catching teeth and said, "Take me to the city and I'll show you."

So they went, and in the nights she danced with men and he danced with men because it was summer and there was always dancing to be found, and in the days he showed her how to coax earth and cajole water and importune wind, although this last was not a talent much used by river creatures and he knew it mostly in theory. And after a few days, when his skin looked dry and his legs began to pain him, the girl knew it was time before he said it: "I must get back to the river before the waters recede and I am stranded—

The argument had been rising at the edge of Zaya's hearing for a minute or two, but words began to slice through the story, hurled as hammerblows by a man who meant to wound and was learning, as he hurled them, that words wouldn't do the damage he was seeking: "—*you* or any other *cop* can tell me who I can *talk* to—"

"Get up," she whispered to Cerminir, "find the alley off of Kaizo Street with the smashed gargoyle waterspout and *stay there*—" And she was on her feet, flying toward the sound, thinking only of speed, speed and dark shapes like holes in the world grinding people into paste between teeth adapted for the horrors of some other home. Too fast, she saw; the cop's partner clocked her coming, reached for something at her belt, and Zaya slowed and spread her hands. Then the other two turned toward her, the cop in the argument and the Kayalim man who'd started shouting. The story was still going. The shouting man's hands looked strange, almost dirty. Not dirty; they were covered in a tracery of dots and lines, combining in the aggregate so that changes in their density seemed to form some kind of contour. He looked long and dumbly at Zaya, then up at the cop. "What do you want me to do?"

The two cops locked eyes for a moment.

"You meat-gob idiot," said the one close to him, and he drew and gutted the man with the yliaster tattoos while the other called "Goety! Secure the area!" and then, in the stretching second while the Kayalim man collapsed, the cop with the bloody sword moved on Zaya.

She'd seen it coming; her mind *reached* for minds to enlist help, but the crow wasn't fast enough and the bushpig wasn't brave enough and the monkey was smart enough to understand what it meant when a human cut another human down like a sunflower in the street and wasn't having it—

Shozo hit the cop coming toward Zaya like a bull rhino; the other one keened as bees went for her eyes. There weren't that many, Zaya knew, but two bugs on anyone's face feels like a million, and Amiko had more than two to throw. A thought formed in some back-brain eddy: *Guess Angonoka's message didn't get through.* The crow and the bushpig and the monkey weren't going to save Zaya today. She dropped the connections to them and came back to her body.

The shouts and screams soaked her; she staggered; Shozo lashed once more with the chain-whip and stepped back from the prone cop, whose sword was gone. Shozo's face was the purple-pink of rare beef—he looked like he'd slept all day in the sun—and there were fine dark dots on his face and shoulders, and a dark stain spreading from one bicep. He moved a hand to his ribs and winced.

"Get out of here," Zaya said; but he shook his head, and then the other cop wiped the bees away from her face and ripped a sword from the sheath at her hip.

The air between her and Shozo froze, a gulf of cool and calm in the roil of the crowd. Her face was swollen with stings, but she didn't seem to feel them any more. Amiko cursed and then there was a cloud of bees all over the cop, but she just kept wiping her face and stepped toward Shozo. They didn't even need beekeeper outfits, Zaya realized. Their augmentations were enough. Zaya *reached* for the cop's mind and found nothing, which would be a good joke if they all lived. Silver glinted from the cop's chest from a familiar amulet. She was wearing a psionic damper, the kind they'd made Zaya wear to race not long ago. Had it ever occurred to her that a damper could stop psionics from coming *in* as well as going *out*?

She *reached* for Shozo and tied off the pain in his arm and torso.

"Thanks," he said out loud, not looking at her. "Now go."

Amiko couldn't spare more attention than a pained look at Zaya, but it said the same thing.

Then the cloud of bees all pulsed at once, and Shozo's eyes looked behind her, and she felt a hard hand on her shoulder.

No, she said inside, even though she'd been about to refuse to run from death. *Not yet.*

But when she looked up, it was Kemreen, a wicked knife already out in her other hand.

"All of you had better get out of here," she said, stepping around Zaya and interposing herself between Shozo and the swollen-faced cop with the sword. "Even you," she said easily to the cop. "It doesn't have to be this way."

The other cop sized Kemreen up. Her sting-swollen face soured and she stepped back. Zaya put a hand on Shozo's shoulder and hustled him away as fast as he could move. They put their left shoulders against the plate-glass window of a bakery and crept along the wall toward Kaizo Street.

Police with clubs and chains reaped pain around them.

When they made it to the alley, Zaya counted: Cerminir, Kirono, Taavi, Gilthiniel, Vanako, Jaliki, Enwë, the fucking ker. One too many, three too few. "Eäril bolted after you," said Kirono, seeing what she was doing. "Minshoon and Yyrreen are out there looking for her. What happened to Shozo?"

"Forget that," said Shozo. He turned around. "We need to find Eäril."

"What you need," said Zaya, "is to lie low and leave town. Any cop who saw what you did will kill you out there. Vani and I can go."

"They saw you too," said Shozo. "And they have dampers."

Shit. He was right. "You lucked out when you took the one down," said Zaya. "Now you're hurt. They will kill you."

Shozo drew a breath to reply, then reeled and steadied himself with a hand on the alley wall. He spluttered some wet noise, then let himself fold in until he was sitting, leaning on the bricks. "My legs just gave out," he snarled. Amiko and Vanako knelt by him, joining Zaya in his mind, and Amiko's voice sliced into Zaya's skull, peppery and bitter: *Let Vani help find your girl. She wasn't a witness, they don't know her.*

Vanako shot a glance at Zaya, questioning. *Did you—*

Of course I did. Let her go before he figures it out.

Zaya nodded at Vanako and she ran out of the alley, not looking back. Cerminir and Kirono shouted and leapt up to follow; Zaya blocked their way. "I told her she could go," Zaya said. "She's an empath. Even if the cops have dampers, she can still find Eäril."

"She's a kid," said Kirono.

Cerminir looked unwell, but she shook her head. "No she's not."

Kirono held Zaya's eyes for a second, turned, and hit the alley wall once with the heel of his hand, exhaling some breath that would have been a curse if the kids weren't around. His shoulders trembled. Cerminir reached out a hand. He took it and squeezed;

then, without a word and never letting go, stepped over to her, leaning his forehead on her upper arm. His face was crumpled, as if in pain. Zaya had to look away.

Amiko had already taken a position at the far end of the alley; Zaya took the Kaizo Street end. She felt a tentative presence at her elbow, and Jaliki's hand crept into hers, moist with heat or fear. She held it for a moment, firm but not too tight.

"What's going on?" Jaliki asked.

"It'll be OK, Jali," said Gilthiniel. "Cops just getting crazy, like they do sometimes."

Zaya turned to look at him, taking him in. Gilthiniel had been older than Jaliki was now when he and Taavi joined the family. Thinner, too; she'd forgotten how thin a kid could get if they weren't being fed. Their mother had come to Yemareir to study from an Ililuë amalgam to the south, but Taavi and Gilthiniel had come, the father had gone, and the mother had ended up on the dole. She'd chosen life on the street rather than the dole-flats, scavenging rather than the refectories, and her children over her own health; they ate when she did not. Which was part, though surely not all, of why she didn't last.

He was too old to be the son of Zaya's body, but she summoned him with an open arm, and when he came, she drew him to her and kissed his forehead like a baby's. "No point in lying to your brother," she said. "This is about yliaster. They wanted to show it's dangerous, they gulled some poor fool into pretending he was summoning a demon so they could bust our heads and be big heroes." No point in lying; but no point, too, in dwelling on that poor fool's fate. "They're not crazy. They know what they're doing."

"Fuck," said Gilthiniel.

"Language," Zaya said automatically.

If they'd been in the house, there'd have been a shitty, disproportionate teenage retort and probably a fight. As it was, Gilthiniel just laughed quietly through a close-mouthed smile. "If they want to teach us a lesson, might as well summon an actual demon."

Kirono shook his head. "Demons aren't what they want us to be afraid of."

The night was warm, but Taavi was crossing her arms across her body, gripping her own shoulders. "It's too bad? I wanted to know how the story ends?"

"There's not much more to it," said Zaya. "With the irukaama's magic, the girl starts growing enough food to start selling it in the city. She can finally buy medicine for the pig. Then a couple of soldiers come from the city and tell her she needs to pay a tax. She does, but it goes up, and eventually she has to stop the valley from flooding so she can grow enough to pay."

"But then she can't see her brother," Jaliki said quietly.

"That's right. The irukaama can only come when the valley's flooded. But the girl has herself and her mom and her pig to protect. This goes on for years, until her mom dies. She asks for a break on the tax, so she can flood the valley and let the irukaama come in to say goodbye—that's not what she tells the soldiers, she says to pay for a funeral, but really that's why. And the soldiers laugh in her face and say her mom doesn't deserve a funeral, and then they kill the pig."

Jaliki squeezed Zaya's arm. It brought her back to the scene. This really wasn't the story for the moment, not when they themselves were one wrong move away from getting killed like pigs by armed people no kinder or more merciful than the soldiers in the story. She should have pivoted to Wing Windtwister.

"What happens next?" Jaliki asked softly.

"She calls the water and drowns them," Kirono said flatly. "Then the irukaama comes. He offers to stay, help defend her against the army if they come again, but she says no. And they go to seek their fortune in the sea."

"Huh," said Taavi.

"What?"

"The title says she's a queen?"

"She is," said Kirono.

The shouts and screams had died down, but smoke was on the wind. Minshoon turned the corner, Eäril in his arms; Kemreen and Yyrreen were close behind.

Eäril wasn't obviously harmed, but she clung to Minshoon like a tick. For his part, he seemed windburned, distant; he staggered a bit under her weight. There was a stipple of blood on both of them. Zaya walked up to him, put her hand on Eäril's back. "Hey, baby girl," she said. "Everyone's OK. Me, Papa Kirono, Mama Cerminir, Taavi, Gil, Vani, Jaliki. We're all here."

Eäril shook her head and burrowed farther into Minshoon's shoulder.

"Come on," said Kemreen. "Not healthy for anyone to be too close to this."

"Are we just leaving?" said Gilthiniel.

"You want to stay?" Kemreen asked.

Gilthiniel's jaw set. "That square's full of Mrineen cops cracking Kayalim heads. I'm not getting hustled away from it by a Mrineen cop."

"No," said Zaya. "You're getting hustled away by your mother."

"You can't let her push you—"

"No, but *you'd* better let *me* push *you.*"

"Veraamaka navo," he said. "What a load of horseshit."

Kirono stepped up to Gilthiniel. He was shorter and broader than the boy; there was no new force or authority in his manner; but when he spoke, something in the softness of his voice demanded attention. "Talk when we're safe," he said. "Until then, quiet."

They left the alley, Shozo picking up the rear in case anyone came after them from the square. Zaya kept her hand on Eäril's back, hoping she might pry the little girl away from Minshoon if only she reminded her that she was there; but eventually Eäril swatted Zaya's hand away, and she did not put it back.

CHAPTER 17

A FEW DAYS BEFORE BELL THE CAT

"—YOU ABSOLUTELY CANNOT BURN until it's time. Understood?"

Cerminir's arms were circled around Enwë, guiding the baby's arms through the motions of cutting mango. Her brow was headed with sweat; her back was bowed. Zaya wasn't sure whether it was the knife skills lesson or the 'stream guidance that was making Cerminir's face contort into a scowl like you'd see on a hyena defending a carcass.

"I know, Cer."

"I mean absolutely seriously, you might not finish the race if you do."

"OK."

"You're mouth is saying 'OK,' but I feel like your mind isn't grasping what it really means."

"I don't think anyone actually knows what 'OK' really means," said Zaya. "O what? K what?"

Enwë slipped a mango-lubricated hand out from under Cerminir's, heedless of the knife, and *glomphed* a chunk of fruit into her mouth, laughed in triumph, and choked in the middle of the laugh. Cerminir made a strangled noise, dropped the knife with a clatter, and slapped Enwë on the back. Pulped mango *slorped* from Enwë's mouth, followed by a wet cough that peppered the cutting board and counter with a spray of mango shreds. She looked up at Cerminir in a moment of wide-eyed shock. Then the wailing began.

Zaya had reached the scene at this point, ready to help. "Baby or cutting board?"

"Mamaaaaaaa!" Enwë said, reaching for Zaya, and Cerminir moved her mouth silently in the shape of a string of curses and said "Baby."

So Zaya took an armful of sticky, keening baby, and Cerminir cut the mango and cleaned up. It didn't take more than a few good sobs for Enwë to lift her head and look over in curiosity at what was happening on the cutting board. "Mama hit," she said, turning her head to meet Zaya's eyes with a solemn stare.

"Mama wanted to make sure Enwë didn't choke on the mango," said Zaya. "So Enwë could breathe."

"Enwë breathe." She looked at Cerminir, then back at Zaya. "Bad word."

"Mama's in her feelings today," Zaya said. "I'm not sure why."

"Old Cheesefeet brewed that liquor just for us," said Cerminir, bringing the board full of cut mango to the table. "People can't drink it. If you screw this one up, he won't be able to sell it to 'streamers either."

"You want the baby to just eat off the board?"

"No baby!" yelled Enwë, pushing Zaya's cheek with a sticky hand.

"If no-baby wants to eat off a dish, no-baby can wash it," said Cerminir.

Zaya brought Enwë over and plopped her in a chair. Cerminir sectioned off about a third of the mango with the blade of her hand, then sprinkled the rest with chili, lime, and salt. She popped a chili-dusted chunk in her mouth while Enwë stuffed her cheeks with the unspiced mango. "You can have some," she said to Zaya with her mouth full. "But it has no-baby spit all over it."

"No-baby can have it," said Zaya, sitting to Enwë's other side. "Why do you care so much about Old Cheesefeet's business ventures anyway? Not that he hasn't helped us, just…" Zaya shrugged. "I didn't think you were close."

"We're not close," Cerminir said. "But, one, if this works, he'll do it for us again. I've been thinking about this for a while, there's a whole world of interesting possibilities with methanols, between the increased physical stress potentiating the somatoplasticity and a few weird genetic pathways that might be primed by the metabolites—"

"In dumb person language," said Zaya, "that sounds like we want to get Old Cheesefeet into the magic potion business."

"Telenór," said Cerminir, rolling her eyes. "Whatever. More importantly, he's connected to a kulustatina."

"What dat?" asked Enwë, showing everyone the yellow sludge on her tongue.

"*You* sound *just* like Mama Zaya!" Cerminir said, bugging her eyes at Enwë as she tickled the baby's belly. "It's a *mutual aid fund* where *everyone* kicks in a *share* and the *members* take turns *borrowing* to fund their *projects!*"

"What dat?" asked Enwë.

"I knew that," said Zaya, who had known it, sort of. "So, what, is there some special equipment he needs extra funds for? Or some ingredients?"

Cerminir was wiping off the yellow dots of mango that Enwë had spluttered on her face while laughing. "No."

Zaya waited a moment in case there was more coming. "So why is it important?"

Cerminir's eyes grew briefly distant in a way Zaya recognized; she was pulling back to get a wider view of the conversation. It was something she did when it had gone a way she didn't fully understand. When her focus returned, her face settled into her "patient teacher" expression. "Right now, Old Cheesefeet does most of his business in the community. Olive and Chartreuse and Celadon. If this works, now he's pulling sherds and plates from rich Mrineen 'streamers. Three flinders of every shard go into the fund. Before, he was just shuffling money around in the Greens. If this works, he's bringing new cash in. And spreading it out." She seemed to realize she was lecturing; she looked at Enwë and shrugged. "You know? It's good for their economy."

"Sure," Zaya said.

Cerminir seemed satisfied to take Zaya at her word, and grasped another chili-dusted mango chunk in her chopsticks.

"If I'm honest," Zaya said, "I had no idea you were doing any of that, and I feel a little shitty about it."

"Sorry?" said Cerminir. "I wasn't trying to keep it from you."

"No, not your fault," said Zaya. "I should have known, but I wasn't paying attention."

Cerminir shrugged and licked chili and mango juice off her fingers. "If it makes you feel any better," she said, "I kind of got the idea from you."

Zaya smiled. Cerminir was looking away, but that was fine. "Thanks, Cer."

The door banged open; Vanako and Jaliki lurched in. Jaliki's leg still wasn't fully healed, so he leaned on Vanako for support. "Letter, Mom," said Vanako, dumping Jaliki into an armchair. She brought it over to the table. "Don't touch it with mango hands, it's fancy. Did Ziyuki-kana invite you to the prom or what?"

"Ew," said Zaya, grabbing the letter. "And I don't have mango hands. Enwë slobbered all over that, I'm not touching it."

"Grmph," Vanako said around a mouthful of chili mango she'd just learned something about that she'd never wanted to know.

While Vanako went to rinse her mouth and Jaliki lobbed taunts from the armchair, Zaya looked at the envelope. It was sealed in black wax, with a knotwork pattern impressed; the knot was open-ended, with one end tapered to a point and the other a stylized snake head. Letters in Old Mlin circled the knot.

Cerminir leaned in to look. "Taipan or Krait?"

"Krait."

Chapter 18

The day before Bell the Cat

THE MEETING PLACE LOOKED like a building she'd once seen on shore leave in Herez, across the Little Strait; long, high-windowed halls, all tile and cut glass. It was a little too rich for Vermilion Precinct, so Zaya knew she'd come to the right place. The great double doors were locked and no one had answered to her knock or shout, so she sat on the stoop like a neighborhood aunt and tried to will the sweat from soaking through her shift. The mental effort probably didn't make her sweatier, but it felt like it.

She'd dressed more Kayalim than usual, wedding/funeral kind of stuff: fine linen dyed brightly in simple shapes separated by thick lines that resolved, when you looked hard enough, into the cruciform shape of a Dawn Wyrm viewed from below against a bright, cloud-studded sky. She'd had Papa Zinji do her hair to match—orange, pink, and purple, he'd said she didn't have enough length to work with blue as well—and she hadn't needed Kirono to tell her she looked amazing. So although it probably wasn't espionage or telepathy that had led Shanhoon Krait to leave her wilting in the heat like a cut rose in the road, it sure felt like one or the other.

He did show, of course. There's no point stranding someone you hate in the oven of a summer afternoon unless you get to see them after they've cooked a while. Krait was unarmed; his bodyguards, broad-shouldered and narrow-hipped, moved with the twitchy speed and ease she'd learned to associate with cops and other enhanciles. They had shining swords with two-handed grips slung in baldrics over their backs and broad-bladed knives on their belts. Zaya guessed they used the knives more often, if they used any of it. All three were dressed in black from the wide open collars of their loose-sleeved shirts to the gleaming toes of their knee-high boots, and if Zaya couldn't actually feel the cooling charm pouring off them like steam off a hot stone, that didn't mean it wasn't there.

One of the bodyguards tossed her a medallion. She knew its weight from its arc, the feel of its chain from the shape it made as it flew; it brought a wave of thought-deafness with it, the idle chatter of passing minds suddenly hushed. "Just a precaution," Krait said. "My people insisted. They've heard stories about what you can do with a stray bird or monkey if you put your mind to it."

"I count eight edges on four blades," said Zaya. "You're a foot taller than me each. And you're scared of my little brain?"

"I'm not stupid, Shearwater-cha."

"No," Zaya said, looping the chain over her head. "But you are a skinny little bitch."

She pressed her lips together to spit the *b* as hard as she could, let them bounce into a sneer as she said the rest. She saw it land. These Mrineen scions liked to fence with words; they weren't much for brawling. "Call it what you like," Krait said, as if he hadn't felt it, but he absolutely had.

Silence hung for a long moment. One of the bodyguards wiped a drop of sweat from his barely-gleaming brow, and Zaya suddenly felt the spreading damp patch between her shoulder blades. "You want to make your pitch?" she said. "I'm dying out here."

"I don't know."

Krait's frankness was weird. It sat ill on him, like a man's hat on a little boy. It was obviously an imitation of her own bitter forthrightness, but that didn't have to mean it was an act. Zaya decided to repay it, more or less.

"I mean, you know me well enough to know this is probably a waste of your time," she said. "I hate you. Maybe you like to think you don't hate me but, take it from me, you do. I'm campaigning against your cop friends and your shitty owner society that lets rich Mrineen hoard power and pretend to be nice by redistributing some of the crumbs, and *I've already turned down an offer to work for you.* Taking a job with you would go against every last scrap of what passes for my personality."

"I don't even know what you want," said Krait. "The answer to a question?" That's what she'd written, in the letter that had gained this invitation: *All I ask in exchange is the answer to a question that I can't set down here.* "If you believed anything I had to say, it'd be the first time since Candlegrass Stand."

"But you're here," said Zaya. "And we both know why. Because you know I'd be an incredible addition to your stupid company. Especially since you haven't replaced Zetaala te-Kaneva." *After you killed him so you wouldn't lose to him,* she thought so loudly she hoped even he could hear it. "And because your stupid company has access to yliaster, which is the only thing between my son and being eaten by a dog from another dimension. It attacked him again a week or so ago, he still can't walk on his own."

Krait closed his eyes, looked down, and shook his head. "Scathe and Ancalagon," he said, "let's not do this on the street." When he looked up, he had a key in his hand.

***

THE DOOR TO THE vermilion-tiled building opened with an echoing *clank*. The air that poured out was musty with newness—sawdust, tile dust, the earthy fug of grout and mortar. When Krait's bodyguards stepped forward to follow, he held a palm out to halt them.

"M. Shearwater hates me too much to murder me on a construction site," he said. "She has to defeat me in a way that validates her narrative arc, otherwise it doesn't count."

The bodyguard who'd tossed Zaya the damper shrugged off his baldric and held it out.

"Oh, come on," said Krait.

"Boss. She's armed."

Krait looked at Zaya's waist; the saddle-knife hung from her belt in a plain leather sheath. "Huh." He looked at her in some perplexity. "Were you actually planning to murder me on a construction site?"

She meant to say no, but it came out "I like to keep my options open."

The bodyguards gave her looks of profound disappointment.

Zaya held her hands up in conciliation. "No, I was not planning to skin your boss and wear him as a leotard. And if I was, congratulations! Now he's got a big metal chungus to beat me up with. *Thanks to you.*"

Krait sighed. "Just ditch the knife, please. If you would."

"You already leashed me with this damper. Plus you've got a foot and a half and fifty pounds on me, plus Lengthy Boi there. I'm not going in there damped *and* unarmed unless you leave the chungus behind."

It was going to be a pain if he agreed. But he wouldn't. Because he knew she might get the damper off in time to reach an animal of some kind with her mind; might, in fact, have arranged for just such a creature to be nearby; and, if she'd gone to that kind of trouble, he might find himself glad of Lengthy Boi the Chungus against, say, the mad rage of a chimpanzee or the sting of a Wyrmbane Wyvern; and he wasn't sure how good he felt, at all, now, about the fact that he'd kept her waiting in the heat, with time to prepare the site in ways no one but her, now, could possibly know. But, for all that, he wasn't going to do the smart thing and just bring the bodyguards in, because he knew or at least thought he knew how little they thought of him, in what contempt they held his carefully maintained slimness and his polished words, and he was damned if he'd give them one more reason to think him weak, especially not when that reason was the bullshit of some undersized Kayalim girl.

"Fine," said Krait, and entered, slinging the baldric over his back as he did so.

Zaya followed, waggling her fingers at the guards, then gently kicking the door closed behind her with her heel.

She should wear his skin, the swine.

He'd looked right at the saddle-knife, and he hadn't recognized the thing at all.

***

THE ENTRANCE OPENED INTO a tiled lobby with high-vaulted ceilings, girders soaring like steepled fingers. A massive desk rose from the floor at the back, dominating the room. Behind it, flanked by entrances to two broad, curving stairwells, was the same knotwork symbol from the seal on the letter inviting her to this meeting.

It wasn't the one on the knife. She'd known it wouldn't be; but the confirmation had stung anyway.

"You want a pitch?" Krait said. "Welcome to the new home of Taipan Invotechnic."

He was looking ahead as he said it, and he didn't look back, only waved with his head in the direction he was about to walk. The hall let light in through skylights two stories up; the second story was split by a mezzanine railed in wrought iron, the rails in the shape of twined serpents. The finely finished design around them faded into schematicity as the hallway progressed; the heavy doors windowed with wire-strengthened glass were unglazed and unpolished, the massive stone tiles gave way to subfloor. Zaya guessed she was not the first person who'd been ushered in to be dazzled by the work.

"You wouldn't work here, not at first," Krait said. "The space won't be physically ready for a year, and it may take longer before it's political for work on yliaster to happen in Vermilion Precinct. The public's going to need reassuring that we won't unleash a flood of demons in here."

"That's not on the business plan?"

"Not in the city limits."

Zaya laughed, politely she thought, and Krait turned to meet her eyes. He looked very serious. "Outside is another story. If we're able to ward the city walls, mass goety could have defensive applications. No one's going to want to invade a city surrounded by loose demons. Are you sure you have the belly for this, Shearwater-cha?"

"I'll worry about my belly. What else?"

"Theoretical metallurgy and alchemy," he said, gesturing at the offices. "Development and quality assurance across the way. Production will start there as well, then move to the facilities in back—even that won't be long-term if we grow the way we'd like, but it'll hold us for the first few years. Behavioral testing upstairs—that's you."

"Behavioral," Zaya said. "Does that include ker-warding?"

"You're paying attention," said Krait. "It will. Not at first, but not long."

"If I'm there, it starts on day one."

Krait's chest twitched with one of those short laughs that comes out *hm*. "Maybe," he said. "We're not set up for it."

"Come on, Krait."

"Kers are invulnerable teleporters," said Krait. "Not everyone in here will be willing to risk getting attacked by something like that. Translocation baffles will help, but with a ker or something else that spans other dimensions you run the risk of an unpredictable rotation." Krait looked up and did something with his eyebrows. "Which is potentially a good thing, if we can get it to rotate in a part of its surface that's vulnerable..."

"You think you can kill them?" Zaya said.

The too-loud words rang from the tile, hung from the girders. Krait smiled, that strange cramped little smile that Gilthiniel used to make when he'd done something unexpected and wonderful, like bake bread all on his own. "I should lead with the ifs and the qualifications," he said. "But yes. For the purposes of what we, in these dimensions, recognize as 'alive,' for the purpose of there not being an invincible animal hunting your kid any more? Yes."

Zaya imagined House Shearwater without the ker always in the corner of her eye. She imagined never worrying about missing an appointment for the next protective tattoo; she imagined Jaliki's two tattoos standing alone on his arm, imagined him growing tall and broad-shouldered without a spreading carpet of dots and lines colonizing his skin like a fungus.

Until a moment ago, a life's worth of warding tattoos had felt like an unattainable dream, the apex of perfection. Now it felt like another kind of death sentence.

Maybe the ker would die in this building. Would that be "development" or "production"? It seemed impossible they would dispose of such an exotic corpse like a common dog—but Krait had mentioned theoretical metallurgy and alchemy, not biology or physiology.

"I want to see it happen," she said, each word breaking into pieces in the tightness of her throat.

"I can't."

"Kill Jaliki's ker in front of me," she said, as if Krait hadn't spoken. Wasn't this how it was done, how heroes faced down gods and captains of industry ran roughshod over economics? Clarity of vision and force of will and cussedness down to the marrow of their deepest bones? "After that, anything. Name your bullshit, I'm not too good for it. But first, kill his ker."

There it was. She had offered him everything. And now he would smile sinuously and find a soft home in her belly for the knife—not the one on her belt, which she had almost forgotten, but the conditions, the ones that would make her howl and curse her name as they ripped her into pieces, the ones that would make her regret she'd ever offered all of herself to a man like this.

And that would be fine. Because the ker would be dead.

But he wasn't smiling like a snake would if it could, wasn't tasting the thought of shooting his venom into her bare heart. He was looking at her like a teacher who'd caught an error in her times tables that she was supposed to have studied away by now. "I can't," he said again. "The science isn't tested, it could take years to figure out—and the pieces of it we think we know are massively expensive. That's money we don't have."

"Don't even try. Your company literally has 'Taipan' in the name."

"Yes, it's called Taipan Invotechnic. Not Taipan Money Furnace. The whole point of this is to make enough money for the House that there's enough left over to fund the risky projects. If you want the risky part, you have to deliver the money part."

"They built you this!" Zaya flung her hand wildly to indicate... this. "There's money!"

"I know there's money. If a stranger on the street had asked you yesterday whether House Taipan would spend thousands of slabs out of the goodness of their hearts to save your little boy, what would you have said? All I'm telling you is that yesterday and today aren't as different as you seem to think they are."

"Holy shit," Zaya said, "are you right about that."

Her hand dropped to her belt. His eyes went wide. She unhooked the sheath as his hand drifted, disbelieving, back to the hilt of Lengthy Boi the Chungus; and he started his draw as the sheathed knife arced, unturning, through the air.

It hit Krait in the chest, pommel-first, then clattered to the floor.

Krait unhanded Lengthy Boi and looked down at the knife. "What the fuck, Shearwater."

"Returning lost property, Krait."

Krait looked at Zaya, then down again at the knife. "If that's a punch line," he said, stooping to pick it up, "someone's going to have to explain it to me." He drew the blade out of the sheath.

When he'd bared about two inches of the steel, he dropped it like a hot pan.

An arctic wind blew up from Zaya's heart through her throat and came out in the shape of words. "Weren't expecting to see that again?"

"I've never seen that in my life."

"For once, you're not doing well at playing dumb."

Krait's lip curled. "I don't have a thing to hide from you."

"Then *tell*."

"Seven years ago,' he aid, "Arhoon Pogona came to my brood-brother Kanivoon and asked if there was a way to take away a 'streamer's edge."

Krait drew breath to continue; but that would be enough. He might be bringing the memories to the front of his mind to tell the truth about them, or to trim and prune, or to lie; either way, they were at the front of his mind, where she needed them. He was starting the next sentence, but Zaya didn't hear it. She allowed herself one gloating thought before she got to work:

For all you hate psionics, you sure don't think very hard about what it can do.

There were ways to do this without the subject knowing. They took time and skill, and were known only to elders too respectable to spend any time with *her*, daughter of an unclean union, mother in another. Instead she snapped the chain of the damper and tossed it down the hall. She held tight to "Seven years ago" and hauled as hard as she knew how; and, like a hooked sailfish bled of fight, up came the rest.

***

PROLOGUE: SEVEN YEARS AGO (said the mind-voice, the one he heard inside his head, higher and clearer than Shanhoon Krait's true voice) I was fifteen, and Kanivoon was ten feet tall, and made of gold, and his voice was like high tide.

***

CHAPTER 1: I WAS FIFTEEN.

And Kanivoon was my brother and I was on his ground crew and I didn't know what I could do to be like Kanivoon. Kanivoon rode a dragon and had a future in the House and talked like an equal to Mrineen like Harshaan Ora and Jenirain Gila. Kanivoon wasn't a tryhard failson like *some Mrineen scion Zaya didn't recognize* or a doomed bellyacher like *some other name blurred to Zaya's understanding* or a washed-up clown like Arhoon Pogona.

I wanted to be like Kanivoon and Arhoon Pogona was a washed-up clown:

***

CHAPTER 2: I WANTED TO BE LIKE KANIVOON.

So when *another damned Mrineen name* in Theoretical Alchemy started talking about yliaster-the-substance-that-unifies-body-and-mind I paid attention.

They said: There is a known source of materials outside the city.

They said: Pharmacological sources would never be pure enough to support psychokinesis.

They said: Mental applications are too dangerous.

They said: You can flip the unifying principle with a simple *tangle of alchemical concepts that Zaya had no hope of untangling* and wasn't that an interesting theoretical curiosity.

They said: As a practical matter, we're all locked inside our skulls anyway, no need to bar the door.

They said: Ha ha ha.

I thought about the bright-haired girls on the mangy Dawn. The pretty quiet one in back and the thick-shouldered one who lived on cheap beer and bar noodles at the losers' parties. The girls who'd edged out tall golden breaker-voiced Kanivoon in the Gate-to-Shore and run away with the Cold Point Chasse.

Not everyone was locked in their skulls.

But maybe some people needed to be.

***

CHAPTER 3: ARHOON POGONA WAS A WASHED-UP CLOWN.

When he started sucking up to those girls, I figured he was just really terrible at starfucking.

And then Kanivoon came to me and said Arhoon Pogona was looking for a way to take away a 'streamer's edge.

Just for the short term. Nothing permanent.

The Bisai was coming up. I knew what that meant. And who.

***

CHAPTER 4: I COULDN'T MAKE A DAMPER.

Or maybe I could, but I was fifteen and working in a home lab and I couldn't do the *tangled alchemical concepts* yet. But I remembered reading about dreams.

Everyone who'd experimented on themselves or anyone else talked about the dreams. Bring the mind closer to the brain, fill it subconsciously with unprocessable thoughts from other minds, and the memory-making process turns all that disjointed foreign thought-matter into monstrous, endless dreams.

It took a couple days to work through all that, and I asked Kanivoon if Arhoon could give them a gift.

And he said yes.

Too bad it didn't fucking work.

THE END.

***

"It worked," Zaya said hoarsely.

"You pulled that out of me like guts out of a bushpig," Krait said in stunned wonder.

"She woke up screaming every night. She never slept. We thought it was the baby."

"You kept winning."

"She's dead, you child."

"That was an accident."

"How do you think accidents happen?"

Krait had been reeling from the shock of watching the story he'd been planning to shape yanked whole out of him like an onion from the dirt; but she could see his feet come back under him, his face harden. "Attacks like that are a risk for everyone in the Bisai. She wasn't the first one killed by a baby Vore and she won't be the last. It could have happened to Arhoon as easily as her." He pointed a finger at her; if she'd been closer, she might have seen if she could pull it out of its knuckle. "Speaking of which. It wasn't my idea. Arhoon went looking for it. Arhoon sneaked it to your wife. I was just a kid trying to prove myself. What did Arhoon Pogona need the Bisai for? He didn't need the money, and no one who mattered would give a shit."

"You did prove yourself, didn't you?" said Zaya. She could feel echoes of it, as if the roots of Krait's story had clung to the dirt of his memory and some had come with it when she pulled. "You perfected the reversal eventually, you figured out how to use a metallic inlay to integrate it with amplifiers and other thaumaturgic effects." She heard the words come out misshapen, as though she were reading them from a distance. She'd never said the word "thaumaturgic" in her life; she'd wicked the phrase from his mind like a cloth dipped in water. "They saw the value in..." She was not looking at anything in particular, but still she squinted. "Corrections."

It was only a word, the context had dropped off completely. So it took Zaya a moment to connect sound to meaning.

"You never did give me the chance," Krait said into the silence that followed, "to talk about what you'd be working on when you started here."

She hadn't, Zaya realized. She'd skipped straight to what she wanted, enchanted by the feeling of standing in this palace of glass and tile and steel and being courted by its prince. Krait had told her he needed to make money. She hadn't given much thought to how.

Who cared? Working for Shanhoon Krait would be the great defeat; the rest was just details.

"It's always been a problem," Krait said, "how the work crews manage psionic inmates. With sorcerers, we can work with the guilds, but empaths?" He shrugged. "Mostly we just tell them to stay in line, and mostly they do, and every so often a crew will just get massacred by a horde of apes or all the supervisors will die of snakebite in their sleep and that's just how the game is played, you know? There aren't that many really strong empaths on the work crews to begin with. But now, every would-be 'streamer is also a would-be empath. Thanks," and *this* was where the sinuous snake smile came out, "to the highly visible successes of certain very charismatic empaths."

"You know I'd never do that for you," Zaya said, because what else was there to say?

Krait's smile was easy, but his shoulders were tight, and Zaya realized that this was what he had wanted from this meeting—or, at least, what he knew he could get. To show her that her victories were nothing but fuel for his success. That every time Kayalim power or influence grew, even in something as inconsequential—as illegal!—as the 'stream, there would always be money on hand to rein it in again.

Or maybe not? Who knew how a mind like that thought about other people? Maybe he thought she was a law-and-order person beneath it all, maybe he thought she'd see this as an obvious operational necessity for orderly government in Yemareir and not as forcible mass mind control. Who knew what he thought he was doing?

She could pull it out of him, of course; but she was already going to have to live with the guilt of having done it once.

"I didn't know what was more important to you," said Krait, "your son's life or your folk hero image. Now I do."

"You killed my wife to cheat at the 'stream and never said a word about it to me until I forced it out of you. I should be glad a person like you doesn't understand me."

"Arhoon Pogona cheated, and a juvenile Cinereal Vore Wyrm killed your wife."

There was a satisfaction in the way he said it: not smugness, for once, but a sense of fit, like a deadbolt clicking in a doorframe. He'd been living with this for years, never talking about it, letting the facts swim around in the dark and chew at his conscience. Now they'd come out into the light, and he had found the words to fence them off forever.

Arhoon cheated. The Vore killed Kiriki. Two sins, two sinners, and Shanhoon Krait clear of all of it.

Yet again, Zaya had won, and yet again the spoils had gone to Krait.

He hooked a toe under the sheath of the saddle-knife and kicked it to her. She stopped it with her own foot before she could think to let it go by. "Big race tomorrow," Krait said. "Normally I'd say you should get some sleep. But if you've been carrying that around all day, it might not be such a good idea."

Zaya picked the knife up and hitched it back on her belt. She folded her arms across her chest, looked Shanhoon Krait directly in the eye, and did not speak.

"All right," he said. "I'm done here. Sorry I couldn't convince you to join, but I suppose it's all for the best."

She waited.

"Fine," Krait said. "Show yourself out. Try not to break anything, though. The Vermilion Police know where to send the bill."

Zaya looked up, as though she'd taken a sudden interest in the architecture, and let her ears tell her he was leaving.

In truth, she had taken an interest in the architecture. Every finely balanced girder, every lovely pane of glass, every perfectly placed tile: She wanted to remember all of it, weigh it all up against the mass of minds choked and lives unsaved that would pour invisibly out the doors and windows of this building and pool on the streets of Yemareir, and the streams of slabs that would drip tidily into the counting-rooms of House Taipan. This was what a factory of money and misery looked like.

When it was a heap of smoking slag and shards, there would be those who'd mourn it. But Zaya would remember what it had been, and know the ruination had been cheap at the price.

Chapter 19

On the day of Bell the Cat

Fly fast enough and even warm air becomes cool. The leather jacket didn't do much for the cold of the slipstream—air at that speed could go through anything, even the pores in tanned goatskin—but still Zaya's back and armpits sweated where skin met skin; so she was damp with sweat and also cold at the same time. She poured herself into Bandit's mind, feeling the ache of its great wings as it hauled the air, the sweet rawness of its lungs as they strained to keep the fire in its muscles from going out.

Black wings flanked them; black feathers taunted them, too, from just ahead. She could not tell whether the gap was closing.

She'd thought going into Bandit's mind—into its well-feathered body—would take her mind off the cold; but there was a great chill in Bandit as well, growing and spreading from her gut. A black cold, a void that threatened to pull her ribs inward, snapping them like toothpicks; to displace organs, distorting their shapes, rupturing connections. The image of splintered bone, ragged tissue, leaking blood and bile, overwhelmed her in its detail. She couldn't see any more; she'd lost sight of the black wings. All she felt were the boiling cold, and the crumbling wall of time standing between her perfectly whole body and the scene of ruin that had seized her mind.

The boiling cold, the crumbling time, and a blessed soft warmth, nestled between her shoulder blades like a lover's hand.

Before it could leave, she struck: her head twisting around on a supple, powerful neck, taking the thick warm thing between her teeth with a hot rush of salt and copper. It banished the cold void like steam off hot stones.

And then it all came anyway: The thrust of staved-in bone into defenseless flesh, the tearing of dimly-felt structures knowable only in destruction, the panicked flight of blood.

She stared down her bright-feathered muzzle into her own fading eyes and screamed through two mouths at once.

***

AND THEN HER EYES snapped open and her whole body stiffened as if bracing for a fall. Her hands probed her mouth, then her belly, but there was no blood at either. The ceiling was a shade lighter than it had been the last time she'd screamed herself awake; the sun was starting to rise.

"Zaya?" Minshoon's voice came from the hall. He was doing his best not to be angry. His best was pretty good, all things considered.

"I'm awake."

"Same."

"I'm sorry," she said.

"It's OK." It was not OK. "Go back to bed."

She wouldn't, if she could help it.

If she wasn't going to get any sleep, may as well not ruin it for the rest of the house.

Everyone had woken up at her first scream, the dream where she'd sprayed fire over Kiriki from her own mouth. By the second, only the adults woke, reflexes still attuned to out-of-place nighttime noises. Only Minshoon had awakened for the third—and, now, the fourth.

She'd get breakfast. If she left in fifteen minutes, she'd be able to pick up fresh bread from the market and fritters from the good fritter place, over the Chartreuse border, and get back before Eäril and Enwë were awake. Hopefully before anyone else was awake either.

She leaned out the window to watch the sky lighten. A smooth, speckled curve caught her eye from amidst the irises in the window box. There was still no disturbance of the plants around the egg, no sign that it was being cared for at all.

"Fuck it," Zaya said, and reached for it. She hefted it in her hand and looked down, not wanting to splatter anyone with a most likely rotten egg.

She felt it stir in her hand.

Or maybe she didn't? Maybe a muscle in her hand had twitched, maybe she'd been about to drop it and accidentally caught it. The exhaustion of a sleepless night full of tailor-made horrors was already weighing on her eyelids and her shoulders—maybe she'd faded into a microsleep. Certainly now that she'd been shocked into paying attention, the egg wasn't performing for her.

Maybe it knew it didn't need to.

"Aww, egg," she said, and made a nest for it in her blankets. She piled them high right below her pillow, so she'd not come back and forget there was an egg in her bed. Which was still probably rotten, even if she wasn't willing to toss it out the window.

She stepped out of her room—Minshoon had gone back to sleep, thankfully—and over to the door to rummage around for the right bags (waxed canvas for fritters, thick twill for bread). Of course, the ker was curled up right under them. She tried to tell herself she wasn't looking forward to seeing if she could land a kick on its ribs before it teleported—right where the skin was thinnest was where she was planning to aim—but as she approached, it opened an eye.

"Good morning, fuck you very much," she said.

She didn't realize how strongly she'd been anticipating what it would do, until it didn't. What should have happened was this: The ker would close its eyes as if Zaya wasn't there. She'd observe all the forms of subterfuge, neither quickening nor slowing her pace, stepping neither heavily nor lightly, until she was in striking distance. Her toe would snake out and, if she was lucky—maybe once in fifty— she'd connect, earning a yip and a whine in the split second before the thing teleported. The other forty-nine times, it would teleport before the kick landed without opening an eye, reappearing at a safe distance without a hair out of place.

Instead, it opened its other eye, then the middle one, then got up to sniff at her calves. Then it looked directly up into her eyes. Its cilia undulated gently, glowed faintly.

"The pleasure's all yours, fuckpig."

It held her gaze another moment, then walked to a far corner of the room and settled its chin on its paws.

A wave of fatigue weighed down Zaya's eyelids. She shook her head, then opened the door into the corridor. "Bastard must know it's race day."

***

"THIS IS NICE," KIRONO said, checking Bandit's feathers.

"I did that side," Zaya said. "If there are any thin spots on the other side, they're Vani's fault."

"Liar!" said Vanako, mock outrage covering a somewhat smaller quantity of real outrage.

"Who are you going to believe," said Zaya, "me? Or some snot-nosed kid?"

"The wax job is good," said Kirono. "But I meant..." He made a broad gesture with an arm to indicate *all of this*, not taking his eyes off the feathers. "It feels more... like it used to feel."

Zaya knew what he meant. More common wyrms, less well-behaved—that is, more that had come up wild. Fewer spikes, less barding. More Kayalim, more Ililuë.

The scions tended to sit this one out. How likely they were to do so was a function of how high their house sat in Yemareir's unwritten hierarchy, and how likely they were to win. Kanivoon Taipan had never raced in Bell the Cat; neither, Zaya imagined, had Shanhoon Krait. Lerikaan Boomslang, a strong 'streamer from a middling house, was not there, but Ajiroon Ora absolutely was. So was Yaulë, an interesting choice—as a strong 'streamer, he was likely to be near the head of the pack at the midpoint of the race, where they'd buzz the Yemareir City Police headquarters in Ivory Precinct.

That was what you did in Bell the Cat: Be among the first to buzz HQ, and hope the same speed that got you there would outpace an angry cop on a fresh Argent Swordwing. Or hang back, and hope the cops would clear out the leaders, or at least harry them out of the lead.

Or you'd do what Zaya was going to do.

"More like it used to feel is good," Zaya said. She wished she had an excuse to put her goggles on; the sun was blinding.

"Standing right here," said Vanako.

Cerminir was tossing loaves of bread to Bandit, who caught them nimbly in midair. Eating them one by one, she'd explained to Zaya, was better for the wyrm's digestion; if she gave it a bucket, it'd swallow them all at once. Enwë watched from a wrap on Cerminir's back, kicking gently and looking very serious. "Remember," Cerminir said, "you absolutely cannot—"

"—burn before we're ready," said Zaya. "We know."

Vanako caught Zaya's eye, then looked left and right, at the 'streamers around them. *Crap*, Zaya thought, and gave a theatrical shrug to show she knew what Vanako had meant. She checked a few of the buckles on the double saddle, which were fine, but she tightened them a hair anyway.

"Hey, Cer," she said. "Can you see who's organizing the winner's party and try to have it at Razaai's?"

"No," she said. "I don't know who does that stuff, and the last thing I want to do is drag a baby through a crowd and try to find out."

"But if you won't do it," Zaya said, "Kirono has to do it. And he doesn't just hate talking to people, he's actually bad at it."

"I'm bad at it!" said Cerminir. Enwë gurgled. "I talked all night about fascist bees to that one guy and now Yyrreen won't share air with me."

"Listen to these grown-ass adults," said Vanako. "Just find Tuuro at the finish. He'll get it done." She looked at Zaya. "But why?"

Kirono smiled. "Razaai's was where we went for losers' parties in the day."

Zaya's heart melted a little bit at that. It was true, but she hadn't expected Kirono to remember—he'd hated those losers' parties, even though he'd gotten laid more often than not when he did go. She let her smile agree for her.

The smile was real, but the agreement wasn't. Razaai's was popular for losers' parties because it offered dirt-cheap food and well drinks in massive quantities; which they did, in turn, because they made it up in volume. Because they were able to pull in musical acts that normally wouldn't consider playing Damask Precinct. Because, a hundred years ago, the original Razaai had had a sister who'd been one of the few Kayalim ever to join the Gentlewights' Club for Physical Magic. And, before she'd gotten killed trying to resolve a scientific dispute with the Society for Refined Inquiry, she'd helped her brother build one of the few enchanted stages in Yemareir, where anyone in the bar's expansive courtyard could hear any sound made with the intent to be heard.

Zaya didn't know if anyone was playing tonight. This wasn't a plan; she hadn't gotten good enough at those yet. But she wasn't worried about getting on the stage. And then, before the fryer oil had ceased to gleam on the white bean fritters, she'd finally—*finally*—do something with her power that was better than channeling slabs to Electoral Politics.

"'Streamers," the announcer cried, "mount up!"

"Good luck," said Kirono.

"*Don't burn early,*" said Cerminir.

And, when they were seated in their saddles, Vanako: "Are you OK?"

"Wyrms, find your marks!"

"Just tired," Zaya said.

Vanako didn't say *You don't have to do this* or *I'm worried about you* or *You'd better keep your nodding-off-ass head in this incredibly dangerous game*, but it all came through, and not by accident.

"Steady!" shouted the announcer.

"I've got this," said Zaya. "After all, you've got my back."

And she felt the pulse of sweetness in Vanako's mind, and she felt that it was not enough, and the announcer shouted "To the air!" and they were there.

***

FIGHTING TO THE FRONT of the pack was like getting the drop on a drunk pissing on a light post; two easy dodges, a few well-placed wingbeats, and it was sorted. Even Carnaug, whose bulk usually was a serious obstacle, seemed unprepared for Zaya, Vanako, and Bandit.

She felt the unease in Vanako's stomach and wanted, more than anything, to ignore it. "It's fine," she said instead, trusting Bandit's mind to carry her words even as the slipstream took her voice. "They all want me to be the sucker at the head of the pack. Same as the market where we're about to win a fortune."

Maybe, Vanako thought back.

The rest of what Zaya caught, Vanako wasn't trying to communicate: Images of Shanhoon Krait, spreading the word among 'streamers. Images of police on gleaming Argent Swordwings, waiting to take them down early.

"Stay with me," Zaya said. "We don't have to do this much longer."

Her mind reeled, then snapped back behind Bandit's eyes; Vanako had seized control of Bandit for a second, pushing it to swerve in front of Carnaug before the elephant-eater wyrm could overtake them.

There was a strange mind-silence, one Zaya had never experienced with Vanako; as though each could only think of the other, and the only thing either of them cared about was making sure the other didn't catch on.

"It's fine," Zaya said after a moment. "You were right."

Which didn't much help; because what was Vanako going to say? No?

"I'm tired," Zaya said. "I didn't sleep well. I need you to do what you just did again, if that's what it takes to win this."

That got a quick pulse of assent. Which meant that they were back to some kind of normal, the give and take of getting a thing done. Good enough.

Carnaug was lengths behind now, using its bulk to stop any eager young 'streamers from overtaking, conserving its own energy. There was a balance here, with a sucker designated to bell the cat. Just because you'd ceded the top spot to the cat-beller didn't mean you didn't need a good position to start from when the cat came calling. So Yaulë and Carnaug were focusing on crowd control, which suited Zaya just fine; and Zaya, as sucker, could set the pace. Which would save Bandit the energy it would need later.

They sailed north through Sepia Precinct on a road whose name Zaya didn't remember. The view from the front was almost peaceful, if you could forget the rotten-egg smell wafting past from Bandit's nostrils and the dozen or so fire-breathing wyrms keeping pace behind them. Sepia was the buffer between the city's White Heart and the brown precincts to the south, and you could see privilege seep into the architecture as that road stretched north, green-adorned townhouses and wide-windowed shops starting out as punctuation and shading into the mode. The precinct police station jutted out into the street, no doubt to force speeding wyrms like the small army boiling up toward Ivory Precinct into slowing down.

This part of Sepia did look familiar now, come to think of it—there'd been a specialty wine shop, that was it. Ports and brandies and ice wines, all the sticky abominations you'd expect from a bunch of interlopers from a pile of rocks in a frozen ocean barely into the post-sheepfucking phase of their cultural history—or at least that's how Papa Kaalo had described it. Which had been some of why Papa Zinji liked the idea: If the stock was expensive, and Kaalo wasn't going to save any for personal use, that made the return on the job that much more attractive. Papa

Zinji liked drink as much as the next man, but he didn't have Papa Kaalo's rhetorical gifts, which meant he didn't share his ability to convince himself to ignore the value of cash in hand—

—and then she was *back*, not sure where she'd gone, and Vanako's mind was an electrical storm, all gas and sparks and nothing to hold onto—

—*police*, though, she was thinking *police*, had they already passed the Sepia station? How long had Zaya winked out for?

It was Bandit who gave her the image, clean-lined and schematic. The building jutting out into the street; the flash of silver as they whipped by; the shape taking to the air behind them, a shining blade of a wyrm, as fluent in the air as any shark in the sea, an indistinct lump of human between its wings. It had inserted itself between Bandit and Carnaug as smoothly as if the maneuver had been choreographed. Which, of course, it had.

"Relax," said Zaya. "We're winning."

Vanako came back with an image: Some shifting number of Argent Swordwings, two or three or four, coming not behind them but straight at them, with this early Sepia Precinct wyrm merely the rear claw of a talon closing on them.

It was a guess, not a premonition. But it sounded right.

"No shit," said Zaya. "The point stands."

What are we gonna do?

"We just need to time it right."

Zaya seized the image in Vanako's mind, clarified it, and began to set a scene.

The Sepia wyrm on its own couldn't do shit to them. That was the keystone of the idea. It was a hunting dog—not the kind that actually kills game, but the kind that drives quarry toward the hunters who actually do the shooting. An aristocrat's plan, flawed by an aristocrat's scorn. Zaya and Vanako weren't guinea fowl or bushpigs. They knew what they were up against.

The aristocrat's plan relied on Zaya and Vanako being afraid of the Argent Swordwing behind them. Fear would make them strain to get away from it, separating them further from the other 'streamers, making plenty of room for the talon to close without interference from any other wyrms in the race.

"But I'm not afraid of that Swordwing," said Zaya.

Vanako didn't directly think the words *I am*, but her meaning came through.

Zaya played it through: They would slowly drop speed, forcing the Swordwing to slow down if it was going to keep its place in the talon. The other 'streamers would close, almost unavoidably—the ones in back wouldn't just obligingly hold their terrible positions, they might not even know what was happening up front.

When the foreclaws in Ivory Precinct began screaming down the Road of Veils to meet Bandit, they wouldn't find a single, desperate, exhausted wyrm to pluck from the air. They'd find a cloud of feathered chaos that outnumbered them more than three to one.

At that point, whether they chose to peel off or close, Zaya didn't care. If they peeled off, good riddance. If they closed...

... then the plan was what it had been all along; Drop altitude, brake hard, and use the one burn that Cerminir and Old Cheesefeet had given them. Use the pack, now in front of them after the break, to foul the pursuit; fly ahead, unfollowed; win.

The image in her mind changed: Four Swordwings, ridden by giants with long, glinting swords, charging directly into the mass of 'streamers. Cobalt-and-cadmium flames; smoking flesh and feathers; wyrm-scream and human-scream; flashing teeth and talons; blood on the streets.

"*Wyrmspear* is fiction, Vani." Per the plan, they'd slowed; a glance back from Vanako showed that the Sepia Swordwing had closed, but not as much as it could have. The rider was a slight young Mrineen man in Sepia Precinct uniform. That surprised

Zaya; she'd expected Narioun Angonoka, or her stooge. "These are police, not Old Mlin wyrmlords. Their version of dogfighting is against scared thieves or smugglers. We could outfly them blindfolded." Oh well; if Sepia Precinct wanted a cut of the glory, they'd get a cut of the pain.

That's not what you're thinking, said Vanako.

And, fuck, it wasn't.

Zinji and Kaalo had only ever tried to rob a store in the White Heart once. It had been before Zaya was born, but Kaalo had flashed the memory at her in such bright detail that she'd had headaches and nightmares for days. The Eggshell Precinct police had arrived, just one cop on one Greater Gyrdrake; terrified, Kaalo and Zinji had mounted their Dawn Wyrm and tried to run. They hadn't known anything about flying a wyrm, and the Gyrdrake had kept pace with them easily while the cop sent crossbow bolts screaming through the thick summer night until he'd holed a wing. Then the Gyrdrake had done what its species does: climbed in the air and come down on top of Zinji, Kaalo, and the hurt Dawn from a two-hundred-foot stoop.

Every line of the scene was cut into Zaya's memory with scalpel clarity, and every emotion Kaalo had felt sang in her heart and gut. The hot breath of a wyrm as its head shot past to sink its teeth into the Dawn's neck, the hot spray of blood, the slicing of knife-sharp feathers and the crushing weight of the wyrm and the awful jolt as the Dawn's body plowed over the unyielding cobblestones, feathers sanded off like sawdust: All that was bad enough. But it was nothing like the terror they'd felt as quarry.

"My dads had no idea what they were doing," Zaya said. "We do. *You* do."

Vanako was about to reply—something in her mind, anyway, seemed to be reaching in the direction of a reply—when her thoughts disappeared, cut away like a carrot top.

Terror sang again in Zaya's heart as she looked back.

Vanako was there, and for a dissociated moment Zaya thought she had changed clothes—she was bulkier, somehow, and glowing in the late morning sun. The next moment, she looked for the spear, the shaft, the blade, anything that might quietly have stolen life without announcing itself. The next moment, she understood what she was looking at: a mass of pearlescent ropes, wrapped around Vanako's upper body, hampering her arms and eliciting a terrified squirming that marked her, blessedly, as both having mental experiences and very much alive.

Buildings were giving way to a small copse of forest. Part of how Ivory insulated itself from Sepia: All the arteries connecting the precincts of the White Heart to the rest of Yemareir had something like this, something you couldn't quite call a barrier, to make a person think twice about crossing the border. If Yyrreen had still been talking to her, they'd have discussed strategy for this environment, how to use the closing trees to their advantage.

There were glints of silver up ahead. More Swordwings.

So this was where they'd take her, if they timed it right; boxed in by trees, cut off from the minds of her wyrm and her co-pilot by some kind of new damper you could make into a net. If that wasn't the newest product of Taipan Invotechnic, it would only be because Shanhoon had made it on the sly in his bedroom.

She tried to think, but the weight of sleeplessness was like a yoke and the fear was like a wall forcing her to walk in circles. There was still a way to win this. Even facing up five cops on Argent Swordwings, even cut off from psionics.

Yes. There was.

No time for buckles; she drew her saddle-knife, cut the straps binding her to Bandit, and carefully turned to face Vanako. She crept back on Bandit's spine—if she could sense its thoughts now, she was sure it would be protesting with whatever passed for anxiety in a reptile—pressed the knife into Vanako's hand, and shouted as loud as she could over the slipstream:

"We're here to win this, right?"

Vanako, sawing away at the damper-net, nodded.

"We can still win," Zaya said. "We have to. That's what I'm asking you to do, all right?"

She turned away to see what was coming. The great thing about giving your big speech to someone tied up in a damper on the back of a dragon is they can't get in your mind, can't come after you, and pretty much can't make themselves heard. Vanako was surely screaming all the questions any sane person would think to ask after a bit like that, but for a little while longer, Zaya was running the show.

She crouched between Bandit's wings and grabbed handfuls of feathers. She wished she could reach its mind, but this net was stronger than the old dampers; even with Zetaala's old counter-measure, she could only manage the barest trickle of contact. She'd have to trust Vanako to do the explaining.

Bandit surely understood that something unexpected and probably very bad was unfolding, but she didn't have a way to give it even a hint of what she was going to do about it, and she didn't have the time to figure one out.

Act your age, she thought. *This won't hurt.*

She squeezed her knees and pushed with the heels of her hands in the signal every well-trained dragon knew for *drop and brake.*

Bandit dropped; Bandit braked.

The Sepia Swordwing passed over them, then wheeled, the fastest, tightest turn Zaya had ever seen a dragon make outside the Yemareir Air Guard. Her jaw actually fell open for a moment's pure appreciation.

It hit an onrushing Eyrie Shrike that Zaya didn't know. An explosion of bright and dark feathers hung in the air for a moment, like some painstakingly hung sculpture commenting on the ephemerality of perfection and the differences that inhere in similarity.

Before Zaya could hear meat hit the ground, she hauled up, and Bandit ascended toward the canopy overhanging the road.

Wyrms shot around her, too slow to brake or maybe seeing an opportunity and surging for it. Zaya made herself as small as she could and tried not to think about Vanako, immobilized, slowly cutting herself out. The feedback loop between herself and Bandit was too slow now; nothing she did could help. All she could do was trust it to make the climb.

Wyrm after wyrm plunged past her, and neither they nor the cops on Swordwings from Ivory Precinct had any idea what to do about it. A Dawn ridden by a team of Kayalim she didn't know tried to tag one Swordwing with a lash of flame; but that wasn't a fight the Dawn was interested in, and the flame fell short. The cop, in turn, half-wheeled to give chase, but either wyrm or rider remembered their mission, and the pair turned back toward Zaya and Bandit.

She looked through the torrent of dragons as Bandit climbed. All the remaining Swordwings were moving, carefully but surely, toward her. And the back of the pack would pass soon, and the air would be clear for them to come.

Bandit was close to the canopy now, close enough that she could grab an arm-thick branch if she stood. Standing on a dragon's back high in the air was a terrible idea, of course. Even the Yemareir Air Guard didn't do that kind of stunt.

She stood and blindly reached.

Her hands closed around the branch.

With her heels, she gave Bandit the pressure-signal that meant *Burn.*

Her hands tightened; her shoulders hauled; her wyrm surged forward, and her feet dangled with nothing but a hundred feet of air between them and the road below.

She couldn't watch Bandit and Vanako recede. She couldn't even watch the Swordwings rise up to meet her. All she could see was the rough brown bark of the tree she clung to; the puckered craters where twigs and branches once had been, the grey offshoots of rotten limbs that would betray her if she seized them, the whitening of her hands' trembling flesh as it clung and ached and, not slowly at all, began to falter.

The burn would carry Bandit back to the front of the pack. That was its purpose: Once the police had been flushed out, to put the pack between them and Bandit. The pincer trap had only modified things slightly. There were enough of them that one might get through the pack; and if one had had anti-psionic countermeasures, they all would.

So, change of plans. Wrong-foot them with a deluge of wyrms they didn't care about. Take that moment to separate the person they were theoretically searching for from the wyrm that they'd been chasing. And every second that passed was that much farther away for Bandit to travel; whereas the human was hanging right here. Arms screaming, legs swaying, soon to be road meat; but here.

She squeezed her stomach and back as hard as she could, thinking she could kip her feet up high enough to cross her ankles around the branch like a sloth or, you know, some other mammal that had spent millions of years evolving for this kind of maneuver. Her feet barely got above her waist. If she'd thought about this ten seconds ago she might have been brave enough to try to swing her feet back and forth, get some momentum to swing them up, but as it was she didn't think her grip could take the jolts.

Of course, her grip wouldn't last much longer, jolts or no jolts. She caught a flicker of hunger from one of the Swordwings circling beneath her. It was too well trained to act on it, of course; but the Swordwings were sprinters, not persistence hunters, and the urge to close and make the kill practically radiated from it.

… which she could feel. Because Bandit had flown off with the damper.

And these idiots hadn't hit her with another one. Because they thought that, just because she didn't have *her* dragon, she didn't have *any* dragon.

"Idiots is me," she said. Out loud, because who could hear her? "I'm idiots."

She seized the Swordwing's mind then, kindled that hindbrain urge to approach until its training crumbled into ash and it heaved its bulk up toward the canopy as surely and lightly as a cat hopping on a bed. She suppressed its urge to flame its prey, tweaked the flight path a hair, damped the pain of her screaming arms, and waited for three eternal seconds.

Then she let go, neatly straddling the Swordwing a few feet behind its rider.

The Ivory Precinct cop turned and stared at Zaya as though she was a tarantula on their dinner plate.

Zaya lunged for the pearlescent net hanging off a hook on the cop's saddle. By instinct, the cop went for it as well; but for all their augmented reflexes, Zaya was, just this once, faster. She sent the damper-net skirling into the open sky.

Zaya sized her foe up in an instant. They were bigger than Zaya, their center of mass higher; for all their quick reflexes, they were off-balance, they hadn't caught up to what Zaya was trying to do. It would be a heartbeat's work to jab their vestibular system, soften the tension in their knees and back that kept them balanced. Then one good twitch, the world's briefest seizure, and they'd follow the damper-net down…

And Zaya would have to cut her hair again.

There would come nights—that day's night would be the first—where Zaya would look through the unmoonlit dark at a ceiling built not to shelter, but to contain, and think about what that image had done to her: Bleach-roughened hair, dyed by her father's hand, floating to the floor. She had not cut it since she'd killed the bandit for whom Bandit's Breath was named. His breath had been the last thing she'd stolen, not for lack of trying.

She was sick to death of stealing.

Zaya held out both her palms for the cop to see.

The shade of the mahogany trees cooled the afternoon air to perfection. The wyrm under her coasted, its feathers smooth as steel against her legs. The police officer before her sat as still as stone, their eyes wide open in the face of what they had thought, until a moment ago, was death.

"Congratulations," Zaya said. "I surrender."

PART III

Chapter 20

Four weeks before the Skua

"I keep telling you," Vanako said, hearing her own voice as though a far-off mountain had thrown it back in echo. "I can't tell anyone what to do."

Krait appraised her, not without theater. "No dragon, no young lover," he said. "Maybe you can't."

Vanako didn't notice she had sat down until she felt Minshoon sit beside her. Her shoulders hurt from where her arms had been pinned back as if she'd been a child about to hit a sibling with a stick; the dullness of the damper still hung like a scum on her mind. She closed her eyes and saw red, yellow, and blue: blood, wyrm-fire.

Words might have been said, but she didn't know what they were. She only knew enough to wrap her arms around the neck of the person who picked her up, both arms under hers, squeezing her to him like a bag of sand. They moved with small, awkward steps, and then the humidity of the garden wrapped her, and with a couple of teetering steps down the front stairs they were where she had landed those vast minutes ago, before two pieces of her heart had been torn free.

"I'm sorry, Vani," Minshoon whispered. "I have to put you down now."

She squeezed harder, and he didn't put her down. After a minute, she felt his arms start to tremble, and she let go.

She looked up at him. She never got this close to Minshoon—he was so tall, and solidly built for a Mrineen, with a strength in his chest and arms she'd never really thought about. He was just Minshoon, he cooked badly and paid bills and coached Taavi on betting in the 'stream and rocked babies to sleep and talked people down off ledges. But he'd carried her like a little child.

"This was really bad," she said.

"Massively."

"It's my fault."

"Some." He looked down from such a height. "But you didn't invent strong people scaring themselves into killing weak people."

"They're going to take him away."

Minshoon's face fell, like someone finding himself needing to explain to a small child that death is forever, and he looked away; but only for a moment.

"Bandit's gone," she said.

He put his arm around her shoulder. "Let's go home."

And it was the right thing to do, if for no other reason than that the cops would absolutely come after them any second now if they stayed. So she went with him. And she saw, down the path to the road, just the other side of the property line, House Shearwater had waited: Taavi, Cerminir, Jaliki, Enwë, Eäril, Kirono, and even, her heart leapt to see, Gilthiniel, who was covered in dirt and leaves and purple smears of what had to be lipstick. Cerminir looked at Vanako with fire in her eyes; she was mad as hell. But she had waited.

"Bandit knows where to go," said Minshoon as they walked toward the rest of the family. "We can go see it in the morning."

CHAPTER 21
NINE WEEKS BEFORE THE SKUA

ABOVE THE ROAD FROM Sepia Precinct to Ivory, wind tore at Vanako like a pack of starving dogs.

Her goggles hadn't come off, but it barely mattered; her eyes were streaming anyway, with pain and anger and bewilderment, although at the speed Bandit was moving it all felt like one thing and the thing it felt like was fear. She wanted to rip the rest of the pearly netting away from her body, but the only thing worse than the screaming pain of clenching every muscle in her body around Bandit was the thought of what could happen if she let even one fiber of those muscles slacken.

At some point, Bandit slowed down to a speed that she was used to; there was a moment when she felt her body and felt the air against it and realized that its force against her skin was a force she knew, not the terrible rending gale it had been when Bandit started the burn, and she let a hand creep up to tear at the net and did not fall.

The ball of netting fell away into the slipstream, and Vanako's mind slid into Bandit's like a child's hand closing around their mother's finger, and she felt it welcome her.

"Where's Mom?"

I don't know, Bandit replied. *I couldn't hear her thoughts when she came off. But I could feel that she didn't fall.*

Zaya had taken them up to the canopy. *We can still win*, she'd said. *That's what I'm asking you to do.* "We have to go back."

She told us not to, said Bandit; but its wings slowed.

"We can't leave her."

Bandit's thoughts didn't resolve into words, then, but in the cool silver contours of its reptile mind the scene was clear enough. Five razorwinged foes slashing through the air; five clouds of blue-and-yellow flame licking from all sides. And, threaded through that image of death, a willingness to risk it; not because Bandit wanted to die for Zaya, but because it trusted Vanako not to waste its life.

What a mistake.

Bandit's mind was grave and worried, but she felt it shimmer faintly with whatever passed for a chuckle in a dragon.

Fine. If Bandit was going to make the mistake of trusting Vanako with its life, then Vanako would make the mistake of trusting Zaya with her own.

She wasn't sure that made sense. But she was more afraid of explaining to Minshoon how she'd lost Zaya than she was of dying in a storm of flame and talons trying to get her back.

So she'd do what she was more afraid of.

Or at least that's what she told herself, as Bandit's wings carried her away from where Zaya had done... whatever she'd done.

***

THEY WERE SAILING DOWN the broad lanes of Ivory Precinct, she realized, Bandit's Dawn plumage as out of place among the stately porticos and columns as an orchid at a fishmonger's. Oh, there were wyrms here, carrying those who could pay through the fine late summer air; but many of them were rare wyrms, an Iron Glisterwyrm and a Melanic Shrike and a grizzled Argent Swordwing, and even the common wyrms were Dusk Stalkers and Eyrie Shrikes with plumage picked to harmonize with the calm whites of the architecture.

It was all Vanako could do not to pull another burn out of Bandit, to fill these smug streets with the heat and color they so badly needed.

But Cerminir had said no. Vanako wasn't sold on Cerminir's philosophy on life, but she wasn't about to contradict her on weird chemical things happening inside the guts of dragons, and Cerminir had said this was a one-burn race; anything else would put Bandit's health at risk, and make losing more of a certainty than if they didn't burn. At least Vanako could entertain herself imagining the expressions on all these sleepy taxi-pilots' faces when Carnaug came roaring down these comfortable boulevards like an avalanche wrapped in feathers.

She whipped past the Iron Glisterwyrm, ferrying some pair of scions in the colors of House Honu, and saw the exact expression she'd been thinking of.

Vanako didn't have to look behind them; Bandit already had. The image of Carnaug filling the street behind them was unmistakable.

Like a breaker, panic drenched Vanako and then moved on. There was a reason Carnaug was always in contention and never first across the finish: It was too damn big. Yaulë, whoever they were, wasn't a good enough flyer to get around that basic fact. Zaya could beat them; Shanhoon Krait could beat them; Lerikaan Boomslang could beat them. Tuuro and Zetaala had beaten them.

And Vanako knew where she could gain some ground right now.

She reached out to dull the ache in Bandit's wings and shoulders, careful not to overdo it. Managing the wyrm's pain was one of the first things Zaya had taught her, one of the rear-saddle functions that had evolved from her and Kiriki's partnership. The front saddle was about tactics, the long-range forethought and split-second decisions that added up to a race. The rear saddle was about maintenance and monitoring, keeping the wyrm's mind and body within parameters and making sure any relevant information about the wyrm or the race was in the front saddle's mind before they needed it. Pain was tricky because it was both a drag on performance and an important signal. Damp it too much, and a trusting wyrm would injure itself irreparably doing what its rider asked for.

But damp it just enough, in the right moment, and you could squeeze out an edge out that transformed defeat into victory.

So she damped Bandit's ache, pushed it on the next few wing-beats, and banked hard to buzz the station.

This was supposed to be the main hazard of Bell the Cat; your wyrm had to circle the City Police headquarters three times before it continued on, giving the finest cops in Yemareir the chance to saddle up and give chase. Vanako didn't even know if they'd do it; presumably the good pilots were all in that small forest between Sepia and Ivory, doing things to Zaya that Vanako didn't even—

—but if some of them did plan to respond in the traditional way, chances were they'd be ready. Their colleagues had been, after all.

Luckily for Vanako, managing the torque of three tight turns around the headquarters was something Carnaug was absolutely going to suck at. She just needed to spend as little time as possible in those turns with Carnaug.

On the first revolution, she looked in windows, trying to find faces to memorize. They'd be the wrong faces, but fuck it. Any face she could spit in, scream at, rake to pieces with her nails and then throw vinegar in or whatever. (Forget that the last time she'd squared off with a cop in the street, he'd nearly broken her shin with a kick so fast she didn't know he'd moved until the pain began to blossom.)

On the second revolution, she looked down at the penned Swordwings and thought dark thoughts. Could she plant a seed in their minds such that they'd flame Carnaug from the ground? Or eat the next human who came in to mount up? Zaya could do it, she was sure. But that would be cheating or, as the case might be, murder; and although Vanako was closer to wanting all that to happen than she cared to think, she wasn't actually there yet.

On the third revolution, she tried to squeeze as much torque out of Bandit as possible without blacking out.

They shot away from the headquarters at least a length before Carnaug even started its own turns. It let out a glass-rattling roar that very nearly knocked Vanako out of the saddle, and the burn that came with it palpably heated the air, but fuck it; she and Bandit streaked out onto Ftaroon Tuatara Street unpursued, with precisely fuck-all breathing down their collective seven or eight feet of neck.

They took every corner like a pack of flying sharks was on their scent, and every straightaway like they'd never eaten a dinner but someone had told them they could have it if they got there fast enough.

Scarlet, Incarnadine, Rust, Damask. The thing about having Carnaug behind you was it really was, in most ways, like running ahead of an avalanche: You felt sorry for yourself the whole time, because it's no fun to spend every waking second thinking about what it feels like to die in an avalanche, but at least it was the *only* thing you had to worry about.

Tuuro would tell her, when he thought enough time had passed that talking about this race was something that could be done with Vanako, what it was like to watch the finish: Carnaug hulking and roaring behind her and Bandit like it was about to swallow them whole, Bandit's brilliant plumage a rebel jewel against the sand-and-water bulk of the huge Ranger, Vanako pressed tight against Bandit's back to minimize drag while Yaulë sat high and thrashed the reins with his massive arms, the roar of the crowd pouring unabated into the same volume of air so the pressure of the noise seemed to crystallize it into hard-edged clarity.

And, in response, Vanako would tell Tuuro "Get out," not kindly or patiently—not because she didn't care… no, on second thought, precisely because she didn't care about Tuuro's adolescent swooning over any of that shit; because her only memories of that finish line were pushing an exhausted wyrm just past its limits and using its eyes to see because she was weeping into her goggles. Because that finish line was the one she never wanted to cross, because on the other side of it people would start to *ask* and there would be a few, the ones she loved and feared the most, that she would have to *tell*.

Because, when she slid off Bandit, her knees didn't wobble and her balance didn't waver. There was no terrible period of forgetting how her human body worked, no stumbling and thrashing as she tried to move two featherless arms and two talonless legs and no tail through space using a dragon motor schema. When she stood, she ached but did not falter.

She hadn't even been there for the race, then, not really. Bandit might as well have taken them to first place on its own.

***

THERE WERE CHAOS AND strangers and gifted food and *meetings* in the House Shearwater living room that night, because of course there were.

Kiri and Vinaali's chicken with chocolate was fuel for the sinews, balm for the wounded soul, and a reason to wash dishes. It paired badly with the bottles of ice wine that Zayeni brought, but nobody cared. Vanako recognized at least two candidates for the House of the Stars, plus functionaries from the party apparatus of both the Thread & Mortar Front and the Travelers; Yyrreen and Minshoon were handling the four of them in a complex pattern, swapping off with Taavi and, miraculously, Gilthiniel, who Vanako had expected to be either stunned, disgusted, or otherwise removed from sociality, but who instead seemed to be managing to set the players at ease with his dumb sense of humor and a hail-fellow-well-met attitude he must have picked up for a chipped flinder at Yemareir's worst thrift shop. Likewise, Cerminir and Kirono had handled bedtime for the littles, but were now working the floor, although it was mostly in the way of making neighbors feel seen and updating them on what anybody knew about Zaya, which other than Vanako's jumbled dump of swiftly fading images was actual fuck-all.

Jaliki, for his part, was leaned against Vanako with his tear-tracked face in that fleshy territory under her collarbone, between shoulder and breast, snoring and drooling.

He'd been at the finish line, and Minshoon had said he'd been the first to notice Zaya was missing—no one else had detected it until Vanako dismounted (and no quantity of ice wine or chicken with chocolate had dulled the shame of that dismount, her body perfectly at home in itself, no trace of the draconic motor schema lingering in her brain). Since then, Jaliki hadn't left her side. He'd gone to the stable with her, walking uncomplainingly on the leg that now seemed to have strengthened as much as it was going to. He'd helped where he wasn't asked, refused to do what he was asked, and made himself surprisingly useful anyway. Whenever a hand of hers had been free, he'd taken it, and sometimes he'd take her hand anyway, although he wouldn't whine or pursue it if she snatched it away, just wait patiently for an opportunity at another angle of attack, like a hyena persistence hunting a hurt wildebeest or some damn thing (Vanako was a city kid). He'd sat with her while Yyrreen, Minshoon, and one of Kirono's professor friends scraped every detail out of every fold of her brain, and then while Vinaali and Taavi and Zayeni offered the comfort of a sympathetic ear (of which she did not avail herself) and of their presence (which she forced herself to tolerate), somewhere in there he fell asleep, which gave an excuse for people not to talk to her because, hey, sleeping kid.

When Zinji settled down next to her, she figured he wouldn't care about that, and she was right.

"Zinji-kana."

"Vanako-ko. You lost my daughter."

"Game recognize game."

Zinji's eyes widened for a half second; then he slapped the couch and doubled over, wheezing. Eventually he straightened back up and said "hoooo!" as if to exorcise the laughter. "You're mean," he said.

"You started it."

"In my head, that was a moment of wisdom," Zinji said. "You were going to look at me with puppy eyes and I was going to explain how one twig of a fourteen-year-old girl can't possibly be to blame for a dozen cops on dragons hauling her mother away. You were very grateful," he said, wiping a tear away with the knuckle of a forefinger. "In my head. But instead you came at me like a pan of hot grease. Just like your mother."

"That's a compliment."

"Yes ma'am."

"I know it wasn't my fault," Vanako lied.

"It's not your fault," Zinji said, "but you don't know it."

"You teaching me about forgiving myself is like Jaliki teaching me how to drink whiskey."

"Oh, come on," said Zinji. "I know more about it than that."

"Maybe," said Vanako, "but the point is it isn't something you *should* know enough about to teach me."

Zinji's face had cleared of amusement. "The first one I asked for. The second one I deserved. The third, I won't stick around for. Which isn't much of a threat, I know. But I did come to be with you while we both sit in fear and loss. Even if my teaching moment wasn't as great as it sounded in my head."

Vanako moved her hand from Jaliki's hip to rest her fingertips on Zinji's shoulder. He covered them with his own.

"She pays for my apartment in Azure," he said. "I think she pays for Jaliki's treatments too? And of course she pays for most of this. I know Kirono helps, but it's mostly her."

"No one will talk about that," said Vanako. "I brought it up, but all anyone will say is not to worry. But all that means is they don't know what to do. Except even though they don't know what to do, they know enough to think that me worrying is going to get in the way."

"And you're not even a strung-out old fart with a track record as a fuckup," said Zinji. "But you've still got to sit on the couch with him while the grownups try to move and shake and make things happen."

"I'm a fucking veraamaka," Vanako said softly. "I got Jaliki his treatments before anyone in this house could do it, even Mom. I was in the saddle when she won her first race since Kiriki died and every one since. I won this one half on my own." *And you worked so hard that you didn't get even a little tusk-mad,* said a voice inside; but fuck it, she was making a point.

Zinji smiled, laughed, burped. "That," he said, "that's all Kaalo. I mean, I know you're not his blood." He waved a hand sloppily, brushing Jaliki, who snorted and stirred; the ker at his feet spluttered and smacked its chops. "But that's all him anyway. So conscious of his own worth, so... insistent that the world recognize it. Were you like that before you came to live with us?"

She made a noncommittal noise. "Yeah? I guess."

"Not everyone has that gift, you know. Not me, not Jaliki, not poor Kiriki. Not your fathers here either, not Cerminir. Eäril, maybe—a lot of little ones are like that, not all of them stay that way. You. Zaya. Ziyuki."

Vanako laughed. "Ziyuki doesn't give a shit about what anybody thinks."

"She does. But Ziyuki has a particular idea of who counts as 'anybody.'"

"That tracks. What's the point of clawing yourself away from the poors if you can't forget about them once you've fucked off?"

"It's not about money with Ziyuki," Zinji said. "She cares what family think. Her new family and her old. She doesn't want us to know. But we know."

"Does she care about family getting disappeared by Ivory Precinct police?" said Vanako. She felt her skin crackle, like she was about to get hit by lightning. "Why isn't she here?'

Zinji made a *pfff* noise that was wetter than it should have been. "She can't be seen in company the likes of this."

"She got herself seen at our victory party."

"Did you have a bunch of dissidents and opposition candidates at your victory party?"

"Her *sister* is *gone.*"

"Her *brood-sister.*"

Vanako wasn't prepared for the bitterness in Zinji's voice, or the pain in the lines that deepened around his eyes.

"I should know better," he said hoarsely, after a moment. "I can keep it light for a long time, Vani. All day, most days. I can pretend that Ziyuki leaving was just a silly thing she did, a silly fantasy that helped her get rich. I can wink about it, like you and I know the real truth. But Ziyuki knows the real truth. She left her *brood*-family to join her real family." He looked at Vanako, then looked at his hands in his lap. "Maybe you don't understand. You do all this Mrineen stuff too." Something dawned on him, and he turned to her with fear in his eyes. "I didn't mean—I mean *you*, of course—I didn't mean *you*."

"What?"

"Nothing."

"No. Say it."

"I didn't mean you're not real family," Zinji said miserably.

"Oh. That is kinda what you said. Isn't it?"

Vanako felt like she should be angrier. But it was Zinji. She'd seen him play with Jaliki, read to Eäril, feed Enwë. He was stoned, he was out of his mind with fear and worry. And even if he had kind of said it, he hadn't meant it.

But it wasn't good that he'd said it.

"When you're old enough," Zinji said, "you can find yourself knowing two things that can't both be true. I know this is my family. You and Jaliki and the rest." He ran a hand over Jaliki's scalp. "And I know you can't make a family that way. It's how I was raised. I guess that's why it's so hard to know what to think about Ziyuki leaving. I believe that she's part of my family, and I believe she isn't any more."

If this was how Zinji got every time he robbed a liquor store, Vanako was starting to understand why Zaya had put him at arm's length. "That sounds hard," she said.

"It is hard."

"Confusing." To show she'd been listening.

"That, too."

"Do you ever see her?"

"Ziyuki?"

Vanako let her silence answer *yes*.

"There's a little place on the eastern edge of Copper Precinct, just across the Alabaster border. She told me to go there if I need her."

"The Sweet Soldier?"

"That one," said Zinji. "I wait there. It takes a little while, sometimes; but she comes, or she sends someone. If she comes, it takes longer. They don't like having me there, I can see it, but they always keep me fed if it's a long wait."

"Did Mom ever go?" Vanako asked.

"I don't think Ziyuki ever made the offer. She told me to come if Zaya needed anything."

"When are you going?"

Zinji sighed. "Why do you think it took me so long to get here?"

Vanako would have grabbed his shoulder if there hadn't been a sleeping kid between them. "What's she going to do?"

"She doesn't know where Zaya is or what she might have been charged with. She's going to learn more and figure something out."

"When will we know?"

Zinji shook his head. "Vani, if she's doing something to help Zaya, she's not going to tell us about it. House Amphisbaena won't be understanding about any rules she might be breaking. They don't recognize that Zaya's her family, even if Ziyuki does." Zinji's tone made it clear he wasn't so sure she did. "We'll know what she does when it works. Maybe."

"Horseshit." Vanako made herself hiss so people wouldn't stare. "That's not an answer."

"Vani. It's been a couple hours. Nobody knows anything. Even if Ziyuki were the Empress of Yemareir, she'd have to know where Zaya *is* to know what she could do."

"She doesn't have to be Empress to do better than that." Vanako began struggling her way out from under Jaliki.

"Where are you going?"

"To my room." She looked at Zinji through a red wall of anger: At him, at Ziyuki, at Yemareir, at herself—but even that red wall couldn't hide Zinji's fear. Kaalo, Jaliki, Zaya, herself: One was dead, one doomed, one gone, one flipping out. The losses must just be piling up in his mind, the way they shouldn't if you were an old man. and everyone in your family was supposed to have more life ahead of them than you. But Vanako didn't have the fucks to reassure a stoned old man who used kids as emotional crutches and thought her family was some kind of bullshit 'Mrineen stuff.'

But he wasn't some old man. He was Papa Zinji. So she found a couple.

"You can walk me if you want," Vanako said. "I promise I'm not about to sneak out and do something impulsive."

"That's the kind of thing Zaya would say if she had a crazy idea, but she felt like she'd thought it through."

"Sit outside my door if you want," Vanako said, remembering to lead with how tired she was and not the coppery resolve crystallizing in her chest. "I'm not going anywhere tonight."

That seemed to quell whatever anxiety she'd kindled in Zinji. "Going to sleep?"

"Going to draw for a while," she said, and it was the absolute truth.

Chapter 22

Nine weeks before the Skua

Breakfast the next day was amazing: Minshoon and Kirono had, somehow, managed to both go out for sweet rolls without telling one another, so Vanako got a full sage-blossom-glazed raisin bun from the Foundry instead of splitting it with Eäril, and Cerminir had taken a rare morning turn in the kitchen to adapt last night's chicken into some kind of amazing hash with chunks of potato, onions, peppers, and at least six different spices only Cerminir ever used in cooking, possibly because of a need for precision dosing to avoid weird psychotropic effects. Though Vanako wasn't sure how precision dosing could be possible, given that she'd eaten a total amount of chicken hash about equal in volume to an actual chicken. At some point she noticed she was the only—well, the oldest—one stuffing herself, and slowed down a little. Maybe she should pick at her food like Minshoon, or beg off like Gilthiniel? Would that be more... respectful? Or at least make it seem less like she was fueling up to execute an ingenious stratagem?

When everyone had at least a few bites in them, the three parents stood. Minshoon spoke. "We all know that Zaya-kana is gone. We're pretty sure she was arrested by Ivory Precinct police. We don't know where she is, and we're all very worried. But we also know your mom is tough, smart, and a very powerful empath. And we know that lots of people know she's been taken, and they want her free almost as much as we do. Which is great... but it may make the government not want to say where she is until they decide to let her go.

"Jaliki, Eäril, you two won't be in school for a few days. Gilthiniel, Taavi, Vani: We talked it over for a little while, and it's up to you. It will, honestly, probably make your lives easier if you go. The less you draw attention, the less likely any of this gets talked about, the easier it is for you to just... get along. And having something to distract you may be more valuable than you think. But your mother is gone. It hasn't even been a day. We're not going to make you go, especially not today."

"I've got my apprenticeship today," said Vanako, after what felt like a suitable interval of contemplation. "I want to go. Ora-shan is going to need an excuse if I don't, and I honestly don't ever want to fucking talk to him about it."

"Kids at the table, Vani," Kirono said mildly.

"What's wrong with don't ever want to fucking talk to him about it?" said Eäril, who was interested in boundaries.

'You shouldn't give people the silent treatment," said Cerminir. "It's passive-aggressive and doesn't send a clear message."

Eäril nodded seriously.

"I'll just study here," said Gilthiniel.

"I'm with Vani?" said Taavi, giving Vanako the brisk nod that served them better than a wink. "Loggerhead-shan's not as racist as Ora-shan, but she's inquisitive and means well?"

Kirono shuddered ostentatiously. Cerminir said, "Have you ever considered just not going back?"

Minshoon turned to Kirono and Cerminir. "Six children look to you two for guidance on how to navigate this world of complex personalities, customs, and laws—" ... it felt like some kind of prolegomenon, but he couldn't seem to summon the will to continue. He turned to the kids instead. "Two more things, then no more speech. One, please know we are doing everything we can to find

Zaya-kana. It might not look like it, and there may be things it's better for us not to share. The second thing is, if it hurts, you don't have to be alone with it. Some of you are probably more used to coming to Zaya-kana with hard stuff. I can't say we can give you everything she gave. But we will try. And Zinji-kana will try, and I'm sure our neighbors will try if that's what you want. I'm monologuing again. Whoever you need. Please. OK, finish up." He looked at Vanako and Taavi. "You two especially, you're going to be late."

"Go easy on Vani?" said Taavi. "She barely got the chance to eat?"

Vanako's cheeks were full of chicken hash, so she deployed the only weapon at her disposal: An open mouth full of half-chewed food. Taavi said "Bleucccch," Gilthiniel said "Rude," Jaliki laughed, and Eäril quickly stuffed a roll in her mouth and did the same, although the roll wasn't chewed enough to be nearly as disgusting as the hash. Enwë crowed and clapped anyway. They left the table in a welter of chaotic laughter and reproving word-shaped noises from Minshoon, and that was Part 1 of Ingenious Stratagem done and dusted: Separate Taavi From The Group.

***

IT WAS BEAUTIFUL OUT, just the barest edge of cool in the morning air, the parakeets on Laurel Street mimicking the brooms of the street-sweepers. Vanako looked to the mural of Zaya on Bandit that decorated the low wall around the apartment, and saw Chashu and Amiko standing very still on either side. "Morning, ladies," said Chashu.

"Hi Chashu? Hi Amiko?" said Taavi, while Vanako looked at the mural. She felt like something had to have changed, some acknowledgment of the enormous and horrible thing that had happened to her family overnight. But she could find nothing.

"Starting to flake a little," Chashu said.

"I'll touch it up some time," said Vanako, realizing she meant it. Touch it up and add to it. She'd need to figure out what would go—what could be superimposed on a detailed, complete, stylistically unified painting that already covered the entire surface, without actually looking like a late-coming addition.

"I'm sorry about your mother," Chashu said. "Rest easy though, we'll get her back."

Amiko gave him a look of reproach: *How?* But if Chashu was paying attention, he didn't show it. Vanako and Taavi waved and moved on.

Once they were off Laurel Street and onto Ashthereen Honu Street headed toward Heliotrope, Taavi asked, "How late do you need to be?"

"Two hours, I think. Tuuro had to move out of the Viridian dole for brooding, so they're all the ass out in Damask now. You?"

"An hour is fine?" Taavi was seeing a boy named Vaisho who lived at the north end of Lilac Precinct. He was possibly almost as smart as Taavi, not half as pretty, and not a tenth as worth talking to; but he was studying biology at the Tuatara College for Natural Philosophy, which made him interesting to Taavi in ways that Vanako was neither able nor willing to get her head around. "Less would be better? I just want to let him know I'm OK? But he's going to have to ask for details and offer his shoulder and ask a couple of dumb questions to make sure I'm not dying inside?"

"That sounds worse than getting grilled by Ora-shan."

"It's fine? It's kind of sweet." Based on tone, Vanako estimated the sweetness level at maybe fifteen to twenty percent, the fineness around fifty. "He needs to feel like he knows what's going on and he's helping a little, that's all? Otherwise he might start writing me letters? Or, like, showing up?"

Taavi had never said outright why she didn't bring Vaisho around, but only because it was so obvious: Cerminir and Gilthiniel would have to be drugged or gagged to keep from swallowing the poor kid like a buttered snail and then burping in triumph for an hour while he digested. There was an unspoken rule that you had to be nice to the grownups' partners, but that didn't extend to kids.

"What about Tuuro?" Taavi asked. "He's going to be mad as fuck, right?"

"Yeah." A conversation with Tuuro was a pretext *within* Ingenious Stratagem, but not an actual stage *of* it, so Vanako hadn't mentally prepared for one, which was possibly a mistake. Or maybe Taavi was out of order here; she mentally prepared for dessert. "Mad but possibly kind of happy? He's going to feel like other Kayalim teams have more of a shot with her out of the way."

"Will they?"

Vanako made a *pfffft* noise with her lips. "They're not ready to go up against Shanhoon Krait, or Yaulë, or Lerikaan Boomslang. Tuuro and Zetaala weren't either, really, and the rest of them aren't at that level yet."

"Why hasn't Tuuro found someone to race with yet?"

Vanako raised an eyebrow and ran the fingertips of one hand down from her shoulders to her knee to indicate the reason.

Taavi chuckled. "He wants to race with you? No wonder he's going to be happy Mom's out of commission?"

This was both a true fact and an obvious one, and since Vanako had not mentally prepared for the conversation with Tuuro that wasn't actually going to happen today, she was processing its implications much later than she should have been.

"Want me to say three hours?" Taavi asked.

"I want to cancel, now." It was getting too easy to forget this conversation wasn't actually happening today... because Taavi was right, it was absolutely going to happen at some point, and Taavi and Gilthiniel were probably going to ask Vanako's dumb ass about it tonight. "Keep an eye out for a nice apple-sized rock, I may have to make a quick getaway."

"Be nice," Taavi said. "He cares about something you care about. He wants to be with you. That means more than you know."

Which was an opening if ever there was one; but Seven Goats Street was where they split off, and Vanako was in a rush to implement Part II of Ingenious Stratagem. Taavi kept on down Ashthereen Honu Street, and Vanako went up Seven Goats Street, toward the lab.

There were times Vanako wished she were smart enough to work in the lab. It was a small office building that had been wrapped around the back and sides in a cloak of glass; all kinds of green things grew in it, and blossoms shone from behind the fog of condensation on the panes. Professor Loggerhead—Loggerhead-shan—was much nicer than Ora-shan, Vanako's own master, and the lab was, unusually, full of Ililuë employees—although Taavi said they were "techs," which sounded pretty advanced to Vanako, but context suggested that being a "tech" was not actually as cool or prestigious as being a student; which made no sense to Vanako, since she was already a student, which sucked, and which hadn't brought her within a ten-mile radius of even thinking about some day knowing enough biology to be a tech. The only people who ever came into Ora-shan's atelier were city planners (Mrineen), landowners (Mrineen) and builders, who might occasionally be Kayalim but, if they were, were inevitably men with cropped hair who had learned to make a good impression one the Mrineen they worked with by not speaking much, and who inevitably took in Vanako's long, bright hair with looks of cool appraisal that... well, if they ever followed the looks up with, say, a friendly word, then Vanako would gladly forget about the looks, but since the Kayalim gentlemen all cared more about maintaining a decorous silence around their Mrineen colleagues than about showing a shred of humanity to the apprentice, the looks were all she had to go on, and the outcome of the appraisals never seemed to be "worthy human, would save from quicksand" (Vanako remained a city kid) but always seemed to settle closer to "shoe-bottom scum, would not warrant effort of defenestration."

Not that Vanako ever dwelt on this or anything.

But this wasn't the atelier, it was the lab, and Vanako swiftly buttonholed Felúndirwë, an unusually short Ililuë tech with a flat of flowers and someplace to be, with the message that Taavi would be an hour late. She'd felt a little bad detaining Felúndirwë, who kept looking at the flowers as though they were about to dissolve or possibly explode, but something about the tech's light eyes and wide mouth and their maybe waist-to-hip ratio had made Vanako decide long ago that she'd cheat on Tuuro with them in a hot second and not be sorry; but she was pretty sure they saw her as a kid, so she needed to start making inroads.

But! This was a morning for Ingenious Stratagems, not dallying and flirtation, and anyway Felúndirwë's body language had started displaying signs of genuine anxiety after about a minute of awkward small talk. So, with a perhaps overly chummy "Hope that your harvest gives you a, ah, big-ass yield, or whatever?" Vanako was back on Seven Goats Street, sweatier and hornier than she'd have liked, and heading south and east.

She'd have preferred to take a wyrm, both to reduce sweatiness and also to save herself half an hour or so, but she found a bike first and discovered it felt good to move her legs, to coast down boulevards, to lose herself in the strategy of getting through space to a destination at a certain rate of speed. Sort of a horniness to sweatiness converter, she thought as she wove through the morning tourists at the Grove of Colors, although maybe the exchange rate wasn't great.

She got rid of the bike in front of Saavero's stable in Rust Precinct.

Most of the wyrms were still there and most of their riders weren't, which made it a normal morning. Vanako greeted Gerain Leatherback and Nannygoat, a pair of gentle souls who were just happy to be there, and didn't greet Zaji sho-Ganeka, who was very focused on giving his Dawn Spinnaker a rubdown, and who'd looked right at her once without saying hello even though he absolutely knew who she was. She'd have gotten past this easier if Spinnaker's stall wasn't where Aubade used to live; but it was, and on Tuuro and Zetaala's behalf she was having trouble getting past it.

On second thought, though: She turned, leaned in, and said "Hi Ganeka-cha!" in as non-fake a tone as she could summon. He looked up, blinking, and put on a perfectly polite, warm smile and said "Hi Shearwater-cha" back like any normal human would who hadn't decided to occupy your boyfriend's dead dragon's home *on purpose* or anything. And now Zaji had seen her and Gerain had seen her and Saavero had heard her, which meant that they could definitely tell her family exactly when she'd come and left, because Saavero was like that. Which was maybe not crucial to Part II of Ingenious Stratagem, but might set some minds at ease, because on this uncertain day it was far from impossible that Vanako and Bandit would disappear separately, and she'd probably take a bit less grief from the parents—on grounds of incrementally reduced familial angst & anxiety—if it was clear that they'd disappeared together.

Bandit was happy to see Vanako, in its cool but guileless reptilian way, and showed it by sniffing at her waist for anything tasty she might be carrying. "Sorry, floof," she said, ruffling feathers on the back of its head. "No sauce today."

An image of Zaya rose, unbidden, in her mind: tiny, as though viewed from a height, and colored with a scent and a feeling of welcome weight between the shoulder blades and a quiver of inquiry. "No Mom either," said Vanako. "Wish I had better news."

What will happen to her? Bandit said. *When will she come back?*

"We're going to fly somewhere so I can figure that out."

The image of Zaya surged back, inquiry now replaced with a cautious excitement.

"Sorry, chicky. We're not seeing her today. But!" She said, before the inevitable mental pout, "You are getting a bonus for helping." She walked over to the crank that opened the skylight and began hauling on it.

Zaya's better at that than you, Bandit observed.

"She's heavier than me."

Stronger.

"Well, I'm lighter. You should be grateful."

Are we racing?

"Not today."

Bandit gave off a pulse of benign indifference, a mental shrug, blue and cool.

"Your bonus," Vanako said, not without a hint of labor in her breathing, "is as much fish as you can eat."

Bandit shared a sensation of mealy, tasteless mouthfeel and a rocklike sensation in its gut, all shot through with spiky contempt.

"No, you turkey," said Vanako. "*Live* fish."

✳✳✳

VANAKO LEFT BANDIT ON the beach in Cerulean with instructions: Eat all you want, don't get in fights, and don't let the Copse out of your sight.

The Copse was a stand of argan trees that grew, unaccountably, about two hundred feet out past the low-tide line. Vanako had never dived deep enough to reach their roots, but she'd seen the coachman fish and knight crabs that lived among the close-set trunks, and had nutshells thrown at her by the colony of gibbons that lived there, subsisting on argan nuts, seafood, and washed-up beach trash. It wasn't the best landmark for them to meet at, unless she wanted to swim, but if Bandit didn't stray too far then it would see her on the shore when it came back.

It had been a funny parting. She'd thought an afternoon of freedom would be a welcome gift, but she'd felt Bandit's trepidation when it realized what she was proposing.

I don't know how to catch fish, it had told her.

"Watch how the wild ones do it." There were a few Dawns coasting on thermals; more were out on far rocks or sleeping in the dunes.

It could be dangerous to get too close to them.

"You sound like a human, chicky."

Chicky was probably the wrong nickname for the occasion; it was short for "death chicken"—itself only mildly offensive to dragons, who didn't care what they were called, but the human connotation of "chicken" might have leaked through. *I've never been with wild ones before*, it said, a little frostily. *When humans run into unfamiliar humans, they invent reasons they should be killed. As if stealing a mate or food wasn't enough.*

"Okay," Vanako said. "What cowardly, squishy little animal should I compare you to that isn't human?"

Bandit didn't dignify that with a response, choosing instead to stagger Vanako with the wind from its wings as it took off closer to her than it strictly should have. "I love you!" she called into its wake, and she knew from the petulant pulse of middle-finger energy she got back that its mind had heard.

So much for Ingenious Stratagem Part II: Lay A False Trail At The Stable. Vanako trudged over the dunes, already sweating, and began to look for a bike.

The three-phase structure of Ingenious Stratagem was built on a principle she'd come to realize after a less ingenious stratagem of hers had broken open months ago: If you want to hide what you're doing, hide it behind something else it looks like you're also trying to hide. The thrill of catching you out will make people feel smarter and better than you, and that satisfaction will blunt the urge to look further.

That one had broken open because she'd lost her nerve, and because she hadn't meant to get caught in the outer lie: She'd just sneaked around figuring she could keep all of it from the family, and she'd been as surprised as anyone when they believed the desperate lie that she'd been dealing worldvine extract rather than yliaster. Or... they hadn't really believed it, they'd figured it out eventually. It had been a desperate lie after all; she'd kicked herself for not saying blue instead, which you didn't have to transport in charm-sealed boxes. But the satisfaction of the story—Vanako did a bad thing, screwed up, and got caught—had let even the dumb, desperate lie stand basically unchallenged for weeks.

That lie had also come close to bankrupting the family, and they still hadn't recovered from the financial damage it had caused, and maybe if Vanako hadn't gone to see Ziyuki that first time then she wouldn't be coming to her this second time, even if this time she was using a much sturdier, better-planned, and generally more Ingenious Stratagem.

This one would work, though. She'd used her apprenticeship as an excuse to get out of the house, used her arrangement with Taavi to delay when Ora-shan would raise the alarm, and gone out, *very* irresponsibly, to fly Bandit alone, risking an encounter with police who might not feel like capturing Zaya was enough. They'd trace it all that far, and that would make a good outer lie: Vanako sneaked out to do something she wouldn't have been allowed to do if she asked, and then she screwed up and got caught.

That was a story everyone could believe. No need to dig deeper.

She pulled up in front of the Sweet Soldier, knuckled the last of the water out from under her eyes, and slung her kit off her back, immediately feeling the breeze begin to dry her sweat-blotted shirt.

Shaved ice places hit peak occupancy on summer afternoons. This one had a couple of midmorning patrons, mostly nursing iced coffees or chatting over fruit plates, but there was plenty of space for her to set up. She probably should have just gotten a drink, but fuck it, she'd been biking and crying and scheming all morning; she ordered a bowl of shaved ice with fruit, condensed milk, grass jelly, and rice flour pillows, and set up while they made it. The easel went into a corner by the cake case, so anyone who entered could see what she was doing, and the smallest table she could find came up next to it to hold the food, and then she put up the thin board she used to draw on, then unrolled a piece of paper over it and clipped the edges so it laid flat. Pens, ink, and brushes went on the table by the shaved ice—it had come while she was setting up—and the sketch of her subject got clipped over the lower right of her paper, so she didn't have to turn her head to see it.

Vanako didn't have the talent for life drawing that some of her classmates had. Her teachers always told her to draw what she saw, but you can't; drawing was a double trick, as far as she could see, tricking a bunch of faithless marks on paper into the kind of arrangement that could trick the eye into thinking they were an actual thing. But those tricks were about consistency as much as detail; a photon-for-photon rendering of a brick wouldn't do much for you if the rest of the house was just a sketch. Like any other con, it was mostly about holding a vision in mind long and faithfully enough to see it through. Reality was a source of inspiration and obstacles, but whether the eye bought the trick was about the vision.

So vision was what she'd worked on last night, when she'd drawn the study she'd be working from today. It felt a little more familiar to her, weirdly enough: Architectural drawing was about creating a vision and drawing it in cross-section, and this was a little bit like that. She began sketching the bigger contours, using light strokes of charcoal she'd overbrush later to finalize. For the purposes of Ingenious Stratagem, it was important to get the main idea in early, so the people who'd recognize her subject would have a chance to pass the message along sooner.

The hair she left schematic—that would be brushwork, there was no point laying in more than an outline—but she got to work first on inking the eyes. Easier to develop the contours of the head around the eyes than try to squeeze the eyes inside the head. Capturing the gleam of an eye with a well-placed omission of ink was something any student artist learned to do swiftly enough, but the bags under the eye demanded more thought: How to make them an essential feature of her subject's identity without seeming to center the portrait on them. Likewise the lines of his forehead. Overwork the incidentals and you'd destroy the consistency. She'd given up on conveying the salt-and-pepper of his perpetual stubble; but here, with her materials to hand and a night's sleep on the problem, an approach took shape, and she intermingled orange flecks of salt with purple pepper, echoes of the flowing hair that was to come, in the smooth and vivid blends that only he knew how to create. It matched Zaya's, or how Zaya's had looked when she was taken. Vanako took a scoop of shaved ice and found it almost all melted, so she took a long slurp from the bowl.

She'd meant to pay attention, see if anyone had left the cafe, but she looked around and of course she didn't know who'd been here and who'd just arrived. She turned back to the work. It didn't really matter. Zinji te-Zuuno's face came into focus on the page, ten times larger than life, unmissable and unmistakeable.

***

VANAKO FILLED IN THE outline of Zinji's hair, painstakingly mixing inks and testing them before she applied them, knowing her own color blends would be clumsy and abrupt compared to Zinji's. They turned out all right, she thought, abrupt for sure but true, at least, to the vision. It took her over an hour to finish the hair, but Ziyuki had not come.

She slurped down the rest of the bowl and ordered some chicken with rice, the only actual food the cafe sold. "It's bad," the cashier whispered behind her hand when Vanako asked for it, but she was too jittery for more sweets and persisted. It really was bad—dry, overcooked, underspiced. Vanako choked it down anyway; and still Ziyuki had not come.

She started to work on the eyes, using the same orange, purple, and pink she'd brought for the hair. It was an interesting effect, but she realized she'd overdone it. The stubble had been enough; bringing the same color to the eyes gave the whole portrait a sameness she didn't love. Still, Ziyuki had not come.

The afternoon rush was starting to pour in. The cashier shot Vanako a series of less and less subtle looks, which Vanako met with a politely uncomprehending stare. At last the cashier made a pointed gesture of rubbing her fingertips together and jerked a thumb at the tubs of toppings. Vanako gave up and got another shaved ice, this time with berries, red bean, and half condensed milk. She got death stares from a group of girls about her age who were eating while standing. When she got back to her table, a

Kayalim well-dressed in the Mrineen style—tight black top and a slim, calf-length purple skirt—was at her table. "There wasn't anywhere else to sit," they said.

"OK," Vanako said, "but I'm waiting for a friend. You have to move if she comes."

"Fine," they said. They were drinking black coffee and eating something with so much fruit piled on, Vanako couldn't see the shaved ice. The two of them ate in weird silence, and still Ziyuki did not come.

Vanako stared at the painting for a while, ignoring her churning stomach as best she could. There were a couple of strokes she could touch up, and she did, but the thing was, it was done. It felt like she should be working, because otherwise why have Zinji stare at the poor patrons of this cafe all day? She was cautiously proud of his expression, sad and amused and perhaps quietly judging, or at the very least a pretty good rendition of the beat-up-but-not-quite-beat-down quality of his prematurely old face, but it wasn't really the right mood for this cafe. Or the right colors, for that matter.

She took out a fresh sheet of paper and began trying to draw shaved ice. It was hard to figure out the strokes that conveyed the texture. "That looks more like mashed potatoes," her tablemate volunteered.

"That's a nicer word than the one that's in my head."

"Well, I hardly know you."

"My name's Vanako." Should she have given an alias? Too late, anyway.

"Haanen ze-Keiaza." They took a sip of coffee, which seemed to have mysteriously refilled since they'd sat down.

Vanako stared at the coffee for a minute.

"Thirsty?" said Haanen ze-Keiaza.

Vanako sighed. "Ziyuki-kana's not coming, is she?"

Haanen ze-Keiaza turned their attention back to their book. "Give it a little time to clear out. In about half an hour, they can close without losing too much business. Then we can talk about it."

"It's just, I think I need to talk to—"

"Shearwater-cha." Their voice rose in a chiding singsong. "Leave it for half an hour, please."

So Vanako experimented with marks for half an hour, trying to draw shaved ice. She drew things that might as well have been haystacks, piles of hair, mountains of gravel. It felt like no one would ever leave. And then the host was gently touching the shoulders of the last couple in there, saying something apologetic in low tones, and they were getting up to leave, and Haanen and Vanako were alone.

Haanen set their book down. "Are you hungry?" they said. "Thirsty? It's on the house."

It took Vanako a second to realize they'd meant the House. "No," she said, stopping herself from asking if she could be reimbursed for two shaved ices and one bowl of terrible chicken and rice.

"OK," said Haanen. "First things first. This stunt shows creativity and initiative but not good judgment. The Baronet has maintained this way of doing business with your grandfather because it is a way to contact him that does not draw attention. Your approach does not succeed on that front—no need to make excuses," they said, raising a conciliating hand. "It's a difficult time, you did what seemed right. But you didn't think about it from our side. Pair that with the fact that you've hung out here all day creating a very striking portrait of a man that, up until now, our regulars thought of as just another random vagrant... it's cause for concern." Haanen's tone remained quite mild and reasonable. "Going forward, the Baronet's proxies know to look for you as well as your grandfather, so there won't be a need for this. Please come by sparingly and only in cases of serious need. The Baronet has been reluctant to set hard and fast boundaries with your grandfather because she knows that need can strike twice in a week, for example, and it can take the form of something that might seem frivolous. I'm not."

"You're not... frivolous?"

Haanen smiled, and although it was an entirely cool smile, it did seem to partake of sincerity. "I'm not reluctant to set boundaries. No more than one appeal per month and three per year, for example. It's a good way for me to make sure we're not getting too distracted by this. But it's not a good way of ensuring she's available when need strikes you. So let's not make me have to do that."

"If you weren't reluctant, wouldn't you just do it now?"

"You might be right. Do you want a lesson about the difference between being right and making good decisions?"

"No, ze-Keiaza-cha."

"Correct."

Vanako looked at her for a few minutes with what she hoped was a penetrating stare. "What are you?"

Haanen raised an eyebrow. "I get that a lot, but not usually from Kayalim with long, purple hair."

"I didn't mean how to call you, I know how to ask that."

"Ah."

"Uh... how do I call you, though?"

"I go by 'they,' thanks. You?"

"'She.' I meant what are you to Ziyuki-kana?"

"That's another area where the Baronet prefers not to create delineations. She asks me to do things; I do them. Do these things have things in common? Sometimes. Is this, what we're doing now, generally the kind of thing I do? Maybe. Am I deliberately cultivating whhat seems like an accidentally annoying air of mystery, so as to seem a little bit less badass than I'm making myself out to be, so you'll let your guard down? Who can say?"

Coming from a Mrineen, this sort of horseshit would be intended to elicit fawning or sparring. Vanako supposed she should read it the same way from Haanen ze-Keiaza; but since fawning and sparring felt like the same thing in conversations with Mrineen, and she didn't have the belly for either, she settled on stony silence, with only her mind's eye rolling.

Haanen sighed. "Sorry, Vanako-cha, I'm exposed to a lot of bad examples and I'm developing all kinds of bad manners. The Baronet is pretty sure she knows why you're here. A run-in with the law, mutual acquaintance, unusual circumstances... ?" They wiggled their fingers while raising their hand, presumably to communicate flying. Vanako made an assenting noise. "You understand, of course, that the Baronet is constrained in her ability to intercede directly in this type of situation." They deepened their voice as if caricaturing the phrase. "House Amphisbaena doesn't like competing with her brood-family for her loyalty. That said, if all the Baronet had were regrets, she'd have sent a letter."

Vanako felt her shoulders drop with relief.

"So," said Haanen ze-Keiaza. "Three facts you should know.

"First, your mother's alive, conscious, unhurt, tried, and sentenced. I probably should have led with that earlier, I'm sorry."

"Bad manners," Vanako said.

"Right. On the bright side, that was technically five facts for the price of one."

"It's funny," Vanako said. "I guess as soon as you didn't say anything about it, I assumed she was alive."

"OK, well, hopefully that's the last time you put that much trust in someone from the government. We're not good people. Second fact: The Chief of Corrections in Yemareir is named Zaailo Merganser."

Vanako blinked. "What's a merganser?"

"It's a duck that looks like it's seen some shit. Don't lose the plot."

Vanako wasn't sure if she imagined a wink. "Did you just wink at me?"

"The plot, Vanako-cha. Third fact: A journalist named Shenireen Agama wrote a piece not long ago on your family and Yemareir politics for the Damask Free Press. Say them back to me, please?"

"Mom is OK but in jail. Zaailo the duck runs the jails. Shenireen Agama published the secret to springing Mom in some journal I'm supposed to read."

Haanen looked at the ceiling as if hoping to find a rope ladder, or maybe a cauldron of boiling oil. "No one said anything about jail for Mother; she is sentenced. Not to death, though, I should have said not to death. That's not widely known, we're sharing it with the family as a courtesy, to alleviate anxiety. In case anyone asks, which they won't, because we're not shouting it from the rooftops, are we?" Vanako shook her head. "Merganser. Chief of Corrections. If I'd just wanted you to know that some duck guy was doing jaily stuff..." She looked around. "I'd probably be stewing tomorrow's red beans in the kitchen of a shaved ice shop right now instead of embroiling you in thrilling political skulduggery. And, yes, read the article, which was published in—"

"The Damask Free Press."

"And they say poor listening skills are destroying job prospects for the youth."

"So what's my job?"

"With ears like that, you can be anything you set your mind to."

"I'm serious," Vanako said. "You're actually going to walk in here like... like the Halftongue Prophet or something? Three facts and you walk away?"

Haanen cocked their head and stared at Vanako. "I'd have thought you were a little old for Wing Windtwister."

"It's all-ages entertainment. Something for everyone." She debated saying the next thing. "Also, the Baronet's brood-nephew is apeshit for it. Literally the one annoying thing about the kid."

"I feel like we're building trust here," said Haanen.

"Totally."

"Guess we need to work on those listening skills after all." Haanen pursed their lips for a moment in thought. "The Halftongue Prophet is cursed by the Chief of the Sky, either because he seduced the Chief's son or, if you're an all-ages kind of person, because creating puzzles and ambiguity is a useful plot contrivance to keep the audience engaged, and nothing creates ambiguity like only being able to say every other word in a sentence. But me, Haanen ze-Keiaza: not nearly stylish enough to get in bed with a demigod, also a political operative of unknown but probably impressive scope, probably pretty good at taking the shortest path to the point in clear, plain language. What's my curse?"

Vanako leaned back in her chair. "You like torturing teenagers in shaved ice shops?"

"Let's stipulate that the curse is operationally relevant and not some annoying kink."

"You have no idea what to do and you're throwing shit at the wall?"

"That," Haanen said with an index finger pointed straight at Vanako, "is excellent critical thinking, and you should keep the possibility in mind at all times. But also, give me some credit for not just being a bag of walking coin flips, I do actually have an unusually well-informed perspective on shit in general and my actions are always at least a little bit goal-directed. You, on the other hand."

"Are you saying I have no idea what to do and I'm just throwing shit at the wall?" Vanako scoffed. "I'm a teenage criminal. Tell me something I don't know."

"That's my girl," said Haanen, standing up. "You've learned two facts that were public knowledge, and one you were going to assume was true anyway. What a useless meeting, right? All that for basically no information. It's like I didn't help you at all."

They were halfway to the door before Vanako could think of a follow-up, so she settled for "I hate you?" With the question mark intended to convey, perhaps, the potential for reparations, or maybe just a general acknowledgment that Haanen ze-Keiaza was, although hateable, also a badass whose approach to cool Vanako would absolutely be studying like an architect trying to reverse-engineer a blueprint from the outside of a structure. (There was a reason architects didn't actually try to do that; but she wasn't going to focus on that just yet.)

"I believe in you," said Haanen, not looking back.

***

No sooner did the front door bark shut than the door to the back room opened. "We're closed," said the owner, or at least the middle-aged Kayalim woman Vanako thought was the owner. She grabbed a broom, flipped a few chairs up on tables, and started sweeping.

Vanako began to pack up. The owner watched for a moment as she rolled up the portrait of Zinji. "Your uncle OK?"

"Grandfather. As good as he ever is. He's not in trouble."

Thee owner nodded, the went into the back. She came out with a grease-spotted paper bundle and placed it in Vanako's hands, still warm. It smelled like cheese and yeast. "For him." She gave Vanako a stern look. "Don't sneak any. He doesn't eat enough."

"Thank you," Vanako said.

"Don't mention it."

"You don't sell pão de queijo here," said Vanako. "You made these just for him."

"Common decency," the owner said. "Don't mention it." She looked at Vanako a little longer. "OK, look. If you ever decide the lifestyle is too much for you, you can always come here. We can find a place for you."

Vanako blinked. "The lifestyle?" She was about to say something about the 'stream, but bit it off; this woman obviously didn't know much about their family, and a packet of pão de queijo maybe wasn't a good trade for the keys to the front door.

"You know. Living like Mrineen do. Boys with boys and that. It's not for us, we know it inside. Your grandfather... well, maybe he's too old to admit it. But someone like you, maybe you see things differently. And we can find a place for that. If it's what you want."

Words collided in Vanako's mouth: *Fuck you*, obviously, and *No thank you*, and *Get away from me* and *How absolutely dare you* and even, small and sharp like a bone chip in a piece of fish, *Yes, please*. Acid boiled in her belly. She wanted to puke it all over this woman; but not as much as she wanted to be gone. "I'll give him the food," she mumbled, not meeting the owner's eye, and darted out of the shop.

***

VANAKO FOUND HERSELF RUSHING to Cerulean Precinct and made herself stop. It wasn't important for her to get back a few minutes earlier; that wouldn't stop anyone from being angrier or more worried than they already were. She didn't need to rush, she needed to think.

There had been three parts to the Ingenious Stratagem, and the third had been the one where she didn't know the payout in advance. She hadn't fooled herself about that. What she hadn't expected was that she wouldn't know the payout even after she'd gotten it.

Then again, how many options had Haanen really given her? She could try to talk to the Chief of Corrections of Yemareir, but the daughter of a currently incarcerated criminal was the kind of person they'd see out at spearpoint. Maybe there was some technicality of the appeal process that Haanen was pointing her at, but she could figure that out if she needed to. Meanwhile, reading a newspaper was easy. Maybe Shenireen Agama's article would tell her what to do next.

It had to. Ziyuki was the smartest person Vanako had ever talked to—or at least the person whose intelligence was most tangible; everyone nodded along when Cerminir and Kirono said things, but they might as well be making up words most of the time for all Vanako knew. If the whole idea was for Vanako to be able to figure it all out on her own—she remembered Minshoon talking about "plausible deniability" once, when Eäril had lied about sneaking a date cake from the counter—then she'd be able to figure it out.

Of course, sometimes really smart people didn't realize how dumb other people were.

Cerulean Precinct was beginning to hum with the approach of sunset, the residents recognizing as one that the time for nightswimming was coming to an end, that the ocean breezes would grow brisk and the sun would cease to linger. There were Dawns out over the water, still. Vanako couldn't tell whether Bandit was among them. But the particular contours of the wyrm curled up nose to tail just inland of the Grove looked familiar.

The Damask Free Press article would tell her something. It had to.

***

Taavi was waiting in Bandit's cell at the stables.

"Tiamat," said Vanako.

Taavi closed her textbook with an audible clap.

"Cerminir sent you, didn't she?" Vanako asked.

"My idea," said Taavi.

"I needed to get out of there," said Vanako. "They were never going to let me fly. I needed to get in the air."

"They didn't want you to get disappeared by the cops, dipshit?"

"I outflew the cops *yesterday*."

Taavi stood up. Vanako had always known she was tall, but she'd never had Taavi standing with her arms crossed over her breasts, six inches away, looking down at her with flared nostrils and fire on her brow.

"Mom is gone, you little weasel. And you *lied*. To *me*."

Vanako hadn't expected her to take this well, exactly; but this was a Taavi she'd never seen. When she breathed in, she felt her throat shake. "Taavi," she said. "I had to. They already took Mom. I had to know they couldn't take this too."

"*They could have.*" Taavi covered her eyes with her fingertips. "Vani. You're in such shit. Dad is practically laying eggs. I'm pretty sure Cer was sharpening something. Chashu said he was going to trawl the riverbed."

"He just said that because he wanted me to feel like this is serious."

"It's serious."

"I'm sorry," Vanako said. "But not for what I did. Just for making life hard for you."

"And for lying?"

"And for lying. To you."

Taavi drew a deep breath through her nose and let it out, as though she were trying to blow a bad smell out of the air. "You're only getting off easy because your mom got arrested?"

"Lucky me."

"And I'm the only one letting you off easy?"

"I mean, I'd hate for Cer to sharpen something just for me and then not get to use it."

Taavi turned to go. Vanako sent a soothing pulse of farewell to Bandit, whose face was snout-deep in a pile of some kind of dried fish. *Thank you, chicky.*

Bandit replied with an image of soaring on thermals, riding up and down where the air took it, nothing on its mind but the flash of scales in the water and the ache in its wings. Vanako ran up to Taavi and snaked an arm around her waist, tucking her shoulder into Taavi's armpit. They walked that way for a few steps, clumsy and tangled.

Chapter 23
Nine weeks before the Skua

THE THOROUGHNESS, HARSHNESS, AND efficiency of Vanako's grounding were... not surprising, but impressive.

Not binding, though, strictly. She had supplies for a stealth charm. But those were limited, and risky to work with in a room where there weren't any doors. And since she'd used stealth charms to sneak out when she was dealing for Tjaroon, it would probably be retraumatizing for the parents if she used one again. No deal-breakers there, quite, but downsides.

She immediately requested to go back to school, words she'd never thought she'd say, but Cerminir had apparently already requested a week's assignments on the pretext of "extreme agitation and nerves" that required regular access to special tinctures and calming baths at home. They'd allow her back after, with conditions, but for the next few days it was home, punctuated by market trips with Minshoon.

The run-up to the election was in "full swing," apparently? The night after Zaya's arrest, there hadn't been nearly as many neighbors over, but a lot more strangers. Yyrreen directed traffic until the candidates and parties had cornered her again, and then there was a lot of sitting and staring until Yyrreen got five minutes with Minshoon to start handing out paper again. Some of the paper was propaganda, some of it was assignments to do things in places. Vanako didn't really know, because she was cutting chicken into chunks with a cleaver and scraping seeds out of pumpkins with Vinaali, who bossed her around in faster Kayalshō than Vanako could easily follow and criticized her knife skills, which he compared variously to "a drunken sea lion," "a blind snake," and "if a lumberjack and a rockslide left their bastard baby in a kitchen."

Still, it wasn't too hard to pick up the broad strokes of what was going on, since Yyrreen and the Thread & Mortar party flack considerately summarized them in a screaming fit that had the Lilac Precinct cops at their door to break it up.

Mostly (Vanako gathered, her ears ringing and her arms aching, while she ground roasted cocoa pods into powder) it came down to who should do what where. Thread & Mortar wanted to compete hard in some districts where the Travelers were likely already leading; they wanted the Travelers to step in in a few districts where they had no chance, to draw votes away from Brightest Scale. Yyrreen said, to a first approximation, "please help yourself to this sack of dicks I baked for you," which was by way of reminding the Thread & Mortar flack that the Travelers were in this to give Thread & Mortar a coalition, not a majority; and, contrariwise, fucked if Yyrreen was going to deviate from the strategy already agreed on in prior negotiations without a change in the actual facts on the ground.

But there had been a change, the Thread & Mortar flack argued, loudly: The Travelers' mascot, and one of their major revenue streams, was now in the custody of the city of Yemareir.

Then Yyrreen really got into it, like "hard to understand the words you're using" levels of into it, and Vinaali set Vanako to chopping some really fiddly little herbs, and she lost what little of the plot she'd had. But the parents' misery was palpable the following morning; and she'd gotten out of the house faster than she had in a long time, especially on the first day of school after a break, and picked up a copy of the *Damask Free Press*.

***

IT WASN'T THE RIGHT one; when she asked the street hawker for a copy of a months-old back issue, they looked at her as if she'd asked for a slice of smoked moon on toast. So she'd bought the day's issue in embarrassment—which she must not have hidden too well, because the hawker's look smoothed out into pity (though not before the flinders hit their palm) and they advised her to hit up the Laurel Precinct Free Library. They also gave her directions there, which added insult to injury. But Vanako was too focused on the injury to dwell on the insult, and scuttled off like a crab in a seagull's shadow.

She'd mostly shaken off crustaceanity by the time she actually hit the library, although the not-entirely-approving eyes of Ms. Shaava the head librarian kept her a little scrabbly still; Vanako had worked up a reputation for minor disorder and excessively irritable question-asking, mostly when Jaliki insisted on spending hours looking for the one Wing Windtwister book he still hadn't read, hoping a copy might have appeared somehow. But the side-eye fell away when Vanako asked for something age-appropriate, and in two minutes she was seated at a long table in the adults' section leafing through a broadsheet.

The reading was tough going, a little. Dr. Agama, if she was a doctor, was a little bit up her own ass about the like *nature* of what she was doing, and the people she imagined were reading, and the state of politics in the city, and, extremely weirdly, about Vanako's family. She barely remembered running into this woman outside House Shearwater—she'd been imperially hung over the night after the Shadowrun—but the idea that this weird story about cops and murder and magic and politics had come from Shenireen

Agama following Zaya around to trawl for quotes about the 'stream was... not comfortable. It made Vanako feel like there were eyes on her.

It made her feel, for the first time, like maybe haring off to fly on her own the day after Zaya's taking had not been a good idea.

But the evocation of Inundinir Square brought back the fear and chaos of that night in a way that made Vanako feel sick, but also seen; and the slow-build sense of dread as it became clear what was happening outside the *Free Press*... she could appreciate the suspense, if she could make herself forget that it had really happened. The piece ended on a cliffhanger, and Vanako found herself hoping Agama was OK.

She could see why Ziyuki had directed her this way. Shenireen Agama understood politics, knew people, and sympathized with Zaya's cause. She could publicize Zaya's disappearance, could maybe figure out the pressure points that could get her back. Vanako could figure out the details... if she could just talk to her.

She couldn't get to Damask Precinct, to the Free Press' offices; she was way too grounded for that. But she could get to the letter-box.

And so she'd sat down at her desk to write a letter.

CHAPTER 24
NINE WEEKS BEFORE THE SKUA

Dear Dr. Agama,

I very interestedly read your recent article on my family, the Shearwaters of Lilac Precinct. As you may know my mother Zaya Shearwater was recently arrested by police on a race I was also in. I would welcome the ability to talk with you about this journalistically interesting event at a time that works for you.

Yours,

Vanako Shearwater

***

"Vani," said Gilthiniel, "why are you writing like a child?"

Taavi threw a pillow at him. Vanako raised an eyebrow, but inside she was cringing. "I'd ask you why you dress like one," Vanako said, "but it's not nice to insult little kids."

"Three out of six," Gilthiniel said. "Needs work. I think this pillow was supposed to have a letter attached to it with some gentle correction of my manners?"

"It was supposed to have a rock in it," said Taavi, "but you hid all of them in your skull?"

"Four out of six." Gilthiniel looked at Taavi for a moment; something passed between them. "Sorry, Vani," he said. "I assumed you wrote it that way on purpose."

"I assumed you paid girls to date you," said Vanako, "but at this point I figure there must be blackmail involved."

"Four and a half? I am actually sorry, though. But, look—Agama's a writer. You want to impress her with the writing. Like I think the 'journalistically interesting' part can be implied, for example."

"I want to explain why she should be interested," said Vanako, trying to sound like a smart person making a subtle point and not a girl worried about looking like a dumb baby in front of her terrible brother, who was apparently five out of six at insults even when he wasn't trying.

Taavi and Gilthiniel weren't the kind of twins who did everything together and finished each other's sentences, except in certain acts of psychological warfare against deserving teachers and exes. They had independent interests and friendships, they had secrets from one another. What they didn't have was their own rooms. Vanako did, but the parents had taken the door off months ago (for cause) and she hadn't quite worked up the courage to ask for it back. It seemed like a bad time to do it now, when she had something very specific she wanted to hide.

But even if she'd had a door, Taavi had pointed out, Gilthiniel would get suspicious if they were suddenly spending a lot of time behind it. And Taavi trusted both his intelligence and his discretion. Vanako... well, she trusted Taavi. So she let Gilthiniel in on the quest from Haanen too.

There'd been immediate consensus that this was the kind of thing they shouldn't keep from the parents for too long, and equally immediate consensus that it was definitely something they shouldn't spill immediately. "One," Gilthiniel had said, "they're already crazy busy following up on their own leads that they're not telling us about. And, two, as soon as they know you tried to talk to Ziyuki-kana, the actual hammer comes down."

Which, Vanako had had to admit, was an analysis that showed both discretion and intelligence.

"I get you," Gilthiniel said, in a friendly and open tone that Vanako recognized as the one he used when he was deliberately softening his voice to communicate something difficult to a kid, like when Jaliki had misunderstood the rules of a card game in a way that was about to lead to crushing defeat. If it had been a teacher, she wouldn't have bothered keeping the miserable expression off her face and stopping herself from looking down at her lap; but this was her stupid brother, whom she'd seen sloppy drunk and getting slapped by girls objectively below his league, and fuck everything if she was going to cower in front of him like she'd gotten seven times eight wrong again. "It's just, she's a professional, you know?" Gilthiniel said. "She knows what she thinks is interesting."

"OK," Vanako said. She had agonized over the choice and order of words in that letter. "If you feel that strongly about it, we can revise." She put a dry twist on *strongly*, like why was he being such a baby about this, but she didn't think it connected. That was fine; the thing was to make the effort.

CHAPTER 25

EIGHT WEEKS BEFORE THE SKUA

Dear Dr. Agama,

I hope this letter finds you all right. I know you must get a lot. I thought it might help to mention that I actually show up in your old article, although I did not talk to you much then. Looking at what the rest of my family said, I now realize that must have been frustrating because journalists can not do much without their source material, so it is a little like my dragon refusing to fly in a race. I could try to run it myself, but I would not do well.

If you would like to meet, I would be delighted to tell you about any part of the stream (The Brimstone Slipstream) and what it is like, that you are interested in.

Sincerely,

Vanako Shearwater

***

"Sure," said Gilthiniel. "Fine."

"You can be honest," said Vanako, straightening her spine. "I want your honest opinion."

"Why, though?" said Taavi. "His opinions suck on average?"

"Look," said Gilthiniel, "I could correct it, but why bother? People in real life care about intention, not style, and most of them suck ass at writing and it doesn't matter."

"This is the literal opposite of what you said about the last one?" said Taavi.

"You think it sucks ass?" Vanako said.

"I think your prose style is an acquired taste," said Gilthiniel, "and I'm a slow learner."

"Was that supposed to be nicer than telling me it sucks ass?"

"It was objectively like three or four percent nicer than telling you it sucks ass," Gilthiniel said with a straight face.

Taavi turned to Vanako. "And what have we learned today?"

"Don't ever ask Gilthiniel for an honest opinion," said Vanako.

Taavi laid a hand on her shoulder and nodded gravely.

"It shows you've read the article," said Gilthiniel. "And that you really want to talk. Maybe that's all it needs to do."

"Did the other one not do that?"

"In my experience, saying you've read something is not the same as showing you've read something."

"He means his teachers can tell the difference?" said Taavi.

"This sucks," said Vanako. "I should just go over to the Corrections Department and find Zaailo Mer-whatever."

"They'll toss you out like a leg-humping dog," said Gilthiniel. "And if they don't, what then? What are you going to ask this duck guy?"

"Where's Mom, how is she, what's he going to do to get her out?"

"The exact things every convict in Yemareir wants out of this exact guy. You know you're not getting answers, even if they don't jet you like a wad of used tobacco."

"What's with you and gross metaphors today?" asked Taavi.

"If Vani can have a prose style, I can have a prose style."

"This is style like Eäril wearing Kirono's vest and getting greasy fingerprints all over it is style?"

"See?" Gilthiniel said. "It's catching on."

"Eugggggh?"

"Like when that one boy gave all your friends the monkeypox."

"I'm never going to be able to compare anything to anything else again, am I?" said Taavi.

"She was jealous," Gilthiniel said to Vanako, "because he didn't give *her* the monkeypox."

"There has to be something I can do," Vanako said. "I mean, obviously the idea here is that there's something in that article that a Doctor of Journalism or whatever can connect to Duck Guy in Alabaster Precinct and give us a lever. There can't be that many hidden steps here."

"He gave the other girls monkeypox by kissing them," said Gilthiniel. "So you can see why Taavi would be jealous."

"Haanen went out of their way to say it's public information," Vanako said, trying to ignore him.

"Much like Taavi getting passed over for monkeypox transmission activities."

Taavi hooked an ankle under his chair and yanked. Gilthiniel squawked and crashed to the floor in a tangle of arms and bad language.

"They didn't tell me anything I didn't already know," Vanako said. "They practically said that. All I have to do is figure it out. Why do I need some sportswriter to figure it out?"

"Agama knows things we don't?" said Taavi. "She might understand why something's important based on, like, decades of experience that we don't have? Like maybe the merganser guy used to be a 'streamer? That'd be ironic, right, a former 'streamer putting a current one away for the crime of doing exactly—"

"Exactly," said Vanako. "Like actually absolutely right."

"... I'm pretty sure Merganser-cha's not a 'streamer," said Gilthiniel, sharing a confused look with Taavi.

"Probably not," said Vanako. "But this is the shit, right? This is the kind of thinking we need. And we don't need a journalist to do it. We're smart enough to figure it out."

"I didn't figure anything out?" said Taavi. "I made something up?"

"Just read it."

"... okay?"

"Read the article. Both of you. There's a copy in my room. And then do *that*."

"What?" said Taavi.

"Make things up that make sense. If it doesn't work, whatever. But you guys..." Vanako sighed. "You're smarter than me."

"Vani," said Taavi.

"Don't argue," said Vanako, who wasn't sure she could take a supportive compliment right now. "The thing is, you're smart like Ziyuki-kana. When she thought up this stupid puzzle, she was thinking how a person like her would put things together. But I'm not a person like her. You are."

Gilthiniel laughed. "Do you really think that?"

"It's true."

"Vani," said Gilthiniel, "we are struggling with university entrance exams. And we studied our asses off to get this far! Ziyuki-kana is one of the hundred most influential people in the city. Whatever she's got going on, it makes what we've got going on look like eagles dropping turtles on a rock."

"Read the article," said Vanako.

"Fine." Gilthiniel showed his palm in concession; but Vanako could tell that, under the tolerating grin, there was a real one hiding.

***

SCHOOL WAS A SHITSHOW, of course.

Vanako had two friends, more or less: Zayeni, with whom things had been a little weird ever since Zaya had threatened to make a monkey eat her boss' face while she was sitting right across from him in a booth in the Blind Beggar; and Varaana, who smoked up like *a lot*-a lot. Vanako had made friends with Varaana early on because she'd been the person everyone pointed to when you asked who you could bum some weed from. She'd only wanted a smoke, not really a friend; but it turned out that, in Lilac Precinct, when you asked around about a smoke, no one other than the dealer would be friends with you. It wasn't the smoking that was a problem, but the asking. The girls who'd come with her back to Lilac from Celadon Precinct had apparently known this instinctively, but they hadn't bothered to tell Vanako, and they acted like everybody else when her reputation as a dope fiend got around. Most of them smoked more than her, because they could afford to. They just kept their purchases better hidden.

So it wasn't like Vanako wasn't used to the stage whispers, the knowing smirks, the tiny origami gifts that unfolded into notes that now said "CRIMINAL" instead of "JUNKIE" and "DYKE." There was more of that than usual; but since she'd sat dragonback with Zaya Shearwater and won, none of it had burned quite as badly as it used to. What she couldn't take was the sympathy.

Every girl who said, sincerely, how sorry she was, or offered help, or asked how Vanako was feeling, was an unknowing survivor of a vengeful force that would have whirled her to red shards of flesh if Vanako had let it. Not the insincere ones, who didn't mean anything they said, or the ones who were just there to twist the knife; Vanako was used to treating those girls like slugs on the road—not much fun to have nearby, but they'd dry out in the sun soon enough. Only a girl who was pure in heart could drive Vanako insane enough to want to seize her by the ears and scream I HAVE FLOWN THROUGH THE AIR LIKE A METEOR ON THE BACK OF A KILLER LIZARD WITH A GUT FULL OF FIRE, THERE IS NOTHING I COULD DREAM OF NEEDING FROM YOU.

So when she did exactly that to Vinda te-Kaleivi, it should have been a problem.

Vanako would have settled for a slap, a scratch, a barbed riposte, a grappling match that went to ground, a sobbing retreat. She wasn't picky. But Vinda te-Kaleivi just put a warm, firm hand on the muscle of Vanako's upper arm, that spot where it swells out just below the shoulder joint, and said, "I know. You're so strong. But you don't have to be strong all the time."

In the howling eternity of this moment, Vanako had two options. One was the simultaneous release of all the molecular bonds joining the atoms of her body, washing the Lilac Precinct People's Lyceum for Young Adults in a pulse of clean, white fury that would leave nothing but a glass-walled hemispherical crater and a cloud of fine grey ash to mark its passing. The sweetness of this option was almost too overpowering to pass up... but the downsides were substantial; and anyway, a truly perfect molecular disaggregation was hard to arrange, and it never paid to half-ass a chain reaction.

The other option was even uglier. But Vanako gritted her teeth and chose life.

"There might be... just possibly... one thing you could do."

"Oh yeah?" Vinda's face betrayed just the faintest touch of dismay, which Vanako clutched to her heart like a puppy. Vinda wasn't really pure in heart; she just had an image to keep up. The unceasing interior soul-scream dwindled to a high whine.

"What do your parents do for a living?"

Chapter 26
Seven weeks before the Skua

Esteemed Dr. Agama,

I know it has not been long since the last two letters you received. Perhaps they are still on your desk unread. Which is all right! However, in the absence of your learned council, I have started a research project that you would maybe be interested in.

My fellow students of the Lilac Precinct People's Lyceum for Young Adults are mostly the daughters of construction workers (there are boys there as well but we are not permitted to socialize). This is because we are a mostly Kayalim school and that is the best job most Kayalim in Yemareir can obtain, if they can become a foreman at least. However there are a few who do other jobs. A number are on the dole, which is not a job, but I am writing in pen here. One does caravan guarding, which my mother used to do. One of them runs a bunch of food carts, and another one works for him (these are all men by the way, my mom told me a lot of traditional Kayalim couples are very sexist and I guess I should have believed her). Two of them are bond traders, which has to do with buying debt but is different I guess from the kind of people I used to know who do that, or maybe these ones just do not tell their daughters about the kneecaps they go around breaking.

But one is a deputy warden at the Viridian Precinct Correctional Center!!! His daughter says she does not know anything about the inmates, which is a little weird actually because she is a very nosy person. I am not saying her dad is hiding something, but I think we should not rule it out, although it is also possible that she does not pry because he is discrete or his job is boring.

Anyway, I do not actually know what to do with this. In my last two letters, I tried to tell you that I had something for you. But someone very smart told me what I should have already known, that you know a lot more about this city than I do and you probably have ways to make connections between things that I could never understand. So I have told you all I know and you can try to do something with it. The actual truth is that I do not know what I can do for you. I am hoping that you can do something for me, and I am willing to try to make it worth your while, but I do not know how. Only I don't really know how you can help me. But someone very smart, a different very smart person, sent me to

*you, and I believe they know what they are doing. If
we could talk, maybe we could figure something out.*

With deepest appreciation,

Vanako Shearwater

****

"Are you going to tell her," said Gilthiniel, "or should I tell her?"

"I know I misspelled 'counsel,'" said Vanako. "I realized as soon as I wrote it."

"And 'discreet,'" Gilthiniel said.

Taavi rolled her eyes. "Not that? Dipshit?"

"Then what?" said Vanako.

"Vani," said Taavi, "did you read the article?"

Vanako packed as much umbrage into her scoff as it could hold. "Did I," she intoned, "read the article."

"The whole thing? Including the little author bio at the end?"

"The part that talks about what her job is or whatever?"

"That's not all it said."

Vanako was starting to feel very antsy and stupid. "That's not part of the article."

"It is when it says her whereabouts were unknown at press time."

Vanako felt a weight pool at the bottom of her belly. "It's months old," she said. "She's probably resurfaced or whatever."

"I went down there," said Gilthiniel.

"You wish a girl would let you," said Vanako.

"You two were in trouble," he explained. "That was the whole reason for this letter-writing thing to begin with, you weren't going to be able to go to Damask and check up on it." He waved the letter at Vanako. "I didn't know you were working on this, or I'd have waited to bring it, just in case."

"It was my pivot," said Vanako weakly. "I got all vulnerable. It was a new angle of attack."

"It was a big improvement," said Gilthiniel. "You should be proud. I am."

Vanako edged her chair closer to his and put her head on his shoulder. She put on a fake-blissed-out expression and closed her eyes, which helped keep the tears back.

Gilthiniel tousled her hair. "Don't get comfortable. I still owe you a burn for your bad cunnilingus joke."

"Don't be a fuckbucket," said Vanako.

"Always asking for the impossible?" said Taavi.

They stayed like that for a moment, Gilthiniel's hand still resting in Vanako's hair.

"Are the parents doing, like…" Vanako searched a heartbeat for the word. "… dick? About anything? Except the fucking election?"

"Of course they are?" said Taavi, at the same moment Gilthiniel made a sort of shoulder-shrugging noise that clearly said "I don't know, but probably not."

"Gil," said Taavi. Vanako couldn't tell whether she was shocked, mad, or too shocked to be mad.

"I'm not saying they don't care," said Gilthiniel. "But what can they do? They went to all the jails. None of them will admit they have her. All the prisons and crews say she's pending assignment.

Their lawsuit just got slapped down in the precinct court. We've got the only lead, and we're not sharing."

Vanako could feel her jaw slacken as she looked at Gilthiniel. "How do you *know* this shit?"

"Kirono will talk about it if you ask," Gilthiniel said. "Minshoon sometimes. They're not hiding anything."

"Ziyuki-kana didn't tell Zinji-kana," said Vanako.

That was what she'd said to Taavi and Gilthiniel: After Taavi had taken her home, after the parents had bitched her out and grounded her, after she'd spent two hours trying to sleep in her doorless room and finally barged into the twins' to tell them everything. Zinji had come to Ziyuki, like he'd told Vanako after Bell the Cat, and Ziyuki hadn't told him what she'd told (or what Haanen had told) Vanako. There was a reason she'd held it for Vanako. There had to be. Because Minshoon, Cerminir, and Kirono were all way the fuck smarter than Vanako was, and if Ziyuki wasn't telling them, there had to be a reason.

"I know," said Gilthiniel.

"Are we doing the wrong thing?" said Vanako. "Should we tell?"

"I don't think it's wrong or right," said Gilthiniel. "It's about control. We're not powerful in this family. We can get latitude to operate if the parents don't know what we're doing. Once they know, they take control. That's not something we want to give up."

"Yet?" said Taavi.

"Yet," Gilthiniel agreed.

"But if we can't get anywhere—" said Taavi.

"Then we tell," said Gilthiniel. "Of course."

"Can we get anywhere?" said Taavi.

"There's always Zaailo Merganser," said Vanako.

"The Chief of Corrections for Yemareir is not going to want to talk to an inmate's kid, Vani," said Gilthiniel.

"Haanen was really hung up on his name," said Vanako. "They wanted to make sure I knew it."

"Maybe they were trying to emphasize that he's Kayalim?" said Taavi.

"With a name like Merganser?" said Gilthiniel. "Half, tops."

""You're one to talk?" said Taavi, laughing.

"We are half," said Gilthiniel. "But fair enough, the number of times I've wished I was te-Normalguy or ze-Bend-in-a-River or..." He noticed Taavi and Vanako looking at him. "OK, I'm starting to see your point."

"No one else uses bird names," said Vanako. "No one. It's literally a thing Mom and Kiriki-kana did as... like a double fuck you to their family bullshit and this city's bullshit."

"Pretty sure the city bullshit boils down to Ziyuki-kana's bullshit?" Taavi said.

"Whatever," said Vanako. "This has to be something." She looked to the twins in turn. "Doesn't it?"

"I wasn't there for the conversation with Haanen..." Taavi began.

"... but yes," said Gilthiniel. "They gave you so little. We have to look at everything. This can't be a coincidence."

"So what do we do with it?" said Taavi.

"We ask someone who'd know," said Vanako.

CHAPTER 27
SIX WEEKS BEFORE THE SKUA

GETTING OUT TO THE Azure Precinct apartment had been easy. The parents and Yyrreen were desperate to get anyone out of the house that they could. There was some thing happening with the Travelers that wasn't going to include the Thread & Mortar Front and the secrecy was stressing everybody out. It wasn't warm enough to swim, but it was warm enough to play in the sand, and the weather was always right to see Zinji-kana, so the trip to Azure Precinct hadn't been hard to sell. Getting Zinji alone at the apartment was as easy as waiting for Enwë to get cranky: Gilthiniel stayed on the beach with Jaliki and Eäril, with carte blanche to blow all their cash on food if that's what it took to keep them outside, and Taavi and Vanako had taken Enwë to the apartment to sleep. Five minutes in Zinji's arms was all it had taken to get her down. She was snoring gently under Zinji's none too freshly laundered blanket.

When he'd put her down, both Taavi and Vanako had been staring at him; but when he'd asked what was going on, they only looked to each other. Finally, Vanako had sucked in a breath deep enough to lift her shoulders almost up to her ears, and asked, "What's the deal with Zaailo Merganser?"

Zinji's face grew sullen and suspicious. "He's your great-uncle."

Taavi and Vanako looked at one another again.

"He's the Chief of Corrections in Yemareir," Vanako said.

Zinji grunted.

"He has a bird name?" Taavi said.

"If you're going to insist on talking about Zaailo, you'd better explain where you're coming from," said Zinji. "I'll tell you right now, no amount of bird name is going to get him to help your mother, if that's what you're hoping. He was probably happy to lock her away."

"Why?" Taavi asked.

"Same reason we don't talk. He's a bigot."

Zinji was over in the nook of counter and cupboard that passed for a kitchen, a bottle in one hand while he rummaged for a glass. He poured something clear that Vanako could smell from across the room. "Kind of a cliché, isn't it?" she said. "Drinking to forget."

Zinji fixed her with a sharp eye. "It's not to forget," he said. "The more we talk about this, the more mezcal goes down my neck. That brings the conversation to a natural stopping point. Don't waste your questions."

"Zinji-kana?" said Taavi. "We can back off if you need us to?"

Counterpoint, thought Vanako, *the fuck we can*; but Taavi's hand was on her shoulder, and Taavi knew Zinji a lot better than Vanako did.

Zinji sighed and looked at his glass, turning it in his hand. "There's never going to be a good time to talk about it," he said. "I learned that with the girls. How much do you know about Kaalo-kana's family?"

Taavi and Vanako let their blank looks speak for themselves.

"All right," Zinji said, and looked into his glass.

***

KAALO WAS BORN WELL off (Zinji said), but by the time he was grown, he was properly rich. The family always lived in Crimson Precinct, they always had work. Kaalo's grandfather had been tight with the alderwight for Madder Precinct; they'd done a lot of construction jobs that got the in the government's good books, and they just kept working that vein. Beachfront chalets up on the north coast, nice little apartments for visiting merchants over in Amber Precinct. Eventually Kaalo's father got into city planning. That was never Kaalo's thing—he liked money, he liked numbers, he wanted to work the bourse or trade bonds.

The poor bastard, he met me.

I told you his people were from Madder Precinct, originally, and they still prayed there, back then. And, for the briefest while, so did we. My mother and I were in Madder for a year, we'd been on the dole out in Khaki for the longest time and then the Thornwyrms started brooding, so they moved us to Madder.

I was stricken the moment I saw your grandfather. I don't think it was ever like that for him—I never did ask. I didn't really want to know. I'd try to get next to him during the haka, so I could touch him by accident, or at least feel his breath after. And I'd see how he tried to do the same with the boys. I was passing as a woman, then, and I was eating even worse than I do now; but even if I'd been out as a man, I didn't think he could possibly want me, some stringy no-account poor who'd never set foot in a place like Crimson Precinct. Not when I saw how he looked at the fit boys, the ones who stomped the hardest, with voices like golden bells.

But I had the advantage of not knowing anything. The other boys knew that they weren't supposed to flirt with boys; but I didn't know I was a boy. And they knew better than to talk about something as Kayalim as psionics with the rich boy from Crimson Precinct. Rich boys were supposed to have Mrineen interests, like dueling and finance and the 'stream. But all I knew was that his family was in construction. I just figured he'd be interested.

And he *was*. But no one else would talk to him about it.

So we talked. I took him out to the beach and taught him the basics of empathy on wild creatures. And, of course, it would have been irresponsible to let him try to guide a dragon on his own, so I taught him to coordinate with me.

I didn't have to tell him how I felt. About him, or about myself. When we were on a wyrm together, I couldn't hide those parts of myself, any more than I could hide the stars.

And he...

... Kaalo stayed with me all his life. You have to understand how much more a marriage, a life, is, than those early moments. But I think he stayed with me right then because he thought he'd won the lottery. As far as his family knew, I was a woman. But that was just a dress I could take off when we were alone, he thought. I thought so too. And when we were close, I could even make him feel me the way I saw myself. You're not supposed to use empathy that way, but I couldn't make myself care. It was like the perfect crime.

His family was never going to approve, of course. I could hide that I was a boy, but everyone knew I was poor. So we got pregnant.

That was when I started to realize we might not have won the lottery after all.

Zaya was an easy pregnancy, if you were all right with being a woman. But... the best way I can explain it is, I could feel my body growing away from me. Changing in ways that made me feel even less welcome, more trapped.

It's such a selfish thing to say. You'll tell me it isn't, and you're right, but it's so different if the baby's already there. I always cherished Zaya, from the first moment I felt her move. What kind of parent was I, if I didn't want to be in the body that she needed to survive?

I'd been doing spells on construction crews and training in fencing, anything to thicken my arms and shoulders—but I couldn't do that any more. I'd been taking barrenwort because that's what the boys who wanted to get big did, but I didn't know if that was safe for Zaya. I could dress how I wanted at home... but not with his family. And the gender charms—even if I could afford them, it would mean I couldn't feed Zaya when she was born. I was trapped in my skull, watching myself change in ways that were ten times as wrong to me as puberty ever was.

... I'm dwelling. Being pregnant was bad for my brain. You get the idea. And giving birth...

... I'm dwelling.

Nursing. Bless the mothers, and leave it to them.

It was the nursing that tore it, really. I never begrudged her...

... enh, don't let me lie. I always gave her what she needed, and I was mostly gracious about it. But I couldn't be around his family any more, putting on a show. Letting them call me the wrong name, dressing in drag all the time. It didn't feel noble the way it had, like I was protecting our family. Exciting, even, like I was undercover. It just felt airless now, like I was suffocating under a pile of pebbles and someone threw another one on every time they called me something I wasn't. Which was all the time.

And Kaalo, bless him, didn't have the option to pretend it wasn't exactly as bad as it was. Because his husband was an empath, and I let him know every fucking day.

But we were still cowards. So we let Zaya out me.

It wasn't hard. We just never taught her the wrong words for me. And so she got old enough to talk, and she used the right ones.

I thought, though. I thought, in front of her, they'd be kinder. Maybe we could start off civil; and, maybe, if we did that, we could keep everything from falling apart. They didn't love me, they never would. But they loved Kaalo, and they loved Zaya. Didn't they?

They loved them, but not enough.

I haven't said anything about Zaailo yet, have I?

Well, he's Kaalo's brother, you'll have guessed that. Younger. Kaalo was the oldest. I'd say he dreamed about tying the family fortunes closer to the city government, but the truth is that was always Kaalo's ambition too, even after we were married. No thought about how we'd square that with having to be around his family all the fucking time if we did that. He just assumed things could keep going. Such a weird thing to think, that I'd have put up with that shit from a husband back then, but I was too in love with the food in the kitchen and the roof between me and the rain. Getting disowned probably saved our marriage.

What a long lead-up to a short story, huh? But that's really all it was. We told them who we were, and they showed us the door.

And the only thing that Zaailo in particular had to do with it—he was married, then, still is; his wife was pregnant. And there was a moment when I thought Kaalo was getting through, I thought his father might be coming around. And I saw him look at Zaailo, and Zaailo just put his arm around his wife and looked at her belly and gave him one of those looks. Eyebrows up, like he was expecting something.

I never got Kaalo to talk about that look. I saw him see it, but he'd never admit it. But I'll tell you what I thought it was in that moment. I thought it was a little speech: *Dad, remember what we talked about. Remember all the foremen, all the workers, all the empaths you need to work cheap to do your job. Remember that, now, working for Seafarer Joists & Girders is a feather in these men's caps—but it won't be, if they think a fag is going to inherit the business. And remember Zaya's a girl, and my baby's a boy.*

Well, I can't prove any of that. But that look was the end of the conversation, and the last time I saw the inside of that house. And the baby was a fucking boy.

I got an invitation to his wedding last year. He married into House Boomslang. The other groom's name is Jenihoon.

***

VANAKO LOOKED AT ZINJI'S glass. He hadn't taken a single sip.

***

"HE WON'T HELP ZAYA," Zinji said, still not touching the glass.

"He doesn't have to let her go to help her—" Taavi began, but Vanako cut in. "Horseshit. He will."

Taavi flinched and shot Vanako a look of genuine hurt and confusion. Well, too bad; she'd explain later. "If he won't let her go," Vanako continued, "there's no point."

"No point in what?"

Taavi stayed quiet and looked guilty, like she was supposed to.

"Zaailo won't do it just for the asking," said Zinji.

Vanako shrugged and grunted.

Zinji put a hand on her shoulder. He was just her height, she realized; he used to be taller. "Please don't ask him to do this."

"He should see who he's hurting," Vanako said. "He can't just make people disappear with no consequences. No one even knows where she is!"

"He's going to tell you he doesn't write the sentences, and it's true," said Zinji. He went still for a second, looking into Vanako's eyes. "And you know that. You think you've got something on him."

Vanako set her jaw and tried to look like she was looking for words. She saw Taavi shoot her a quick glance of what she was just going to assume was admiration. Zinji's grip on her shoulder grew firmer—he wasn't squeezing something out of her, just trying to tighten the feeling of connection. Vanako let an image slip from her mind to his: a crowd of angry Kayalim in front of an ornately gardened white marble house, carrying torches and chanting Zaya's name. If he hadn't been looking for impressions from her mind, he'd have noticed the little push she gave it, just enough to get into his skull; but he would be looking, and would not be suspicious of how easy it was to read her.

He looked at Taavi. "Do you know what she's cooking up?"

"No?" This was technically a lie, but in practice it was close to the truth; Taavi was losing the thread. Nerds had a lot of uses, but you didn't get much practice holding onto complex lies when you could wrap the teacher around your finger just by showing up and sincerely doing your best. She was getting out of her depth here.

"Protests," Zinji said. "Outside Zaailo's house? You clearly haven't been there. The gardens aren't nearly that nice, and it's brick."

He was feeling smug, which was incredibly annoying and absolutely essential. "I could get a hundred people there," said Vanako. "Two. Easy."

"I don't believe you," said Zinji. "But also, you haven't thought this through."

"OK? Think it through for me."

"If you threaten a city official, they'll come with dragons."

"What?" Vanako said. She was sure this was true, but the implication was surprising. "They've done that for the yliaster protests. But they don't use them."

"To protect the government, they will. If you threaten the Chief of Corrections, they'll roast people in the streets. People like Kiri and Vinaali know this. They'll make sure it gets around. Which is a big part of why I don't think you'll get a hundred people to a protest like this. And you should be thankful for that—because, if you do go through with it, you and the half-dozen idiots you pull in won't get much worse than some broken bones and a bit of light internal bleeding. Which is bad enough that I wouldn't wish it on anyone, but miles better than being burned alive."

"We have dragons too," said Vanako. "You literally can't throw a stick without hitting one. They'd be starting a war."

"You think the 'stream are going to war against the government?" Zinji said. "Most 'streamers are weekend warriors, they don't care about Zaya except as competition they don't have any more. The rest of them might care, but not enough to die." He saw something in Vanako's eyes; she wasn't sure what. "This isn't how things get better, Vani. It's like when the street bully asks you to armwrestle. You can put in a good showing, get their respect. But if you actually get serious about winning, you're gonna find one of their big friends on each arm and a knife in their hand."

Vanako realized she'd forgotten what she was supposed to be doing here. The shock at what Zinji had said was still there, and she let it leak into his mind; the disbelief was fading, and she let that through as well. The decision not to send crowds to Zaailo Merganser's door took a little more care, since it wasn't as new as it needed to seem, but the thought of people burned alive by police lent a fresh distress to her thoughts that would help put the right shine on it.

"I see you're starting to understand a little of what you're getting into," said Zinji, as gently as he could. "Or... not getting into?"

Vanako glared sullenly at him and didn't speak.

"I feel like I missed something?" said Taavi, who in this instance absolutely hadn't.

"Your sister's emotions are running high," said Zinji. "Her mind's giving away a little more than she'd like. It's one of the prices of learning psionics—there were months when I could read Kaalo like a book, before he learned to control where his thoughts went. He hated that. He was always in love with the idea that he was unpredictable." He smoothed the hair on the top of his scalp.

"Words, though, Vanako-ko. Tell me you won't try this. I don't think you will, but I need words."

Taavi sighed. "We will not send our friends and neighbors to get fricaseed in the streets in front of Zaailo Merganser's house?"

Zinji looked to Vanako.

"Fine," Vanako said. "Screw him, anyway."

"And don't get any ideas about going to Ziyuki with this," said Zinji. "She can't take a hand in this directly, any more than—"

"Fine!" Vanako shouted, and Enwë moaned, then began to cry. Zinji went to her, and she stuck her arms out to be comforted, and Zinji lifted her and folded her into a warm embrace. He rocked her gently, hips and knees bouncing; and he must have been right, a little, about Vanako's thoughts leaking, because he sidestepped over to her with Enwë still in his arms, and put an arm around Vanako's shoulder. She let herself lean into the rhythmic motion of his rocking, and if Enwë's tiny fist was wrapped a little too tightly around her hair, she was content not to pry it open.

CHAPTER 28
SIX WEEKS BEFORE THE SKUA

HOUSE SHEARWATER WASN'T FULL when they got home, slightly on the wrong side of a dusk that still felt too early coming; but neither was it empty.

The table was, again, scattered with food, most not cooked on the premises; Shozo, Chashu, and Amiko were manning doors and windows; Cerminir and Kirono had retired, it seemed, or maybe were just recharging, but Minshoon and Yyrreen were still talking over beers with a leathery woman Vanako recognized from previous meetings, as well as the two vertical meat stacks who never seemed to leave her side. There were a couple of other Kayalim as well, some neighbors and some not. There was a flurry of introductions, since the children couldn't be packed away unobtrusively, and of course Enwë began wailing for Cerminir and Eäril insisted on sitting on Minshoon, and the ker worked itself into the proceedings for all the world like a normal dog, although the glowing cilia and the extra eye meant its new would-be friends reacted to it mostly with alarm and disgust; they knew what it was, and the fear of contagion, however groundless, was all over their faces. The leathery woman stretched her smile farther than her face seemed to want to go, and said "the young 'streamer" in tones that were meant as a compliment but sounded like greed.

When the pleasantries were over and the younger children had exhausted their parents' willingness to allow them any more left-over dessert, there was a general movement in the direction of the bedrooms in back; but Yyrreen put a hand on Vanako's arm and said "Stay a moment, will you?" So Vanako got a second helping of some kind of bread pudding thing that she'd have absolutely annihilated if everyone would just look somewhere else for a few seconds, and took a seat in the living room, and gradually the adults all settled in around her.

Minshoon spoke first. "Vanako, we've been thinking about what you and Bandit should do while we work on finding and freeing Zaya. You know the cash she was making in the 'stream was an important piece of the political work we're all doing, trying to build a coalition in the House of the Stars so we can make yliaster legal."

That wasn't all it was supposed to be good for, and Minshoon knew Vanako knew it. "If you think I'm going to race like she could race," said Vanako, "you're in for a disappointment."

"No one's going to be disappointed no matter how you do."

"Minshoon's speaking as a father, of course," said the leathery woman. "The rest of us need that money."

Minshoon shot a quick glare at her, then turned back to Vanako. "There's an opportunity," Minshoon said. "We've got access to two 'streamers with experience in paired flight, but they've never flown on the same wyrm. They're young—"

"—they're in love," the leathery woman cut in.

"Kaana," Yyrreen said, chiding gently—but only gently.

"There's no sense pussyfooting around it," Kaana said. "Zaya's a hero in spite of being a gay woman who dated a cop—people like that she's a mother, and they really like that she's a widow. Having Zaya's daughter and her lover pick up the banner—"

"Ugh," Vanako said through bread pudding.

Kaana smiled, something genuine taking shape behind those creased features. "He's a boy. You're too young. I know. But that's the story people like. Young lovers bravely defying the odds."

"I think of it more as taking advantage of the variance around the point estimate of the odds," Minshoon said.

"That's why you have no friends," said Yyrreen.

"I love having no friends. It lets me focus on embarrassing my family."

"You said you need money," Vanako said to Kaana. "Putting me and Tuuro in a race because we're cute is going to leave you with none money."

"We believe in you," said Kaana, lacking a certain depth of sincerity.

"Shanhoon Krait, Yaulë, Kshalain Honu, Lerikaan. There are probably a few Kayalim teams with a shot at beating us, too. The safe bet is you lose every flinder of your entry fee. I'm not giving up, I'm just being honest."

"We have an interested party who's willing to fund your entry fee in exchange for a share of any takings," said Kaana.

"That seems weird," said Vanako.

"I'm afraid I can't say anything more about it."

This made Vanako briefly furious, but a cooling peace quickly flowed over her. She wasn't the only person getting up to behind-the-scenes bullshit and hiding it. It was just that the grown-ups could refuse flat out to tell you what they were doing and you had no way to force them.

"It's your old boss," said Kirono.

Kaana and Yyrreen looked daggers at him. Minshoon just sighed.

"I trust her," Kirono said, as if it was all that needed saying. He looked at Vanako. "Don't tell anyone. The guy's a criminal, you know."

"He's footing the entry fee in exchange for a cut of the earnings?" Vanako said. "That doesn't add."

"He also gets all of his own bets," Minshoon pointed out.

Who's gonna throw their race now so the cute couple can win? she almost asked, but the wrong people were in the room. "So Tuuro and I try to win some races and spend the rest of our time making out where people can see us, and the organized crime boss foots the bill?" she said instead. "Just trying to be clear what my very protective family is asking me to do."

"You're not getting your door back any time soon," said Minshoon.

Kaana cackled. "I was going to say you should just be yourselves and act like a normal couple. I'm starting to think you may have to pick one."

"Yeah, it's almost like you should have asked me whether it made any sense at all before you started throwing orders around and trying to use my relationship with a teenage boy as a prop for your campaign or whatever."

Kaana gave Vanako a frosty look. "A teenage boy? What are you, a creepy schoolteacher? He's older than you."

"Dating teenage boys is cradle-robbing no matter how old the woman is. But don't let me keep lecturing you."

"If you're trying to goad me into calling the whole thing off," said Kaana, "you're doing a pretty good job. Unfortunately for you, I'm desperate."

Why? Vanako wanted to ask; but Kaana would give her a withering look, point out that it had all been explained already, and proceed to repeat herself anyway. Or, worse, Minshoon would do it, thinking his gentleness would be better than whatever weird mix of pushy, caustic, and selfish passed for Kaana's personal style; it would not. "Fine," Vanako said instead. "I'll meet Tuuro tomorrow and we'll get some practice in. I assume someone here knows what our next race is and when?"

"There's an Arc in a few days," said Minshoon. "Good practice. We'll sign you up tomorrow night."

"Sign me up for all of them. The more of Tjaroon's money we can blow on entry fees, the better."

"What I like about getting you back in the 'stream," said Minshoon, "is that you'll be off the streets and out of trouble. Or that's what I thought; and then you started thinking of ways to antagonize the organized crime boss anyway."

"See?" said Kaana. "It's like she was born for the Travelers. She already knows that rich people are the enemy. She just has to learn that the law-abiding ones are worse than the criminals."

"I'm going to bed," said Vanako. "It'd be a shame if they put me on my first mural with bags under my eyes."

"Wonderful to meet you, Shearwater-cha," said Kaana.

"I bet it was," said Vanako.

The right thing to do would have been to help clean up some food; but Vanako's legs and back hurt from biking, and her head hurt from information, and even though she thought she didn't dislike this Kaana person as much as she was acting like she did, she was definitely very much over this interaction.

She half wanted to process this with Taavi and Gilthiniel, then realized that "half wanted" meant she wanted to process it with Taavi and not Gilthiniel; so, screw it, another time. She passed her door, passed theirs, and went through Zaya's.

It had gotten to be a habit since Zaya had disappeared: Checking the window box of irises for letters. That was how Zaya had summoned Vanako to their first race together, months ago. Zaya had asked her to water the irises, and she had, and one night there had been a pair of goggles and a note.

That had been the Angels' Tribute, where Tuuro's grandfather Zetaala had died. The course ran through the Necropolis, which conjured visions of the dead. Vanako had seen her mother, who'd been killed by a fox ker. She wondered who Tuuro had seen; whether, if he ran the course again, he'd see Zetaala.

But there was nothing in the irises. She left the window open, even though the night was chilly, and sat down on the edge of Zaya's bed. She moved the weirdly mounded blanket from the pillow, then lay her head down and covered herself. She only meant to lie there for a minute; but the deep draught of air she drew through the pillow seemed to perfuse her brain like a cooling mist, and she was asleep before she could begin her exhalation.

Chapter 29
Six weeks before the Skua

Merganser-kana,

Please forgive the personal correspondence at your workplace. I was unable to obtain the postal address of your domicile. I hope we could find a venue of mutual convenience to discuss a matter that is professional to you but personal to me. I know the weight of obligations must compel you to great selectivity in sharing the hours of your day; still, I hope my parting signature will lend clear and compelling justification to such a meeting.

Cordially,

Vanako Shearwater

***

"There," Gilthiniel said. "He'll lap that up."

"There," Gilthiniel said. "He'll lap that up."

CHAPTER 30
SIX WEEKS BEFORE THE SKUA

THE CRIMSON PRECINCT HOUSE was brick, as Zinji had said, but he'd been wrong about the gardens: They were lush and strange, with broad, deep green leaves that shone like leather, and elaborate orchids big enough to be pollinated by pigeons. There was a kitchen garden positioned to look as if it had been tucked away, but the vegetables were so huge and perfect that Vanako was convinced they were for display just like the rest of it. She could feel eddies of heat and humidity from sorcerous microclimates, although she couldn't see them.

The door opened silently, a full two minutes after her knock, and there stood… someone, anyway? They were dressed in Kayalim cuts and colors, loose and rich; their skin was smooth, light, and strangely tight at the corners of the eyes and mouth, and their hair was tidily cropped, but dyed a purple that was richer than Vanako's fading hair. They didn't seem like they could be as old as Zinji, which meant they probably were. Vanako had dressed in her best, but she felt as shabby as an ungroomed dog next to this person.

"I'm Zaailo Merganser," he said. "You may come in if you like, but I thought we'd walk around the grounds first. You should know this place. It's only because of my family's cowardice and bigotry that you don't. Mine included, I suppose."

"Hi," Vanako said, blinking.

Zaailo Merganser hopped off the stoop, onto a path Vanako hadn't realized was there. She followed, taking a careful step down so she didn't crush any precious plants or possibly any irreplaceable rare slugs? Who knew what a family like this left lying around?

Once she was off the stoop, the heat and humidity really hit her—this garden was almost like Cold Point, she realized, the boundaries of the sorcerous microclimate just permeable enough to permit air flow, but effective enough to create sharp shifts in temperature. "We keep fruit trees near the front door so I can do things like this," Zaailo said, picking a lumpy yellow-green fruit from a nearby tree and handing it to Vanako. "That's a custard apple. They're from Kayazē. Pain to eat out of hand, we'll bring it inside."

He grabbed another for himself and took her farther along the path, pointing out a few more trees and flowers, every one from Kayazē. "Nobody's gone back there, you know. This is all from seeds and little gardens that our people have maintained here over the centuries. Things our ancestors brought over. It's an amazing feat of preservation—thousands, really, of amazing feats of preservation. Lecturing," he said, with a conscious emphasis, as though he knew it was a swift left turn and was signposting it on purpose, "sets me at ease when I'm nervous. The Mrineen guests I do this to have a script for occasions like this; they offer lots of compliments and platitudes, 'how exotic,' 'what dedication to your heritage'—it's all puffery, of course, I don't expect that from you and I don't want it. This isn't for them anyway, it's for us. But I don't think you've spoken yet, and you wrote to me for a reason. What was it?"

She'd been lulled by the lecturing, and more than a little stunned by the garden—was this what Kayazē was actually like? The Queen who Flooded the Garden—had her garden looked like this? But there was an answer to Zaailo's question; it was one of the few she'd planned for. "You have a bird name."

"You know a lot of people with those."

"Not who live in Crimson Precinct."

"Your mother's brood-sister lives in Argent."

"Her name is Amphisbaena, not Shearwater. And she doesn't talk to me."

"She did once, over shaved ice." Her look of surprise wasn't entirely feigned; Zaailo laughed. 'We see each other from time to time. Legislators and city officials, it's unavoidable. She's how I recognized your name; I might have thrown your letter away otherwise. Didn't say what she'd talked to you about, only that she'd met the newest Shearwater and was impressed."

That could be a lie, Vanako told herself. Probably was.

"So," said Zaailo Merganser. "I have a bird name. What does that mean to you?"

"I think it means you think your family can be more than just your brood-family."

"In Mrineen families, it can be less too."

That was a warning: *Don't expect me to treat my brood-brother's daughter like my* real *niece.*

"Mrineen families have reptile names," she said. "We have bird names."

"And birds care for their broods," he said. "Is that it?"

It hadn't been—all she'd meant was *We're not the same as them*—but it sounded pretty smart, so she shrugged her shoulders and cocked her head as if to say *I didn't make the rules.*

"So you want me to acknowledge my feathery instincts," said Zaailo, "and intercede on your mother's behalf?"

"Yeah, I want that," she said. "But I know better than to ask. You can't just free someone in your custody because she's related to you. That's corrupt."

"You don't really believe that," said Zaailo.

"But you do."

Zaailo nodded sadly. "I do. It is. My orders come from the courts—at least in terms of the sentences I have to execute. It's been widely known for months that Zaya stole the wyrm you two were racing with, and then of course there was that business with the girl at the University. Lilac police didn't think they could maintain order in the precinct if they broke into a house full of children to apprehend her, and then there was the officer who died chasing her at Cold Point; that made a lot of officers nervous about engaging. But the tip about—Bell the Cat, was that the race?" Vanako nodded. "I run the work crews and jails, you understand. The police don't consult with me on operations. But that was an opportunity for two precincts with strong flyers to join forces in capturing her. Says a great deal about their respect for her abilities, whatever you may think of her guilt or innocence. Yours too."

"What does it say about my innocence?" Vanako thought she kept her voice calm, but blood roared in Vanako's ears; she thought the thrashing of her heart might knock her off her feet.

"Your abilities," said Zaailo. "You were on the wyrm with her, weren't you? What did you name it, Bandit's Breath? I'd like to hear the story there one day, if I could."

"You'd have to ask Mom," Vanako said. "I wasn't there when she named it."

"'Mom.'" Zaailo seemed to be rolling the word around in his mouth to taste it.

"Zaya-kana." That felt weird.

"I know. You know, Vanako, there aren't many 'streamers on the police force, and fewer empaths. Those skills are in demand. It could be a path out of..."

He trailed off; she thought she could guess some words he'd decided not to use. "Of what?"

"Your family's done well for themselves," said Zaailo. "A flat in Lilac Precinct is something a lot of Mrineen families would love to have. Two of the young adults in House Shearwater are university bound, to all appearances, and one of the heads of household is a professor. For such a small, new House, it's a respectable set of accomplishments. The next scion of the House should be looking to her own future." Vanako realized he was watching her face very closely. "Or have I misunderstood why you're so interested in Kayalim Houses with bird names?"

Her heart accelerated again, but not in fear this time. "I don't know if I see myself in law enforcement," she said, the understatement leaving her throat tight.

"Take some time to reconsider," said Zaailo. "But I understand."

"I've been training as an architect," she said. "I've been told that's the family business? Seafarer Joists & Girders?"

Zaailo laughed; he seemed genuinely taken by surprise… then genuinely mortified by his reaction. "I'm sorry," he said. "We've got a feeder program, all the masters in Lilac Precinct know to recommend their best apprentices." His face moved as if to say more, and Vanako could see him struggle to put it into words that wouldn't cut: *If you'd been any good, I'd know you already.*

If anyone had asked Vanako yesterday whether she'd care that Ora-shan hadn't recommended her for a "feeder program" to some builder she'd never heard of, she'd have looked at them like a dog at a card trick. Here, in a humid garden full of plants that were supposed to feel like home, with no one but her long-lost… great-uncle?… who was rich enough to collect them, and capable enough to run a business to keep him rich while he worked full time for the government… she felt her throat swell, her eyes sting.

He looked at her appraisingly, and obviously the appraisal found her wanting. She tried to write her exit speech in her head, but she was finding it hard to improve on *Fuck you.*

"Can you meet me in Madder Precinct tomorrow afternoon?" he asked. "It turns out there's an architecture project I could use your skills on."

"Your studio's here."

"For a certain, limited conception of 'studio,' that's true," Zaailo said. "Here's the real truth, though: Your master might speak about 'rough' drawings and 'finished' drawings, but even the most finely finished drawing is a blank page. That's no slight to your work, any more than it is to the papermakers of the world. But it's what the world writes that makes your drawing finished." He grinned, and alongside the good humor in it there was a sharpness, each tooth flashing even in the low light of the rain forest garden. "And you get more world for less in Madder Precinct."

CHAPTER 31
SIX WEEKS BEFORE THE SKUA

"THAT'S A CREEPY THING to say?" said Taavi.

"Pretty normal thing at the business factory," said Gilthiniel.

"The business factory is creepy?"

Gilthiniel shrugged. "It all seems like appropriate business. If I needed to throw some money away on property for R&D, I'd do it in Madder Precinct."

"OK, but at least you'd be able to understand when someone bitches you out in Kayalshō for ruining the neighborhood?"

"I think that sort of understanding would compromise my ability to do a business."

"Zaailo's Kayalshō is better than mine," said Vanako. "He's read all the history, he knows all the epics…"

"Sounds like a huge dork," said Gilthiniel.

"The word you're looking for is 'cultured'?" said Taavi.

"That's what I said."

"What am I supposed to do with this?" said Vanako. "Am I snooping around for dirt on him? I'm not going to his house, and I don't know if I could stand to sneak around it if I were. Does he even have a clue about where Mom is?"

"I think Ziyuki-kana knows where she is?" said Taavi. "Why would she send you to find that out?"

"Why would she send me to find anything out?"

"Maybe it's not what you know that she doesn't," said Gilthiniel. "It's what you can say that she can't."

"We have to trust her?" said Taavi. "For now anyway? You just met Zaailo-kana, how could you possibly know what you're looking for?"

Zaailo-kana. That hit her ear awkwardly, like the sound was the wrong shape. But she was the one who'd said all that crap about bird names being different from reptile names. Had that been real? Or just a way to get what she wanted from the conversation? Being the only family with a bird name had meant a bird name was just what her family was. Now that there were two, there were some things about a bird name that were what they had in common, and some things about a bird name that they didn't have in common because one family or the other was doing it wrong. Was being rich and successful one of those things? Was this just a wake-up call that "House Shearwater" was nothing more than a bunch of people pretending to be Mrineen and doing just an unbelievably bad job at it?

She looked to Gilthiniel, then to Taavi. "It's not time to tell, right?"

"That you've got a business meeting with the Chief of Corrections in Yemareir who also happens to be Mom's uncle?" said Gilthiniel. "No way. Not now. Not when we're on the actual verge of maybe learning something."

"It's her decision?" Taavi said.

"She asked us," said Gilthiniel. "I assumed that meant she wanted our opinion."

Taavi turned to Vanako. "If you feel like it's too much," she said, "we can tell?"

"Gilthiniel's right," Vanako said. "I just wanted to check with you guys. In case there was something I was missing."

It felt true. As soon as Gilthiniel had spoken, it had been clear to Vanako that he was right. But there was no denying that she'd hoped to hear the opposite: That they were out of their depth, that it was time to call in wiser heads. When Gilthiniel, the least fucks-giving human of her acquaintance, said it was time to tap out, then it would have to be true.

Whatever. Zaailo Merganser was cultured and powerful and intimidating and smart, but he was basically an old paper-pusher. Put him and Zinji in an alley with a knife between them and she'd bet on the Ministry of Corrections having to consult its succession plan. The Madder Precinct visit was going to be fine.

***

"AND IT *WAS*," SHE said to Tuuro over a mouthful of churro and cinnamon cream.

They were at the food cart near Bandit's stable in Rust Precinct, the nominal purpose for her visit to the south of the city that day.

"Now I know you're lying," said Tuuro. "Creepy old kashaaizo invites you to the ass-end of nowhere to help with his 'business' and everything's fine? That's like you and me being at my place for an hour alone and me telling my dad he's *not* about to be a grandfather."

She poked his shin with her toe. "Voya sho, perv. People will talk."

"What else people should say about me? If they talk about my report card, I can't show my face in public. Much better they talk about my girlfriend." He was joking, of course. They hadn't had sex; she hadn't asked to, he hadn't pressed. She'd had a lot of thoughts about that, many in contradiction of one another, but mostly she was relieved not to have to worry about it.

"I was kind of creeped out at first," she said.

"Good."

"They have this... maze."

All joking fell off Tuuro's face as though a trap door had opened under it. "Vani."

"What?" she said, wide-eyed. "What's so scary about a harmless little maze in Madder Precinct, where no one can hear you scream?"

She joked now, but it had been a moderately terrifying experience. To stand at the entrance to this broken-windowed warehouse, with its roof crudely torn off and its interior visibly reshaped with battered cinderblocks, and be told by the king of Yemareir's prisons that she'd be helping them with "data collection."

"Now you're going to tell me they had some honking gaizu in there," said Tuuro, "so you can blow it off like it's no big deal."

"Not some honking gaizu," Vanako said. "Animals."

Tuuro leaned his head back and wiped his hands down his face with a moan. "You're not even alive right now," he said. "You absolutely got murdered in this rich kid's death maze, you just haven't realized it yet."

"He's my grandfather's age," she said. "And the animals were in cages. Well," she added, waiting until he was just about to express a drop of relief, "some of them were just walled off in glass. Or chained."

"But the only one they actually let run around loose was a starving tiger. Right?"

"I'm a dragonrider, kashaaizo; what you're worried about?" She took the last half churro and scraped the remnants of the cinnamon cream up with one end. "A starving tiger isn't my enemy, it's my freaking bodyguard."

"Let me handle the guarding of the body." Tuuro's grin flashed for the barest second.

"As soon as I let the dog handle the guarding of the pot roast." Vanako smiled as she said it. "But no. No big predators." That might have been strictly an exaggeration; there had definitely been a couple of wild dogs, and a hyena that looked stringier than it should. But nothing as big and dangerous as a tiger or a leopard, especially not roaming free. One tricky aspect of this, Zaailo had explained over mate after, was the different empathic receptivities of the animals in question; there wasn't much evidence as to what level they'd be looking for or how much variation to expect, and an animal's level of empathic receptivity wasn't correlated with anything simple like brain size, so they had to just shuffle the locations around, repeat the exercise with lots of different empaths, and hope for the best.

Which had made for one experience that was somehow creepy and boring at the same time: Take five steps, answer the question. Take five steps, answer the question. Try to tune out the animals' vocalizations, so out of place to a city kid; try not to turn around every time a weird noise came from behind. Take five steps. Answer the question.

And, of course, Zaailo had been very clear on what the question meant. "What do you feel?" had nothing to do with the unease of walking a roofless maze in Madder Precinct with two wild dogs and a hyena locked in with her. All it meant was "What other minds can you sense from where you are?"

But none of that really mattered. This, finally, might be something she could actually tell her parents. Maybe she could even pull in Zinji to help with the project. Maybe this could be how the estranged bird name families of Yemareir finally made peace.

And if by "made peace" she was also thinking about how House Shearwater could benefit from that peace, well, screw it. They hadn't had a good financial month since the last time Zaya had gotten paid for long-hauling—not with Zaya throwing all their money at elections. No one else looked at all those papers Minshoon was forever scribbling on, but Vanako did and it was easy enough to figure out the score. Things had been bad even before Zaya was captured; at this point they were practically living on savings and donations, Kirono's faculty wage didn't even come close. And—this, at least, the parents had been straight about—they hadn't yet reached an accommodation with Tjaroon for Jaliki's treatment now that Zaya was out of the picture. He would need his warding tattoos refreshed in two weeks.

She put a hand on Tuuro's, heedless of the churro grease. "It's for Jaliki," she said. Her voice caught, but she didn't care. "They've got yliaster on the walls. No need for tattoos, you don't have to let a bunch of random people get their hands on yliaster. They're using the maze and the animals to map out the psionic interference fields." She leaned into Tuuro, let her voice drop to a whisper. "They're building a hospital for the hunted."

CHAPTER 32
Six weeks before the Skua

When the churros were done, Vanako and Tuuro took Bandit out to Madder Precinct and flew.

It wasn't quite that simple, but it was nearly. Bandit had to acclimate to Tuuro's scent and weight, but Vanako's referred trust went nearly as far as earned trust would have, and the pleasantries are pretty well over in five minutes. The only sticking point came when Tuuro tried to mount up between Bandit's shoulders. It shied away and projected a strong multi-sensory image of Vanako instead.

"I flew front before," Tuuro said to Vanako, puzzled and annoyed. "You know back. What's the problem?"

She knows me, Bandit said. *She'll guide me better. You need to learn.*

Vanako felt, more than saw, the anger rear up in Tuuro: equal parts a child's bright outrage at being thwarted and a man's hot shame at being questioned. Bandit felt it too, she knew, but it merely watched, cool and still, to see what would happen. Vanako wasn't afraid of Tuuro in that moment—she wasn't afraid of Tuuro at all—but she did envy Bandit, who could watch Tuuro's rage as though he were a monkey chattering at the theft of its dinner, a gutful of flame ready to wash away any hint of danger. But Tuuro strengthened his back and cleared his face and said, not too stiffly, "I understand. I'll work hard enough to make you want me up on point. You'll see."

Bandit didn't intend its usual reptilian impassiveness as a burn of any kind, much less a sick one; but it was hard, Vanako discovered while pushing down her laughter, to unlearn the primate point of view.

To distract herself, she mounted up. Tuuro followed suit, and they were airborne.

Bandit hadn't been wrong. Tuuro needed to learn. Aubade had been older than Bandit, bigger all around, with muscle-heavy shoulders that could fling it forward at amazing speeds… but it had tired quickly. Bandit was well shaped for long flights, its shoulders broader but less powerful, its lean haunches better suited to tucking away on a long haul than seizing a human-sized shark or tuna. Tuuro's work with Bandit leaned too hard on managing discomfort it wasn't yet experiencing, not enough on managing the force he was asking for during agility maneuvers, and Aubade's motor schema still colored every impulse he sent to Bandit's brain.

But she could feel him improving, adapting bit by bit to the information about Bandit's body plan as he absorbed it from Vanako's command, and viewed it directly as he passed commands to Bandit.

Her own adaptation wasn't nearly as quick.

It wasn't a matter of knowing Bandit's body, its capabilities, its quirks—all that was second nature, front or rear. It was the decisions.

Vanako was used to executing commands from Zaya; used, even, to anticipating what she needed, to adjusting Bandit's perceptual-motor parameters in response to its fatigue or frustration or confusion, to feeding back the information she knew Zaya would need. But what information did *she* need? She was more comfortable, she came to realize, working mostly blind—looking back occasionally, if Zaya and Bandit couldn't, but otherwise working from a sketch of the course ahead already marked up by Zaya's expert attention. In the chaotic flow of the actual world hurtling toward them at killer-lizard speeds, Vanako had to choose where to place her own attention. Which, it turned out, she was crap at, overloading Tuuro's mind with unprocessed input and making him occasionally sick to his stomach.

Vanako could feel him wanting to take the front saddle. Of course he did; he'd done this before. But he never asked.

They wove through columns of closely spaced trees, ran full revolutions around dry fountains clockwise and counterclockwise, practiced rapid ascents up the sides of abandoned tenements and staying below roofline in neighborhoods with buildings of varied height. It was Tuuro who eventually called it. "Not your fault," he assured her. "Switching wyrms isn't supposed to be easy. But I paid good money for that churro. I don't want to see it on the street, you know?"

After a practice session, Vanako and Zaya had usually sat against the slowly pulsing flank of a resting Bandit and debriefed. But it had always been Zaya who led the conversation. Her memory of spots both rough and bright had been perfect, or so it had felt; and if she'd asked Vanako for a lot, she'd always mixed it with her own history and weaknesses, so Vanako could understand that Zaya had understood that she was human and would learn like one, imperfectly.

That was something the teachers at the Lyceum never did, Vanako realized. Whatever their own journey might have been in mathematics, philology, or history, it was only important because it had given rise to the person in the front of the room, not because the students could possibly learn anything from it. Maybe the teachers were embarrassed? Maybe they'd tried to share their paths, long in the past, and their students had looked at this person who through no real right held power over the use of their time, seen a crack to their soul open, and taken aim. It was something

Vanako would have done, if she'd ever had the opportunity. Maybe they were ashamed that the path hadn't taken them higher, to the life of a professor or scholar or writer, instead of teaching kids who didn't want to be there in a school that produced construction foremen and factory supervisors on its good days, not mathematicians and philologists and historians.

Or maybe there was no path. Maybe teachers just showed up at the school with an empty belly and a glimmer of uncared-for aptitude, and if it was on a day where the school had money for them, they got hired.

"So how'd we do?" said Tuuro, leaning in with a smile, and Vanako let herself sink into the kiss and stay for a while.

A giggle snapped them out. There was a knot of local kids standing well away from Bandit; some were as young as Eäril, some could have been older than Vanako. "Veraamaka navo!" One of the younger girls called. She got a smack on the head from an older boy and squealed in protest. "That's not her," he said. "She's in jail. That's her daughter."

"If it's not her," a girl said, maybe eleven, "how do you know it's her daughter?"

"I saw them fly once, it's her. Kinda tall, skinny, long purple hair, no boobs."

Vanako *reached*, and the smallest blue tongue of flame licked from Bandit's mouth. Several of the kids screamed, including the little girl.

"Boobs are off limits in this conversation," Vanako said. "Don't even try for butts." This to the older boy, who was clearly composing a riposte; he looked annoyed, but swallowed it.

"With hair like that," he said instead, "you're supposed to be kissing girls."

"Hair like this says you don't get a vote," said Vanako. "But even rude little shits are allowed to pet a dragon, if they move slow and touch gentle. Unless you're scared."

Tuuro, who'd been hoping they could shoo these kids off and get back to business, sighed only a little bit theatrically, leaned his head back, and closed his eyes.

The older boy, not thrilled but not able to back down, got out in front of the rest of the group. He was followed by a sleek, glossy-furred tortoiseshell cat, which might not have stood out in Lilac Precinct but drew notice here in Madder; it was well groomed and well fed, with two perfect eyes and two perfect ears. When the boy reached his right hand out to touch Bandit, Vanako saw it was mangled, the forearm crosshatched with fine red scars.

"Hey," she heard herself say softly. "Just so you know. We're fighting for you. OK?"

He retracted his hand from Bandit's feathers and looked at her as if she'd recited one of the old epics backwards.

"That fucking cat," she said. "I know what it is. When we win the election this year, that thing will never touch you again. I promise."

He looked away from her. "I don't know what you're talking about," he said. "It's just a cat that follows me around."

"Then kick it," she said. "Throw something. Scare it off."

The kid took a couple of steps back, disgust all over his face. "You're crazy," he said, louder than he needed. "I'm not doing that to a cat."

His friends all looked at him.

He looked back, sensing leverage. "You can pet the dragon if you want," he said, "but I wouldn't get anywhere near that lady. She's crazy. She said I should kill my cat. Fucking crazy!"

The kids' eyes all turned toward Vanako.

She was about to explain what she'd meant... but something stopped her. These kids couldn't possibly not know what the cat was. Kers were good at disguise, but something always gave them away eventually: a stray teleport, an accidental show of invulnerability, or just a sustained disinterest in eating that rang false in any domestic animal that wasn't terminally ill. They knew what it was—but there was a deal, terms unsaid, that they didn't talk about it around their friend. Around their friend, it was just a friendly little cat.

Unless veraamaka navo broke the deal.

She looked at Tuuro. He shrugged. She looked at the cat. "It's half dead and smells like a slaughterhouse," she said. "You should put it out of its misery."

She got up; the kids erupted in protest, defending the cat. She and Tuuro mounted up, the calls of "Cat-killer!" and "Fucking crazy!" following them for longer than she thought possible, then finally fading as they rose.

***

WHEN VANAKO APPROACHED HOUSE Shearwater in the gathering dusk, there was a man leaning against the mural.

This wasn't unusual, necessarily. Maybe a little disrespectful? But it was a nice, smooth wall, and it was near both a thickly-leafed tree, which made it a good place to wait when it was sunny or raining, and a gaslamp, which made it a good place to wait when it was dark. The figure of the man struck a note of recognition, one that took her a moment to pin down. She'd have liked to say it was his look of almost-hidden vigilance that she'd picked up on, the subtle and undisguisable quirks of posture that marked a man on the lookout for something. And maybe it had been; but the thing she noticed herself noticing was the pad of paper in his hand, held close by his side like it was no big deal, he definitely wasn't trying to hide it or anything.

She'd met someone else in that spot, carrying that same pad by her side, a few months ago. And now that person's mailbox was full of her letters. Which shouldn't explain why this person, who wasn't that person, was standing outside her house; but although the two things shouldn't have been related, Vanako figured they probably were.

He was a Mrineen man, on the short side—which still put him a head and change taller than her— brown hair tied back in a loose ponytail and bright hazel eyes that were actually a little hypnotizing, or would be if he weren't blinking like a chicken at the snap of her fingers. "Hey," Vanako said. "Here for me?"

He squinted, and the lines around his eyes deepened; he was older than she'd thought at first, maybe around Zaya's age. "Maybe?" he said. "I'm here about some letters."

"Yeah," she said. "Look, I'm sorry about those. I know there's not much I can help you with, and—" She wasn't sure how to say to a journalist, *I've changed my mind, I don't want you to dig into my great-uncle's past after all, I think he's doing good work and I want to help.*

"There is," he said.

Crap. Did he know she'd been visiting Zaailo? If he did—

"Those bond traders," he said. "Whose daughters are your friends at school. Do you have their names?"

Vanako laughed. "Wait, really?"

***

"HIS NAME IS JERIOUN Crotalus," said Vanako, lying back on Taavi's bed. The glow charm was off—it was late, and Vanako wasn't supposed to be here, but the day had been too full, and she was afraid that important things might evaporate from her mind if she waited until morning. "He's an economics reporter at the Damask Free Press. He said he knew Shenireen Agama and that's why he opened her letters—he knew she'd be interested in correspondence from our family."

"Has he seen her?" asked Taavi.

"He says no one has, since Inundinir Square."

"Why does he care about bond traders?"

"He maybe has a lead on a big story, but he can't talk about it."

"Susssss," said Gilthiniel.

"I mean, yeah? But all he wanted were names. He didn't even ask about the one guy in R&D with Corrections. He doesn't care about Zaailo Merganser, or Mom. He just opened Shenireen's mail and found something he thought could help him out."

"Well," said Taavi, "if Zaailo-kana is building homes for hunted people, maybe that's just as well?"

"Also wildly sus," said Gilthiniel. "If he's building for hunted people, why isn't he testing on hunted people?"

"He will," said Vanako. "You can't keep kers in a fixed location, because they fucking teleport. It's easier to map out the interference patterns with controlled senders and receivers—caged animals and empaths walking on directed paths. Then you can get a baseline layout for the dampers. You can test it with real hunted people after."

"Please," Gilthiniel scoffed. "That's..." He did weird things with his face for a minute—searching for words, probably? "That makes sense, actually. You can baseline it faster with controlled inputs, you can sample more densely at high-variance areas. I'm just repeating what you said. OK, shit. Maybe he's really doing it."

"Just wait to hear the rent when the first one's built?" said Taavi, bitterly.

"He's got ten rich prospects waiting on their own places," said Vanako. "That's going to fund the cheaper spots."

"How is he even getting the yliaster?" said Taavi. "Isn't it illegal?"

"He thinks not much longer."

"Really?" said Taavi. "He thinks Mom did it? Brightest Scale is losing the majority?"

"I don't know," said Vanako. "I didn't ask that. He could be thinking longer term than this year. I don't know."

"Damn," said Taavi.

Their quiet let the sounds of frogs and crickets blanket the room. A monkey hooted somewhere in the square.

"But where does this leave us with Mom?" Taavi said. "Why would Ziyuki-kana send us to Zaailo-kana to learn about his new... ker-proof houses, or whatever? I don't want to say I don't care about it, but... this isn't what we wanted?"

"Don't take this the wrong way," said Vanako.

"My nipples just got hard," said Gilthiniel.

"Ugh, shut up," said Vanako. "Go rub one out in my room if you need to, I'll wait."

"You saying something you're worried about Taavi taking the wrong way is all the sexual gratification I could ever hope for," said Gilthiniel.

Vanako kicked up into Gilthiniel's mattress, raising it an admirable half-inch or so; he yipped satisfyingly.

"Don't take this the wrong way," Vanako said, "but getting Jaliki into one of those houses is more important than getting Mom out of jail."

There was quiet for a while.

"I hate it," said Gilthiniel.

"She's right, though?" said Taavi.

"That's why I said 'I hate it' instead of saying 'This'll only hurt for a second' and then throwing Vani out a window," said Gilthiniel. "I can't think about it any more. Is this really what Ziyuki-kana wanted out of this whole stupid quest? Stay out of Zaailo Merganser's way so he can build shit that might help Jaliki one day?"

"When you put it that way," said Taavi, "it sounds exactly like something Ziyuki-kana would do?"

"This was never about getting Mom out," Vanako said. "It was about trading her freedom for his life."

She said it out of, not certainty, but curiosity; were these the words that would make sense of all of it? Hearing them, it seemed like they were. Ziyuki had come up with a distraction for a child, beginning with a puzzle straight out of a Wing Windtwister drama and ending in the lesson grown-ups always ended with: Get out of the way.

"I do have one question, though," said Gilthiniel. "Don't take it the wrong way."

"I won't, but I can't speak for my nipples."

"Four out of six. Have you asked him?" said Gilthiniel. "To get her out? Have you asked Ziyuki-kana?"

"Of course," said Vanako, annoyed. She thought back on her conversations with Haanen, with Zaailo. "I mean, I might as well have. They know what I want. It's not like I was coming to them when she was free."

Taavi and Gilthiniel held a fragile, careful silence.

"It's not a fairy tale," said Vanako. "There's not, like, some stupid little technicality where they have to do something for me if I just use the magic words."

It was clear that Gilthiniel very much wanted to say something; but he didn't.

Vanako sighed, and this time her breath did shudder a bit. "Fine. I'll ask. They'll say no."

"Yeah," said Gilthiniel. "But at least then we can't say we didn't ask."

CHAPTER 33

FIVE WEEKS BEFORE THE SKUA

"SHE CAN'T," SAID HAANEN ze-Keiaza over sweet green bean soup; the air had taken a chill. "The Chief of Corrections reports to the reeve. I won't lie to you and say a request from House Amphisbaena won't carry some weight. But the House doesn't want this, and Chief Merganser knows it."

Vanako sipped on her mate. "Does Ziyuki-kana actually want Mom to go free?"

"Back to distrust, I see," said Haanen, nodding their head encouragingly. "The answer is yes, not that you should believe an answer from me."

"Does she think that this dumb quest she's sent me on is actually going to get Mom free?"

"That's a better question," said Haanen. "The real answer is, the Baronet doesn't know. She thought you'd take this a different way than you did. But what happens has always depended on you."

"Pretty rich, when the Baronet throws up her hands and lets a kid handle it."

"Can't even tell you to your face, right? She has to send her underpaid, powerless flunky to do it."

Vanako stabbed a finger at Haanen. "My entire ass. Tell me you're powerless one more time and I will drench you in soup."

Haanen clicked their tongue, grinned, and flicked their own index finger right back at her.

✳✳✳

"I can't," said Zaailo over mate in the parlor. They'd just finished another walkthrough of the Madder Precinct model; she'd requested an audience after, and he'd taken her on Kazaru, an old Argent Swordwing twice the size of Arhoon Pogona's dead wyrm Ice.

"Can you at least tell us where she is?" said Vanako. "We have no idea how she is, how she's doing. Prisons and work crews all have visitation days."

"Not empaths," said Zaailo. "Security concerns."

"Then at least let us know where she is!" said Vanako. "So we can write." She could see him wavering and pressed the advantage. "And maybe she can write back?"

Zaailo looked strangely at her; some combination of nerves and annoyance. "Your mother's not the only one in this situation. I can't personally courier letters to everyone."

"You could, actually," said Vanako. "Because there's no risk and practically no effort, and there can't possibly be that many people in this particular situation. Right?" *How many people could you possibly be holding in secret jails with no visitors?* she wanted to say, just to drive the point home; but she bit it back.

Zaailo considered this. "You can write as much as you want," he said, "but we'll look over it before we give it to her. Her letter will be short, and we'll take out anything that identifies her location or her crewmates. Possibly some other things. We'll let her know what not to write, so we don't have to black out so much."

Vanako leaned in to press his hand in hers. "Thank you. Just knowing for sure that she's alive and all right will mean so much."

And it was true, maybe the truest thing she'd ever said to Zaailo Merganser; but the taste of it was bitter.

***

"We have to tell," Vanako said to Taavi and Gilthiniel.

They were sitting around the fountain in Laurel Square, eating pão de queijo and drinking coffee. Jaliki and Eäril were drawing on the flagstones with chalk; Chashu was watching from about the same distance as the Lilac Precinct cop on the other side of the square, who seemed to be mostly watching Chashu. It was brisk and clear, the stone of the fountain cold enough to feel wet although it wasn't.

"Yeah," said Taavi.

"No," said Gilthiniel.

Vanako and Taavi both looked at him until he held up his palms in concession. "OK," he said, "I get that you don't feel like we can write to Mom on our own—"

'They would roast us alive over a slow flame," said Vanako.

"And we'd deserve it?" said Taavi.

"We arguably already deserve it," said Vanako.

"All I'm saying is, there might be more we can learn if we—"

"The Chief of Corrections is going to read it, Gil," said Vanako. "It's not like we have a code worked out. Even if we did, we probably couldn't ask something like 'tell us whatever you know about your estranged uncle that we might be able to use to get you out.' It's kind of a niche situation."

"You need to have more faith in yourself," said Gilthiniel.

"If I could do magic, I'd be in magic class."

Gilthiniel's eyes widened. "That's it!"

"The actual Yearner, Gil," said Vanako, "what?"

"That dealer friend of yours. She's doing Fundamentals of Magic with te-Hakaina-shan. She can hide something in the letter."

"Varaana?" said Vanako.

"Sure? She started saying hi to me, so I asked Jeizo who she was, and he said, 'that dealer girl at the Lyceum who's friends with your sister,' and I kind of left it there."

"Huh," said Vanako. "I thought she was just skipping class to deal. Not to go to, like, more class."

"She's not short on customers," said Gilthiniel. "Kids at the Academy have a lot more spending money than they do at the Lyceum, present company excepted obviously. But she could hide something in a letter—"

"You're going to trust *Varaana* to tamper with a letter so the Chief of Corrections can't detect it? Potentially destroying both our chance to hear from Mom and my relationship with the one guy who might be able to get Jaliki into a living situation that..." Not wanting to invoke the specter of death, she let her eyes wander to Jaliki, who seemed like he was trying to explain something to Eäril. The ker wasn't as close as it usually was when Jaliki had no protection at all—it would have been right up with them, sniffing and licking and getting in the way, tracking chalky pawprints back home—but it wasn't far either, lying on the flagstones with its chin on its paws and watching. If it got hungry enough, and the treatment weakened enough, could it break through?

"Fine," said Gilthiniel. "I know someone else who's absolutely killing it in Fundamentals—"

"He knows we have to tell?" Taavi said to Vanako. "This is just how he grieves for things he knows he can't keep? You should see the schemes he comes up with to keep girlfriends?"

"Some of those worked," said Gilthiniel.

"Your girlfriend is who again?"

Gilthiniel threw a piece of pão de queijo into the fountain heard enough that it skipped off the surface tension. A seagull caught it before it went under. He made a fist and shoved his knuckles against his lips, his face tense and tight.

"Gil—" said Vanako.

"It's fine," he said, his voice as taut as his face. "I obviously can't stop you, so go ahead. Whenever you want."

"It's not about just doing it because you can't stop us—"

"Then how is it I was told this instead of asked?"

"Because we can't not tell!" said Vanako.

"None of this other shit should have been a secret either," Gilthiniel said bitterly. "What changed?"

"I asked you," said Vanako. "Over and over." She heard her voice growing hoarse, felt her throat going tight. What the hell, some distant corner of her mind thought; why am I freaking out about a fight with my dumb brother, who I fight with all the time? "If you thought we should tell before, why didn't you say?"

"If my opinion mattered as much then as it does now, it's obviously best I didn't say shit."

"We did literally everything you said we should do until now," said Taavi.

Gilthiniel stood up to storm across the square. Vanako bolted up before she knew what he was doing; Taavi's hand was already on her shoulder.

"To be clear," said Vanako, "I'm not going to prolong the conversation. I'm just going to beat the shit out of him." She decided it was easier to just pretend there wasn't salt water trickling down the planes of her nose to settle on her lips.

"Beating sounds better than more talking?" said Taavi. "But not quite as good as letting him think about what he's done while we talk shit about him over the snacks he left behind?"

"Your brother sucks," Vanako said, allowing herself to be guided back to the fountain.

"Enh," said Taavi. "He's OK?"

"You're his twin. You have to stick up for him."

"But the only reason I'm sticking up for him to you is that I stayed with you instead of going with him?"

Vanako shrugged and took a sip of Gilthiniel's coffee. "You're right," she said. "Stolen coffee tastes better than beatings feel."

Chashu had sauntered up to them. "Sorry to disturb," he said. "You'll stay close to the house? Gil looks like he might do something dumb, I should keep him in my sights."

Taavi nodded. Chashu nodded back, then left.

"I don't have, like, a story for why he's like this?" Taavi said when Chashu was out of earshot. "It was worse when he was in the closet? Having Kirono-kana around was really big, I think. The whole thing was hard, but I remember Mom really wanted to drag her feet and be, you know, 'sure,' and I think Dad didn't but he didn't want to push Mom on it, and Cerminir was a little checked out, kind of that 'we do this better in the Amalgam' attitude she gets even though she hates the Amalgam and she'd never go back?"

"Like Thelendil."

"Only she wouldn't pretend to joke about it? Anyway, it took some time because... you know Kirono-kana, he doesn't like to fight either? Not that it was a fight exactly... but having him there to say, no, even though he's thirteen we need to respect the way he chooses to show his face to the world—I think that was maybe years of pain he spared Gil?"

"Oof," said Vanako. "Mom came at me so hard one time when she thought I was calling him a girl. I never would have thought—"

"Obviously she's done some growing? But—being Gil works better for a boy than it does for a girl. That's pretty clear?"

"I feel like you're giving me this intense look right now, like you're trying to put something in my brain."

Taavi chuckled. "Whatever. Being Gil works better for a boy... but you lose something too? You get more respect, more freedom, people laugh at your jokes. But they don't laugh with you? They don't cry with you? Especially when you've got an... approach... like Gil's?" This time she definitely looked intensely at Vanako, and was definitely trying to communicate something.

"Huh? Oh." Vanako reached for more pão de queijo, but there weren't any. "I thought he left more snacks."

"You get what I'm saying, though?"

"I'm getting that Gilthiniel has trouble getting close to people, because he approaches conversations like a lion approaches a sick antelope."

"This whole project was a chance for him to help you? To get close to you? He's not in love with you or anything," she added hastily, seeing an expression evolve on Vanako's face. "But, like, for the longest time it was just us and Jaliki. And then the babies, but... babies? So it was cool to have you around, and he wants to earn your, like... respect? So he doesn't want to hand the quest off to the parents because then he becomes, like, a marginal figure in the effort? No authority, no respect. Or that's how he thinks."

Vanako thought about this for a while. "When he dates girls," she said, "he sells himself as the low maintenance type. Right?"

Taavi put her head in her hands. "Stop. Yes. Please. No. Do you ever laugh at something and also get incredibly angry about it at the same time? That's my brother and *low maintenance*?"

"Good. Just checking to make sure the laws of physics were still working."

"Every morning I wake up and think, 'Maybe this is the day I turn gay?' But it never is?"

"Do you think Mom and Kemreen were better off?"

"If by the grace of the Sculptor I do turn gay one day, I won't date cops?"

"Harsh," said Vanako. "But fair." She crumpled up the wax paper that had held the pão de queijo, tossed it, and caught it. "So what do we do?"

"We wait for Gil to come around? Then we tell."

"What if he doesn't?"

"He will? He'll hate it, but he will."

"How long?"

Taavi shrugged. "Hours, days? He's good at being butthurt, but he doesn't actually like it? And he knows what has to happen."

CHAPTER 34
FIVE WEEKS BEFORE THE SKUA

HE WAS, BUT HE didn't, and he did. So they told.

Minshoon looked at Cerminir; Cerminir looked at Kirono; Kirono looked at Minshoon. "It seems like only yesterday," Minshoon said tightly, "that Vanako was making huge, dumb moves and hiding them from the family, all in the name of saving someone who never asked for this kind of help from a teenager. I can't imagine I need to remind you that Zaailo Merganser quite literally has your mother under his power. If you'd said the wrong kind of thing, and he'd been the wrong kind of person..." There was fear in his eyes—not for what might have happened, but for what still could. "We've learned the hard way what we already knew—there is no accountability in this system at all, for anyone. We've filed paperwork, we've been to court, we *won* a suit against the Ministry of Corrections. We still haven't heard anything about Zaya's location. If he'd decided—*if he decides* that she needs to have some kind of accident..." He ran a hand over this scalp. "I don't know, Vani. Maybe that's not the kind of thing that happens. But it seems like there's not much stopping it.

"On the other hand, nothing we've done has gotten us the promise of a letter. Much less a letter back." Minshoon sighed. "You and Zaya have a habit of gambling with the family and winning just enough times to want to keep it going. Sometimes I wonder if you remember that losing one of those gambles is the reason she's not here."

"Winning them is why Jaliki's still alive," said Gilthiniel. "Winning this one could buy him a place to grow old. One where that fucking ker can't so much as walk the halls."

Minshoon shook his head. "Gil, you of all people I'd have expected to look a little harder at that hospital project. You think the Chief of Corrections is prototyping a hospital for the hunted?"

"Minshoon—" Kirono said, so quietly it seemed like part of a different conversation.

"He has clients lined up," said Vanako. A thread of sickness vibrated gently in her stomach. "He told me that's what it is."

"Vani," said Minshoon, "it sounds to me like he's prototyping a prison for empaths."

Into the silence that followed, Kirono interjected a sigh. "I was wondering if we should save that for a later conversation."

"You think I'm wrong?" asked Minshoon.

Kirono shook his head.

"He's not doing it for Corrections," Vanako said. "He's doing it for Seafarer."

"OK," said Minshoon, extending an index finger.

"Minshoon," said Kirono.

His head snapped around toward Kirono, scarily fast. "They're old enough to get us into this," said Minshoon, "they're old enough to learn to think their actions through." He turned back to look at Vanako and Gilthiniel. "Vani, maybe there's a hospital in the works. But the work you're doing for him gives him a prison for free. And he runs the prisons. What's an easier play for Seafarer Joists & Girders—going to the free market and finding financing to shelter a bunch of hunted folks who can't make rent? Or going to the budget that Zaailo Merganser controls?"

He'd interrupted Kirono to say his piece—but his voice was so kind, so wise, so patient. He wasn't trying to shame her or make her feel stupid. That was one of the best things about Minshoon, she thought; even in his angriest moments—and this wasn't one of them—he was always a teacher.

"I have to go," Vanako said, and the world blurred with water and motion.

There were voices behind her, steps following her steps down the stairs; when she went over the wall in the courtyard, they got much quieter, and soon she couldn't hear anything at all.

***

THE BIKE RIDE TO Damask Precinct brought her back; she'd been somewhere else, when she was running from her family, chased away from her body by all the shame and stupidity that Minshoon was working so hard to keep her from feeling. Maybe the air-hunger and the burn in her legs were a penance, a counterbalance. They also helped slow her thoughts. Vanako could feel her mind straining to race, but it didn't have the fuel.

She left the bike in the middle of the path in front of Tuuro's dole-flat. He lived on the eighth floor, bunked four to a small room with three of his friends; they shared a small common room with a table and one armchair, and Tuuro didn't spend a ton of time there, but if he wasn't there she didn't know where he was, so he'd better be there.

He was there. The room smelled like food—fried noodles and cabbage, white fish. Jevaano answered the door—he was big, soft, and kind, the sort of boy a boy like Tuuro wasn't supposed to be friends with—and there must have been some kind of wild look on her face, because a look of concern immediately darkened his. "Tuuro?" he said. "Vani's here."

Tuuro got up from the game of dice they were playing at the rickety table. "Hey," he said. "You want to talk about it in the bedroom—" laughs and whistles rose, as inevitable as the morning sun, from Zeiki and Aaro at the table—"or the roof? Or the square?"

Bed would be comfortable, but the smell and the noise and the worry of eavesdropping would make it hard to talk; and Tuuro might take it as the kind of invitation it wasn't. But the roof was crowded on warm nights, and the square would be full of the kind of commerce you couldn't do on the roof, because you needed escape routes. She shook her head. "The bay."

"It's a long way to the beach, Vani. I've got work—"

"Not the beach. The bay. Over the bay."

"You want to practice? Now?"

"No, dumbshit. I want to fly."

****

WHAT SHE REALLY WANTED, of course, was for him to know what was wrong without her saying it. But the moon over the water was beautiful, the clouds were keeping their distance, and moonlight painted the breakers in gently pulsing lines. She couldn't look at Tuuro, but she used his own proprioception as a kind of spyglass, hanging her own memory of his features on his body's model of itself to form a likeness. She fixed that in her mind and let the memories of the evening's conversations flow toward it, opening herself up just enough that he could pull more context if he needed it. He could probably pull more, let in like that; but she didn't care, and he didn't do it. Bandit just rode the thermals and mostly avoided being annoyed at the exchange of monkey memories and feelings passing through its brain.

"So the problem," Vanako said, after it felt like Tuuro had digested all the relevant information, "is I'm too dumb to live."

"No," said Tuuro. "Chief found the lie that made you let him use you. Plenty of men on the dole make a living at that shit. They like when it makes people feel ashamed."

"He has a company full of empaths. Why does he need to fuck with me?"

"Not easy to find an empath who'll work on shit like that."

"Zetaala-kana did," Vanako said.

"Dampers were voluntary."

"That aged well."

Tuuro sent a pulse of conceding energy her way. "Look, Chief can lie to you, but most of the empaths he knows, they work for the business, right? Like you said. They know the difference between a hospital and a prison, they know what halls they're walking. You're a kid. It's not your fault you don't know shit."

"You wouldn't have known either, asshole!"

"No, I would not." His answer's sincerity was absolute. "And you wouldn't blame me for not knowing. Chief saw an opportunity and took it. Nothing to do with you."

Vanako laughed bitterly. "Spoken like someone who knows a good opportunity when he sees it."

"Hell yeah." A few sensory flashes: Her mouth on his, the muscles of her back moving under his hands. It was embarrassing to see herself from his point of view... but interesting to see what he liked, what stuck. She rolled her shoulders, pinched her shoulder blades together. "So how do you get him back?" he asked.

She scoffed. "Please. My parents aren't letting me go toe to toe with the guy who runs all the prisons in Yemareir."

"Sure—only, fuck that. He fucked with you. You need justice."

"Listen to yourself."

"You know I'm right," Tuuro said. "I can feel it."

And he could; because she did.

But it was easy to feel powerful with the bay spread out below like a queen's court, the moon stretched across it like a supplicant. It was easy to know what justice for Zaailo Merganser would look like: A loss of money, maybe, but what he really loved—what he feared to lose—was his position among Yemareir's circles of powers as the city's good Kayalim, the one whose success reassured the nobles and captains of industry that their positions had been earned by sweat and not bought for flinders by ancestors reaping the windfall of old madness and tragedy.

"I don't know how to do it," she said, trusting the empathic connection to convey what she'd been thinking.

"Me neither," said Tuuro. "I'm still thinking about how to make Shanhoon Krait pay for what he did to Zetaala-kana. But you know what that's better than? Thinking about what I could have done to save him."

***

She didn't stay with Tuuro that night, although she would have liked to. Even though the room was airless and the sheets were suffused with the smell of fried food and old sweat and his flatmates would be an arm's length away, she didn't want to leave. But she also didn't really want this to be the reason she stayed over for the first time, either; and she knew, from experience, what it was like when you showed up at House Shearwater after a night where no one knew where you'd been.

The night Zaya had gone missing—the night she'd met Kemreen and stolen Bandit—had been all right; she'd told everyone she was going for a drink with a friend, and it had seemed like every-one knew what that meant. It hadn't been until midmorning that a muted panic had begun to set in, the remaining parents communicating more and more in glances, their answers to Jaliki and Eäril's questions showing the strain of repeating an unworried message they'd ceased to believe. Zaya's mes-sage had made it from Cildinior Amalgam in a couple of days, but not before a visit from Officer Jizeji te-Kaino of the Lilac Precinct Police, who was just checking on behalf of a friend in the Saffron Precinct Police curious about Zaya's whereabouts, and shortly before the visit from Detective Amritain Hawks-bill of the Saffron Precinct Police, who of course was out of his jurisdiction and therefore, by necessity, "just talking." The parents had spared a lot of care for Jaliki and Eäril's anxi-eties—the younger kids knew adults left and came back, but they also knew what police meant. Not much care was spared for the swarming guilt that had soured Vanako's stomach and eaten away at her sleep in her newly doorless room. Minshoon and Kirono had offered their usual, generic kindness, diluted by their own fear and distraction; Cerminir had spent about a week full-on pretending Vanako didn't exist, and although Vanako had never asked, she knew everyone (well, except Enwë) was at least a little bit relieved to see Cer go to Cildinior Amalgam to check on Zaya and maybe bring her home.

Everything that had followed Zaya's return had buried those memories, and the rush of them when Tuuro offered her the use of his flat disoriented Vanako for a moment—not only with their volume and detail, but with their foreignness. Now, she was close enough to Taavi and Gilthiniel to take her worries to them; now, she was secure enough at home to demand better from the parents than they offered, if she had to.

Was she, though? She'd been complaining about them not doing enough, but she hadn't ever taken it to them. She'd fallen back on secrecy, again. Just like Zaya.

These thoughts came slowly on the ride home. It was a slow ride, her legs exhausted from the sprint to Tuuro's and the hour on Bandit and the fatigue of the whole sleepless night, which began to end as she watched, the sky lightening to deep-ocean blue and then blue-grey. The effort of pushing herself across the city wasn't quite enough to blunt the cold. She hoped Zaya was warm that night. In the Olive Precinct dole-flats, she'd seen people with missing toes and fingers from frostbite, caught out on mountain work crews during a cold snap. It didn't happen every winter, but it might happen any winter.

She pushed the thought from her mind. It wasn't winter yet. By the next cold snap, Zaya could be sleeping in her own bed, in a house where the cold could not enter.

Minshoon was asleep on the couch. Vanako looked around, then sat beside him and put a hand on his shoulder. His eyes snapped open.

"You can go to bed," she said. "I'm sorry I ran away. I was feeling stupid and ashamed." She'd practiced the words enough that they were almost easy. "I was with Tuuro. We took Bandit for a ride to clear my head. We didn't do anything that would get me pregnant."

Minshoon laughed, still not quite awake. "I'm glad you're not pregnant. Enwë's not ready to be an aunt." He took a moment to order some thoughts. "I'm not going to talk about what you did wrong. You know what it was and why. I'm glad you're back. And I'm glad you didn't cut us out of the opportunity to contact Zaya." He looked off for a moment, reviewing whether there was something else he was parentally obliged to say in this moment. "There's something I didn't get to tell you, when you ran." He leaned forward and picked up a tube of paper from the coffee table, tied shut with two slim ribbons, one brick red and one bright cerulean. He handed it to Vanako, and she opened it. The paper was thick, bright white, and pleasantly textured; the script on it was so flowing and perfect it was hard to credit to a human hand. "If I didn't seem as surprised as I could have when you confessed about Zaailo-kana," he said, "this is why."

"When did you get this?"

"About a day ago. Two, now. We were trying to decide what to do about it. We thought it should be Zinji's choice, since he's the one who has a relationship with Zaailo-kana." She was surprised to hear Minshoon use the honorific, but then of course he should; Zaailo was Zinji's generation, older than him. "Or that's what we thought."

She turned her eyes back to the paper:

The House of the Merganser throws open the doors of its estates to the scions of the House of Shearwater, their beloved friends, and their trusted helpmeets, on this,

The Immolation of Ashniraan Merganser,

And the Celebration thereof, thereafter.

We request your reservation of the tenth hour of the morning to the second of the afternoon, on the sixth day of Scathe's moon, in this year, 831st in the Calendar of

Yemareir, 5,340th in the Time of Mlinivoun; 16-Mountain, Barley, Rain by the Star-Clock of Kayazē.

With open arms,

Zaailo Merganser

The letter closed with his seal, the stylized head of a duck with a staring eye and wild plumage that made it look like it had been used as a feather duster.

"What's a helpmeet?" asked Vanako. "Is that like a servant?"

"I think any kind of employee," said Minshoon. "If you're Ziyuki-kana, let's say, you might want your secretary around to cross-check any invitations you might get against whatever you've already got on. I'm a little surprised that was your first question."

"All my other ones have bad words in them. And you don't have the answers."

"Try me."

"OK. Why the fuck?"

"You didn't have to start with the hardest one."

"I might possibly not have that many others."

"Any more words I can define for you?"

"No," Vanako said. "I'm good."

CHAPTER 35
FOUR WEEKS BEFORE THE SKUA

THE STARTING LINE OF the arc-en-ciel was a fever dream—hazy, sickly, and forever slipping fishlike out of Vanako's hands whenever she tried to take control.

She'd been through a dozen starts in the 'stream, maybe more; but Zaya had alway guided her through, and she hadn't realized just how much Zaya had been doing when she did it. Pledging the entry fee, swearing to the terms, dickering over her position on the starting line, checking the straps and buckles of the double saddle for their safety and Bandit's comfort, figuring out how to time Kirono's wax touchups with Cerminir's last-minute nutrition so it all got done and no one felt rushed or slighted, feeding priors to Taavi based on nothing but vibes, since none of these 'streamers had a reputation: None of it was hard, necessarily, but it all had to happen, and Vanako wasn't used to making sure it did.

Neither was Tuuro, for the most part. Zetaala might have ridden rear saddle, but he'd navigated the details of the 'stream. But Tuuro pitched in readily enough. He seemed comfortable. Vanako desperately wanted to feel comfortable.

"Hey. Kid."

Vanako turned to face a tall, thickly muscled Kayalim woman with cropped hair, her arms crossed over her chest and her face as still as stone. *Good*, Vanako's mind remarked, *more ballast*. The woman's forearms were tattooed with matching leopards, rendered in the stylized Kayalim fashion. Her Eyrie Shrike eyed Vanako from behind here with a blank curiosity that she could cure easily enough by reaching into its mind; but she didn't. "Hey, Adult," she said, resisting the urge to cross her own arms in imitation.

"Heh." The laugh felt genuine, as far as it went. "Fine. Fair enough. Look, I'm sorry as hell about Zaya-cha. She was the best of us."

"Was, remains, will continue to be."

"Sure. And I don't know you, but let's just say I understand you were a part of that."

"Thanks?" Vanako said.

"So you might come to this race with some expectations."

Ah.

Vanako rolled her eyes. "OK, Adult, I get it. I'm not the crown princess or whatever, I have to earn my victories and I can't expect a tough 'streamer with forearm tattoos to be nice to me just because my mom could beat her like a lame goat. Which, fine, and I'm not even that mad that you felt like you had to say it while glaring down at me like an angry pile of biceps." She saw Adult's eyes flicker over to her own biceps, which flexed a little at the attention. "But let me ask you this: I've never seen you in a real race before. So if you sail away with this candy-ass victory—and you might, because I feel like baked shit out here—let me ask you this: Are you actually gunning to take my mom's place at the top of the real 'stream? Or are you just here to feel good about dominating a bunch of weak 'streamers because you know deep in your biceps that Yaulë would set up shop in your ass and sell your organs on clearance?"

"I'm here saving my winnings for an entry fee, actually," said the pile of biceps, visibly angrier. "If you're really not a princess, how's it so hard for you to tell the difference between 'can't hack it' and 'can't afford it'?"

A wave of shittiness broke over Vanako's head. "Sorry," was all she could summon up.

Adult gave her an appraising look. "I'm Jina ze-Tsuzeki," she said. "That's my sister, Jaisha." She pointed a thumb back, to a slight woman with cropped hair who was adjusting the buckles on the Eyrie Shrike's double saddle. "Might help you to know a couple names in the bush league."

"I guess you know me," said Vanako. "I'm riding with Tuuro te-Kaneva."

"So I hear," said Jina ze-Tsuzeki with a waggle of her eyebrows, and she turned to walk back to her wyrm.

"See?" Tuuro said. "Everyone knows about my girlfriend. And everyone is running scared."

"She didn't seem scared," said Vanako. "Her arms are bigger than your legs."

"She can break my legs after she comes in second," said Tuuro. "That's what she's scared of."

"Maybe because she won't eat without first."

"You can't pack on that kind of muscle when you're starving."

"He said from experience."

"Hell yes, he said from experience," Tuuro said. "You get beat up less if your chest and arms don't look like a parrot with no feathers."

"You can have a snack after the race."

"That's what I like to hear." He leaned in for a kiss; she gave it. If he pressed it just a little too hard, for a little too long—well, it was the image they were supposed to be projecting.

"'Streamers, mount up!" came the cry, and they did, and soon—

***

OFF THE MARK, THE rush of colors and feathers and wyrms all suddenly in motion hit Vanako like a firework exploding out of total darkness; she was flash-blind. She'd handled the flare of information from the rear before, but heavily processed—weighted and winnowed by Zaya's attention, not the whole raw riot of it. Bandit could handle itself at the elements of staying safe in a crowd and making life difficult for the wyrms behind it, but there was no question of coming out of the pack in front, or even well placed. It was all Vanako could do to try to parse the scene and remember the course—how did you even get to Vermilion Precinct from here?

Give some to me, said Tuuro.

"You do your job, I'll do mine."

You're better at my job. I'm better at yours. Give me some so I can help. I can't do much with this shit anyway.

"Fine." She fed him back the visual flow of the race, as unprocessed as she could.

That Dusk Stalker's going too fast into the corner, you can cut in.

"Yeah but—"

She adjusted the force fields of Bandit's wings and tail to adjust for the big Dawn gaining behind them. She felt Tuuro curse in the back of her mind and grinned.

Then Tuuro lurched in to adjust them back; Vanako pulled back in hesitation, and both the Dawn and the Shrike came into the corner ahead.

"What the fuck?"

What the fuck?

She almost shot back her explanation—a bear trap of a thought—but thought better of abusing her co-pilot while they were in the air at skull-splattering speeds; and, while she untangled the bear trap into something less tight-jawed and lacerating, she felt the insight unfold in his mind.

OK, he said. *So the new word is, you do my job and I'll do yours.*

"The new word is, I trust you and you trust me."

They'd closed the Vermiliion border by now, coming up on a narrow side street that would take them into the plaza. She felt Tuuro pushing her to go faster, to put her nose practically on the tail of the Dusk Stalker in front.

"I don't want to die in a fireball before we even get to Jasper."

TRUST ME VANI.

She'd said she would, so she did.

It wasn't her own expectation that was satisfied when the two wyrms sped up faster than they should on the lead-up to a sharp corner; it was Tuuro's. But the referred feeling was just as sweet—sweeter, even, for its foreignness, the way the touch of someone else's hand always felt better than your own. They pulled ahead; she banked into the turn; they braked, but she was already dipping to cut under them, and she felt hair snag on a talon as they pulled under, then up, their breath hot on Bandit's tail. Vanako was close enough to hear one of the 'streamers yell "Fuck!" and she couldn't suppress her own shout in response, an ululating cry that started in the bottom of her stomach, counterpointed by howls of encouragement from the street.

YEEEEEAAAAAHHHH came the cry from Tuuro's mind, but his attention was already on the wyrm entering the square in front of them, evaluating lines where they might overtake, tactics they might use to do it.

"Let's do that again," Vanako said

***

IN VERMILION PRECINCT, THEY did it again.

In Jasper Precinct, they tried to spook a solo Mrineen 'streamer on a Saw-Pinioned Dart with a sudden wyrm-scream from behind.

It didn't work, but a few seconds later they were out on a wide boulevard and Vanako slipped through an open lane before the Dart could adjust.

In Topaz Precinct, they spent their time catching up to the pack. Not much competition coming from behind, but Vanako reminded Tuuro to stay vigilant. She had to do it more than once, but it wasn't exasperating, it didn't feel like nagging; it felt just like reminding herself.

By Chartreuse Precinct, most of the wyrms in the pack were starting to flag; but whatever fire it was that moved Bandit's wings was still burning high, and it felt like those other wyrms gave way one by one, willingly, even graciously, providing lanes out of pure generosity. *Careful there, crown princess,* Tuuro warned, which Vanako acknowledged distractedly. She had a race to focus on.

In Ultramarine Precinct, they drew up on Jina and Jaisha ze-Tsuzeki cruising north on the main drag. Vanako pulled Bandit up on their left, the west side; she felt Tuuro groan—they'd have to turn east; they should have tried to cut in on the inside—but ignored it. They pulled up next to Silence and began pressing to the right, pushing them toward the cliff face. Silence puffed up the feathers behind its jaw and flicked a tongue of flame out of its mouth in annoyance; Vanako felt both Bandit and Tuuro tense up at the threat. *Vani,* Tuuro said, *that's a half-wild wyrm.*

Jina shot Vanako a swift dagger-stare and edged Silence toward Bandit. Vanako gave a foot or two—then sent a twitch through Bandit's tail, gently slapping Silence's. Bigger face-feathers, more threat-flame. Vanako felt Bandit itching to make its own display, and—"Fuck it. I'll allow it." Not great for visibility, but that wouldn't be a factor for long.

Vani, I do not want to get into a dogfight right now.

"We won't."

That wyrm wants to kill you. So does Jina.

"Tough titty."

The road veered a little farther from the cliff face; Vanako let up the pressure just a bit. Silence's wings stroked harder.

"Just one more," Vanako said.

She edged hard to the right; Silence finally surged, hooking right to gain some room for a great haul of its wings, cutting through the spray of a waterfall.

The half-wild wyrm streaked ahead, an arrow fletched in blue and grey, and veered slightly inland to climb the road that would take the ze-Tsuzeki sisters up the cliff face. Vanako was content to hang back a few lengths.

Tuuro sent a wordless pulse of inquiry, some combination of "why did you x" for x including but not limited to "take the outer lane," "rile up a minimally trained wyrm," "play tail-footsie with said minimally trained wyrm," and "let Silence out in front of us after all the shit heretofore enumerated," with a dash of "enrage a woman who could probably crush my head into tiny little bits of fluff like a dandelion clock."

"We'll pass them by Lilac Precinct," said Vanako, and shot him an image back.

Tuuro's mind was silent for a moment.

My liege, he finally said.

***

By Lilac Precinct, Bandit and two others had passed the ze-Tsuzeki sisters... but no one got within two lengths of Bandit; and if the crowd wasn't as large or loud as it was during proper races in the 'stream, there was something about seeing it from the front saddle that made each face more beautiful, each banner and bouquet more colorful, than any crowd she'd seen since.

She knew the script: Tear off her goggles so they could see her face, bring out the saddle-knife so they could see all the totems catch the gleam of the afternoon sun, lean back to the aft saddle for a kiss on dragonback. Cheers and petals flew, and she had to stop her hands from creeping under Tuuro's shirt—they were linked, still, through Bandit, and something about feeling her own shape between his hands, her own tongue on his, made it hard to remember where they were, and with whom, and what they were there to do. And feeling that he felt the same way she did made it no easier. She pushed him away, not easily, and slid down Bandit's flank before proximity to Tuuro could lead to any really poor decisions. The crowd parted enough to let her through to the podium. When the prize came, she took it in her hand, then held it high, long enough for them to go still.

'Some of you are wondering—" Her voice broke, and she paused to regain it. "Some of you are wondering, now that Zaya Shearwater's disappeared, where's House Shearwater's contribution to helping the hunted get treated? Are we still in this fight?" She scanned the crowd, not realizing what she was looking for until she found it; A baboon ker, mostly hidden by the crowd, standing by a thin older Ililuë man whose left arm was missing below the elbow, whose eye were weary and haunted. She could throw this pouch to him, she thought; it wouldn't be enough for a month's treatment, certainly not two, but maybe it would put him over the edge? Or at least let him buy something to help with the pain? However small that was, wasn't it more than it would do in the hands of the Travelers? Wasn't that worth more than a few thousand more pamphlets, a couple of Travelers in the minority in the House of the Stars?

But she was up here in front of everybody. And she'd said half the words already. And Minshoon and Jaliki and Kaana te-Tekko were looking at her full of expectation, knowing exactly what she was supposed to say, waiting for it.

"There are a lot of fights at our door," she said. "We're still fighting for my brother's life. We're fighting to get my mother back. We're fighting everything a family of Kayalim born poor in Yemareir has to fight every day." Those words were true; they came from a bright well of anger inside her that glowed like molten metal and coated her throat with the taste of copper. Why did each one make her wilt a little as it moved through the air and into her ear? "So are we still in this fight? To get the government we need to help our hunted siblings and children?"

The pouch arced through the air; one of Kaana's bodyguards reached out to catch it.

"Fuck!" Vanako shouted. "Yes!"

The curse cut through the air as she'd known it would; she'd never be eulogized as an orator, but anyone could put a little spin on a good curse. The crowd broke out in roars, cheers, and whistles, and if its size made the whole display feel less fervent than polite, it was fine. Polite might be all she could really handle right now. The announcer said a few concluding words that no one listened to, and a procession started flowing toward Laurel Square, where the winner's party had been planned in the event that the winners were Tuuro and Vanako.

They moved vaguely in the direction of Laurel Square, fielding congratulations and tousling the hair of the occasional kid as they went, and Tuuro's hand in hers was hot and tight and the pad of this thumb was rubbing against the outside of hers like... the thought *a dog humping her leg* crossed her mind before she could stop it, and she felt his grip loosen. She tightened hers. "I'm sorry," she whispered, trusting her mind to amplify it. "I'm just—I'm not really feeling it any more."

That's why I'm trying to bring it back.

"It'll come back. But not now." She pulled her hand and mind back, felt him cling just the faintest bit to both. "Sorry," she said. "Just need to keep my thoughts in my own head for a bit."

"All right." But Vanako knew it wasn't.

A tall, solid form fell into step beside them, then nudged into Vanako's space, pushing her into Tuuro. She sighed. "Funny."

"I thought so," said Jina ze-Tsuzeki. "That was a smart move. How'd you know our wax would wash away so easily?"

"Smell," said Vanako. "One of my dads is super into feather-wax. He taught us how to recognize all the common ones. I honestly thought it was the most useless thing until..." She shrugged. "It wasn't."

"Kirono. Of course." Jina shook her head. "Oh, princess."

"I won that race."

Tuuro cleared his throat.

"Sure. You and your footman won fair and square," said Jina. "With the knowledge you picked up as a scion of House Shearwater. You even name yourselves like them." By *them* it was clear she meant Mrineen; or, at least, some other group of people despised by Jina ze-Tsuzeki.

"Why do you have such a bug up your ass about my family?"

"Because you're pretending to be these folk heroes when all you do is cozy up to politicians and rich people and use your advantages to win races."

"Don't forget organized crime."

"I try not to repeat myself."

"Hey," said Tuuro, stepping in front of Vanako to face Jina directly. "We're all on the same side here."

"No," said Jina. "You're on the side that thinks money is more useful to court the Mrineen vote than help actual Kayalim people. Even though they blueball you every fucking time."

"Spoken like a woman who knows all about getting blue-balled," said Vanako. "Speaking of which, we're headed to the winner's party. You're invited, if you can stand it."

Vanako turned and headed in the direction of Laurel Square, shoulders tensed for the one-liner that would destroy her. When Jina ze-Tsuzeki yelled "Enjoy the ball, princess," it was like a warm, scented bath. Not even worthy of flipping her the bird in parting.

***

IT WAS CLEAR ENOUGH, though, that Tuuro wasn't as satisfied as she was with the exchange. "You don't want to be the one to tell me," she said, "but you want me to know she has a point."

"She has a point."

"She's an asshole. I don't understand any of this shit. I'm winning races for my family. Which you want to say she has a point about as well."

"It sounds like you maybe agree she has a point," said Tuuro.

"I don't agree with dick. Helping actual people sounds great until you actually have to hand over a flinder to a stranger. Then you realize the ones who are best at asking for money are the ones most likely to be doomed, because people who aren't doomed don't get much practice asking for money."

"Kaana te-Tekko's great at asking for money."

"Boyfriend points are not currently available for 'setting Vani straight,'" Vanako said. "Don't ask when they will be, the answer is never."

"OK," said Tuuro. "But let me just remind you, Jina ze-Tsuzeki isn't the only person you know who's had thoughts like that after losing to House Shearwater."

"Great," said Vanako. "You also think we're the royal family now? Why are you even here?"

"No," said Tuuro. "I just think it's easy for people who have a little to forget how much a little is. If my roommates knew where you lived, they'd look at you the way you look at Zaailo Merganser. Every time I come by, I wonder if it's the day Minshoon-kana's gonna tell me I can't come in until I get some new clothes."

"He'd never—"

"I know."

Vanako stopped and pulled on his hand so he'd stop too. "He'd *never*."

"I *know*," said Tuuro. "But it's not about what I know. It's bigger than that. You can't do anything about it. Just don't act like it's…" His face briefly wobbled, as though he'd had his toe stepped on but his expression had stopped halfway to where it was going. "Stupid, or whatever."

She laced her fingers through his and squeezed, not sure when their roles in the conversation had switched, or how. She walked to Laurel Square beside him, stepping softly on the cobblestones, as if to keep from slipping on a coat of ice.

Chapter 36
Four weeks before the Skua

"If this all goes wrong," Vanako said to Tuuro the next morning, "I just want you to know you clean up nice."

Goes wrong? he sent back; but the irony he was trying for didn't cover the ember of real worry inside the question.

"You know. We might not get invited to the good parties any more. Maybe have to start selling off the silver."

Her banter didn't much relieve Tuuro. Vanako banked Bandit to the right and down, past a stand of centuries-old trees that surely hadn't stood here for more than a few dozen years and the sorcerous humidity that sustained them, and landed with Bandit's right foreclaw neatly poised on the front step of House Merganser.

She slid down Bandit's flank and sized up the greeter, a gangly black-haired Mrineen who was, in the face of a killer fire lizard on their doorstep, annoyingly nonchalant. "I guess I should know who you are?" they said, glancing over at Bandit.

"It's none of my business if you're bad at your job," said Vanako. "I just need to know if I should stable the wyrm somewhere or just give it the run of the place. It's well trained, won't eat your pets."

"Doesn't your driver have another ride to pick up?" the greeter said, looking up at Tuuro.

"That's not my driver, he's my helpmeet. Essential staff."

"He looks essential," said the greeter, pretending to hide a small smack of their lips. "You seem a little young for him."

Vanako rolled her eyes and brushed past them to enter the front hall.

It was an incredible room: soaring ceilings, walls paneled in rich dark wood, illuminated pictures of mergansers carved into the panels. A Mrineen man and woman, both slender and dressed in tight black-and-silver formal wear, turned to look at her at the squeak from the greeter. The man smiled with a delight that sat a little too naturally on his face—young, sharp, and handsome, framed by black curls.

"Vanako Shearwater, as I live and breathe," said Shanhoon Krait.

"Miss!" The greeter called from behind her. "You can't just leave your dragon here! There's a line forming!"

Vanako glanced out the door, saw Tuuro had dismounted, and *reached* out to Bandit and indicated a shady spot in Zaailo Merganser's toy rainforest where it could curl up comfortably. "Shanhoon," she said, in a tone that at least felt like it was calm and self-possessed, rock steady, not shaky at all. "Excuse me for a second." She stepped back out to the front porch, away from the constructed opulence of the front hall and back to the cultivated opulence of the garden, and addressed the greeter, who was watching Bandit walk off. "I've come to collect this helpmeet," Vanako said, taking Tuuro's arm. "Can you see to the others?"

"Of course," the greeter said, not liking it. "Which ones are yours?"

"Oh, you don't need me for that," Vanako said. "Why, I'd be here all day! They'll tell you."

The greeter looked to the front of the line, then on toward the back—there were dozens of people in it by now. Vanako could practically feel it sink into the greeter's mind that almost all of them were Kayalim.

Yyrreen was toward the front, eye-stopping in a white shift with rows of macaws decorating the hem. Vanako didn't look directly at her; she could feel Yyrreen's eyes like augers grinding bone-dust from her skull.

"It's an unusually large staff," the greeter said. "Perhaps a few of them could—"

"Oh!" Vanako said, looking inside as if she'd seen something she must attend to, which she hadn't. "So sorry, must dash! I won't keep you any longer, you've been *such* a great help—" And she grabbed Tuuro's wrist and dragged him in.

"*What*," said Tuuro, "is *he*."

Vanako looked over at Shanhoon Krait, who was engrossed in conversation with his same interlocutor, and silently said *shit*.

***

BEFORE THE IMMOLATION OF Ashniraan Merganser, Vanako, Taavi, and Gilthiniel had sat down to write a list of titles.

Zayeni was the Deputy Undersecretary of Pharmaceutical Distribution for House Shearwater; her boyfriend was the Assistant to the Deputy Undersecretary. Tuuro was the Vice Chair of Draconic Operations, his roommates were Sub-Vice Chairs. Neighborhood people who'd brought food and drink to political events held various ranks in the invented hierarchy of Procurement Specialists, presided over by Kiri and Vinaali, the Executive Directors. Kaana te-Tekko was Chief Medical Advocate.

She'd chuckled at the title when Vanako had come to her with it. "Not what I'd have picked, but I get it. That's good. But what do you expect to get out of having me there?"

Vanako had polished her answer to a high shine by now. "You're not the only one. There'll be dozens of us. Maybe a hundred, if we're lucky. And we're hoping for two things. One is to remind Zaailo-kana who we are, which is hopefully the same as reminding him where he came from. We don't have servants and staff, but we have each other. We come out for each other. And there are a lot of us."

Kaana was thin-lipped and unapproving. "He's had a lot of time to think about all that, and it hasn't done much. You're not going to convince him he ought to be accountable to a bunch of scraggly Lilac Precinct strivers he doesn't know any more, if he ever did."

"Maybe. But he's also going to have guests there, and there's nothing a Mrineen scion likes more than messy drama. Which is the second thing. If we can get just a couple of them, maybe just one, to get the idea that they should support freeing Mom because it would be *fun...*"

Kaana te-Tekko's head sank, supported by her hand. A weary, disgusted noise emanated from somewhere in her chest, never really getting close to any consonant or vowel in any of the alphabets Vanako was aware of, at least. After a few moments of silence—Vanako braced for the aftershocks—she looked up.

"What a nightmare hole," she said, "what a slime-lined, excrement-encrusted grave-shaft it is in which we live. You're right. It could absolutely fucking work. I'm in."

***

"I'M SORRY," VANAKO SAID to Tuuro. "I didn't know he'd be here."

Which was, strictly, a lie—of course he'd be here. Nothing could be more expected. She just hadn't thought about what that would mean to Tuuro. Which was *so much worse* to say than that she didn't know.

Tuuro was looking across the hall at Shanhoon Krait, who was carrying on his conversation with his interlocutor as if he had no idea that Tuuro's eyes were burrowing into him like daggers. He'd probably grown numb to that kind of stare by now. "It's all right," said Tuuro. "I'll improvise."

"You will absolutely not," said Vanako. "Zaailo-kana runs the jails. This place has got to be crawling with high-ranked cops."

"He has a sword," said Tuuro. "I'll challenge him to a duel."

"He has like sixty inches of sword," said Vanako.

Tuuro eyed the rapier at Krait's belt. "Thirty-six, max."

"You have none inches."

"It's all right. While he studied the blade, I was learning how to make dragons do things with nothing but my mind."

She dug her fingertips into the meat of his bicep. "Tuuro."

He looked away from Shanhoon, finally—but not at Vanako. He was staring at a point somewhere in front of him, and if there'd been anything there, he wouldn't have seen it. Vanako tried to get into his mind, but he'd slammed it shut. Then he *reached* out, and she felt the force of it.

She saw a frown cross Shanhoon's face, saw his hand creep up to his throat. She could hear Tuuro's teeth grind. She dug her fingers in harder. "Stop."

Krait drew a breath—was he working harder than he should have to expand his chest? Tuuro's teeth ground again. It wasn't easy to turn off the brain's life support; the rhythms that drove heart and breath were deeply entrained, resilient to all but the most massive floods of noise. But Tuuro was used to working with much larger motor systems; and Shanhoon Krait coughed, more weakly than a healthy young man had any business coughing.

"You fuckstick," Vanako said to Tuuro under her breath, "you owe me for making me save Shanhoon Krait's life."

She looped one hand around the back of his head and slipped the other up his shirt, then pulled his mouth down to hers so it wouldn't echo off the soaring ceilings and wood panels when he yelped in pain. Which is exactly what he did, into her mouth, when she pinched his nipple between her fingernails as hard as she could.

"Get out of here," she said against his lips before she let him go.

He spoke directly to her mind: *I'll kill him.*

Some other time. Take Bandit. Just get out.

"The lovers!" Krait said jovially, if a little roughly; he and his companion had joined them. "The talk of the 'stream, after yesterday. It's lovely to see you reconciled with your estranged family, Shearwater-cha; Merganser-cha has become quite lighthearted since he made your acquaintance."

"You know each other?" Vanako said. Of course they knew each other.

"Business partners. Talking of, I wanted to show you a new product Taipan Invotechnic has been working on." He leaned down so his face was near hers—he was so tall—and tapped his collar, embroidered with geometric patterns in glinting purple thread. "I had an interaction with a powerful empath recently that left me thinking. Why focus on damping *them* when what we really want is to protect *us*? So now I have a damping field in almost everything I wear. Much more comfortable than one of these amulets the 'stream used to use, and much less obtrusive. Unless, of course, you're an empath trying to get through it. Do I know you?" This last to Tuuro, casual enough that Vanako couldn't tell if Krait was sincere.

She felt hate flare in Tuuro's mind, but all he said was "No."

Vanako worried that she'd have to make him leave; but before she could make up her mind whether to nudge his, he leaned down to paste a quick kiss on her temple and loped out the front door without another word.

Krait watched him go. "Man of mystery."

"You killed his grandfather in the first race I ever flew," said Vanako.

"Did not."

The room had mostly cleared out. No one was watching them except maybe a neighbor from Laurel Street and, unfortunately, Minshoon. Oh well; sometimes you had to look at things you'd rather not.

Vanako drew back a fist and punched Shanhoon Krait between the legs as hard as she could.

Krait's eyes bugged out; veins stood out on a suddenly red face. He clipped her shoulder with his own, almost knocking her down, as he folded in on himself, with a noise like a sheep giving birth.

"And you sicced the cops on my mom," she said to the empty air in front of her, as if he hadn't fallen at all. "Don't come to the ceremony. No one should ever let you near a baby."

***

Vanako was almost out the back when Minshoon caught up with her. "What did you do?" he asked, his calm so close to complete.

"I took an open lane," Vanako said. "Just like Mom taught me."

"This place is *crawling*—"

"—with people who never suffer consequences. And only one of them is crawling right now. But you know he deserves it."

"Vani, it is dangerous to fuck with these people."

They emerged into the back garden, and a wall of greenhouse air slapped them like a wave. The dense trees from the front of the house wrapped around to the back, but here they were smaller, functioning mostly to provide shade and scaffolding to the lianas, bright flowers, and broad-leafed plants that grew on or among them. There were a few clearings connected by paths, and it was in the largest of those that the crowd gathered, vastly overflowing the seating thanks to the unannounced House Shearwater contingent. A priest of the Wyrm Immanent stood beneath a bower of brightwick, robed in overlapping white fabric scales hemmed with gold, draer head adorned with the gleaming remiges of an Argent Swordwing. Zaailo waited to the side with two unbelievably handsome men who must have been his son and son-in-law, and a short, cropped-haired Kayalim woman who was trying to calm the fussing baby, who was reaching for her from their father's arms.

"Speaking of which," Minshoon said, "what the hell is the entire neighborhood doing here?"

"Helping."

"The Dancer's broken ankle," he muttered. "Of course they are."

"It's dangerous to fuck with us too," said Vanako. "The people roll deep."

"Please, please, please, spare me. Vani, this was—" Minshoon looked around, as if hoping all the people who shouldn't be here might happen to have gathered on a handcart that he might be able to push away if he was quick enough, then stopped himself. "You don't have any funny jokes planned, do you? No surprises?"

"We might do a haka for the baby if there's a good time and we can get the space. A *sincere* haka," she added, seeing his face darken. Which was true. Even if it might possibly fade into a sincere plea for Zaya's freedom after the sincere welcome to the baby was over with.

"Fine. Tell Zaailo-kana about it, please, as early as you can. And don't cold-cock any more guests. It's not going to help anyone if you get arrested for pulverizing the balls of the peerage."

"Krait isn't even a baronet."

They took their places in the crowd, standing off to the side so Vanako could see without Minshoon blocking anyone's view. "You're right," said a familiar voice to Vanako's other side, "but he will be. House Krait always creates successful entrepreneurs, it's part of their business model."

"Dad," said Vanako. "This is Haanen ze-Keiaza. They work for Ziyuki-kana. Where's Ziyuki-kana?"

Vanako craned her neck to look at the front of the crowd, but she couldn't recognize Ziyuki from the back. Then everyone turned their heads, and she caught a glimpse of Ziyuki's profile as the proud fathers brought a none too happy baby up to the bower and the priest.

"It's a pleasure," said Haanen. "So what's, you know. The idea?" They made an efficient gesture encompassing the crowd. "I mean, forgive me for assuming these scraggly Kay-alim are all your people, but..."

"Zaailo doesn't care about my mother," said Vanako. "He only cares about the opinions of rich Mrineen scions. This is a way to get their attention—"

"—and if enough of you plead your case to enough randomly selected oligarchs, maybe the idea takes hold and now you have an ally to get under Zaailo's skin. OK. What was, like, the probability you assigned to something like this working? This question's for Daddy Number-Cruncher who wants to act like he doesn't own this because it wasn't his idea."

"It was my idea," said Vanako. "He didn't know it was happening."

The priest had begun to lecture in Old Mlin; Vanako wasn't sure if drae was reading scripture or speaking words of draer own composition. "I can't put a probability on that," said Minshoon. "I've got nothing to go on. I don't know the guest list, any estimate of their baseline attitudes about secret imprisonments, any likelihood we'd actually talk to any given person..."

"Sounds like you'd put money on it being doomed."

"I'd hedge it with one in twenty odds on success if I could get them. But mostly as motivation for Vani to actually get it over the line. If we can put the fear of... anything... into the Chief of Corrections—"

The fathers had taken off the baby's grey ceremonial clothes, leaving them naked except for a grey diaper, and handed them to some ecclesiastic-looking minion in a scaled robe similar to the priest's, only grey with silver edges. The baby was fulminating in full diapason at this point, casting wet, betrayed glances back at their fathers every few seconds to check that they were still there. The priest pronounced some ritual-sounding phrases in Old Mlin and draer hand erupted in blue-and-yellow flames.

"OK," said Haanen to Vanako. "Would you believe me if I told you Zaailo didn't invite you here just to ooh and ahh at his grandson getting ash rubbed all over his chub rolls? Don't answer that, you'd better believe me. That journo you sent sniffing around has him about filling his drawers."

"I didn't send anybody anywhere," said Vanako.

"Fine. All I know is you sent a bunch of letters to the Damask Free Press and now this guy thinks he's got a story about bond traders buying up debt in ventures like Zaailo's hospital, because someone's telling them it's not going to be cheap for much longer."

Vanako blinked. "I don't get it."

"Seafarer's buying them," Minshoon said quietly.

"Not quite," said Haanen. "Seafarer's buying Taipan Invotechnic. House Krait and House Taipan are buying Haven—that's House Merganser's prison project."

"The debt's going to be worth more if yliaster becomes legal and widely available," Minshoon said to Vanako. "They know something."

"What does that have to do with us?" said Vanako. "We're not traders, we don't touch any of that stuff."

"No," said Haanen, "but you can choose how angry your community gets about it when the story breaks. I don't know if the plan's to butter you up or stare you down." They looked around at the Kayalim listening stolidly to the litany of Old Mlin and the squalling of the baby, now nearly covered in ash. "Hopefully stare you down."

"Catch more flies with butter," said Vanako. "Not as satisfying for you and Ziyuki-kana, though, is it? I think you want to see him put me in my place." She tried to conceal the hurt in her voice when she said this. What the hell?

"I don't want to see anything. I want him to feel in control."

"Why?"

"Because then he feels safe. And when he's safe, he's pre-dictable," asked Vanako.

"What would he do if he wasn't predictable?"

"*I don't know.*"

That was hard to argue with, actually. "Fine, whatever," Vanako said. "I can pinky promise not to sic my scary neighbors on him when the bad money story breaks. Is that what you—wait, *what*—"

The priest had finished daubing the baby in ash and was now holding them under the armpits in flame-wreathed hands; as Vanako watched, drae bathed the baby in a stream of cobalt-and-cadmium flame erupting from draer mouth.

This all made the baby very upset, but didn't injure it in any way, and Vanako entertained the embarrassing thought that the baby was some flame-retardant being of prophecy—and that, by extension, so were all Mrineen old enough to walk, and was this the feeling of her life's bedrock crumbling beneath her feet—be-fore settling on the huge letdown of a fact that the flame was all illusion.

"Just like that," said Haanen. "Act like you don't know it's com-ing. Squeak a little."

"I did not."

Minshoon snorted.

"Seriously, though," said Haanen. "In a room with Zaailo Merganser, your job is to cave and promise whatever. He thinks specific threats are scarier, because he's a dumb government functionary who thinks that grown humans who don't live in his house will respond to conditioning-based parenting techniques. So he'll probably threaten you with some concrete bad thing, which you should squeal about to me or your aunt at the earliest opportunity. If he's vague, good news, it means he thinks he can't deliver. If he tries to catch more flies with… butter… then you're taking a bath in butter, the butter has you in its greasy grip and you are powerless to resist. Butter is your new boyfriend, your new life's work, your new skin care routine. You," they said, fixing their eyes on Minshoon's, "stick with her, help her sell it. Vani, you can put up some token resistance if Dad's there, then buckle when he shoots it down."

"I thought butter was my boyfriend," said Vanako.

"You need 'boy loses girl' to really sell the plot," said Haanen. "Don't you read?."

"By flame and scale and talon touched," said the priest, "this child will walk in the succor of the World-Cincture, the Sentry of Waters, the Wyrm Whose Wings Are the Sky; and all who cross their path will know it. Go in peace, I hear there's an open bar."

***

Vanako put her hands up to applaud the end of the ceremony, but no one else did, so she didn't. She looked over to Haanen for a cue, but Haanen was gone. A petite Mrineen woman, curvy and brown-haired, was gliding over to take their place. Vanako could feel a cool front move with her; she was sorcerously dressed for the sorcerous humidity. "Zalsheen Gila," she said. "You'll know my cousin Jenirain, and I know you, of course. You came without your young lover?"

Vanako sighed, for many reasons. "He and Shanhoon Krait don't get along."

"Next time Shanhoon can skip instead. I'll draft a petition. How fascinating of you to bring all your help! You truly are royalty among the Kayalim of Yemareir, I had no idea."

"They're not servants," said Vanako. "We support each other. I owe some of them my life. That's what I'm trying to communicate here, that community's stronger than—"

"—than money? I couldn't agree more; it's why we throw parties even though they're *so* expensive. Your entry fees operate on the same principle, I should imagine. No flinder so well spent as one on community."

"Sure," said Vanako, meaning the opposite, "but it's not about buying—"

"Only, I had—you'll forgive me—a more poetic reading; that all those obliging neighbors could never truly *fill out* a guest list that was missing your mother—even if they do cause a run on the punch. Quite a powerful statement, in my mind. Especially in the very lair of the correctional system! Especially to your estranged uncle, one of the most successful Kayalim in Yemareir!"

Vanako cast her eyes back toward Minshoon, hoping for a way out, but a few neighbors had collared him and he was stooped to participate in their whispered conversation. When she turned back to Zalsheen Gila, she saw the scion looking back at Minshoon as well, her smile gone, an expression of stone-faced probing in its place. The smile returned so intensely that the other face of Zalsheen Gila seemed to have been an illusion. "How engrossed they are," said Gila. "What *could* they be talking about?"

"I have no idea," said Vanako. She tried to figure out where a well-bred Mrineen would take this conversation, but anything she could think of wasn't anywhere she wanted to be. "Look, Gila-zē, I have a very blunt question for you, and I guess I hope you find it charming instead of rude. What do you actually think about my mother's imprisonment?"

Everything in Gila's too-wide eyes, her too-attentive posture, her too-sympathetic simper said she was using her face to soften the blow of some polite non-answer, like *I'm no lawyer* or *I'm not familiar with the situation* or *One must play the hand one's dealt, alas*; but instead she nodded and said "Quite a profound injustice," although she gulped so hard saying it that it looked like she'd swallowed an apple whole.

The entire performance made Vanako want to back away, but it seemed wrong to leave an opening like that unexplored. "I know we've only just met," she said, "and I honestly can't tell how much of your act is just making fun of me in ways I'm too dumb to notice, but if you really think my mom being disappeared by the prisons is an injustice, we could use your voice. Like, if you would actually say it to Zaailo-kana and other powerful people. My family has tried *everything*—"

"They've diligently pursued all legal options to secure her mother's release," Zaailo Merganser cut in. "Grandee, I hope you'll forgive me for interrupting; Vanako hasn't yet met my son and grandson. If I could take you inside?"

"I'd like to meet them as well," Minshoon said from behind Zaailo. Zaailo turned to appraise Minshoon; the solicitous look on his face faded, then snapped back into place.

"Minshoon Shearwater; of course. Please join us. Zalsheen, I promise to return your interlocutor to continue her attempt at influence peddling. I know it's a conflict of interest for me to interfere."

"I'll keep it from the Ethics Commission just this once," said Gila, and she turned with a dainty wave and a rise of her chest that, Vanako was pretty sure, was about to be a sigh of relief.

"She seemed nervous," said Vanako, joining Zaailo to enter House Merganser.

"Star-struck, no doubt," said Zaailo. "You're more formidable than you realize."

Zaailo swept them in through the back door, then through the darkly painted foyer and up a stone staircase with his stylized merganser symbol inlaid in brass in every step. "I'm sorry I didn't invite you to the Vigil for a New Soul," he said. "We had the whole garden lit up, and the food was out of this world. No insult to the cooks we got for today, but it's not the same. Did Kaalo ever cook chocolate chicken for you?"

Vanako was about to remind him she'd never met Kaalo—but Minshoon chuckled with recognition. "He did for me," he said. "Spiciest thing I'd ever eaten, then or since, and he'd just destroy me for it every time. 'You Mrineen all have little baby tongues,' he'd say. 'Even Yyrreen can handle that.' He told me I'd get used to it if I soldiered through, and it tasted good enough that I did. And he was right, over the course of a year or so it got to be tolerable." He blew air out through pursed lips, as though he could still taste the chilies. "Not until he was on his actual deathbed did he confess to goosing my portion with assassin peppers."

Zaailo laughed. "I'd be lying if I said that sounds like the Kaalo I knew," he said. "He was more buttoned up back then. But I'm glad he kept a sense of humor through his life."

"He did," said Minshoon, "but that wasn't it. He said he'd seen what getting too close to Mrineen had done to his family, and he didn't want it to happen to Zaya."

For a moment, all Vanako heard was the sound of their steps in the cavernous hallway.

"Scathe and Ancalagon," said Zaailo. "I guess I deserved that. What a mess."

They'd come down a hall lined with beautifully wrought sconces interspersed with small portraits in plain wood frames. Zaailo paused before a double door. "The nursery, naturally. The baby needed a little time after getting smeared all over with ash and emotionally scarred with fake fire. You know, that ash is made from wood burned by real dragonfire? They have the Air Guard's Swordwings burn down old buildings every so often, just for practice. Then they take the ash and bless it and smear it on the babies. It's a weird world we live in."

He led them into the room, which was indeed a nursery; there was a crib on one side, a bed on the other, a curved wooden wardrobe and a low chest and a shelf full of book with wood or fabric pages. The bay windows looked out on the back garden. The jungle trees still towered over them, even on the second floor.

Vanako hadn't even thought about the fact that there was no baby in the crib until a steel-strong grip pulled her elbow behind her back.

Chapter 37

Four weeks before the Skua

Vanako screamed and kipped like a hooked fish; she heard Minshoon roar and a scuffle break out beside her. She felt fabric come down over her face, and for a moment she felt as if she was choking, no actual air-hunger but a terrified certainty of it coming; but then there was light again, the fabric pooled around her neck—it was a shirt, rucked up over her shoulders like a collar—and a strange silence came over her like a blanket, even though she could hear perfectly. She could feel the warmth of a bare chest behind her.

Zaailo was rubbing his forehead with his fingertips as though he had a headache. "I know this will probably ruin our relationship," he said. "But I didn't bring a fucking army into your backyard, so forgive me if I don't show a ton of disappointment."

A corner of Vanako's mind was spitting out a venomous riposte—*I weep for your canapé trays,* or something—but all that came out of her mouth was "What army?"

His glare was pure venom. "We're not doing this, Vani. There's enough police on their way to handle your people. What I need from you is to get that fucking dragon off my property. It goes peacefully, they go peacefully, you go peacefully."

"What?" said Vanako, still trying to catch up. "Of course everyone's going peacefully. No one's here to hurt anyone."

"Whatever. Tell it to the newspaper, that's what you like to do. I just want my guests to leave without getting murdered or barbecued—"

"Zaailo."

He stopped talking and looked at her, but his face might have been carved from teak.

"Zaailo-kana. Tuuro left on Bandit before the ceremony. No one here is armed. Think about this for a second."

Zaailo shook his head. "No further thinking necessary. Here's what we're doing. The police are going to surround this place, they're going to have wyrms overhead. Once that happens, we'll get you all out of here in an orderly fashion. What you need to do is keep your people in check until that happens, and get your dragon out of here."

"It's not *here*. Ask anyone."

"That had better be true."

"It's true!" said Vanako. "No one is here to hurt anybody."

"Good. We're going to open this window now. We'll walk you up to it, and you're going to say the following—"

"No," said Minshoon.

"Here it is," said Zaailo. He turned away from Vanako toward Minshoon, his eyes bright with fear and anger. "The statistician's going to tell me how I got the math wrong."

"She's not their queen," said Minshoon. "If we can quietly spread the word that it's time to go, they'll go. 'Hey, the proprietor's a little spooked, we better leave.' Right? No one wants to be here for trouble. But if Vani says to stay in one place because police are coming, they're not going to do it for her. They care about her, but not enough to stand still and let themselves get surrounded by cops. They're going to do what they think they need to do to survive. And they're *not armed*—" he gritted this out through his teeth—"so they'll run if they can. But if they're cornered, I don't know what'll happen."

"They don't need to be armed. They're empaths. But if they're peaceful, all they need to do is show it."

"Some of them," said Minshoon. "Look, Zaailo-kana, a bunch of cops and a bunch of scared folks from Rust and Damask are not going to mix well. Someone is going to get the wrong idea. Maybe one of them, maybe one of your guests, maybe someone in this room. What if it's some Alabaster Precinct cop up on a Swordwing? They could burn your whole garden to ashes if they think it's in the public interest. This house could be a pile of smoking sticks on top of all our corpses. The wrong kind of mind on that Swordwing looks at this party, sees, the highest-ranking Kayalim in the city administration and the only Kayalim in the House of the Moon…"

Vanako threw her mind against the damping field, hoping she might get through, knowing she wouldn't. *That's not the move,* she wanted to say. *He can't let himself believe that.*

But maybe he could, or couldn't stop himself; because the doubt in his eyes kept growing. Maybe Minshoon could do this.

She felt the warm, hard-muscled presence behind her move in a measured rhythm; A shaking of the head, whose chin brushed her scalp with each arc, stubble catching on a few of her hairs. The accidental intimacy of the gesture made her feel sick.

"Chief Merganser," said the voice of Shanhoon Krait from behind her. "Your plan is fine. If we were wrong about what House Shearwater is doing—and I hope we were—then no one gets hurt. I'll write the letters of apology with my own hand. But if we were right… then they'll try something before the cordon gets here. *That's* the situation where something unpredictable happens. That's what we have to stop, by showing them we have her. And we have to do it soon, because we don't know when they're going to find out they're about to be surrounded."

"The two of you are going to get people killed," Minshoon said quietly.

"Don't be ridiculous," said Zaailo; and if the doubt was not gone, there was something over it now, a brittle, surly hardness. "We're going to open these windows, and you're going to tell your people to stand ready for an orderly departure, assisted by police. And then you and your foster father here can go."

"*Foster* father?" Vanako said. "Careful, Zaailo-kana, your Mrineen mask's falling off."

She felt Shanhoon Krait's chest jerk just slightly against her back: A silent chuckle.

His stubble caught against her hair again. He was orienting to something. She saw it herself: A splash of orange and magenta, flying in a swift pass at the level of the nursery.

Dawn Wyrms were diving hunters; their eyes made small things huge and blurry things sharp. Bandit would have no problem seeing her face through the bay window, if it were looking.

"I think you're about to lose control of this situation," said Vanako.

Zaailo's face shrank into a mean suspiciousness, and he opened his mouth, but Krait spoke first. "She's right," he said. "Her little lover's on the Dawn, and they've just spotted us."

"You said the wyrm was gone," said Zaailo, his voice shot through with bitter spite.

"Relax," said Krait. "This is exactly why we had the cops bring Swordwings. Probably he'll see the better part of valor, but if not, he'll be shown it. No great shakes on wyrmback, if memory serves; this one's the dangerous one." He twitched Vanako a bit, as if reminding Zaailo she was there, or maybe just reminding Vanako that he could.

"My son and grandson are out there," said Zaailo, staring at a spot a few feet in front of him.

"Get them to safety," said Krait. "I can keep things in order here."

A flash of magenta and violet descended past the window with an audible *thump*; there were a few squeals from outside.

"He's landed," Krait said cheerfully. "That'll give the cops the high ground. So to speak."

Zaailo started for the door; Minshoon's voice stopped him. "You have to tell Tuuro what's about to happen," he said. "If this turns into a dogfight between him and a pack of police wyrms, anyone here could die. Anyone."

Zaailo stared at Minshoon for a second, then two. Then he bolted.

Krait began walking Vanako forward, toward the bay window.

"I'm not saying anything you tell me to," she said.

"I don't need you to say a thing," said Krait. "Just want to watch events unfold."

"You fuckpig. You planned this."

"I planned for you to bring a million of your closest neighbors to an Immolation I didn't know you were invited to?" said Krait. "Please. Speak to the Chief of Husbandry and Agriculture if you don't like reaping what you sow."

They were at the window now. Bandit was still and alert, its head high, eyes scanning the air. A knot of Kayalim had gathered around Tuuro, and more were moving toward them as they noticed their neighbors talking to one another in the dragon's shadow. A few Mrineen admirers were gathered what must have felt like a safe distance around Bandit, pointing and chattering. Haanen was at the edge of the crowd of Kayalim around Tuuro, listening in. Vanako couldn't see Zaailo, his son and son-in-law, the nurse, or the baby.

"I don't think Zaailo told te-Kaneva the cops were coming," Krait said. His voice was oddly muted; it took a second for Vanako to realize he was talking over his shoulder, to Minshoon.

Tuuro pointed up to the bay window, eyes following his hand. His gaze met Vanako's.

Haanen's eyes followed as well, and Vanako seized them too—or tried—and mouthed "help" as widely as she could.

Vanako could practically see the whispers ripple through the crowd. Tuuro began moving with a purpose; behind him were three of their larger neighbors, all broad-shouldered men with darkening faces, and Amiko, whose face was carefully blank. She looked for Chashu, found him with Cerminir and Enwë; Shozo had found Kirono, Eäril, and Jaliki; she looked frantically for the twins.

A uniformed trio of household staff moved to intercept Tuuro. Their hands were on the scimitars at their sides. Tuuro's jaw set. Bandit swung its head to cast a yellow eye at the household guards and shifted its weight to its pinions, then began striding over behind Tuuro. Among the Mrineen guests, decorative swords came loose from their scabbards: one, two, four, a dozen, some slow and awkwardly held, a few moving as smoothly through the air as snakes.

"Stop!" Vanako shrieked, trying to break the glass with her voice.

The Merganser guards wavered but did not break. They didn't draw either—they didn't have to, Vanako realized. As long as Tuuro didn't go through them, their job was done.

Tuuro said something. Smoke trickled from the corners of Bandit's mouth.

Tuuro, Amiko, the neighbors, and the Merganser guards all stood very still.

The door to the nursery slammed open; Krait and the bodyguard holding Minshoon whipped their heads around. "Let the Shearwaters go," said Ziyuki Amphisbaena, her voice filling the room to the farthest corner.

"I'm a law-abiding person," said Krait. "Why don't you go pass a bill?"

"Fine," said Ziyuki.

The nursery carpet did a good job at silencing footsteps, but Vanako could hear them anyway, accelerating as they approached.

Finally, Shanhoon Krait let go and turned to face Ziyuki.

Vanako heard the sound of a palm on Krait's face. She could have looked back to savor the slap, but her mind was on one small, ugly, glinting thing: The locking mechanism that kept the bay window shut.

It was no trouble at all to unlock, the simplest thing in the world. But somehow her fingers kept slipping.

A shadow passed over the grounds. Everyone looked up, even Tuuro.

Vanako gave up on the lock and ripped Krait's shirt over her head. Mind-sound flooded in. "Get out!" she shouted, or began to; but before Vanako's words had any chance to reach Tuuro's mind, she saw one of the Merganser guards rip his scimitar from its scabbard. She imagined the high thin song of a freed blade; saw him take one step, then two.

By the second step, Tuuro had seen the attack coming. She felt him *reach* out to Bandit, cadmium-and-cerulean flame shining at the front of his mind.

Then his eyes flickered up toward her, and his mind pulled back.

He took the hit on crossed forearms, and pain blackened her vision, and blood flew, and she screamed, and he fell, and through the absence where his body had been there licked a tongue of that same cadmium-and-cerulean flame, and the Merganser guard sang as high and thin as his sword had done in the long-ago moment when the destruction of bodies had been a worst-case scenario and not a brooding reality, ready to multiply.

***

ALL ACROSS THE GARDEN, swords struggled free, none in Kayalim hands.

A few of House Shearwater's helpmeets ran for the edges of the garden; most, not wanting to cross the path of an armed Mrineen scion, gathered close to Bandit. For its own part, Bandit was visibly off-balance, trying to keep one eye on the threat of the Merganser guards to Tuuro and one on whatever was happening in the sky. As she watched, it reared up on its hind legs, although rather than fan its wings it held them limp in front—sharing the pain of Tuuro's mangled arms. At least there still was pain.

A hard hand grabbed her elbow—Minshoon. "Let's get out of here."

"Wait."

He jerked her arm. "Come on."

She pushed him off with a jolt of neuromuscular static and *reached*.

Dislodging Tuuro's connection to Bandit's mind wasn't hard; Tuuro was frantic, hurt, weakening. She felt Bandit relax, just barely, at her familiar presence. Gently she pried its attention from the Merganser guards and turned it fully toward the sky. The Swordwing was at the height of its arc; it would hang there for a moment, then swoop for another pass, this time with cause to use its flame. And Bandit's own thoughts were full of flame as well, and the taste of dragon's blood, and the feel of feathers parting under teeth—

"No," Vanako said. "You'll die."

Bandit began to form a thought composed half of inarticulate resignation, half of bloodthirst. The Swordwing turned at the top of its arc.

"No. This is what you do." She showed it.

Protect Tuuro. Fear made it inarticulate. *Protect you.*

"You can't. Fucking do it, Bandit. So you can see Zaya again."

The Swordwing was halfway down. Bandit looked up, puffed its chest, and let out a roiling cloud of flame.

The gleaming silver wyrm was well out of range; Bandit had flamed too early to injure it.

But not to blind it.

The diving wyrm screwed its eyes shut. The cop on its back threw an arm over their eyes. And Bandit took to the air at an angle—not to meet the Swordwing, but to cut under it, where it would have to risk throwing its rider to follow.

Vanako searched the air with her own eyes and Bandit's. There was another Swordwing coming, but it was too far off. It was faster than Bandit, but it wouldn't catch up before its own wind gave out.

Keep the sun to your left until you lose them, she told Bandit over the fraying thread of their connection. *Then go to Saavero's. I love you.*

If there was any reply, Bandit was too far away to make her hear it.

It had only been a few seconds since she'd pushed Minshoon away. Haanen and a thickly built Mrineen with green hair were standing across from Krait and his bodyguard, unarmed but springy at the knees, their weight on the balls of their feet, ready to move.

When Vanako and Minshoon broke for the exit, Haanen stepped back, the need to threaten gone. Ziyuki stood, unmoving, arms across her breasts, feet rooted as mountains.

***

Vanako and Minshoon took the stairs down to the foyer two at a time, not even seeing the white-tunicked police of Alabaster

Precinct until a deep-voiced cry of "Stop!" rang off the walls. They managed to stop just before they'd have run into the shouter, whose short, thick-bladed sword was bare and ready. More police streamed through the front door and into the garden. Vanako wanted to scream at them to stop, to stand down, to hold back their blades and bows; but her chest would not move air for the words.

There was noise coming from the back already, and not good noise. "Scathe and Ancalagon," someone said, surely looking at the blood and burned meat that had been whole flesh a minute earlier. Then: "Back away from him, all of you. *Now.*"

"You have to let me see him," Vanako said to the cop pointing a sword at her.

"You're staying right here," said the cop.

"There's at least two crossbows on us, Vani," said Minshoon, as if he'd known she was about to *reach* into this cop's mind and dissolve all muscle tone from the neck down, which he absolutely had, because she absolutely was. She imagined plucking crossbow bolts from the air like misarranged flowers, setting them on more harmonious trajectories. The mental image was as sharp and vivid as that of dropping this fucking cop, which was kind of frightening, since one was something she could do and one was actual magic.

"I can't stop crossbows with my mind," she said, and repeated it once to herself: *I* can't *stop crossbows with my mind.*

There was more shouting from the backyard—there was barking, there was cursing, there was a roar that could have been a roar of pain but wasn't. But there was no screaming.

Then the crossbows' line of fire shifted, and Cerminir marched through the back door with her hands behind her head.

Enwë was wrapped at her chest, wide-eyed and squalling. Cerminir's eyes poured over Vanako like ice water.

She led a procession through the front door: Eäril and Jaliki, holding hands; Shozo, Kirono, Chashu; Naaka ze-Kijani, who ran the millinery on Myrtle Street; Venu te-Venu, who taught history at the Lyceum; Taavi, finally, and by the Dancer, Vaisho, scared white and not even trying to hide it; a string of faces she only knew from the campaign; Yyrreen...

No Zinji. No Gilthiniel. No Tuuro.

When the last of the procession had passed through the dark-paneled foyer, the cop at the bottom of the stairs stepped aside to let her and Minshoon through. "Your turn. Get out."

Minshoon moved to go, but Vanako said, "Where's Tuuro?"

The cop swung his head to a counterpart out back for the answer.

"Is he the burned one or the cut-up one?"

"His arms were hurt," said Vanako.

"We're taking him to a medic to patch him up. Then we need to talk to him."

"Where?"

"He knows how to find you, right?" the cop at the bottom of the stairs said.

"So when you're done talking, you'll let him come find us?"

"Depends on what we hear."

Vanako did her best imitation of that look Zaya did that said *I'm mad and you'd best not make me explain why.*

"You can find him in a holding cell at the precinct station if we need to keep him around a minute."

"Can I go with him now?"

"No."

"Why?"

"Because one empath is too many already." The cop turned; Zaailo Merganser had come in the back door. "Hi, Chief," the cop said. "We were just clearing these folks out."

"It's all right. They're family."

The cop looked at Zaailo, then to Vanako, then back to Zaailo. "Not much of a resemblance."

"Family. Not brood."

The cop had the grace, or at least the presence of mind, to look embarrassed. "Of course, Chief. We'll be out of your way."

"You did good work today. This could have been much worse." But Zaailo's tone made it a dismissal.

Dismissed, the police left; and then it was the three of them, standing in the dark-paneled lobby, stylized mergansers staring down at them with wide eyes. Zaailo stepped aside, and Zinji entered the room.

"I invited you here so you could share an important moment in my grandson's life," Zaailo said. "Your grandfather insists that you had no ill intentions. You only wanted to make a scene. You didn't think about what it would mean to bring an army to my home."

"*Your* people were armed, not mine!" Vanako snarled.

He went on as if she hadn't spoken. "I don't really care what you were thinking or planning. I should count myself lucky you did so little damage." He shook his head. "But in all honesty, I had you here to tell you something, and thanks to your little stunt, I never got to say it."

"Were you actually going to admit that you were using me to troubleshoot your psionic-proof prisons?"

"Why would I tell you what your pet journo's already spilled? Don't you check your people's work?"

"Because you're sorry for lying to a girl who thought you'd invited her into your family," said Zinji. "You daft old fart."

"I don't have a pet anything," said Vanako. "I didn't even know you were a slimy old liar when he came to talk to me. I wanted him to write a story about Mom, to put pressure on you to at least tell me where she is. But he didn't care. He just wanted to know which girls at my school had dads who were bond traders. So I told him.

Am I not allowed to tell him whose dad does what? Why do you hate me so much for talking to this idiot about something that has nothing to do with you? What *does* it have to do with you?"

Zaailo stared at her as though she'd asked what blue had to do with the sky. He moved his eyes back and forth from her to Minshoon. "You really…" He fixated on Minshoon. "All this, and you have no idea. I could have saved…" He shook his head again and let out an unsteady laugh.

"Oh, come on, Zaailo," Shanhoon Krait said from the balcony. "It's all out there anyway. Don't make them put it together. It's been a tough day for everyone."

Oh, great, Vanako thought as if from a great distance. *Two grown men discussing how to put a knife in my heart.*

She looked up. Krait had put his shirt back on. She wondered where Haanen and Ziyuki had gotten to.

"Our ventures," said Krait. "They're risky ventures, so the debt comes with a chunk of interest. To compensate the lenders for the very real possibility that the companies might not be around to pay them back."

She didn't think it was intentional, but the act of explaining had drained Krait's voice of anything mocking or sardonic. It was still the voice she hated most in this world; but it made her wonder, for a moment, what it might be like to be a child of House Krait, and have Shanhoon for a mentor.

"Lately," he continued, "it's been noticed that a few financial concerns have been buying up said debt. A vote of confidence in our businesses that isn't shared by the rest of the market. And the question that your 'idiot' is asking, in many forms and guises, is merely 'why so confident?'

"There are good answers and bad answers. A good answer would be that these financiers possess unusual good taste and discernment. A bad answer would be that someone told them a secret nobody else knows, and they're cheating. The good answer won't sell copies of the *Free Press*. So, we imagine, the bad answer is what he'll write. And people will get angry."

He let the last word hang. He seemed to be waiting for an answer, but it wasn't Vanako his eyes were on, or even Minshoon; it was Zaailo. Who, indeed, seemed to be searching for something buried too deep in the folds of his brain to be dug out. Krait sighed and continued.

"Forgive your great-uncle; he's usually better at this, but shame's overcome him. Or a minor neurological event. What he brought you here to tell you, before all this unpleasantness, is that, when your people get angry, you should be very careful how you use the powers of your folk-hero station to influence that anger. For example, it would be better if they didn't do something like stage a protest outside this house, or vandalize facilities under construction. I can't imagine I need to tell you why."

"I keep telling you," Vanako said, hearing her own voice as though a far-off mountain had thrown it back in echo. "I can't tell anyone what to do."

Krait appraised her, not without theater. "No dragon, no young lover," he said. "Maybe you can't."

PART IV

CHAPTER 38
THIRTY MINUTES BEFORE THE SKUA

"It's a long story," Vanako said. "Fly toward the sea and I'll tell it."

The young Ranger Wyrm turned—she felt the roll of its shoulders; Saavero had been right about its strength—and Vanako dredged her mind for the things her teachers had tried to make her learn, back when she was young enough that they felt some responsibility.

"Long ago, before any human or dragon who's alive now had been born, there weren't any of these buildings, or people, or ships. There was just... jungle, maybe? I don't actually know. It couldn't have been desert, I guess, or they would have picked another spot. Veldt, maybe."

The image of *veldt* sparked hunger in the dragon's mind, and Vanako realized she was about to lose her audience.

"The point is it was nice, and there were people who would come and stay for a little while. They didn't live in one place, they roamed all over the continent, but they built things here and stayed for a few months each year. They didn't build nearly as much as you see now, but they built an amphitheater and a graveyard and—you'll like this—they built all the broodspires."

The wyrm didn't like this. Bad memories flashed through Vanako's brain: Shattered eggs, claws in flesh, a wing stuck to a stone floor by its own blood. Pain, hunger, darkness.

"Sorry, my bad." She felt a little guilty for getting its attention this way... but that's what storytellers were supposed to do? Right? "No one really knows why they built the broodspires. Like, couldn't dragons breed just fine on their own? But maybe it was easier for them to do it somewhere..." She decided not to say *safe*. "Secluded. Out of the way, you know? But no one really knows.

"Anyway, you can see from the old buildings that little communities developed around all of the broodspires. And you can see from some of the graves that for a while, it was pretty normal for people to get killed by dragons... but eventually they figured out how not to do that, which we know because most of the bones with burns and bite marks are really old. And then there's this one tomb, in the Necropolis—the big graveyard—"

???

"A place where you bury dead bodies."

why?

"Because humans are scared little monkeys who get grossed out by dead bodies. And also we figured out the germ theory of disease."

ok.

Good enough. "So we found this one tomb in the Necropolis—a *tomb* is like a building where you put dead bodies—only there weren't any dead bodies in it. It actually looked like a bath house—like a place where you can go wash, like a warm little lake inside a building." This was as exhausting as explaining something to Eäril—only more so, because Eäril would absolutely have noped out by now and Vanako could have stopped. But the Ranger Wyrm was still paying attention, in its way. "The point is it was covered with tiles on the inside. And each tile had a black, like, thumbprint, pressed into the clay while it was still wet and varnished over so you know it was on purpose. These were little tiles, there are hundreds of them. And at some point one of them fell off, and someone split it open along the thumbprint so they could test what the black stuff was, and it was the ash of a human body."

The wyrm's attention, steadily blurring, snapped sharp. Burned mammals were interesting.

"Then a while later"—decades, centuries? She couldn't remember—"they tested it again, and it turns out it actually also had dragon ash mixed in. If you go there now—and you can—OK, I don't know if *you* can—you'll see this set of long tables, built exactly for the size of the tomb. And each of them has just stacks of little tiles on it, even smaller than the ones on the walls. Those ones are reinforced with metal edges so they don't break, and there's a book there so you can look up names and find tiles for a particular person. When I went there with my class, there were some kids there who had names to look up, ancestors of theirs from early in the Mrineen colonization. Not me, I don't even know all my grandparents' names.

"Anyway, the wall tiles were for people—and maybe dragons—who got killed by a brood of Cinereal Vore Wyrms, before the magical barrier around Ashen Precinct went up. Those were the ancient season-city people, we still haven't figured out how to read their writing. And then the table tiles are for people and dragons who got killed by the first brood of Vore Wyrms after the city was settled by the Mrineen from Old Mlinivoun, before we knew how dangerous it was to be around them when a new brood hatches.

"There are a lot more table tiles than wall tiles. Like, a lot more.

"And the teacher was... proud of that? Like, see how quickly we managed to settle this place so densely that a lot of people got killed when something bad happened in a pretty small location. They built up Ashen Precinct to be the heart of the city in six years. Before they even dragged my ancestors' terrified asses across an ocean to help with the construction. For a hot second, it was called Radiant Precinct.

"And hundreds of years after, they still add a table tile every so often. My mom's wife Kiriki has one. I haven't gone to see it yet.

"What I think a lot about now, though, is that you make memorials for things you want to remember. You don't know Mlin so maybe you don't know how stupid that sounds—they're practically the same word. But you know who lives in the heart of the city? The people that people care about. When we fuck up and kill a bunch of rich people, they get tiles on a table in a tomb. And then when normal people die the same way as those people, maybe they get a tile too.

"But if Jaliki gets killed by his ker, there's no special tomb for him. He'll just disappear into a grave no one cares about, and eventually the river will drift and his grave will fall in."

The sensation from the Ranger Wyrm's mind was a little bit like being patted on the shoulder by a baby, if instead of a fat baby hand it was a cool talon guided by a predatory intelligence that viewed socialization as a regrettable and dangerous necessity. It was very much the thought that counted.

"Thanks for listening, Apple," Vanako said, with as warm a pulse of appreciation as she could manage. "You're a good dragon."

you're a weird monkey who spends all your time in your head. how do you spend all your time in your head.

Vanako was pretty sure there was some affection in there, or at least whatever passed for it in the draconic mind.

"My brain is spacious and full of comfortable folds. You're just jealous because yours is like a little pebble rattling around in your skull."

The image got through, but not the insult. It felt like Apple was about to start with a *?* but then quit trying.

"Whatever," Vanako said, and she reached out to start the wyrm's descent toward the bay.

CHAPTER 39
FOUR WEEKS BEFORE THE SKUA

THERE WAS NO WAY Vanako was going to sleep the night she lost Tuuro and Bandit; still, though, it was easy enough to pretend she was exhausted. She shambled to the doorway of her still doorless room and lay face down on the bed as though she'd fainted, and no one came to wake her. Why would they? She'd need her rest to deal with being hated by literally the entire human race in the morning.

Don't flatter yourself, Shearwater, some voice said in her head; she wasn't sure whose. *Only the people who know you hate you, and almost no one has any idea who you are.* She heard every shout, thump, and rustle of bedtime in a big family through her absent door: Jaliki's grave obedience, Eäril's overtired hyperactivity, Enwë's inconsolable wails consoled finally by nursing. Taavi and Gilthiniel had done what Vanako had done, only with an actual door, and if she wanted to know why Gil's eyes looked so weird and haunted from his brief disappearance at the Immolation, she also knew she wasn't ready to hear some of the things it might be. Kirono had Eäril because even though he didn't usually do bedtime, Zinji had come home with them, and Kirono would rather work with Eäril than Zinji, so Minshoon was setting Zinji up on the sofa and rolling with his random crotchetiness.

Vanako didn't feel herself fall asleep, or wake up, but the period from evening bustle to evening peace passed faster than it should have. She listened for a minute to see if anyone was still up and about, then rolled over. Stinking dog breath hit her face: The ker was staring at her, tongue lolling. She squeaked and swatted at it; it teleported two feet back, just out of range. "Limper make off with you," she muttered, and it put its head down on crossed forepaws and looked at her as if she'd kicked it. She swung her legs over the bed and headed toward the door—the door-hole—at top speed, but Jaliki was in it, rubbing his eyes. "Hey," he said.

"Hey yourself. Did I wake you?"

Jaliki shook his head. "The ker did. Sometimes I see what it sees now." *Is that bad?* Vanako thought. *That has to be bad, right?* "Where are you going?" Jaliki asked.

"Out for a walk," Vanako said. "Can't sleep."

"When I can't sleep, Mom says to count backwards from a thousand." Jaliki's face fell. "Or she used to."

"Sorry, kiddo, I can't count that high."

Jaliki stepped forward, wrapped his arms around Vanako, and squeezed. She could feel the set of his shoulders, the spread of his feet. "You can't go."

He'd gotten so tall—his face was planted squarely, unselfconsciously, between her breasts—and she smiled as she reached behind her back to separate his hands. But he clenched his arms against the separation, and she realized she didn't quite have the leverage to pull his hands apart, and his goaty boy-smell curdled in her nose. Her heart hammered against her ribs—against his face—and her stomach began to turn. "Jali," Vanako said, and thought she could hear her voice shaking. "I need you to let me go."

"You can't go." He tightened his grip.

Her lips skinned back from her teeth, and she dug her fingernails into his forearms; and, when that didn't loosen his grip fast enough, her toe found the wound in his calf.

Jaliki stumbled, his leg giving way beneath him—but he still clung to her, even though his face was crumpled in pain and he was wheezing like he'd been punched in the stomach. But his grip had weakened, and she broke it; and when he fell, she could not make herself catch him. She had to force herself not to kick him. She was breathing fast and shallow; she was furious. He held his chest off the floor with skinny elbows, sobbing, and when he looked up at her all she could see was the smooth, perfect curve of his nose, the hugeness of his eyes. Like Eäril's, like Enwë's—a child's face. He was just a kid, he wasn't Shanhoon Krait holding her against her will. He was just a kid.

"YOU CAN'T GO!" he screamed, and she felt an iron gate slam down in her chest.

"I can," she said. "I am." She stepped over him, ready to shake an ankle loose if he grabbed for it. He didn't. He only wailed, raw and wordless, and let his arms collapse so he was flat on the floor, his back heaving up and down with the effort of weeping. Zinji was sitting up on the couch, or trying to, tangled in his blanket. "What's going on?" he asked. "What's wrong with Jaliki?"

"He's perfect," Vanako said. "Ask him what's wrong with me."

She was out the door before he could reply.

***

FOR ALL THE GOOD it did. Bandit's cell was empty.

CHAPTER 40
THREE WEEKS BEFORE THE SKUA

VANAKO CHECKED BACK EVERY day, but Bandit didn't return to Saavero's. She checked at the dole-flat every day, but Tuuro wasn't there. There was nowhere to check for Zaya. Vanako did check the irises every so often, as if Zaya might have found a way to get a letter there. But there was nothing.

The nights grew longer, and they cooled. Perfect weather, as warm as a late spring day flirting with early summer—but no warmer.

Brooding began at the Damask Precinct broodspire, and now there was nowhere to check on Tuuro. His roommates had told her, oddly apologetically, where they were going: to Madder, to Rust, and to an overflow dormitory in Olive Precinct, where they'd be four dozen to a room until the Ranger Wyrms' new cohort was hatched and fledged, probably sixteen months. She went back to the Damask apartment once, after the precinct had cleared out, but the door to the dole-flat was locked. The Rangers were daytime hunters, and she had gone at night, but still one tailed her through the precinct, only peeling off when the lights and noise of Ochre Precinct came into view.

The nights grew longer, and they cooled. Arms went bare still, but now they were crossed over chests after sunset, palms warming biceps, voices pitched high to comment on the chill in the hopes of taking its edge away. Vanako didn't do either. She deserved the cold, and if that was possibly the most teenage thought one could think without shattering the laws of physics, well, fuck it; not letting the cold get to you was badass. And anyway, she did deserve it.

Vinda te-Kaleivi walked up to her in school, a week or so after it happened. "It was you, wasn't it?" she asked. "Who sent that reporter around to talk to my dad?"

Vanako looked behind her. The two girls who were about to grab her arms shrank back at her regard. She dipped into their minds—one then the other—and kindled the tiniest uncomfortable sensation, just to let them know she was there. She turned back to look at Vinda, whose mind she hadn't yet trespassed on. Vinda crossed her arms over her chest defiantly; but, to hear her face tell it, her stomach felt just like her friends' did.

"How bad did they hurt him?" Vanako asked. "If they beat him up, you can have a free shot anywhere but my head. Two if they broke a bone. If they killed him, you can hit my face."

Vinda cast an appraising eye at Vanako. "For payback, that's pretty fucking crap."

"They're free shots. I set the rates."

"Maybe I don't have to settle for free."

"Your girls back there just realized you do," said Vanako. "Catch up."

"Oh right. That's convenient."

Before Vanako could question the choice of words, a hot, blunt presence parted the surface tension of her mind as easily as water and every joint below her navel yielded to gravity. She folded forward like a jackknife snapping closed. Vanako caught herself before the flagstones met her teeth—even in the rush of the moment, a corner of her mind said *she let you do that*—and she knew what happened when you were down and your opponent wasn't, so one arm folded over her face and her stomach and back tensed all at once.

It was her stomach the kick came for, but it just wasn't very good; Vinda was rushing, so the angle was all wrong, and there wasn't much power in it. Half of it bounced off Vanako's ribs anyway, so it didn't really take her breath, didn't bring her gorge up to distract her.

Vinda's technique improved on the next kick; she took some time to square off and aim well. It spoke highly of her attitude, Vanako thought. She'd clearly been disappointed by the first kick and was making thoughtful adjustments. But Vanako wasn't that interested in continuing to get the crap kicked out of her, so she grabbed Vinda's leg on the backswing and jerked.

What that was supposed to do was pull Vinda down. But Vanako wasn't in a very strong position, so all it did was make her hop to keep her balance. One of the ambush cowards laughed—which, objectively correct, Vanako had to give it to her—and some combination of physical imbalance and humiliation loosened Vinda's mental grip on Vanako's motor schema; so she got her legs under her and drove Vinda's leg into her hip with all her strength, which did exactly what it was supposed to do. Vinda hopped back, lost her balance, and—

***

"This sounds a lot worse than skipping class and a uniform violation?" said Taavi, her voice floating up from the bottom bunk.

"She started crying after I hit her a couple times," said Vanako.

"What's the compliment for good hitting?" Taavi wondered. "Well punched? Top whacks?"

"It wasn't like that," said Vanako. "You know how something bad can happen, and that can upset you, but you're not really upset about the bad thing? It's just kind of what pushes you over the edge into getting upset about something else?"

"Ripping pugilism, old chap?" Taavi mused.

"Anyway, Vinda's dad got fired. For talking to Jerioun. That guy from the *Free Press*. Teiali and Shizako's dads too, all three of them. I said at the going rate, I'd buy them a drink and we'd call it even."

"What?" Taavi said, outraged. "That's burglary! You should have taken the beating?"

"Meh," said Vanako. "It was cheap peach arrack, and they all drank too much and walked in reeking and falling over each other. So they're out another week for drinking during hours." She shrugged. "Who knew Lyceum girls couldn't hold their liquor?"

"You are the actual Limper?" Taavi was obviously trying to hide her admiration... but not that hard.

"It was kind of nice," said Vanako. "Passing a bottle, listening to someone other than me worry about whether they'll have to leave Lilac Precinct. Vinda's dad is mad, Teiali's dad is worried, Shizako's dad is depressed. Normal stuff."

Vanako hadn't had much to say, of course. There hadn't really been room for *my mom is missing, my boyfriend is hurt and missing, my dragon is gone.* But that had never been what she was going to get from that moment. The point hadn't been to share, it had been to pretend.

"I'm still going to Ora-shan's, at least," Vanako said. "So if you need cover to visit Vaisho, let me know."

"We broke up."

The statement left Vanako feeling weirdly bereft, and it took her a moment to figure out why, because she absolutely did not give a shit whether Taavi stayed with that stuck-up nerd. It came to her quickly enough, though: What she'd wanted Taavi to say was *Don't do that for me, you're in enough trouble already.* "I'm sorry. How are you feeling?"

Instead of *Thanks* or *OK* or *Great* or *Terrible*, silence hung between them.

"That good?" Vanako asked. "Speechless? With freedom?"

More silence. Taavi broke it with a sniffle.

"Aw, sis."

"Stop," Taavi said, speaking as if around a pebble lodged in her throat. "Look. You lost Tuuro and Bandit in the same day. And now I guess you're getting beat up in school. I can't even imagine what it's like to be in your head right now. But." She sniffled loudly again, then cleared her throat. "He broke up with me. Because his family thinks our family is a bunch of dangerous troublemakers, and he doesn't see a future for us. And he's right."

"Damn right he's right," said Vanako. "Fuck those shits."

"Before they took Mom away, I would have said exactly what you're saying."

Vanako blinked. "Wait a second. Your insufferable dork boyfriend and his stuck-up family decide to cut you loose because a bunch of cops curb-stomped *my boyfriend*—" She knew this was inaccurate, but she wasn't doing revisions right then—"and you figure that means you get to do a little victim-blaming, as a treat?"

"I'm saying they don't want their son to marry into a family where people are constantly disappearing and getting hurt and getting in trouble? And I'm realizing I don't blame them, because they're right, it fucking sucks? And you should know that better than anyone, because you've lost more than the rest of us?"

"What are you trying to say?"

"I don't know? Nothing?"

"Horseshit."

"If you're asking what I already said, I already said it?" said Taavi. "But if you're asking what I'm going to do, or what I think you should do? I actually don't know."

"Then why are you talking?"

Vanako heard the ties of the bedsprings creak, then the scrape of a chair on the floor, and Taavi's face was in hers; she must be balancing on the frame of the lower bunk. "You don't have to say sorry for blowing up my relationship, or getting those girls' dads fired, or whatever? I know you're still facing up to what happened? But if you're going to act like everyone else's problems are, like, an *inconvenience*—"

Vanako planted two fingers in the middle of Taavi's forehead and pushed.

Immediately images sprang forth in her mind: Windmilling arms, a crack of impact, a pool of blood haloing a blind-eyed face. As it was, Taavi tipped, lurched, and stepped off the bed to keep her balance. It bought enough time: By the time Taavi was ready to unload, Vanako's back was to her, headed out the door.

CHAPTER 41
TWO WEEKS BEFORE THE SKUA

BY THE TIME THE election came around, Vanako had put her door back on. Not that it helped much. The neighborhood and the Travelers started filling the living room starting at about lunchtime on election day, and the crowd only increased as the sun set, the night deepened, and the counts came in. It was as good an excuse as any to stay in her room and draw. She did worry for a second that the likes of Kaana te-Tekko might want to make a spectacle out of her, but the worry was needless: No one outside her family had any interest in talking to Vanako. She could sneak food and alcohol back to her room like a ghost. Her family didn't seem too interested in talking to her either, if she was honest.

Not that she blamed them. The loss of Tuuro and Bandit stood between her and them like a wall of brambles. When the knock sounded on her door, she figured her moment had arrived—most likely as a sacrificial lamb for having thrown the election to Brightest Scale once again. She answered it anyway.

Haanen ze-Keiaza stood outside the door.

"Can I come in?" they said, and Vanako stood back, more than a little confused, to let them by. They looked around the room, taking in the art scattered in drifts on the desk and floor. "Where's Zinji?" they asked.

"What?"

"That portrait you drew. The Baronet told me she wished I'd hung onto it. If it's precious to you, I'm authorized a small appropriation to commission a copy." They flashed her a quick grin. "If you're willing to part with the original, the appropriation's still on the table, as long as it doesn't look like it's been used to line a latrine."

"I gave it to Zinji," said Vanako. "I'll do another for Ziyuki-kana, you don't have to pay."

"Yes I do," said Haanen. "The Baronet said so."

They were smiling when they said it, but the smile faded. Vanako could see Haanen's facial muscles trying to cling to it as it left.

"It's election night," said Vanako. "You're not here for my art."

Haanen shook their head slowly. Vanako could see the pain on their face. Her blood froze. "Mom."

"No," Haanen said immediately. "Sorry, I should have—no. Or." Vanako's thawing blood re-froze. "Nothing new, is what I meat. We think she's all right, but we're not sure. Same as before."

Vanako should have felt relieved, but she couldn't. "What, then?"

"You're getting your divided government."

Vanako knew what those words each meant on their own, but the arrangement was confusing. "Is that... something I asked for at some point?"

"Brightest Scale is losing the majority."

"That sounds like a good thing.

Haanen let the silence hang.

"But you're about to tell me why it's a bad thing."

"Yeah." Haanen sighed. "OK. You know Zaya was throwing most of the earnings from your races to the Travelers, right?"

"Yeah. Are you saying they won?"

Haanen actually spluttered with laughter. "The Travelers have a ceiling of maybe ten precincts if circumstance are absolutely ideal. They won six, which is mind-blowing. Or. I mean, they're going to."

"They're going to? Did Ziyuki-kana rig the election?"

"She did not, and don't say stuff like that where people can hear you. We just have some good information about who was going to do well where, and all the close calls are in. So the Travelers won six, and the Thread & Mortar Front won 24, and you can math out the rest."

Vanako twisted a lock of hair between her thumb and forefinger and looked off into a corner, narrowing her eyes as if she was deep in thought. "But imagine a world where I couldn't."

Haanen rolled their eyes. "In that unimaginable world, some infinitely patient civics teacher would tell you Brightest Scale is slated for 27 seats."

"Which is less than 24 plus six."

Haanen's chest dropped in what Vanako recognized as a very quiet sigh of relief. "Which means?"

"No one has a majority?"

"Yes. Which means they have to form a government."

"And that was... the plan all along?"

"Pretty much," Haanen said.

"And the plan is bad, actually?"

"If you math it out, in the situation where there are three parties and none of them have a majority, any two of them can form a government."

Vanako frowned. "But Brightest Scale wants to keep yliaster to companies the houses control, and Thread & Mortar and the Travelers both want it for everybody."

"No. Thread & Mortar wants it for all Mrineen. And Brightest Scale knew the houses weren't going to keep hold of it forever.

Keeping control with the houses did two key things. It lined the pockets of the houses, or at least some of them. But it also kept them in the good graces of the police. Which is important, your patient civics teacher would tell you, because only owners vote, and owners like police. A lot."

"I'm still not getting to bad, actually," Vanako said.

"Thread & Mortar and the Travelers now form a governing majority that wants to let common citizens have yliaster. If you're Brightest Scale, you have two problems with this. First, you lose the money the houses have been skimming off the black market for price-gouged yliaster… but, like I said, that was going to happen anyway. But second, you lose the faith of one of the key constituencies keeping you from getting eaten by your citizens. Imagine if Zaailo Merganser had gotten his house guard out during the Immolation and the police hadn't shown to back him up."

They gave Vanako a moment to let that sink in. It did.

"So," Haanen continued. "You're Brightest Scale. You don't want to get eaten by your citizens. The money you were getting from yliaster is a write-off at this point; you're not getting it back. What if there were a way you could appeal to the Thread & Mortar front *and* appeal to the police?"

"It would… slap?"

Vanako recognized the look Haanen gave her less by its appearance than by a sympathetic echo in the muscles of her own face: withering derision.

"It would suck?"

"You make it available to everyone," Haanen said. "But you put a layer of supervision on it. In particular, you let police opt to withhold it from anyone they consider to be at risk of doing something dangerous with it."

This, Vanako did not need spelled out for her. Who was at risk of doing something dangerous? People who were desperate. People who had committed crimes. People who'd migrated in from outly-ing amalgams and conurbations. People who weren't friends with police. All ways of rephrasing "Ililuë and Kayalim." "How do you know all this?" Vanako asked.

"When the fix is in, people start talking."

"And why are you telling me?"

"Because we didn't want you to hear it through the grapevine and be up nights wondering."

Vanako blinked. "Wait, really?"

"Well, no. I actually had a secret ulterior motive, but now that you've said 'Wait, really?' I've decided to tell you."

Maybe Vanako couldn't stop herself from looking mortified, but she at least didn't have to act it. "Fine," she said. "No need to be shitty about it."

"Only half shitty. I do have a secret ulterior motive."

Vanako stared at them.

"No fooling," Haanen said.

"Why would you not open with that?"

"I wanted you to have a little warm feeling about how nice I was being before I told you about how I wanted to use you. Also, I wanted to keep you off balance a little bit."

"What is your problem?"

"I'm from the government. Want to hear our ulterior motive?"

Vanako did. And Haanen told her.

***

AFTER VANAKO SAID NO, and Haanen told her the offer would be open for a few weeks yet, and Vanako said fuck no, and Haanen said "OK" but so you knew they were thinking "just you wait," and Vanako said "fuck your smug little smirk, I said no and I meant it and you know I meant it, get the fuck out of my room," and Haanen didn't get what you'd call *the fuck* out but did get basic, unmodified out, Vanako went out into the bustle of the common room and told Minshoon.

Not about Haanen's offer, which felt too new and raw to share, but about the deal they'd said Brightest Scale had cut with the Thread & Mortar Front. Minshoon looked over at Jaliki, asleep in his armchair, the ker sprawled out on its back with all four paws in the air, apparently asleep as well. The pain on his features hit Vanako with a pang of jealousy. One day, maybe she'd rate that kind of care from these people.

Then he looked at her, and the pain on his face was the same.

"This is going to be hard for you," he said.

"It's been hard."

"I know."

You don't, Vanako wanted to say, but of course he did. Zaya was gone for him too. Jaliki was hunted for him too. He'd lost Kiriki, he'd lost Kaalo, his daughter had endangered a hundred or so of his neighbors for no evident return.

She told him Haanen's offer.

Minshoon looked away and rocked back on the back legs of his chair.

"I'm not going to do it," she said.

"Don't make promises you can't keep." He looked back at her from the wobbling chair; his smile was real, and his voice, which words like that should have made sharp, was as gentle as she'd ever heard it. Which was always. Or, if not always, at least every day.

"We'll get them back," he said, after she didn't speak. "Zaya, Bandit, Tuuro. We don't abandon family." *We didn't abandon you,* he was saying; and he was saying, *Keep faith that this house will be whole again.* But she didn't believe it.

CHAPTER 42

ONE WEEK BEFORE THE SKUA

THE NIGHTS GREW COOL enough that coats made their way to hooks by the door, and people wore long sleeves when the sun was out. Instead of going out to visit Zinji and take in the sun on the beach, Zinji came in to visit them, fleeing the cold winds off the bay that crept (he said) through the gaps between window and frame, between the boards of the salt-battered wall that faced the water.

The House of the Stars convened its new session. Jenishoon Terrapin had lost; Kaana te-Tekko and Yvvvoun Leatherback had been elected. So had Yyrreen. Minshoon, Vanako was dimly aware, had been preparing the neighborhood, the campaigners, for the Thread & Mortar Front's betrayal. Word was spreading. The community already knew. And it seemed like maybe they were, if not OK with it, at least not mad at her in particular.

Or that's what she thought until the night the law was announced, and crowds began pounding on their door. From her bedroom, she only heard the side from the hallway; Minshoon's answers were too low to make out from behind her door. For all the words in the air, nothing was really said: *You did this; we're fucked; we knew this would happen all along;* and when Minshoon had done all he could with these accusations, which couldn't have been much, they said: "There's no point talking to this Mrineen. Get veraamaka navo."

Vanako opened her door, not at all ready to face the mob but ready to do anything other than what she was doing. But it opened on a tall, broad back and an explosion of black hair that scraped the top of the doorframe.

"Let me go," Vanako said, before she could remember that Cerminir both hated and terrified her.

"I might like to," said Cerminir. "But Zaya would kill me if I let a mob rip you to pieces. Anyway, fuck those people. My baby sleeps here. Even if you almost got her killed, at least it wasn't on purpose."

"They're right," Vanako said. "They should get to say their piece to my face."

"It's not like you're *not* on the list of people who fucked up here," said Cerminir. "But above you there are a lot of people with full-grown brains and tits, and most of them are elected officials. If you want these baby-wakers to see your face, draw them a picture."

Chapter 43
Five days before the Skua

It wasn't the first time Vanako had seen protests in Laurel Square, although it was the first time she'd really followed why they were happening. They were bigger than usual, the chants louder, the prevalence of torches and candles greater; there were four Lilac Precinct police there instead of just Sergeant te-Zaulanen. They stood apart from the protesters, though—unlike the Sergeant, who was chatting people up around the edges, especially if they were from other precincts. Vanako noticed this, from the window of her bedroom, long before she thought about it, but the answer was quick enough in coming: This law made the officers kings over anyone who was hunted, or had a hunted relative. Or who ever might; which was all of them.

And that was also why this didn't feel all that different from some other precinct complaint, new construction or new taxes or expanding the moat around the Dawn Wyrm broodspire to keep children from exploring it. The damage was theoretical. Lilac Precinct was full of well-off professionals, and its police force was majority Kayalim. Most people in Lilac Precinct wouldn't face any obstacle to having an yliaster allocation approved, if they needed it.

At least if they behaved in front of the police.

And they did. And by the time Vanako opened her door to leave a second time, Cerminir had gone to bed, and so had the protesters and police alike, leaving barely a stick of litter in the square to mark their passing.

***

In Celadon Precinct, the bars were fuller than usual, but there wasn't any action in the streets.

In Crimson Precinct, a couple of block parties were winding down. That would have been normal for summer; in mid-autumn it was a little out of place.

Vanako should have cut through Sepia Precinct, but she couldn't make herself do it, so she coasted along the border on the Crimson side until she hit Coral Precinct, then sped through a few sleepy blocks to Rust Precinct, where everything that wasn't upside down and on fire was in the process of being turned over, torched, or both. She quickly abandoned the bike she'd taken this far; there was too much jetsam in the streets, too many streets fully or half-barricaded. The sheer profusion of objects felt like a latecoming miracle for Rust Precinct, where abundance of any kind was rare and veiled. There were chants, but far away; they came from all sides, the different rhythms shifting in and out of phase. There were people nearby, but they were all on their way somewhere, hands full of hard and jagged things, mouths full of words and teeth. Vanako supposed the scared people were all indoors by now.

She picked her way around a wet, scorched spot where glass crunched underfoot, then around a street sign battered and bent like a poorly hammered nail, then over a pile of chairs, benches, and beds taller than Cerminir. When she dropped over the other side, it took her a moment to recognize the square up ahead. The fountain in the center seemed to have changed shape.

Then the darkness between her and it pulsed and stretched, and a cold wind blew from her heart down the halls of her arteries, riming the wall of every capillary. A rasping sound came from the darkness' direction—half moan, half scream. If there was an emotion in the noise, she could not hear it. Water filmed on Vanako's forehead and over her eyes, but all the heat of her flesh seemed to have deserted through her skin.

She could turn around, climb back over the barricade. It could be no more dangerous to go around the square than through; the thing probably hadn't perceived her yet. There was no reason not to backtrack and go around.

… except she would have to turn her back to it. If she did die—and who knew what that thing would do, when her eyes were off it—it would be while running from her death.

Which was the story that took shape in her head, but she knew the truth: She was just too scared to take her eyes off it.

So Vanako stepped forward, as slowly as if she were approaching a terrified cat, each step as silent as she could make it. The demon, still nearly unmoving, was slightly to the left side of the fountain—the cart, since Vanako was facing south—so she put her back against the face of the building to her west. No lights burned in windows; if anyone was in the upper apartments, they knew not to draw the thing's attention.

Step. Pause. Breathe. Step. Pause. Breathe. It was so, so still. Vanako had seen demons as corpses, and seen them full of furious, killing life; she had never seen one at rest. She turned the corner into the square; her back was to the plate glass window of a barbershop, not broken. She took a step away from it, closer to the demon. *It stands to reason,* she told herself. *I should shorten the path to the other side. The longer I stay here, the more risk that it gets hungry.*

As if the word "hungry" in her head were an incantation, she noticed the foot hanging out of the fountain.

Its sole faced Vanako, its toes pointed down; its owner, or what was left of them, must have been face down in the fountain. When the demon pulsed, its body moved the foot gently. Vanako braced herself to hear a wet crunch or a slurp, to see the foot move in a peristaltic jerk as the demon pulled it in. She made herself step and pause and breathe. The demon rasped again, but its movement remained gentle, regular. The foot moved with the demon.

They didn't eat people, of course. They just seemed like the kinds of things that would eat people. They killed—why? They killed because...

Because, if they killed their summoner, they could go back. Because although they were strong here, fast and lethal, they couldn't live. Because this world drowned them as surely as air drowned a fish.

Was that what it was doing, draped over the lip of the fountain? Drowning? Vanako felt a rush of guilt, even felt herself take a step toward it—

"No closer."

The voice sounded from directly in front of Vanako, clear as a bell in the cold, empty air. She started and jumped back, and the demon heaved toward her—but the effort didn't even bring its bulk fully out of the fountain. After the single heave, it did not move again. Something dragged at Vanako's attention, drew her eyes to the roof deck of a block of apartments. A human shadow, bald-headed, their chest bare or perhaps clothed in a form-fitting top, their legs covered by a skirt or billowing pantaloons.

"It's no danger to you unless you come close," the same voice said. "You don't have to sneak around. Just get out of here."

"I've gone up against these things before," Vanako said, a little stung by the dismissal. "They can cover a lot of ground fast."

"Not this one. It's dying."

"Did you hurt it?"

"No. It just ran itself ragged. They can't survive here very long, you know."

Vanako squinted at the figure on the roof deck, but it didn't help her see anything more. "You're a sorcerer."

"Sure."

It sounded like the sorcerer might prefer a different designation, but if they weren't going to insist, Vanako wasn't going to ask. "Can't you send it back?"

We've never seen one die in conditions like this. Normally we have to banish them or kill them."

"But this one was in a Kayalim neighborhood, so you made an exception."

The sorcerer laughed, not very sincerely. "No. You think this was the only demon summoned in Yemareir tonight? We got here when we could. All the guilds are out tonight."

"So you just chose to come here last."

The sorcerer could have contradicted that if they wanted, but they didn't.

"Send it back," Vanako said. "What are you going to learn from watching it die?"

"Which tissues are deteriorating and how fast. Which parts of its body it needs to sustain life. What chemicals or radiation it's reacting to—"

"Do you hear what comes out when you talk?" Vanako said. "You sound like every evil sorcerer in the books you and your friends probably complain about over beers after work."

"And much like them," the voice said, annoyed, "if you get close enough to that thing to fuck up my measurements, I will very literally vaporize you."

The square suddenly felt huge, the gently pulsing demon very far away, and the tiny silhouette of the sorcerer very close indeed. The sorcerers' guilds all had codes of ethics, of course, and preventing the murder of non-magical humans was the main reason why. But Vanako didn't know if those codes extended to interference with the gathering of valuable data; or if they really applied on dark nights in precinct no one cared about, where the street were literally full of monsters.

She pulled her jacket close and ran. If the demon lunged for her, she did not hear it; if the sorcerer had anything else to say, they kept it to themself.

***

THE NEXT FEW BLOCKS of Rust Precinct slipped by as quickly as a dream. It was a terrifying dream: there were bonfires and piles of embers, there were weapons lying in the street—some improvised from found objects, some filmed with dark and gleaming evidence of use, some shattered—and there were people: people lying still, people nursing the wounds of other screaming or sobbing people, people losing battles against shockingly small numbers of Rust Precinct police, people chanting and breaking windows and hiding in back alleys and the corners where stoops met facades.

And then Vanako crossed into Damask Precinct, where all was dark and quiet, and even the soft wings of Ranger Wyrms didn't disturb the night. Vanako kept to the sides of the streets anyway, creeping like a mouse along the floorboards. She was still a city kid, but even a city kid could reason that a dragon used to hunting in broad daylight on the veldt might have difficulty finding prey at night if it wasn't out in the open. Reason or hope, whichever it was.

It didn't take her long to reach the broodspire. The Dawn broodspire in Lilac Precinct was surrounded by a moat and a guardrail, and a precinct police officer patrolled Kazako Square from dusk to dawn to ensure no one went in. The concern was less about people getting eaten—although it was never impossible that a wyrm or two might shack up in the spire outside of breeding season—and more about respecting the dragons' habitat, and keeping the spire from attracting squatters and shady goings-on.

None of these impediments existed in Damask Precinct. Vanako could just walk up to it, lay a palm right on the stone.

She did. Then she walked around the perimeter, keeping her eyes up to find an entrance. Broodspires were perforated with entrances all around their circumference and up and down their height, but only those built in the Arnkerrth-1 style had entrances at ground level. This one was a Caiman-Agama spire—similar to Arnkerrth-1, but the slates were more uniformly crafted, joined with green mortar mixed from Emerald Dunes sand and enchanted (or so she'd been forced to memorize in her history classes) for longevity with a more sophisticated charm.

And, of course, no ground-level entrance.

But the stacked-slates construction made for plenty of finger- and toeholds. The lowest entrance was maybe twelve feet up. Vanako reached it without much difficulty. Her toes lost their grip briefly more than once; but after surviving a riot, a demon, and a sorcerer in the last half hour alone, the lurch of her stomach barely registered. The rim of the entrance was clad in smooth black tile—another small difference from textbook Arnkerrth-1 spires, whose untiled apertures were gradually widening as generations of dragons' talons chipped flakes of slate away—and Vanako's grip nearly slipped as she scrabbled over the edge.

The interior was softly lit by charmed stones in the ceiling. The short tunnel of the entrance opened onto a corridor that went up to the left and down to the right. She decided to go up. If she had to run away from a dragon, she'd rather do it downhill.

The corridor corkscrewed up the spire's height, opening on to a bower every several dozen steps. Each bower was about the size of

House Shearwater's common room, with a gently sloped depression in the floor that could fit a handful of eggs each the size of an infant... all of which Vanako knew from memory, not by sight, because each such depression was entirely obscured by a pair of Ranger Wyrms.

They didn't sleep like mammals, their chests swelling and collapsing with deep breaths that rustled out of their noses. They were stone-still and silent. They slept nose-to-tail, but Vanako wasn't sure if that was a natural behavior or just due to the small size of the bowers. Then again, was there a difference? Did dragons breed in the wild at all? It must have happened at some point; as a species, dragons were older than humans. Weren't they?

Vanako's thighs began to ache as she climbed the spiral tunnel up the broodspire. One thing she hadn't reckoned on was the smell of charred and rotting meat, which thickened as she climbed away from one entrance and hit a peak about halfway to the next, where her distance from the entrance below and the entrance above was equal. Dawn Wyrms were fish-eaters and rarely hoarded food; on the occasion they caught an especially large shark or dolphin, they'd either eat it whole and sleep for a week or, occasionally, share it with others. But Rangers were more apt to squat on a carcass and nibble until it was gone—possibly because the species had a reputation for turning to cannibalism in lean times, and a week's torpor was a bad risk when your neighbors might eat you. In all events, the smell got steadily worse as she climbed.

But every bower had two wyrms curled around the eggs. Vanako didn't know why this surprised her. She'd even rehearsed the possibility on the bike ride over—for every kid who really stole an egg from a broodspire, there were probably a thousand who said they did, and ten who'd actually tried and died doing it. And with two parents protecting the eggs, it didn't really make sense that they'd ever be completely unguarded. Especially at night, when Rangers slept. But it was possible.

Or it had seemed possible.

Well, fuck it. If she was going to climb over a Ranger Wyrm's tail to get an egg, she should do it closest to the lowest entrance; less distance to carry it before she had to climb, less distance to run if she had to. This was what she should have done to begin with. Forget leaning on blind luck—she could just use her empathy to keep her safe. She turned around and began the march down.

Down went more quickly than up, of course; Vanako didn't realize she'd passed the lowest entrance until she'd gone by several bowers and realized the freshening of the air she'd come to expect wasn't coming. She hadn't planned to look in the bowers below the lowest entrance. But now that she was here, she might as well.

When she checked the closest, there was only one wyrm.

It took her a moment to realize it; the wyrm's back was to her, hiding most of the bower from view. But there was no nose by its tail. It was alone.

Vanako made herself check the other four bowers, just to make sure fate wasn't laughing at her by stashing even better luck a few steps away. They all had two wyrms.

This was the best shot she'd get.

She tried not to think too hard about the fact that the other wyrm in the pair might be on its way back now. Might, as a daytime hunter, be returning to its mate with talons empty; might be angry, might be hungry. She took all the mental energy that would obey her and concentrated on the egg.

Her cover story for the egg was all worked out. The weekend warriors in the 'stream flew wyrms bred from the hatch for racing: trained to work with human riders as early as they could support a child's weight, fluent in the pressure-signals that Bandit had known, but with bodies adapted for speed in a way Bandit's had never been. Kayalim teams, without the money to pay breeders, sought out third- or fourth-cohort wyrms from the mountains or the veldt or occasionally the jungle or, most often, the bay. Vanako and Zaya had beaten all of them on Bandit. How much better could they do on a wyrm trained to work with them from birth?

It wasn't a bad story. It made sense, as far as it went. But the best thing about it was that she could tell it for eleven years.

Properly fed, a Ranger Wyrm could grow big enough to carry her, at least, inside eleven years. So, for eleven years, that wyrm would be her exit. It would need her, first for sustenance and then for guidance. And she would have to meet that need, and take all the time it would demand. Because you don't pull an idiot stunt like going into a small, enclosed space full of fire-breathing killer lizards and then let the opportunity you stole there go to waste.

Vanako rounded the solitary Ranger Wyrm's dusty yellow back and stepped over its tail, her eyes fixed on that depression in the middle of the bower.

Thoughts about how to pick a healthy egg clattered to the floor of her mind like plates tipped off a table. The depression was a sticky, yellow ruin; the eggs inside had been smashed thoroughly enough that Vanako couldn't count how many there had been. She said "shit," but only with a motion of her mouth, and she had the presence of mind not to back away, which would have tripped her on the dragon's tail, but instead to creep to the side.

It didn't really matter, though. The wyrm's eyes were open, and the one facing Vanako was fixed directly on her.

A menacing plume of bright white steam trickled from the corner of its mouth—a threat display for Ranger Wyrms, if not as threatening as, say, the thing where they open their mouths all the way and puff their crests out to remind you how fucked you are if they decide to take you out. "I didn't do it," she said, and closed her eyes.

When she opened them again, the wyrm was looking directly at her.

Dragons didn't show suspicion on their faces, but that didn't stop Vanako from seeing narrowed eyes, a curl in its lipless mouth. *i know*, it said, or near enough. It wasn't like Bandit, whose thoughts had been shaped by contact with humans since it was a hatchling; the movements of its mind weren't so neatly contained in words. There was something in the tone of those movements, though, that she recognized from a few interactions with Bandit: a cool despondency, a hollowness.

"Show me?" Vanako said.

It took a moment for her meaning to seep through. Dragons didn't have the sociality of mammals, and Rangers less so than Dawns. But she felt it bend its concentration to the task, felt comprehension dawn. An image formed in her mind: A wyrm's tail crashing down on the clutch, shattering the shells in three deliberate strikes. Two sky-and-sand wyrms facing off over the wreckage like cats in a crate; the scorching pain of blue-and-yellow flames, the tearing of fangs and talons, the bludgeoning of wings. Eventually the other wyrm left, either to abandon the broodspire or to try its luck with another mate. Vanako caught herself inserting those speculations; the wyrm was incurious and indifferent.

"I'm so sorry," Vanako said. "I can't imagine how that must feel, to have your eggs destroyed."

She felt like an idiot as soon as the said it. Dragons didn't care what you could imagine. Then again, her imagination seemed to have annoyed this one; its irritation rattled against her like a shower of marbles on her skull. The tail came down again in its mind, once, twice, three times, and this time Vanako noticed what she had not before: the impact of the stone on the length of the tail, the cool of the air on the yolk in its feathers.

It hadn't been the mate that had destroyed the eggs. It had been this wyrm.

"Why?" Vanako asked.

The feel of wings against air was the Ranger's only reply.

"Then why are you here?" she asked; but the question was answered before the last word left her lips. There was a rent in the middle of its right wing.

Vanako had more questions—if it hadn't wanted a clutch, why had it come here? Why had it mated? And then she looked at its size, and she understood. It was a second-cohort wyrm; if it were a Dawn, it would be huge for its age, but for a Ranger it was merely a little on the large side. It didn't know what the broodspire was for—what mating, for that matter, was for. Maybe it had enjoyed the weeks of gestation, resting with its companion in this space its instincts had told it to come to. Or maybe it hadn't, the feeling of disquiet growing and growing, until at last the eggs came and the cause of its unease could be identified, located, and destroyed.

Vanako loved Bandit. She would always love Bandit, the wyrm who'd made her a 'streamer, who'd given her the sky. But her love for this wild, selfish thing was like the first sliver of sun over the desert, pure and searing and unstoppable.

"Come with me," she said.

Another shower of marbles bouncing off her skull. This time the Ranger actually lifted its wing, showing where the feathers were torn free and the flesh wept, letting Vanako feel the dull ache and bright piercing pain that came with the motion. For a wild wyrm new to human minds, it was quickly learning to communicate.

"Not like that," Vanako said. "You need to use your legs and pinions like a stupid monkey." Vanako sent it an image of a baboon, walking exaggeratedly on its legs. When the wyrm didn't under-stand, she changed the image of the baboon to a Ranger Wyrm. It definitely didn't wrinkle its snout in disgust, but Vanako saw the gesture anyway, translated by her primate brain, as clear as day.

"Don't be a princess," Vanako said. "If you want to fly again, get your scrawny chicken carcass out of this pile of bricks and come with me."

***

Walking through the ruins of a riot, Vanako discovered, was a lot more fun with a dragon tagging along.

The streets by Saavero's weren't any less on fire than the rest of Rust Precinct, although at least the food cart outside the stable had disappeared before it could be stripped for parts. Saavero themself was unrattled by Vanako's appearance with the young Ranger. "Still paid up on Bandit for a few months, I suppose," they said, summoning girl and dragon in. "Will it follow the rules?"

"While it's here." *No fighting*, she said in the Ranger's mind. She thought it assented, but it was hard to be sure.

"It's not staying?"

They were walking past the other wyrms, which were taking more notice than usual. Was it just that the Ranger was injured, or did they somehow know it was supposed to be in a broodspire?

"Have I done something to offend?" Saavero asked.

"Huh?" Too late, Vanako realized the question wasn't serious. "No, of course not. It just needs a place to stay while its wing heals."

"You're not riding it?"

The distaste in Saavero's voice was mild, but unmistakable. Vanako realized she hadn't even thought about riding the young wyrm. "It's too small," she said.

"It's a Ranger. Look at those shoulders."

"It's wild."

"They all start that way. Six months of hard practice and it'll carry two."

Vanako didn't know what to say about this. The young Ranger seemed about as biddable as a tiger. More, though—with Tuuro and Zaya gone, with Bandit gone, with glares shooting at her from every shop and street corner in Lilac Precinct, Vanako didn't think of herself on dragonback. Of course she didn't think of herself on dragonback.

Only—why shouldn't she think of herself on dragonback?

Saavero threw the door to a stable open. "You'll stay, of course. While I fix up the wyrm."

Vanako hadn't thought about it, but she'd have to. Saavero wasn't an empath; they couldn't approach a wild wyrm alone. She entered the stable, summoning the Ranger wyrm after her with a quick gesture of her mind. It followed, not without concern, but without hesitation. Without thinking, Vanako shot a swift flash of warmth in its direction. Bandit usually replied to those mammalian gestures with its own pulse of cool affection; it was a shock to feel the young Ranger freeze at the unexpected emotion. But she felt it consider the new thing, felt it probe the memory of the feeling, felt its glassy mind settle into something like acceptance.

"What shall I call it?" said Saavero, taking a roll of clean cloth and a brown bottle from a cabinet in the cell.

Vanako's first thought went to yliaster. reached back to the Cerulean Precinct yliaster garden, and then to Cerminir's drunken monologue to Jenishoon Terrapin. *The flowers who bloom for the defenseless vagrants, the crazy ones who chase the light*—or whatever it had been. "Thornapple," she said.

CHAPTER 44
FOUR DAYS BEFORE THE SKUA

VANAKO GOT HOME BEFORE anyone was awake, or at least before they'd left their rooms. She wasn't sure at first what felt wrong in the common room, but it hit her soon enough: The air was cooler and more mobile than it should have been, the sounds from the square closer.

The brick was on the floor, under a window frame now rimmed in jagged glass. The note wrapped around it said VE-RAAMAKA NAVO FUCK YOU.

"Vanako." She jerked her head up to see Cerminir coming out from the hallway, Enwë on her hip. Enwë pointed at Vanako and squealed. Cerminir was glowering as usual. "How long have you been sitting there?"

Vanako shook her head. "I don't know."

"Why are you sitting there?" Her eyes flickered over to the window. "What happened?"

"Someone threw a brick."

Cerminir stepped closer. "Don't put Enwë down," said Vanako. She got up and began picking up shards. "Sorry."

"What? No. Be careful. I won't."

"Won't what?"

"Put Enwë down," Cerminir said. Vanako piled shards in her palm.

Cerminir seemed to be at a loss; she brought Enwë to the kitchen and found a couple of pots. "I'm putting her down, actually. She's got—"

"It's fine. I'm almost done."

Cerminir started cutting pineapple. Enwë clattered pots. Vanako piled shards.

"What does the note say?" Cerminir asked.

Vanako told her, spelling out the word Enwë wasn't supposed to hear.

Cerminir dropped some pineapple in one of the pots for Enwë to eat and walked over to Vanako. She squatted to put her face on Vanako's level. "Get rid of those and go sit down," she said.

"You don't have any shoes on," said Vanako.

"By the time I was eight, my feet were harder than your teeth. Go sit down. Have some pineapple. You were out all night, you need some sugar and water."

That was correct, which was annoying. Vanako moved to the kitchen to pick Enwë up with one arm and the cutting board of pineapple with another, then brought both to the table. She set Enwë down, then the fruit, then herself. "Who says I was out all night?" she asked.

"You smell like smoke, and you look like a tired child."

Vanako took a bite of pineapple; the burst of sweetness blinded her for a moment, and the cool juice washed a dry sourness off her tongue she hadn't realized was there. The world felt brighter, sharper-edged.

It wasn't what she wanted. The edge of her fatigue sharpened; so did the edges of the glass shards she remembered in her hand; so did the edges of the words in the note.

Enwë was squeezing cubes of pineapple into pulp. Vanako got a fork and fed her. Enwë grabbed the fork and started pushing pineapple around on the cutting board; Vanako pushed most of it out of her reach. Cerminir had gotten rid of the shards of the pane somewhere and was preparing mate. Vanako ate a cube of fruit, then gave one to Enwë, putting it on the end of the fork so the baby could try to feed herself. Enwë knocked the pineapple off the fork with her chin trying to eat it, and Vanako caught it before it hit the floor. Enwë crowed at the catch, and Vanako popped the pineapple in the child's mouth. "Nice one," Cerminir said, pushing a cup of mate toward Vanako while she sat.

"That means a lot, coming from you."

"God, you're a bitch."

"Very meaningful also," said Vanako.

"I feel like we could." Cerminir pointed at herself, then Vanako, then herself, then Vanako. "You know. Like an equilibrium. Just bounce the same words back and forth."

"You're being nice to me."

Cerminir studied her for a moment. "You're using a statement as a question."

"Guilty?"

"Sorry. That was more like." Cerminir twitched a fingertip down, then sharply up, a check mark. "Keeping score. Not against you," she added quickly. "Just for me. Getting it without being told."

"You should do a fist pump instead."

Cerminir shook her head—barely a twitch, really, just the one jerk right, then left. "Because I'm trying to soften a blow."

"What?"

"Is the answer. To the question. That you asked with a statement."

Vanako blinked, then shook her head, expelling a laugh like a hit of broken tooth. "What blow?"

"Give me a minute," Cerminir said.

Vanako gave her a minute. The pineapple disappeared, chunk by chunk.

"You have to leave," Cerminir said when it was over.

Vanako pushed away her mate and shifted her weight to her feet.

"Wait," said Cerminir. "This isn't about how I feel."

"What if it was?"

"We can't have that conversation," Cerminir said.

"Why the *fuck* not?"

"Because you're not ever going to believe my mind has changed," Cerminir said. "That's on me, I've said some shit to you and I have to live with it. But it means I'm not going to waste your time trying to convince you I don't hate you when I'm also saying you have to leave."

That was a pretty fair response, Vanako had to admit.

"What I'm trying to say to you," Cerminir continued, "is *that* crossed a line." Cerminir pointed to the window, then snapped her fingertips closed to shush Vanako. "Don't make some clever comment. I don't mean it was a bad thing to do, that's obvious. I mean my people have told me they won't let children of the Amalgam come to harm through my association."

"Won't let—"

"They'll take Eäril and Enwë and Jaliki."

Vanako blinked. "That's kidnapping."

"I know words, Vani."

"They can't just—"

"It's not completely impossible that they'd just surround the house," Cerminir said. "If they think precinct police are pushovers, or just indecisive enough to let them finish the kidnap before they can pull together enough resistance. Kind of a high-variance approach, but it has the advantage of getting all three children at once. I think it's more likely they'd just snatch them while we're out, though. Plays to their strengths. Cildinior warriors aren't complete strangers to penetrating fortified positions, but they're better at stalk and ambush. But then all the kids have to be out in the same place at the same time, with enough warriors in range to do it quickly. We could maybe buy a couple of days if we keep the children home, but they'll figure that out. If they do it here, though, it'll be worse. We'll try to protect our home, and they'll probably have to hurt us to get to the children. You're appreciating that I've thought this through."

Vanako sorted through that for a bit.

"I feel," Vanako said, "like a lot of people are coming to me with disturbing information about things that I can't do literally shit about."

"Huh? Oh, you mean Ziyuki's little goblin dropping the news about the vote on you. Minshoon told me about that." Which was, weirdly, a relief, because it was how things were supposed to happen: Parents were supposed to gossip about kids behind their backs, for their own good. "But this isn't out of your control."

"How—oh."

For several seconds, the only sound in the kitchen was Enwë smacking on pineapple.

"So," said Cerminir, "I think you're thinking something about how you think I've always hated you and isn't this suspiciously convenient, coming from the perspective of someone who's always hated you. Which I don't, by the way."

"You don't love me."

"I love Minshoon, and he loves you. I love Kirono, and he loves you. I love Taavi and Gilthiniel and Jaliki and Eäril, and they love you." She jerked her head in Enwë's direction. "Enwë probably loves you too, but her standards are incredibly low."

She didn't take the last step, state the false equivalence. Vanako appreciated that. "I'm not responsible for your people's kidnapping bullshit," Vanako said. "They don't get to steal my family just because I messed up."

"It's not because you messed up. The yliaster vote had nothing to do with you. People are blaming you for it because you messed up at Zaailo's. That's not fair. But it is real. And the danger of that brick through that window is real."

"Then Cildinior Amalgam can come help keep us safe."

"They could," said Cerminir. "But they won't."

And that, at the end of the day, was all it was. Cildinior Amalgam could fuck all the way off whenever they liked, but they wouldn't. The Lilac Precinct window-breakers could keep their bricks to themselves, but they wouldn't. The House of the Stars could allow anyone who needed it to use yliaster, but it wouldn't. The police could ignore the criminal history of anyone who asked for yliaster, but they wouldn't. Zaailo Merganser could release every prisoner in Yemareir, but he wouldn't. Cerminir Shearwater could keep decisions about the safety of the house off of Vanako's bony, aching shoulders.

But she wouldn't.

"The one thing every idiot in this stupid fucking family agrees on is that we stand up for each other even when the odds are bad," Vanako said. "But when it comes to me, you lie down every time. Minshoon and Kirono would never ask me this." She realized she had forgotten a name. "Zaya would never ask me this."

Vanako could tell she'd hit home; Cerminir's eyes lost a fraction of their focus, and she could see a shade of unsteadiness in the set of her mouth. "Maybe," she said. "But I did ask you. And I explained why. So now you have to make a decision. Not about whether I'm a good person or it was fair to ask you what I did. But whether what I asked you to do is the right thing or the wrong thing."

Vanako played through scenes in her mind: Minshoon, Kirono, or Zinji, sobbing as they explained how Enwë or Jaliki had been taken. The common room of House Shearwater, wrecked after a lost battle to keep the children.

"You know," Vanako said, "For certain. That what you said would happen, will happen."

"There's a group from the Amalgam in Laurel Street right now," said Cerminir. "I saw them from the window. We can speak to him now if you like."

"Yeah," Vanako said. "Yeah, I think so."

***

Vanako picked up Enwë before Cerminir could. That didn't sit well with Cerminir, but fuck Cerminir. Enwë squirmed, and Cerminir told Vanako "Relax your shoulders," and Vanako did, and it helped a little bit, and Enwë planted a sticky hand on Vanako's collarbone to twist her small body so she could face forward. She smelled like pineapple and breast milk, which wasn't going to be Vanako's new favorite scented candle, but she made herself focus on it rather than ignore it. She might not smell it again. She descended the stairs with Enwë already making her arms ache, and the bricks of a future seemed to fall into place.

When they emerged onto Laurel Street, there were three Ililuë who looked like they were from out of town, two men and a woman. Vanako recognized one. "Hey, Thelendil," she said.

"Hey, Vani," he said. His face was older, leaner than it had been when he'd lived with them, not that many months ago; his shoulders had broadened, his arms thickened. She wondered what he'd been doing, to spur that growth. His eyes moved to Cerminir. "I feel like this conversation is either going to be shorter than I expected, or a whole lot longer."

"She's up to speed," said Cerminir.

Thelendil's chest rose and fell; the sigh was audible. "That's good, probably. Vani, I'm not going to make excuses. We have the power to do this, and it's gotten harder and harder to justify not doing it. This particular thing probably shouldn't be the last straw. We should have stepped in any number of times before now. But this is your *house*."

"You know that doesn't mean what it does out there, in here," said Cerminir.

"I know," said Thelendil. "But, first, that doesn't really play at home. And second... we should have done this before now." He looked at Vanako. "I know how close you are to Jaliki. I'd never separate him from you and Zaya unless I had no choice. If we'd done this earlier, he could at least have stayed with you." His eyes swung back to Cerminir. "And he could. We could take you all in, you know. I'm just saying it's still on the table."

"Our life is here," said Cerminir.

"Yeah," said Thelendil. Back to Vanako. "You could come out too. Just you. It might be cool to have another Sky Eater. It's not a bad life."

"That must be why you have to kidnap kids to join you in it," said Vanako.

"Wow. All right." He shot Cerminir a questioning glance. "You sure she'll honor the deal?"

"Are you sure you'll honor it?" Cerminir asked Thelendil.

"What?"

"We're giving her up to get you off our backs," said Cerminir. "Two weeks from now, you could decide that you want Eäril and Enwë and Jaliki anyway, just to be safe. How do we know you won't? Don't pretend it's not the kind of thing my mother would do."

The two Ililuë standing behind Thelendil shared a glance.

"Just keep them away from dragons and politics," Thelendil said. "There won't be a problem."

"I'm not worried about it," said Vanako. "He knows if he goes back on his word, there'll be a pissed-off veraamaka who can burn down his village any hour of the day or night."

"Amalgam," said Cerminir.

"*That's* what you're going to set her straight on?" said Thelendil.

Cerminir gave him a look that rewrote Vanako's definition of contempt.

"I might have to withdraw my invitation to come out," said Thelendil.

Vanako nodded, since it felt like the crashing of her heart would make her voice quake if she spoke.

"What a mess. "Thelendil said. "Where will you go?"

"I've been a city kid for too long," Vanako said, and her voice was as steady as she could hope. "I'm going to go see the world."

Chapter 45
Sixty minutes before the Skua

The words, tears, and embraces that followed would be some of Vanako's most treasured memories. So she did with them what one does with treasure on a long sea voyage, and put them in a box for safekeeping. It was a box in her mind, of course; but she imagined it polished and gold-banded and locked with a charm, tucked in the bottom of the canvas rucksack Minshoon had bought for her belongings. The rucksack was enspelled to float in salt water no matter what was in it, and to burn the fingertips of thieves and spit indelible green ink in their faces. Resting on one shoulder as she walked into the Ivory Precinct routing office of the Transdesert Corporation, it felt like armor.

The woman behind the desk looked Vanako up and down. "What brings you here?"

"I'm here for an assignment."

"I don't know you."

"I know. I heard there might be an opening."

"Did you." This did not sit well with the woman behind the desk. Vanako noticed a series of gouges in it, like claw marks.

"I think Gretiraan Skink is no longer available?"

"Look at you." The woman behind the desk bent down and pulled open a drawer to fish out a few forms. "Yes, Greti just got a very nice offer to join the security team at House Amphisbaena, and I guess they must have done us the favor of bragging about it to all their little friends. What's your name?"

"Valaaina Gannet," Vanako said.

"Bird name."

Vanako did the best she could to keep her face composed, but the woman behind the desk didn't even look up.

"Mine's Kanireen Hawksbill. We can't allocate a wyrm to this job—Greti had their own. You'll supply yours?"

"What if I couldn't?"

"We'd be done here?" said Kanireen, a little annoyed. "I just said we can't spare one. Do you have one?"

"Yes. That means I get a special contract, right? To reflect the additional risk... I'm taking?" Minshoon had told her to say "to my property," but Vanako couldn't talk about Apple that way.

Kanireen tilted her head up just enough that she could spear Vanako with a look over her bright steel-rimmed spectacles. "Is its parentage attested? Do you have fledging papers, any certification of breed purity...?"

"No, but it's right outside if you want to check its teeth or some-thing."

That got a snort of what Vanako thought was genuine apprecia-tion. "And if I stepped outside to 'check its teeth or something,' the breed of wyrm I'd see would be a...?"

"Ranger Wyrm."

"Which you'll attest is wild-fledged. Cohort?"

"Second. And I can't prove it didn't escape from a breeder. But yes, wild-fledged."

"Fine. That's an extra sherd and a quarter on your per diem, plus point four five percent on the final payout—that's of the whole thing, not of your share, so it's pretty generous and I'm not hag-gling on it. It's actually the rate for a common wyrm from a breed-er, which I'm giving you in appreciation for you showing up as quick as you did and not making me pay some youth to go shake the trees until some down-and-out 'streamer fell into my office." Vanako bit her tongue. "Before you think you've crossed the town line into Free Cash City, though, let me remind you that with your own animal comes your own liability. If your wild-fledged Ranger harms or kills one of your shipmates, you will make them and their family whole. If it damages the ship or the cargo, you will make Transdesert Corporation whole. Detailed conditions spelled out in the contract, of which you, the ship's captain, and the expedition chief will each have a copy. Speaking of which."

She pushed a piece of paper toward Vanako, then an inkwell with a quill resting inside. This wasn't actually a test; Kanireen Hawksbill wasn't actually watching Vanako to see if she signed "Valaaina Gannet" like an actual child who still hadn't learned to write her own name. But that was what it felt like.

Vanako dipped the pen again to do another, already rehearsing how to replicate the signature so it didn't look like four different people signing the same contract, but Kanireen was already gathering the sheets. She looked at Vanako's ready hand and snorted a laugh that might have been meant more kindly than it sounded. "We don't have much here, but we do have sympathy paper," she said. "It's a little pricey, but it pays for itself in lawyers' fees." She looked at Vanako, clearly expecting her to get how that made sense. "Because the sympathy also extends to you, as the signer. There's never any dispute over what you signed. You've not got much experience working proper jobs, have you?

That was insulting and intrusive, which would be less annoying if it weren't also true. "Is that it? We're done?"

Kanireen looked over her spectacles again. "I used to know a woman with a bird name. We worked together a bit—not *together* together, but I connected her with a lot of jobs. No relation to you, obviously; you don't look a thing alike and, you know, different bird. I didn't know her well, but I liked her, and she brought me gifts." She put the tip of a forefinger on the tufts of an ivory statue of an owl and rotated it around on its base. "She stole from the company, though, and we fought about it, and she sent a couple wyrms and monkeys in here to ruin my office." She traced a finger over one of the gouges on the desk. "That's from one of the wyrms, and you can see burn marks on the wall, under the paint." She jerked a thumb back toward the wall behind her, and Vanako thought she could see it, a radial stain showing through the white paint as the lightest, most delicate grey. "I heard she's in jail now."

"Sounds like your friend is kind of a crazy bitch," said Vanako.

It was a reflex: anything to sound like she wasn't Zaya's daughter. The sound hit her ear strangely, as if someone else had said the words with her voice. It felt like something, to have said them, but she wasn't sure what.

"That's what I thought," said Kanireen. "Then I thought about it some more." She looked gravely at Vanako. "Didn't change my mind."

That caught Vanako off guard. She laughed, louder than she might have liked.

"Didn't change my mind," Kanireen continued, "but it did get me thinking. How much time had she spent in the air, just waiting for the miles to pass? What would that do to your mind, just sitting up there with nothing around, nothing but open air in any direction? When you could be home with your family, if only you didn't need the money? Maybe I'd go crazy. Maybe I'd steal. Like to think I'd steal something better than a mangy old Dawn Wyrm, but maybe if I were crazy, I'd think differently."

Vanako shrugged. "Sound like you're overthinking a crazy bitch being crazy. But I guess I'll find out."

"You will." The woman behind the desk filed away the sympathy-copies of Vanako's signed contract. "Anyway, if you ever see my friend, let her know that Kanireen at the routing office misses her, and she's sorry she said what she said."

"How would I know if I met your friend?" Vanako said.

"Bird name," said Kanireen. "Don't see that many of you. You know?"

Kanireen bent back to her work and Vanako turned to leave, a little proud of herself for keeping up the act, but couldn't stop the word "'Fuckpig!" from elbowing its way out of her mouth at maximum amplitude: There was a saltwater crocodile, easily as big as any she'd seen sunning on the delta, lying log-still right by the door. She must have walked right past it when she came in.

And, oh, it wasn't a crocodile, of course. Not really.

She turned around to Kanireen. "I'm so sorry."

"Nothing I haven't heard before."

"No. I mean, for the cursing too. But I meant—"

"It's all right. He keeps his distance now."

"The cops gave you your allocation?"

"I'm a law-abiding citizen," Kanireen said, with just the slightest tone of protest. "Especially now that I'm not buying it on the sly any more. That was a sucker's game anyway. My supplier was short for a couple weeks. Just a couple weeks. But Fuckpig there saw its chance and took it, and now I'm down one heel and half my toes. Kind of thing that makes you grateful for a desk job."

"Is its name really Fuckpig?" Vanako asked.

"Now it is." Vanako laughed again. "My supplier was a little like you, actually. Kayalim girl, same age. Long hair, though, and very pretty."

Zayeni, Vanako realized. "I'm sure all that's better now," she said. "It's in good hands."

Kanireen chuckled. "Maybe I'll introduce you to a police officer one day."

An echo in Vanako's mind: A shattering pain in her shin, the lash of a steel-tipped boot-toe. "That's OK," she said, because she couldn't think of anything else to say; and, feeling like the world's loneliest child, she stepped past Fuckpig the crocodile ker and through the door.

***

ON THE OTHER SIDE lay a tree-lined street, with monkeys chattering in the branches and Merlin Wyrms that might, in different circumstances, be looking hungrily at the monkeys; but their eyes were fixed on the alert form of Thornapple, as attentive and alive as any cat whose ears have just caught the scratch of mouse-claws.

where were you.

"Getting you and me as far away from that broodspire as possible," Vanako said, "We're taking the good ship *Skua* down the coast. All the way down, to the Satin Cliffs and Ennë-Alándor."

Quick flashes of the images Thornapple had shared with her the night they'd met: Fangs, flame, and feathers; talons; blood—and relief at the thought of distance from those memories. Vanako put a hand on its shoulder. It almost didn't twitch away. Bandit had been used to social touch from humans. Thornapple didn't hate it, maybe, but it always came as a surprise.

The saddle Vanako swung up on had been Zinji's gift; a neighbor of his was a leatherworker who knew how to treat hide to resist rotting in the salt air. In the pack given by Minshoon rattled pill-bottles from Cerminir: one bottle that would ward off dehydration, another for hypothermia, another for scurvy, another that would induce vomiting if she ate bad food. Another had been tucked into the saddle with a note in Zinji's handwriting that said "To enjoy with trusted friends"; but it was the same bottle as the other three, the same handwriting on the bottle with the ingredients and chemical composition, the same tightly rolled shape of the pill. Taavi had given Vanako a blank book, with pen and ink for writing—as had Haanen ze-Keiaza, with a beautiful tooled leather cover inscribed with the words "Sailor's Log"; Jaliki had given her an illuminated volume of the Wing Windtwister stories, a little soft-cornered from reading it himself; Yyrreen had given her money. Kemreen had given her a saddle-knife.

So, fuck her eyes, had Thelendil.

Kemreen's gift had been perfectly lovely, a hiltless weapon with a flowing curve and a slightly leaf-shaped blade in the style she typically carried herself. Thelendil's was designed more simply; technically it was just a bone blade mounted on a carved bone grip. But the blade was what was called the finger-blade of an Argent Swordwing—a section of the long, slim, last bone in one of its wings. The sawteeth at the base of the blunt edge appeared to have been knapped, like flint. The edge, as far as she could tell, had not been touched at all. The look of it was almost fibrous, silver streaks running along its length; but it was smooth under her fingertip, and the edge would part cloth at a touch.

Thelendil hadn't joined for her going-away. He knew he had neither the right nor the welcome. The note with the knife read only, "I'd been saving this. But it should see some use instead of sitting around my house waiting for a day that might never come. I hope your day to use it never comes."

Vanako wondered if he'd thought anyone could read that message as anything other than *I made this for my son, but he's probably going to die before he could ever use it, so you can have it.* If that was all he meant, why not just come out and say it?

"Fuck all these idiots anyway, Apple," Vanako said, feeling only slightly bad about saying it with a bag full of parting gifts on her back. She wasn't sure she could call the pulse of cool emotion in return "agreement," exactly, but it was close enough. "Let's get out of here."

She took Thornapple straight up, high enough that she could see the bay even from the middle of Yemareir. Before she could say go, though, a flash caught her eye: an actinic, sun-core white, intense enough to notice even on a sunny morning. She swung her head in the direction she thought it'd come from, and caught it again, with its source. The wyrms were barrel-chested, thick-necked, with the ugliest faces she'd ever seen on a dragon, folds of flesh protecting the eyes. One was ash-grey, the other was brick-brown. The searing white flames lanced from their mouths almost in the shape of bolts or blades rather than flames; but they weren't having much luck getting close to one another, because they were just so clumsy in the air.

Then one got the drop, or lucked out on the turn, and closed in on the other from the side. Vanako flinched in preparation for the inevitable. The white fire flashed out like a blade.

When its afterimage had faded enough for her to see, the other wyrm's head was gone.

It fell as though its body had never known wings, the killing wyrm following it in a stoop as swift as any hawk's. They streaked to the ground together, living wyrm and dead, and the rotting hulks of the buildings among which they fell told Vanako why she'd never seen wyrms like them before. They were Cinereal Vores, confined to Ashen Precinct by ancient and unknowable magic. And their brooding season had begun.

Thornapple was impressed by the speed of the killing, and a touch unsettled by its brutality, but it processed Vanako's disgust with some confusion. *???* was as close to words as its thoughts came, but the question's tone was worry, not confusion, and Vanako couldn't help but be satisfied by it.

"'It's a long story," she said. "Fly toward the sea and I'll tell it.""

END

Before You Go,

A QUICK WORD FROM your humble author. If you enjoyed this book, I'd love it if you'd leave an honest review on the platform or platforms of your choice! Reviews are gold for authors; they encourage readers to buy our books and platforms to promote them.

I publish a monthly newsletter, where I mostly talk about books and similar topics—comics, RPGs, and so on—and provide updates on my work in progress. If you liked this book and want to be the first to hear about new stuff coming out, please click here to join:

https://www.cobblerandbard.com/mailing-list/

Whether you join or not, thank you for reading! Turn the page to sample a draft chapter of the forthcoming sequel, *Snowdrift Starlight*—

Matt

SNOWDRIFT STARLIGHT
Sample chapter

In sight of Yemareir

Northbound

It was just as well that fishing routes weren't something that was taught in school, Vanako reflected. Because, if they had been, she wouldn't have paid attention to them; and if she hadn't paid attention to them, she'd be beating herself up for it now. Which would be a minor addition to her problems, even if she only considered the ones that were indisputably her fault. But she was past beating herself up about that stuff. A new thing could be a major distraction from the business of keeping oneself—and one's dragon—alive on open water.

The dragon was having a better time of it. Apple was used to not eating for a long time; its feathers protected it from sunburn, and it could thermoregulate pretty easily in the heat by dunking more or less of itself in the water. Thirst would be what did it in, if anything. Vanako's useless ape body, by contrast, got both hungry and thirsty very quickly, and didn't do so well in the sun. At least she could take shelter under Apple's good wing, and keep predators with brains away with vigilance and empathy. But there were trireme jellyfish in these waters, which were undetectable with empathy and which could kill her with the merest brush of one of their mile-long tentacles, so it didn't pay to stay in the water too long.

Still, she was probably better off than anyone else clinging to a piece of the *Skua*'s wreck And a lot better off than a lot of people who weren't.

Vanako had dreamed one or two things about the sky-whip, but never that it could tear a ship to actual flinders, like a dog at a shoe. It wasn't the kind of power she'd care to see on land.

Better that than die out here, though. The skyline of Yemareir furred the horizon to the northeast; Vanako saw the odd boat as a roving dot to the north. All it did was underline how far she was from any help. How vast a plain of absolutely fucking nothing lay between her and any human at all.

For the thousandth times, Thornapple bent its head to lap at the water, and Vanako sent a lance of thought to stop it just in time. "I'm sorry, baby," she said, *again*. "That stuff'll kill you."

It was clear from the smooth barbs of annoyance in Apple's mind that it did not believe Vanako. But it did not try again.

***

THE NIGHT DID GROW cold. Thornapple pulled up onto the broken forecastle to let its feathers dry fully and trap the last of the day's heat, which would last it until morning. The snug space under its wing was better cover than Vanako had a right to hope for, out on the open sea. But she couldn't sleep. So she told herself stories.

She had seen Varaunë take to the air before the *Skua* broke apart. Intransigent was more than twice Thornapple's size; it had a better chance at breaking through the sky-whip's devastation. Maybe Varaunë would tell someone about the survivors in the ocean south of Yemareir... but, of course, his relationship with the law had never been tranquil. And he didn't know their coordinates. Or at least, she didn't; and she didn't know why the other wyrm-flyers would have.

Captain Loggerhead had been on deck when it happened, and she'd seen... Vanako shook her head, rejecting the image before it could collect too much detail. But he had the dovecote in his quarters. Maybe he'd sent one out before he came on deck to share in the *Skua*'s destruction. But, of course, she knew where those doves went... and whoever read that message might decide that silence from the *Skua* was worth the price of paying a few more lost sailors' kin.

Antimain and Trillium might have broken free of the storm as well, although Vanako had not seen them on deck when the sky-whip began to rage. Likelier Antimain had been in her cabin. Trillium could have escaped on its own, and so could Counterpoint; but where would they go? And if the right person found them, how would they know where to look? And, of course, Meneánda had been on the *Rejoice*...

... but fuck Meneánda.

The one Vanako thought the longest on was Mik. She had definitely been in Vanako's cabin when the whip hit; she knew about the book. If she'd awakened in time, if she'd understood what was happening, if she'd had the presence of mind to write before the *Skua* broke to splinters under her...

... then she'd still have been belowdecks when it was torn apart. Still under tons of wood, any falling spar of which would have been enough to trap her, to knock her out and drown her, to kill her outright. Maybe it was better to hope she'd made it to the deck, where the prospects of being thrown into open sea were better, where it would only take a mountain of luck to avoid being crushed or immobilized rather than outright divine intervention.

It was only the queasy worry in Thornapple's mind that made Vanako realize she was sobbing loudly enough to wake a dragon.

"I'm sorry," she answered to the question Thornapple's thoughts were not quite human enough to ask. "I miss Mik. I want her and she's not here." She'd gotten into the habit of explaining primate emotional concepts to Apple. It wasn't clear it helped the wyrm understand, but it seemed to find some comfort in Vanako's understanding that it *didn't* understand.

where is mik? it said, or close enough.

"I don't know, baby. She might be dead."

Apple seemed to be mulling over something.

you don't know where anyone is.

"Sure don't."

Apple gave that more thought.

usually you know things.

Vanako reached up and stroked the smooth, hard feathers of its underwing. "You know more than you think."

Apple's mind rang with gentle disagreement. That was fair enough, Vanako thought; it had been more right than wrong. Not because it was inattentive or incurious, although it could be both. It just wasn't much good with primate social cognition.

... miss... varaunë , Apple thought.

"Yeah?"

good leader. felt safe with him.

"Leader" was an interesting term for Apple to use. It didn't have a ready analogue among dragons, who certainly learned but did not really teach. Vanako struggled a few moments with what she wanted to ask. "Remember with me," she decided on at last. "A time when you were flying with Varaunë and felt safe."

The tactile sensation came first: air under the wings, warm weight on her back. It was a cool day but not cold, the sun high. Four wyrms flew in a loose knot: Intransigent in the lead, then Counterpoint, Apple, and Trillium. They were low above the water, and Apple was afraid, because it had seen the killing steam of the sea-wyrm, had seen it breach with frightening speed; airborne dragons might not be its prey of choice, but this monster had ways to make them regret their pursuit. But Apple could feel Vanako's mind search the waters, could feel it find and lock in on the sea-wyrm's brain, and then felt the chatter of monkey talk, faster and more intricate than its own mind could yet understand.

An echo of a response, and Vanako pulled Apple higher into the air, as Trillium and Counterpoint did the same. Intransigent let loose a blast of flame, not close enough to really hurt the sea-wyrm but close enough to annoy it, and Intransigent narrowly dodged the creature's breach, which took the thing's whole body out of the water. Its return sent a splash high enough to mist Apple's belly and underwings; but in no time it was chasing Intransigent, now low enough to the water that a mere flick of the sea-wyrm's neck might be enough to get its teeth on one of the huge Ranger's talons...

"You're right," Vanako said as the memory faded. "He put himself in danger to be the bait because he knew he had the skills to survive, and as the leader it was on him to take the risk." She wasn't sure Apple followed; ideas like "trust" were still a little foreign to the young wyrm. Apple could understand trusting Vanako, but generalizing that relationship to other beings was more of a stretch. But it would never get it without practice. Vanako thought, not for the first time, of Cerminir. All the pointless chatter to Eäril and Enwë, the annoying simplifications, the endless repetition... it had taken on new meaning to her now.

Something else about the memory nagged at her, though. The smell of the water was familiar. It should be familiar—it was seawater, she'd seen nothing else for weeks—but why did she notice that it was familiar?

Well, Apple could tell the difference between different regions by smell. And the smell of the water in Apple's memory was the same as the smell in its nostrils. Because Apple's memory of Varaunë and Intransigent had happened here. Because this was where the *Skua*, the *Scamp*, and the *Rejoice* had come to kill a sea-wyrm. Because these were sea-wyrm waters.

Vanako's unguarded mind must have been touching Thornapple's; she felt a flutter of unease from the wyrm. She *reached* out, half searching and half inquiring, and the image sharpened: Vanako, her limbs convulsing, rolling off the forecastle. "I know, baby," Vanako said, sending as much soothing as she could. It wasn't much; with a solution in mind, she was finally drifting off.

It was all right. Apple didn't much like being soothed anyway.

***

After an hour of waiting in the morning, there was no sign of a sea-wyrm's mind in Vanako's range.

Thinking on it, this didn't seem strange—they'd been out here for two days and nothing had come close enough to their piece of the wreck for Vanako to worry about. It was also worrying, because Vanako could tell her range wasn't as long as it should have been. Exposure, hunger, and bad sleep were already taking their toll. There was a solution to at least one of those problems, and Thornapple was going to love it, but Vanako wasn't.

Sea-wyrms might elude Vanako's mind, but there were plenty of fish in range. Getting one close to Thornapple was easy; getting Thornapple not to swallow them whole was more of an effort. Interestingly, the young wyrm wasn't any more pleased about using her talons to slice still-flopping bream into a mess of guts and chunks than Vanako was about using her handy monkey thumbs to scoop the mess into the water. But it was much more pleased to lick the deck clean than Vanako was to take a share of the chum for herself. She thought enviously about the starving heroes in storybooks who found even disgusting food delicious when they got it; she either wasn't hungry enough or wasn't heroic enough. But she got some raw bream down, kept it down, and felt it strengthen her.

"You're a good Apple," she told Thornapple while they waited for the chum to do its work. "I don't tell you that enough." Thornapple's mind responded with the usual mix of confusion, discomfort, and appreciation.

The chum attracted the odd shark, who would obligingly eat a few chunks of bream and swim away; but nothing large enough to move the chunk of forecastle. They set to chumming again, this time with more fish. At some point, Vanako cast her eyes to the skyline of Yemareir—and didn't see it. Some current must have pushed them south. How long would it last? How large was the sea-wyrms' range, and were they still in it? How far might the forecastle drift, and how fast? All of these were questions it would have been cathartic to scream at Antimain, or Kshanreen, or Mik, or Gilthiniel; but Thornapple wasn't the right audience for that kind of performance, so Vanako kept it, with some effort, to herself.

Three hours later—close to noon—the chumming had attracted nothing but more diffident sharks, and the coastline had noticeably changed.

"We need a more convincing act," Vanako said. There was no one human to talk her out of this, and Vanako keenly felt the loss. Hunger, thirst, a diet of mangled raw fish, and the stir-craziness of spending days on a hacked-off fraction of a ship that had been none too big to begin with would compromise anyone's decision making... but one thing Vanako knew about herself was that she made bad choices when she felt boxed in. She'd stolen yliaster from a crime boss to help her brother, then given it back to help her family (both, somehow, the wrong thing); she'd tried to help Zaya get out of... wherever they had her, only to find herself doing unwitting R&D for an oligarch who wanted to build prisons for empaths; she hadn't had sex with her boyfriend, but she'd gotten him hurt and imprisoned when she'd gone along with an idiot stunt of his instead of saying no. To say nothing of the *Skua*, where she'd lost a friend to Ennë-Alándor, another to a dragon, and all the rest—including a lover and a brother—to the sea.

Thornapple was perceptibly annoyed at these self-pitying rec-ollections, which to it had very little to do with the merits of the plan. *the problem*, it expressed with nearly verbal precision, *is that we will be eaten.*

"Sea-wyrms are weird," said Vanako, "but at least their mouths are close to their brains. If its teeth are in range, then I'm in."

In Thornapple's mind burned an image of blue and yellow, swimming like candle-flames in the deep; of water roiling with bubbles until it exploded into killing steam.

"I've got the range to stop that before it gets too bad," Vanako said, doing her best to project a confidence she didn't feel. "Any-way, we'll be right here by our little house. We can always climb back up if it gets bad."

Another dire image formed in Thornapple's mind, but Vanako pulled back. She cared what the young wyrm thought, but she didn't want to see it. Instead, she shoved the chum into the sea (their third batch, a half dozen sardines) and jumped after it.

The water was cold and tasted not at all of blood, and Vanako despaired for a second. How was it possible that any creature could taste blood from the deep, if she couldn't taste it here? But fuck it; if a hawk could see a mouse from a thousand feet up, a sea-wyrm could taste a few sardines' worth of blood from a thousand feet down. That made sense, right?

Thornapple galumphed into the water, and even its splash sounded reluctant, but the wave of its impact slapped Vanako in the face and she squealed with laughter, less a sign of happiness than a reflex born of memory: Back when she would swim with her mother and brother, the ones she'd had before she lost them, he would flop in the water and splash her with his whole body, just like this. But that water had been warm, and shallow, and she'd sometimes worried about being attacked by sharp-toothed beasts, but never actually tried to attract one's attention.

"Flop around," she told Thornapple. "Make it seem like you're in distress."

It was hard to focus on all the things she needed to do: Keep her head above water, keep vigilant for approaching sharks and trireme jellyfish and especially sea-wyrms, show Apple what a "flop" was, keep her teeth from chattering so hard they cracked. She thrashed as sincerely as she could without going under, and Apple imitated her to the best of its ability, and if its theatric instincts weren't quite there, at least it moved more water. They wouldn't be able to keep it up much longer—Vanako could feel her limbs going sluggish, their strength sapped by cold and hunger, and the motion of the water was hurting Apple's injured wing even as its blood cooled even more swiftly than Vanako's.

"Apple. Get out."

She didn't have to tell Thornapple twice. When it fell in, it tried to scramble back up on the broken forecastle, its claws not gaining as much purchase as they needed on the sea-soaked wood. When it tried and failed again, Vanako began to feel a buzzing in her stomach. The wyrm's limbs began to move more frantically, stiffness and numbness sapping their precision. Vanako slid into the wyrm's mind, calmed its shivering, blunted the pain from its hurt wing, and fine-tuned its focus on its fore- and hindclaws. The third attempt took twice as long and fired enough pain into Thornapple's hurt wing that Vanako couldn't blunt it all without knocking the dragon out, which in turn nearly sent it into the sea again.

But strength and mind and claw and tail added up, eventually, to enough, and Apple was back on the forecastle.

It was only then that Vanako noticed the ravening mind boiling, gape-mouthed, up from under them.

She *reached* without a second thought—but she hadn't reckoned on the foreignness of the marine mind. Vanako felt her own body thrust into some other realm as the cold wet salt dark mapped itself onto sweet, bright, mild air, through which the great blade of a hunter pushed itself with wings that were not like wings at all, and a tail that might have been a fifth and ruling wing, and the song of blood like baking bread in her nostrils, foreshadowing the obliging crackle of yielding bone under unstoppable jaws—

Vanako didn't know how to stop the fins, not without losing the wyrm to gravity. But she could stop the jaws.

Hold on, baby girl, she said to Apple, and the sea-wyrm breached.

It didn't know to struggle to snap its jaws closed, didn't even know there was a mind opposing its own to push against. It surged up under them, open-mouthed, and the sickening moment of elevation never seemed to end. Vanako bounced off teeth that should have cut her in two, caught briefly in the webbing at the hinge of the huge wyrm's jaw; then she was in free-fall, panic and salt spray blinding her to the endpoint: Yielding water, or the wood of the *Skua*'s forecastle?

For better or worse, it was the water. Vanako heard the echo of her own impact, then felt it: The ocean trembled at the sea-wyrm's return. She made herself take one second to feel her own body, to look through the blue until she found the sun. Then she kicked as strongly as she could toward it.

She'd come dislodged from the sea-wyrm's mind, and frantically she beat back the terror of its jaws, its killing steam; but dead by drowning would be no better. The sun shimmered through the sea, and she swam for it.

Vanako surfaced, sucked in air, then looked around: For the *Skua*, for Thornapple, for any sign the sea-wyrm might make before it struck again. Or that was what she would have done—had she not surfaced directly into the sight of Apple and the sea-wyrm, slashing at each other with claws and teeth, churning bloodied water to a boil.

Thornapple was on top of the monster wyrm, of course, like a lion clinging to an elephant's back. When it rolled and writhed to slash Thornapple with its teeth, the Ranger Wyrm used its good wing to get just enough lift to release its hold, then land again, its talons in a new position. The sea-wyrm gaped, and the air went hazy with steam; but Apple either wasn't hit or didn't care. It returned fire, cobalt-and-cadmium flame bathing the far side of the sea-wyrm's head. That was enough time for Vanako to seize the monster's mind—only to reel with fresh pain and disorientation, the scorching-away of half of the visual world.

The rhythm of Vanako's treading faltered; she gasped, choked on spray, coughed. But she kept her hold on the sea-wyrm's mind; and, with all the strength she could muster, bade it *dive*.

Hurt, thwarted, and confused, it obliged. For a panicked moment, Vanako thought of Apple, dragged under with the leviathan; but some movement, some bunching of its muscles must have been a tell, and Apple released its claws and leapt off before the sea-wyrm sank.

***

THEY MADE IT BACK, eventually, to the *Skua*'s forecastle... only to find it battle-tossed, now floating with the prow pointing straight up. Vanako could pull herself up—carefully—on the barnacle-scabbed hull. Thornapple could not. It had slightly better luck ducking under the fragment of the ship and pulling itself up into one of the lower decks, but there was no sun there, no way to dry its feathers. Vanako didn't know how either of them would sleep. She also didn't know how a wet Thornapple would make it through the night.

"I'm sorry," she said to the wyrm, after they'd both scrabbled all they could against the new inhospitality of the *Skua*'s final remnant. "I thought I could control it. I didn't know how different it would be." She was probably lucky, she realized, that she hadn't succeeded in cracking its motor schema; a body plan that size could override her own scarily fast. And she hadn't even thought about the difference in the way it breathed. What if it had convinced her own body that it could live for hours on a single breath? Why had she thought she could do this?

you think so much, Thornapple said.

"Someone has to," Vanako snapped.

A pulse of cool, smooth indifference: wyrm-shrug.

***

VANAKO COULD FEEL THE water cooling. The sun was preparing to set. Her mind was on sharks and sea-wyrms, of which she'd detected none; she was too weak to scan for jellyfish. She'd run a loop to short-circuit the discomfort of her own thirst and hunger, which she'd been taught never to do because she wouldn't know when she was running up against her physical limits... but she knew she was running up against her physical limits. She needed to keep her mind clear anyway. If there was fresh water around for her to forget to drink, life would be pretty great.

She didn't realize she'd drifted off until she woke to Thornapple thrashing in the water. For a moment she thought the sea-wyrm had returned: The young wyrm was practically hurling itself out of the water, getting all the lopsided lift it could wring out of its good wing, bellowing as Vanako had never heard it before, shooting plumes of flame into the air as far as its exhausted body would permit.

"Apple, baby!" Vanako shrieked, struggling to breathe through the roiling water slapping at her face. She pushed her way into its mind, cringing inside at the transgression; this wasn't how 'streamers treated their wyrms. "What's wrong? Let me help—"

Vanako's attention followed Thornapple's—to a strip of sky low enough to the horizon that it was still painted with delicate pink light. There was a flaw against that light, moving too smooth and fast to be a wisp of cloud, too big to be a bird.

"Oh shit, Apple, oh shit oh shit oh shit," Vanako said, sobbing. She inched over through the water to wrap her arm around the wyrm's neck, to push her face up against its tawny-downed muzzle. "You're so good. You're such a good dragon. You did it, I know you did it..."

She felt the wyrm's discomfort building at the primate social contact, and separated from it before it would feel forced to pull away. "I'm sorry, baby." She tried for one doomed second to control her hiccupping sobs, then failed completely. "I just... you saved us. I know you saved us. We're gonna be OK."

Vanako did not know anything of the kind; but, beyond reason, she believed it. Because, against the sunset, Apple had seen a dragon, had had the understanding and the self-possession to signal to it with noise and flame and flying water and every disturbance it could muster...

... and because, on the horizon, lamp lit like a star against the coming dark, there was a ship.

ABOUT THE AUTHOR

Matt Weber is the author of the Streets of Flame series, *The Dandelion Knight*, *Reverie Syndrome*, and *Verso & Other Stories*, as well as short fiction in *Nature*, *Cosmos*, and *Kaleidotrope*. By day, he has worked in a number of data-related professions in academia, digital health, fintech, and government. He lives in New Jersey under a pile of writhing juvenile D&D addicts.

Bluesky: @mattweber.bsky.social
Newsletter: https://www.cobblerandbard.com/mailing-list

www.ingramcontent.com/pod-product-compliance
Lightning Source LLC
Chambersburg PA
CBHW061102310726
48974CB00002B/367